Off the Menu

Off the Menu

Christine Son

NAL NEW AMERICAN LIBRARY

NEW AMERICAN LIBRARY

Published by New American Library,
a division of Penguin Group (USA) Inc.,
375 Hudson Street, New York, New York 10014, USA
Penguin Group (Canada), 90 Eglinton Avenue East, Suite 700, Toronto,
Ontario M4P 2Y3, Canada (a division of Pearson Penguin Canada Inc.)
Penguin Books Ltd., 80 Strand, London WC2R 0RL, England
Penguin Ireland, 25 St. Stephen's Green, Dublin 2,
Ireland (a division of Penguin Books Ltd.)
Penguin Group (Australia), 250 Camberwell Road, Camberwell,
Victoria 3124, Australia (a division of Pearson Australia Group Pty. Ltd.)
Penguin Books India Pvt. Ltd., 11 Community Centre,
Panchsheel Park, New Delhi – 110 017, India
Penguin Group (NZ), 67 Apollo Drive, Rosedale, North Shore 0632,
New Zealand (a division of Pearson New Zealand Ltd.)
Penguin Books (South Africa) (Pty.) Ltd., 24 Sturdee Avenue,
Rosebank, Johannesburg 2196, South Africa

Penguin Books Ltd., Registered Offices:
80 Strand, London WC2R 0RL, England

First published by New American Library,
a division of Penguin Group (USA) Inc.

First Printing, August 2008
1 3 5 7 9 10 8 6 4 2

 REGISTERED TRADEMARK—MARCA REGISTRADA

LIBRARY OF CONGRESS CATALOGING-IN-PUBLICATION DATA
Son, Christine.
Off the menu / Christine Son.
p. cm.
ISBN: 978-0-451-22417-0
1. Asian-American women—Fiction. 2. Female friendship—Fiction. I. Title.
PS3619.O49O44 2008
813'.6—dc22   2008001073

Set in Perpetua   •   Designed by Elke Sigal

Printed in the United States of America

For Michael—without you, I'd still only be fantasizing about writing.

Acknowledgments

I am deeply and forever grateful to the following: My agent, Anne Hawkins, for her unending patience, firm hand and nerves-soothing wisdom. My editor, Anne Bohner, for her keen eye and even kinder heart. The wonderful people at NAL, who made my dream come true. Bonnie Hearn Hill, my writing fairy-godmother. The Tuesdays, the rest of my writing fairy-godfamily. D'lesli Davis and Aimée Johnson, the girls with whom I'd most like to run around New York, and everywhere else, too. Lindsay McCaskill, Maura Brady, Mark Holmes and Pat Reynolds, for their unending encouragement and shared love for snark. Jenny Fogel and Ashley Nadeau, my constant cheerleaders. Shijin Pomales and Betty Soo Terry, for their inspiration. Kristy Kiernan, for her insight and generosity. Jennifer H. Corriggio, for her sisterly care. And most of all, my family—especially my mother, who truly believes that I can do anything.

One

Whitney Lee was rummaging through her desk when the phone trilled, its sharp blasts reverberating against the walls of her hamster-cage-sized office. She stared at the caller ID for a long moment, dismayed to see that Will Strong was on the line. God, she thought, finally reaching for the receiver, did her boss always have to call at seven o'clock on Friday nights?

"This is Whitney," she answered, trying to sound sunny.

"Lee," he shouted, "I need you to—" A faint female voice whined in the background before he cut her off. "Tell her that I'll get there when I get there." Pause. "Like hell it's important. Jesus, can't you see I'm on the phone? What's wrong with you? Lee, you there?"

"Yes." She lowered the volume on the phone base and held the receiver a few inches away from her head. Will never bothered to introduce himself when he rang to shriek at her, and without fail, he managed to include a tirade or two at his secretary while shattering her eardrums.

"I need you to—I'll tell you what, this'll be easier in person. I'll be there in a second." He slammed the phone, sending a piercing ring through her skull, and in a moment, she heard his heels stomp against the marbled hallway.

"This had better be quick," she muttered under her breath. If she didn't leave in the next five minutes, she would be late, and she had a date she refused to break. She shoved two Redweld folders of documents into her briefcase and loaded a banker's box of files onto her rolling cart. It was more paper than she could review in one night, but at least she would be able to work in the comfort of her own home. She could hardly stomach the sight of her office any longer, the mahogany-paneled claustrophobic cave of requisite billable hours, and she was cleaning off her desk with manic energy when she heard someone clear his throat.

"What the hell are you doing?" Will asked, his characteristic irritation giving way to bewilderment at her apparent attempts to escape. With his navy double-breasted pin-striped suit and slicked-back graying hair, he looked every bit the managing partner of Boerne & Connelly LLP, a law firm whose Houston office spanned twenty-two floors of the tallest building in Texas.

"Nothing. I was just trying to clean up a bit. What do you need?" She sat down, grabbed a pen and tried to look like the seasoned attorney that she was supposed to be, if you could call a third-year associate who spent most of her days reviewing documents seasoned.

"Did you get anything from the client? Gary said that he was sending over fifteen boxes of company files."

"Yes, they're right there," she said, pointing to a stack against the wall. He barely glanced at it before his eyes bored into her, and in her gray pencil skirt and white dress shirt, she felt underdressed next to the expensively attired lawyer. The Houston office of Boerne & Connelly had recently adopted a Friday business-casual policy, and all three hundred lawyers and two hundred staff members had embraced the practice. Will alone refused to dress "like an intern" on Fridays, even though he had been the one to promulgate the perk.

"You and James need to review those documents before depositions start rolling," he said. "Plaintiff's counsel's already bitching about the production, so we need to be sure to produce everything that's not privileged by Monday." His voice rumbled like thunder, amplified by the acoustically aggrandizing narrowness of her office.

"Of course." She scribbled the directive on a notepad. "By Monday."

"Don't fuck this up, Lee." His barrel-shaped body seemed to grow as he thought about the assignment. "You fuck it up, and we're fucked. Understand?" He thumped a squat index finger on her desk for emphasis. "Make that clear to James. I can't tell that boy how important this is."

"I understand." She threw in a few nods to underscore the fact that his words made sense. The way he yelled at her, she sometimes wondered if he thought that his Asian employee had learned the English language only last year. From across the room, she could see his watch.

What caught her eye wasn't the Rolex's shiny gold links, but the time. She needed to get out of there.

"Good." He crossed his arms and leaned against the wall and gazed about her office, and his uncharacteristic loitering made her nervous.

"Is there something else you need?" she asked. Her voice caught his attention, and his beady eyes narrowed on her.

"You know, ever since I became *managing* partner"—he never let her forget his two-week-old position—"I've been trying to figure out how to take our firm to the next level. You know what the answer is?" He didn't wait for an answer. "Clients. We need more clients. We've rested on our asses for too long, and the whole world's changed in the last fifty years. I've been telling the executive committee that this office has *got* to get rid of its good ol' boy reputation. It's killing us. Clients don't seem to care anymore about the good work we've always done. Now all of our clients—and more importantly our *prospective* clients—all they can think about is the firm's minority count. How many women it has, how many homosexuals, how many liberals and all that other bullshit."

"God, Will," she said with a heavy sigh. She knew better than to blast him for his political insensitivity, and even if she had had the authority to chastise him, she didn't have the time. "Is there any way we can talk about this on Monday? I have to be somewhere in ten minutes." She fidgeted feverishly, praying that he would go away. She was already late. Even worse, she might miss the Valedictorians' Dinner altogether, and it was the one occasion she refused to pass up. Ten years ago, the only three Asian girls at the otherwise Waspy Loyola Academy had graduated with identical GPAs, making their class the first to celebrate three valedictorians. They had returned to Houston, Whitney later than the others, and even though she couldn't remember exactly when they had begun to meet monthly, she also couldn't remember the last time one of them was a no-show. Come to think of it, in the three years since the inception of the Valedictorians' Dinner, none of them had ever canceled.

"No, this can't wait until Monday," he snapped. "This is important, Lee. You're one of the few Asians—Asian-American—Orient—girls at the firm." They both cringed as he stumbled over his characterization of her. "Shit, you're the only one in our office."

"I know I'm the only Asian woman," she said, helping him along.

"A Chinese *woman* lawyer. You'd think we would've had more than one by now, but there just aren't that many that interview with us. It's a real problem, Lee."

"I'm Korean, Will," she said flatly.

"Korean," he echoed. It was clear that her correction confused him, and he was looking at her so intently that she thought he might argue about her ethnicity. Suddenly, he bolted upright. "Well, I'm going to make it my mission to show the community that we have minorities at the firm." He beamed at her. "You're the wave of the future, Lee. The wave of Boerne & Connelly's future. *Texas Lawyer* won't be able to slam our firm for discriminatory hiring practices anymore once it sees that you're our—what's the word I'm looking for?—mascot."

"I'm hardly a mascot." Giving up on politeness, she stuffed herself into her coat and reached for her bag. "If the firm wants a reputation for diversity, why don't the partners just hire more minorities?"

"It's a problem of perception," he said, frowning. "Minorities—at least the ones we want to hire—don't want to come here because we have no diversity, and we can't tout that we're diverse, because, well, we aren't. It's a vicious cycle, which is why we need to advertise the ones we've got. Perception, Lee. It can be your greatest friend or your worst foe. And you're going to help change people's perception of us." He suddenly smiled widely, revealing the silver crowns that peppered his molars. "A young, attractive, *minority woman* on the cover of our firm press packet. This is the best idea I've had all day. The PR firm's already got copies of your picture from the Web site, so you won't even have to do anything." He smiled even harder, his bizarre expression making him appear like a maniac. "You can thank me by getting to those documents."

She gaped at him, at a loss for words. She didn't challenge his ridiculous plan to prop her up like an exhibit in the foolish hopes of luring darker-skinned law students. He was likely to forget they had even had this conversation by Monday morning. Why the partners had voted the most absentminded, attention-deficient, wrathful man to run the office was beyond her.

"I told the executive committee that the firm needs change," he said, apparently lost in self-adulation. "And, *boy*, change is what I'm going to give them."

She sighed, wondering how long he planned to chitchat. Thankfully, she didn't have long to wait. He suddenly swung his left wrist to his face so abruptly that she winced, afraid that he'd strike himself.

"Shit, I need to go. Get to those documents."

"Yes, sir," she said, relieved that he hadn't given himself a black eye.

He stomped out of her office, his alligator boots ringing against the marble floors of the hall. Whatever his mood, he lumbered across the floors as if he were furious, and his ample girth only magnified the *Tyrannosaurus rex* quakes of his travels.

A mascot, she thought as she turned off her computer. Three years at the firm, and Will had promoted her from his personal slave into an unwilling cheerleader. It was an additional insult, actually, considering that she loathed her job and barely tolerated her coworkers. Had she known six years ago that her life would turn out like this, she would never have gone to law school. She was a twenty-eight-year-old pack mule, as fungible and objectified as the rest of the lawyers at her firm. It was a terrible realization, and one that weighed on her mind constantly. Not that her parents viewed her circumstances as such. As obsessed as they were with professional accomplishments, they were mentally unequipped to understand that she was desperate for a way out, and they were psychologically incapable of comprehending that her true calling was music. They would likely suffer massive strokes if they discovered that she dreamed of leaving the firm for a singing career, one that would allow her to share her raspy, bluesy voice with the rest of the world. Then again, they didn't work hundred-hour weeks like she did, and James did.

As if on cue, James Carothers, the beleaguered fifth-year associate, appeared at her doorway.

"Hey, Whitney," he said with the enthusiasm of a zombie.

"Hi. Listen, we've got to get those documents reviewed and produced by Monday," she said, nudging her chin towards the wall.

"Fine. You staying late tonight?" His bloodshot eyes glazed over her, and in the same gray suit that he had worn yesterday, he looked every bit the person who hadn't slept in two days. Considering that she had barely slept in three, she shuddered to think about her own appearance.

"I can't. I've got a dinner." She yanked her bra-length hair out of the nape of her coat, catching her reflection in the wall of windows that winter darkness had transformed into a mirror. The deep hollows in her cheeks dismayed her, and the almost wild quality of her wavy hair only highlighted the fatigue on her face. She averted her eyes and turned off the Tiffany lamp on her desk before moving towards the door.

"You know my wife's expecting our third kid next month," he said. He didn't look excited. He didn't look anything other than exhausted.

"I had no idea. Congratulations, James."

"I can't even go home tonight, so what does it matter?" He spoke quietly, as if to himself. "What does any of it matter? Some days, when I can't take it anymore, I just stare at the gun in my drawer. I don't think I'd ever use it, but it's there nonetheless."

Whitney froze. If he was kidding, he wasn't convincing her, and their relationship wasn't such that she should know if he had sunk into the kind of despair that required a call to professional help. Or to the police.

"James, please go home," she said, searching his face for signs of jest. "Get some sleep. Play with your kids, have dinner with your wife—do something that won't worry me. I'll look through the documents tomorrow morning, and I'm taking some home with me tonight."

"Really?" His expression remained unchanged. "You sure?"

"Yeah. Don't worry about the project until Sunday. You can pick up where I leave off." She walked through the door and turned around. James hadn't moved. "You *were* joking, right? Because if you need to talk, I'm right here."

"Of course I was," he said, not at all assuring. "I don't have a gun at the office. I don't even have one at home."

"Okay." She continued to study him, still concerned, and as he gazed back at her, unblinking, she got the impression that he wasn't really seeing her at all. "Hey, seriously, if you need some time off, let me know. I can get through these. I'm sure Glenda would help, too."

"Thanks." He trudged out of her office and made his way down the hall, his focus never leaving the floor.

Whitney lingered a moment longer before she dashed into the hallway and strode towards the elevator banks. Waiting for the doors to open, she watched several dozen lawyers scurry about the hallways, all of them as frantic on this Friday night as they were on Monday mornings. Despite their frenetic movements, there was a static quality to them, and they buzzed past one another, as disconnected from the colleagues as they were from themselves. It was as if a part of their souls had died and had been sentenced to solitary hells, and when she stepped into the elevator, she sighed with relief. Lord, she prayed, may she never become like them.

Weaving through a sea of people who were also rushing to escape the building, she made her way through the marbled lobby, burst through the gilded doors and trotted across the street. The January air, unusually cold for the normally balmy city, nipped at her cheeks, and she pulled her coat closer around her, quickening her steps to escape the frigid evening. She spotted her car in the football-field-sized parking lot, and in moments, she was throwing her bag into the passenger seat and plopping behind the wheel. Even before she started the engine, she fished through her bag and pulled out a cigarette while fumbling with the radio until she found a classic-rock station. As she navigated through the interminable traffic with smoke streaming out the windows and Stevie Ray Vaughan blasting from the speakers, she thought about her Friday-night companions. Although she saw them every month formally, and spoke to them at least half a dozen times in between their sacred dinners, she was still eager to hear what was new with them. And considering that one of them was a rising star in the culinary world, and the other was a hero to her first-grade class, there was always plenty to talk about.

"Oh, good, you're finally here," Hercules Huang cried as she exploded into the dining room. Whitney jumped at the rocket launch of the chef's appearance, and when she looked up, the kitchen door was still swinging from her mighty entrance. Dragonfly had opened ten minutes ago, and already a couple of tables were occupied. In half an hour, the entire restaurant would be bursting at the seams, and Hercules would have a prime view of her business's success. She scooted into the banquette where Whitney had just sat down.

"How are you?" Whitney asked before Hercules wrapped her thigh-sized arms around her own reedlike frame and gave a vigorous squeeze. Face-to-face, Whitney had a close-up view of the freckles that scattered across her full-moon face, which melted into her thick cream cable-knit turtleneck.

"Great," Hercules said. "Fabulous. Where's the other little fucker?" She looked at Whitney, her expression instantly apologetic. "Sorry. Where's *Audrey*?"

"She'll be here soon." She wriggled out of her coat. "Since when do you care whether you curse in front of me?"

Hercules grimaced. "Did you read the *Houston Chronicle* last month?"

"You've got to be more specific than that, H."

Hercules rolled her eyes, looking put-upon, but underneath her clear agitation, Whitney sensed a deep worry. "They interviewed me for a feature on up-and-comers, something about being a successful Chinese chef in the South, and they didn't filter out anything I said. Can you believe that?" Her bushy brows arched over her serpentine eyes, and her cheeks flamed into two red spots on her butter-hued skin. "It's like the paper's got a vendetta against me or something."

Whitney chuckled. "I'm sure it's not as bad as you think."

"Do you know how many times I said *fuck*? Thirty times. *Thirty!* And I apparently said *motherfucker* twenty-three times." She shook her head in disbelief, and her frizzy charcoal-colored hair whipped about her shoulders. "My business manager almost had a heart attack. You wouldn't *believe* how many people wrote the paper to complain. A lot of them said that they were going to boycott the restaurant. For what? *Cursing?*" She banged a fist onto the table indignantly. "Sometimes, I freakin' hate Houston. Bunch of right-wing conservatives." She sighed heavily and rubbed her forehead. "Anyway, I've been trying like crazy to clean up my language. It's bad for business."

"This place seems to be doing just fine," Whitney said, watching a crowd edge its way into the front door.

"Where *is* she?" Hercules asked, apparently no longer interested in the article. She bobbed around her seat impatiently, looking fully like a bouncing snowman, as she tried to spot the remaining member of the group among the well-heeled patrons who were entering the restaurant.

The front door swung open, and Audrey Henley, the last of the Valedictorians, walked in. Dressed in a fitted black cashmere sweater, white silk slacks and staggering stilettos, she looked every bit the carefully groomed heiress to a billion-dollar Texas oil fortune. Well, other than the fact that she was a deeply tanned Korean girl with dark crescent-moon-shaped eyes that always gave the impression that she was smiling. She had been adopted into a Caucasian family as an infant, the lucky lottery winner of social circumstances, and from outward appearances, she was as much a Henley as her chic mother, whose picture could be found in most Style sections of Houston's periodicals.

Audrey waved and slid into the booth, the fabric of her pants swishing against the leather as she shimmied into her spot. Hugs and kisses abounded again before a sharply dressed waiter appeared. In keeping with the formality of the establishment, Hercules demanded that the waitstaff dress in black suits with earpieces for increased efficiency. Whitney thought they looked like Secret Service in training.

"Ladies, the usual?" he asked, bending at the knees so that he was eye level with them.

"Of course," Hercules said, and opened her arms wide. "These are my motherf—" She stopped suddenly and cringed. "These are my girls, man. You'd better take good care of them."

He nodded and walked away.

"Lord, Hercules," Audrey said, looking amused, "I don't know what's more painful to listen to—you dropping the F-bomb all the time, or you trying not to curse at all." She shook her head, and her face-framing auburn layers gleamed under the chandeliers' light, drawing attention to the South Sea pearls that studded her ears.

"You don't speak to your dad like that, do you?" Whitney asked.

"Don't even get me started on that man," Hercules said with a scowl. Her cheeks flared, and in a moment, she looked sunburned again. "I wish . . ."

Just then, the waiter returned. Hercules' frown deepened as her session was cut short.

"Ladies." The waiter had returned to the table with a bottle of champagne, and the women watched as he poured three glasses. Once they settled into their drinks, he continued. "Tonight, we've got a lovely four-ounce petit mignon with a red wine reduction, medium rare, as Chef has requested. It will be accompanied by truffle-infused mashed potatoes and ginger honeyed carrots."

"Thank you," Hercules said, proud of her waiter's table-side manners. He retreated, and if Hercules had been about to blast into an all-out complaint session regarding her father prior to his arrival, she was apparently no longer in the mood.

A few silent moments passed, and Hercules' eyes darted from Whitney to Audrey and then back to Whitney, cuing the main feature of their dinners. On these Fridays, they went around the table and nearly unhinged their shoulders patting their own backs. Hercules had begun the tradition after they had rented *The Joy Luck Club* years ago. Using their own achievements, Whitney and Audrey had joined in on the re-creation of the movie's mothers' one-upping of each other, but by the end of the charade, it was clear that neither had any real interest in the silly competition. Hercules, on the other hand, having the most overt, frightening, get-the-hell-out-of-my-way competitive streak, had relished what was clearly a tournament for her. She had dragged the obnoxious one-upping to their monthly Valedictorian Dinners much to

Whitney and Audrey's chagrin, and despite their protests, she refused to let the institution die.

"How's your second restaurant coming along?" Audrey asked Hercules, kicking off the evening's boasts. "Did you decide what you're going to call it?"

"Dragonfly Deux." Her face brightened with pride. "It's a good name, don't you think?"

"Do you think people will associate Dragonfly Deux with this place?" Whitney asked. "Why don't you just call it *Dragonfly*, so people know it's a chain?"

"Because it's *not* a chain," she said, visibly offended. "It's its own concept with its own menu and its own theme."

"Which will be what?" Audrey asked.

"I'm not sure, but it's not going to be upscale comfort food like this place." She motioned to the cherry-paneled walls, oversized sconces and massive stone fireplace in the center of the dining room. "I was leaning towards fusion, but I don't know that I want to get into something that's been done to death." Anxiety flashed across her face for a moment before she relaxed into a smile. "I've got time, in case you're worried, and considering that construction is taking fucking forever, I'll have a menu set by then."

"Well, I wish you *would* make it a chain, because I love upscale comfort food," Audrey said. "I would come here at least once a month even if I didn't know you. Frankly, I wouldn't mind seeing another Dragonfly close to my house."

"Huh." Hercules chewed on a nubby fingernail thoughtfully. "Really?"

"Well, whatever you decide, I'm sure Dragonfly Deux's going to be great," Whitney said, and laid her hand on the chef's arm in support. She was about to reach for her glass when Hercules spoke.

"I'm not finished. This month's a twofer." Her eyes grew larger, and her ample bosom puffed out. "A *very* fancy company has approached me to start my own line of cookware. We've been working on it for the last couple of months, but I didn't want to say anything until the plans were set in stone. We're calling it Hercules Cookware."

"What?" Audrey gasped. "You're getting your own line of cookware?"

"I am indeed. Y'all better start using Hercules Cookware when it comes out and not that Calphalon shit." Her chubby cheeks flushed a brighter shade of pink, and she took another swig of her champagne.

"Where's it going to be sold?" Whitney asked.

"We haven't gotten that far yet, and distribution is another deal altogether. But Macy's is interested."

"Which company are you working with?" Audrey asked.

"I'm sure you've heard of Acceleron," she said, eyeing them expectantly.

"Of course," Audrey said as though every cooking American used the brand. Whitney had never heard of Acceleron, but then again, not having cooked more than a handful of times in her entire life, she wasn't any kind of authority on the subject.

"I'm really proud of you, Hercules," she said. "And I'm not just saying that because you're the most famous person I know."

"Famous," Hercules repeated, pleased by the word. She grinned widely, exposing the snaggletooth that years of braces couldn't correct. "Don't you think that's overstating it a bit?"

"I don't think so," Audrey said. "You have to know that you're something of a celebrity in Houston. Even my mother's seen you on the channel eight morning show, and she doesn't watch much TV."

"Oh, that reminds me, my segment on *Good Morning, Texas* got picked up for another year," she said, even cheerier. "I'll be on the first Tuesday of each month."

"Like I was saying," Whitney said, "famous."

They toasted one another and drank again. Whitney drained her glass completely. Spying her need, the waiter walked over and silently refilled her drink before receding into the background. In a moment, he returned with three oversized plates and set them before each diner. Careful to keep the scalding dishes from burning his guests, he waited for their inspection and approval.

"This smells wonderful." Hercules beamed at the server. "Tell Simon that I've decided against firing him tonight."

"Yes, Chef," he said. "Is there anything else I can get you ladies?"

"Another bottle of champagne," Hercules answered. She looked at Audrey and Whitney with motherly admonishment. "Y'all are a bunch of lushes. It's unnatural for people your size to be able to drink like sailors."

Whitney grinned. She and Audrey had already downed most of the first bottle, and there were still toasts to be had. She marveled at her own ability to imbibe like a college frat boy twice her size when Hercules could barely get through half a glass of champagne without serious consequences. Apparently, alcohol tolerance wasn't proportional to mass, as they had all believed, and a few sips of Coors Light was enough to send Hercules home in a cab.

"Well, ladies, enjoy," Hercules said, and carved into her steak. Famished from her long day, Whitney ate in silence, relishing the perfectly seasoned beef. After a few bites, Hercules decided it was Audrey's turn and faced her. "You're up."

She thought for a long moment. Finally, she shrugged and said, "I'm about four months away from finishing my dissertation. Then y'all will have to call me *Dr.* Henley." She grinned, amused by the idea.

"That's almost a year ahead of schedule, isn't it?" Whitney asked.

"It is." She seemed delighted that her friend had noticed the feat.

"Are you going to do any postdoc work?"

"Well—I'm not planning on it. I'll probably stay on the faculty at St. Mark's, maybe teach a higher grade."

"Why are you getting a Ph.D. if you're not going to do anything with it?" Hercules asked. She frowned severely, as if insulted by Audrey's decision.

"Because I like the process of learning," she said, her cheeks reddening. "And I love English literature." Hercules continued to look skeptical, and Audrey rolled her eyes. "It doesn't have to be a means to an end."

"That makes no sense," Hercules said. "There's always an end. Otherwise, what's the point?"

"You're doing God's work, teaching children," Whitney said, throwing Hercules a reproving look.

"I don't know how you have the energy to keep up with first graders all day, every day." Hercules shook her head. "I volunteered for Junior Achievement once, and I had to teach civics to third graders for an afternoon. What a bunch of monsters. They completely wiped me out."

"I love my kids." Audrey brightened as she thought about them. "Sometimes I wonder if I shouldn't have gotten a Ph.D. in elementary education instead of English lit."

"I can't even imagine doing what you do," Hercules said. "All children, all the time—" She shuddered. "It takes a saint is what I'm saying." Audrey chuckled and turned back to her meal.

For a few wordless moments, the only sounds Whitney heard were the chimes of crystal hitting the smooth surface of neighboring tables, the clanging of silverware against solid plates, and faraway whispers and laughter from people she didn't know. Audrey and Hercules focused on their food, clearly as ravenous as Whitney had been, and after a few more bites, their eyes landed on her. Her shoulders tightened as she realized that she had achieved nothing significant since their last meal together.

"Well?" Hercules asked expectantly.

"Well"—she racked her brain desperately—"the firm's decided to make me its mascot."

"What does that mean?" Audrey asked.

"It means that I'm going to be something of a—"

"Spokesperson," Hercules interrupted, looking awed. "I heard that a lot of large companies are trying to humanize themselves by picking spokespeople. You're going to be the face of your firm, aren't you?" She was clearly impressed. "I told you that you were on the fast track for partnership."

"I don't think so," Whitney said. "The managing partner made it pretty clear that he was using me to bait other minorities to come to the firm with the ultimate goal of attracting more clients."

"What?" Audrey asked, her little eyes rounding.

"This is *Houston*," Hercules said indignantly. "There's nothing *but* minorities here. Don't y'all have a bunch at your firm?"

"I'd say that in all of our offices, we probably have less than a dozen."

"How's that even possible?" Audrey asked.

"Boerne and Connelly is one of the vestiges of the good ol' boy network. Hell, the managing partner's nothing if not a cow-steering, bronco-riding good ol' boy from West Texas. I don't think he's ever known an Asian girl before me. You should've seen the way he was tripping over what to call me." Hercules and Audrey gawked at her, and she felt her face burn. As much as she hated the firm, she realized that she was its mouthpiece to the women, and the embarrassment of its diversity quotient, along with the firm's attitude towards minorities, suddenly felt personal. Even worse, her continued employment seemed like a passive endorsement of what was clearly abhorrent to her friends.

"You're joking," Hercules said, not at all amused. "In this day and age, how can there be people who don't know what you are or what to call you?"

"How can there still be segregated schools in Dallas or segregated proms in Atlanta?" Whitney asked. "The country's not as progressive as you think."

"Why'd you go to that firm of yours, then?"

"They promised a good quality of life," Whitney said with a shrug. "Who knew they were lying?"

"They're *lawyers*." Hercules let out an exasperated sigh, mockingly disappointed by Whitney's naïveté. "Of *course* they were lying."

"So, are you going to go along with your partner's plan?" Audrey asked.

"Depends on what it is that he wants me to do. I'll do whatever he wants so long as it's genuine, and so long as it doesn't misrepresent what the firm's really like."

"Seriously?" Hercules asked, incredulous. "You're just going to take it? Shit, if *I* had been in your shoes, I would've told that boss of yours what I really thought. I would've told him that he needed to catch up on what the real world looks like before he started spouting his ignorance." She shot Whitney an accusatory stare. "Why didn't you tell him off? He probably thinks you're some kind of Asian stereotype. You know, the meek, humble, *subservient* geisha girl who'd fetch his coffee if he asked."

"It has nothing to do with race," Whitney said, certain that the belligerent chef would never understand corporate culture. "*Everyone* does what he says. He's the managing partner, for God's sake. Even the other partners don't argue with him."

"You should start your own firm," Audrey said. "It's unfair that you have to do more just because you're a minority."

"I would *never* start my own firm," Whitney said. "I can't think of a worse way to make a living."

"Still, it's unfair."

"No more unfair than anything else."

"Of course it is," Hercules said, looking at Whitney as if she were defending the Ku Klux Klan. "What you're going through sounds like a bunch of bullshit to me."

"That kind of bullshit exists everywhere," Whitney said. "Maybe you don't see it because you have the good sense to work for yourself."

"I can't believe you're going to sit there and smile and wave, like the freakin' winner of a Miss Minority contest," Hercules said, almost angry. "I would *never* do that. I didn't sign up to be anyone's mouthpiece, and I wouldn't let someone force me into it."

Whitney sighed. They had never seen eye to eye on the issue, and every time she had spoken on behalf of Korean-Americans, Asians, minorities in general, women or lawyers, Hercules had criticized her easy acceptance of society's expectations of her role. Hercules, on the other hand, seemed intent on destroying stereotypes of her own culture by adopting wholesale that of an amorphous other. It was a strange swap, unnecessary and understandable at once, and Whitney wondered what was so odious about being Chinese that Hercules felt compelled to abandon her heritage completely.

The waiter returned with plates of chocolate mousse and a silver boat of hazelnut sauce. After a sliver of a bite, Audrey popped up and turned to them.

"I'd like to make an amendment to my previous monthly update, if I could." She looked at Hercules, who was still affronted, and then at Whitney, and when they both nodded, she continued. "On top of finishing my doctoral program a year early, I'm also taking y'all to Austin for a weekend. The second week of March, actually, since St. Mark's will be out on spring break. Does that week work?"

"What are you talking about?" Hercules asked.

"I was thinking that we should go away for a weekend. Take a break from life for a bit." She was smiling widely, and her cheeks were blazing red, perhaps from excitement and too much alcohol.

"We've never taken a trip before," Whitney said.

"It would be a lot of fun, don't you think? My parents have a really fantastic house in Austin, right on the lake. Since they never use it, they were thinking about selling it, and I want to go there at least one more time before they do."

"What does it matter whether they use it or not?" Hercules asked. "They don't use any of their other houses."

"My dad's lawyers are advising him to dump it, and he's actually listening to them." She leaned forward. "So? What do you think?"

"I'd love to," Whitney said, perking up at the mention of her backyard. She could already hear the pulsing heartbeat of the city, the guitar strings and drumbeats that flowed from Sixth Street to Lake Travis, and the more she thought about the trip, the more excited she became. She pulled her BlackBerry out of her bag and scrolled to her calendar. "I'll block off that weekend right now."

Hercules reached around her back and grabbed a mini day planner from the back of her pants. She always kept one holstered, like a gangster with a schedule. Whitney leaned over and peeked at the weekly agenda, overwhelmed by the number of appointments and deadlines that filled each page.

"That's *perfect*," Hercules said. "I'm supposed to meet Lucas Christensen then anyway. He's in San Antonio, but that's, what, an hour away?"

"Who's Lucas?" Whitney asked.

"A friend of mine from culinary school." She looked at them dreamily.

"*That* boy's going places. He's the executive chef at Buccari in San Antonio, and he turned that place from a toilet into a four-star restaurant in three years. We've been talking about opening a restaurant together forever." She returned to her calendar. "I'll be there."

"Great," Audrey said, delighted. She poured herself another glass of champagne. "We're going to have so much fun."

"Are you going to bring Victor?" Hercules asked. "Or is this a girls' trip?"

"Definitely a girls' trip." She turned to Whitney. "So you can't bring Scott."

"I wouldn't dream of it." She took another bite of the mousse and then pushed her plate away. "Things seem to be going well with you and Victor. Y'all have been dating for, what, two months now?"

"It'll be three next Wednesday," Audrey said, looking even more pleased. "God, I can't believe it's already been that long. I feel like we just met yesterday." She smiled serenely, clearly thinking about her adoring boyfriend, and Whitney reached out and patted her hand.

"You seem happy," she said, genuinely glad.

"I *am* happy." She leaned closer to them and whispered, "I think this is it."

"What's it?" Hercules asked.

"I'm finished looking for Mr. Perfect. I've found him."

"How do you know?" Hercules asked, frowning. "It's only been a few months."

"Because I do. I don't know how to describe it other than—I just feel it in my bones." Her entire face flushed, as if her cheeks alone couldn't carry her happiness. "Don't laugh, but I even pointed out an engagement ring that I thought was pretty. It was a cushion cut with a border of smaller diamonds. Very art deco."

"What did Victor say?" Whitney asked.

"Nothing. But he didn't freak out, either."

"I think Scott would run if I started showing him rings that I thought were pretty."

"Would he?"

"God, yes."

Hercules dragged the chocolate mousse towards her, the heavy plate screeching against the top of the table. She seemed pensive, perhaps mulling over Audrey's and Whitney's relationships. At last, she leaned against the plush banquette, looking uncharacteristically peaceful. "It'll be good to get some sun and float in the lake." She poked Audrey's arm. "This trip's a great idea, Auds."

"It is," Whitney said. They toasted one another again and shared the remaining glass of champagne. In the fifteen years that they had known one another, this would be their first excursion together, and judging from their smiling faces, she knew that they couldn't wait.

Two

"Mom? Dad? Your darling daughter's here," Whitney called as she walked into her parents' foyer. She opened a hallway closet, stepped out of her black stilettos and stuck her heels onto a shoe rack while scanning the area for Scott Yang's usual black loafers. She never missed a Friday night at her parents' home, even if all she could manage was a quick hello before dashing out again, and her boyfriend, aware of her parents' expectations, likewise came by to bow his greetings before taking her out. His shoes were nowhere to be seen, and she twitched her lips, wondering how long he was going to work tonight. She had to be at Billy Bob's by eleven, where she had promised to play the guitar and sing backup for Tate Philips, and Scott or no, she was leaving in twenty minutes.

"In here," her father shouted, his voice echoing against the high ceilings.

Whitney walked into the kitchen and placed a take-out box on the green granite counter. Her father was standing by the far end of it, and she kissed his cheek, noticing that the decor had changed.

"Is that a new cactus?" she asked, pointing to the spindly plant on the counter, complete with a terra-cotta dish and a wooden sign welcoming her to Texas.

"Your mother got it at Costco," he said, delighted. "It came in a box. A *box*. Can you imagine such a thing?"

"Yeah," she said with a chuckle. He pushed his thick glasses up his nose and gazed at the mismatched array of purple flowers, a misshapen bonsai tree and a lone orchid that decorated the ledge.

"It's been almost a year since we moved into this house, but we still have a little more to do before it feels like home."

"It feels pretty homey to me."

"Yes, it does, I suppose," he said, looking content.

She followed his eyes and took in the whitewashed cabinets and stainless steel appliances of the country-styled kitchen that opened up into a cavernous family room and breakfast nook. The central feature of the redbrick suburban beauty had sold her parents on their dream house, and with a Viking range and Sub-Zero refrigerator, her mother had touted that she could show off her culinary abilities while her guests admired her from the comfort of the couch.

"What's up?" Robert asked from the kitchen table, finally looking up from his CAD drawings.

"Hey." Whitney greeted her brother with a small wave. "Where's Scott?"

"He had a few things he had to finish before he could leave. He said that he'd be here by ten thirty." He returned to the oversized schematic that hung over the edges of the table, his lips moving silently as he scratched what Whitney assumed were arduous calculations onto a yellow notepad. To say that he was obsessed with his job was an understatement, and he was working more hours now than he had at the beginning of his engineering career at NASA. He often brought his work home, sometimes inviting his coworkers to their shared apartment to finalize projects, and she felt a screwed-up smile spread across her face as she remembered the night that she had opened the door three years ago to find Scott on the other side.

"Robert, what are you working on?" her father asked, hovering behind him.

"I can't tell you." He circled his arms around the indecipherable chart. "Don't look, Dad."

"I would never." He returned to the counter and sat on one of the stools that faced the sink, unfazed by Robert's cryptic work. He was equally secretive, having left Dow Chemical for a classified position at NASA. What he did exactly, Whitney had no idea, but she knew that the position required multiple advanced degrees and numerous security clearances. Elated by the Lee contingent at work, he often announced that if the space program ever offered vacations to the moon, the family could use their company discount. Only Whitney's mother found his joke amusing.

Just then, her mother emerged from the master bedroom and plodded towards her, her freshly scrubbed face practically hidden behind her large, black-rimmed glasses.

"Hi, honey." She took Whitney's face into her plump hands and kissed her cheek. She held on to her for another moment and inspected her, her watermelon-seed eyes minimized into specks behind her thick lenses. After taking in a soft breath, she clucked her tongue. "Oh, you poor thing. You look tired."

"I *am* tired."

"You must be working so hard." She didn't seem concerned at all. In fact, she looked proud.

"You have no idea." She gently uncurled her mother's fingers. "I brought some leftovers from Hercules' restaurant for y'all."

"What is it?" she asked as she opened the Styrofoam container.

"Chocolate mousse with hazelnut sauce. It's pretty good."

"That's why she gets so fat. She eats like this all the time." She tasted the dessert with the tip of her pinkie, grunted and pulled out a fork. "It's delicious."

"Promise me you'll never call her fat in public," Whitney said, appalled by her bluntness. "It's so rude."

"But it's true," she said with her mouth full. "It wouldn't hurt if she lost a little weight."

"*Mom.*" That her mother would criticize a size 16 woman was ridiculous, considering that she herself was perhaps one size smaller. But she was, as she often said in her defense, nearing sixty, and having spent her life looking after her husband and two children, she deserved to eat whatever she wanted, whenever she wanted.

"I think she looks fine." Robert threw a judgmental glance at Whitney. "Meatier women always look better to me."

"I'll tell Hercules that you think she's *meaty*," Whitney teased.

"I just mean that I don't like girls who starve themselves and then wear jeans around their hip bones. It's not natural, *Whit-ney*."

"I'm so glad that my size is the deterrent of your attraction, *Robert*." She took a seat at the table. "And for your information, I don't starve myself." She patted his bulging stomach. "I just don't eat as much as you." He slapped her arm away.

"So what did you girls talk about?" Her father grabbed a fork and joined her mother at the counter. Standing side by side with identical boyish haircuts, gray cable-knit sweaters and dark-rimmed glasses, they looked like nerdy nesting dolls. Whitney had heard that long-lasting couples tended to resemble each other, but her parents could have been twins. Even their lopsided smiles and frowns were the same.

"Same old things we always talk about. Oh, we're going to Austin in March. Audrey invited us to her parents' house."

"That's so nice of her," her mother said. "What are you going to do there?"

"Relax. Lay out. Take the boat out. Go to a few clubs." The longer she dwelled on their trip, the giddier she felt. The weekend getaway would be her longest break from work in three years, and as short as the vacation might have seemed to anyone else, she viewed it as nothing short of indulgent.

"Clubs?" Her mother frowned. "I don't like that. All kinds of bad things happen there."

"What? How would you even know?"

"I read it all the time in the Korean newspaper. People go crazy and shoot each other. Or they stab their friends because they're drunk." Her little eyes rounded, and she seemed intimidated by her own inaccurate perception. "Everyone takes drugs there. That's why they end up hurting each other."

Robert guffawed, looked up, rolled his eyes and then returned to his work. Her mother didn't seem to notice his reaction.

"Have you ever been to a club?" Whitney asked, taken aback by the ignorant generalization.

"Why in the world would I go somewhere like that?" Her brows shot up, and she shook her head violently, as if to rid herself of the association. "Those places are—they're terrible."

"How can you say that if you've never—"

"Honey, you don't know, because you come from a good family

that made sure you weren't exposed to all kinds of horrible things. But I know that those—what do you call them?—dancing clubs, they're not good places. It's a big problem in Korea right now. America also. Everything with young people is too much these days. Too much sex, too much drugs, too much violence." She sighed heavily, taking the statistics personally. "There was an article in the newspaper of a teenage boy who was shot at one of those places last week." She shook her head again. "Just terrible."

"Mom, not all clubs are like that," Whitney said, already aware how fruitless her argument was. "There are places where you can listen to music without becoming a victim of a drive-by."

She frowned. "No, that's not true. Reverend Lee actually spoke about it last week." She pursed her lips, looking reproachful. "You would know about these things if you went to service more often."

"I would go every Sunday if I didn't have to work like a troll," she said, tracing the deep grooves of the oak kitchen table.

"Oh, you poor thing." She clucked her tongue again, clearly pleased that Whitney was living the American dream of seven-day workweeks. If there was a position she held in higher esteem than a faithful churchgoer, it was a workaholic, and Whitney didn't doubt that she regarded a professional career as a religion unto its own. A moment later, she walked over and joined them at the table, and being a good foot shorter than Robert, she looked like a chubby child next to him. "Anyway, clubs are no good, honey. Drinking, too. Maybe it will be best if you girls just relax and go swimming." She nodded, reassured by her own admonition. "Is this the first trip you're taking together? I don't remember you mentioning any others."

"Yeah. It's kind of funny, isn't it? We've known each other more than half of our lives, and this is the first time we're going anywhere together."

"It's good to keep up with your high school friends." She nudged her thick glasses up her bridgeless nose. "Who knows? Maybe they'll be your clients one day." She looked at her expectantly. "So, are you working on your own cases yet?"

"No." She bristled, annoyed by the pushy attitude. "I'm still in the dungeon reviewing documents. Apparently, no one gets out until his sixth year."

"That's not funny." Her mother frowned again.

"I wasn't joking."

"Well, work harder, then. I'm sure you'll be a partner in no time. Then, you'll have time to have children. After you're married, of course. I think that maybe it's too difficult to have kids before you make partner."

"I'll be thirty-five by then."

"It takes that long?" she asked, surprised.

"I've told you a hundred times that the partnership track's almost eleven years now." She crumpled a napkin in her hands, aggravated.

"Well, you'll make it in much less time." She smiled brightly. "I have faith."

"God, Mom, lay off on the pressure, okay?"

"I'm just saying to work hard and be successful. What's so wrong with that?"

"Nothing. But the way you say it, it stresses me out. Life's too hard as it is to have you push your own agenda through me."

"It's every mother's right to live through her children," she said before looking away. "After graduating from *Seoul-dae*"—she raised her brows, as if to impress the prestige of her alma mater—"who knew that I would have ended up as a homemaker? I could have been anything I wanted. It's really just—" She held her breath, as if the deep-seated yearning would pass. "Oh, what I would give to be able to go to law school."

"You can still go, you know," Whitney said. "You don't have to sit there and wonder what it's like. If you want to go, go. See for yourself how terrible it is."

"How can I?" she asked incredulously. "I'm fifty-nine. Besides, my English isn't good enough to go to law school."

"There are a lot of fifty-nine-year-olds who go to school," Robert said, looking up from his CAD drawings. "And, hello, your English is perfect."

"It's too late for me," she said, waving her hand dismissively. "I already lived my life. My job was to raise two beautiful children. I have no regrets. But if I could do it all over again—" She blinked a few times and then smiled at Whitney and Robert, her apple cheeks squishing against her glasses. "Well, at least I have you two to be proud of."

"You're proud?" Whitney asked, surprised. It wasn't often that her mother said so out loud.

"Of course I'm proud. What do you think I do whenever we see our friends at the alumni reunion? I brag about my children." She looked at Robert affectionately. "Everybody knows Robert has two Ph.D. degrees, like his father. And not from some low-ranked school, like Mr. Jung's son. From"—she paused for full dramatic effect— "*M-I-T*." Her cheeks flushed as she sounded out the name, and she looked wondrously at Whitney next. "Everybody knows my daughter graduated from"—she puffed out her chest—"*Har-vard* Law School, and is going to be a law partner."

Whitney and Robert exchanged exasperated glances. She knew that her parents, both alumni of Seoul National University, or "the Harvard of the Milky Way galaxy," as her father described it, stored up nuggets of her and her brother's achievements to display at their yearly reunion. Apparently, so did their classmates, and perhaps because they found ostentatious boasts about themselves distasteful, they bragged about their children's achievements with shameless vigor. She could only imagine what one of their functions looked like, and she envisioned a science fair of aggressively prideful Korean parents, standing next to their cardboard displays of their children, pictures, trophies and all.

"You know how tired I am of hearing Mrs. Chang brag about her son?" her mother asked no one in particular. "How many times do we have to hear that he's the president of Samsung? Or Mrs. Kim. Again with her daughter becoming the chief of surgery at Cedars-Sinai." She appeared annoyed, but Whitney knew that the accomplishment roll call was her way of alerting them to their competition, and to the standard of achievement she expected from them. "You should see how Mrs. Park brags about her son. So what, he graduated from Juilliard and is now the first-chair violinist with the Philadelphia Philharmonic Orchestra?" She shook her head. "She is too much. So obnoxious."

"Maybe you can tell her that we're musical, too," Whitney said.

"How are we musical?"

"I play the guitar, Mom. You know that."

"What's so great about that? Everyone can play guitar these days. Even Mr. Yu plays at church when we have revivals." She spoke absently, distracted by the TV screen in the family room. Her father was flipping through channels, and he stopped when he found a cholesterol-lowering-medication advertisement, apparently intrigued by its double-blind statistical analyses. The chipper commercial gave way to a new music video by Chantal McKinney, and Whitney's mother frowned, obviously dismayed that they were watching MTV. Immediately, she called out to him. "Daddy"—decades of referring to Whitney's father in the third person had set his identity simply as *Daddy*—"please change the channel. I cannot listen to this garbage."

"Mom," Whitney said, "Chantal's album's been number one for two months. The song's great. Listen to how clear her voice is."

"I really don't understand how you young people can enjoy this." Her eyes enlarged, underscoring her disbelief. "This is not *music*. Beethoven, Mozart, Mendelssohn—*that* is music. This is"—she motioned to the screen—"this is just noise."

"It really isn't," Whitney said under her breath, unwilling to mire herself in a losing argument over current music's value. Her mother's attitude—the quick dismissal of what she considered to be a waste of sound—was the reason she had never shared her passion, never told her parents that she dreamed of performing onstage or that she sounded like a heady mix of Diana Krall, Susan Tedeschi, Alison Krauss and Patty Griffin. They wouldn't differentiate between her solo, folksy style and the highly stylized thumping they deemed to be trash, and they certainly wouldn't accept singing as a possible profession. It was strange that Koreans of their generation should laud classical performances with such fervor while denigrating all other musical genres. Perhaps their unfettered zeal was born out of envy, an emotional relic from their war-ravaged land when a violin equated with wealth, a cello with extravagance. This same generation—denied piano lessons in favor of food—had made them compulsory for their children, and after ten years of what Whitney had considered to be pure torture, her mother had finally relented and allowed her to rest the metronome. The irony wasn't lost on her.

"Oh, good," her mother said, appeased now that Whitney's father had turned the station to a more subdued National Geographic program on shark attacks. She perked up suddenly. "You know who I just remembered? Mrs. Cha. Her son speaks seven languages, but you would never know that if you spoke to her. She's so humble." Her awed expression, complete with raised brows, returned. "Seven languages. Can you believe it? He's a translator for the United Nations. *Seven*, honey." She looked at them reprovingly. "And you can barely speak two. Sometimes I think it was a mistake not to speak Korean at home."

"Maybe." If Whitney was exhausted before, she felt completely drained now, and she wished that Scott would hurry the hell up and get over there.

"You know," her father said, his deep voice cutting through the room, "when we first came to this country, we told ourselves that we were going to be Americans, and that we would raise our children as Americans. We had always thought of this country as the land of opportunity, and when we arrived, it was like a dream. We were so young and idealistic. Everyone in my Ph.D. program at Caltech was the same, sort of free and hippie. Even your mother was hippie. She had very long hair."

"God, I can't even imagine," Robert said.

"Oh, yes," her father said, his lips curling into a soft curve at the memory. "But now sometimes I regret not teaching you two more about our customs. It would be nice if you had more of a sense of where you come from, or what was going on in Korea today."

"Anyway, I'm glad our class reunion isn't until November," her mother said, her focused expression making clear that she was still contemplating what to brag about this year. "It is so tiring trying to keep up with everyone."

"You don't have to go," Robert said. "Normal people don't go to college reunions every year."

"How can we not go?" her father asked. "Everyone always goes, and it's so convenient, since Houston has a local association. It's an honor. It's almost impossible to get into *Seoul-dae*. Only the smartest people in Korea get into our college. It's like—like the Harvard of the Milky Way galaxy."

"Uh-huh," Whitney said.

"I only wish I could say that my children were married," her mother said wistfully. "I've been praying that you two will get married soon and start your lives."

Robert sighed, and his rumbling groan sounded more distressed than usual.

"Believe me, I'm looking." He fidgeted uncomfortably in his seat.

"Honey, I'm starting to worry that all the time you spent studying, you didn't try to find a nice girl to marry."

"I was with Eleanor for three years, remember? I don't think it was for lack of trying." He ran his hands through his hair and then propped his elbows on the table.

"Well, you haven't tried since you two broke up," she said, looking concerned.

"It's been three months, Mom."

"You're almost thirty-two. It's not good to be unmarried still at your age. You should call Gina. She is Mrs. Hahn's daughter. She's finishing her residency in Philadelphia, and I hear she's quite a catch. You two will make a beautiful couple." She nodded excitedly, as though the relationship were already set in stone. Never mind that Gina probably had no clue who Robert was, or the fact that she was thirteen hundred miles away. Never mind that she might be exceedingly busy, married, engaged, pregnant or gay.

"Please stop, Mom," he said wearily.

"I'm just trying to help you," she said, looking hurt. "It gets harder every year to find a wife. At least we don't have to worry about Whitney in that respect. She and Scott are going to get married before we know it."

It was Whitney's turn to object.

"Mom, please."

"Honey, we all know it's true." She rose from her seat, kissed the top of Whitney's head and then moved over to Robert. After planting another kiss on his cheek, she headed to the family room, where the Discovery Channel was now playing silently on the TV. As far as Asian families went, hers was unusually affectionate, and they made sure to kiss one another good-bye, even if they were simply retiring to a different part of the house. They were uncommonly garrulous, as well, unlike the stereotypical reticent, speak-only-in-incomprehensible-metaphors Asians she had seen in so many American portrayals. Still, as expressive as they were, she knew that they weren't flexible in their demands for professionally brag-worthy children, and the realization only weighted the burden on Whitney's shoulders.

"You really look like shit," Robert said, his voice rousing her from her thoughts. She peered at him and then at his designs, and he curled the paper towards him, as if concerned that she might actually understand his work.

"You're too kind," she said.

"Are you seriously working that much? You look like you haven't slept in days."

"That's because I haven't. I had to a get a motion for summary judgment ready this week for a partner I don't work for. Plus, I had to go through eighty boxes of documents by today." He looked at her blankly. "That's a lot."

He sighed heavily. "At least you've someone at the end of the day."

"At least you've got a job that you like."

"Want to trade?"

"Okay." She smiled at him, and he returned the expression.

"Seriously, Whitney, as much as I don't want to admit it, Mom's right. I'm going to be thirty-two this year, and unlike most of the guys I know, I actually *want* to get married. Hell, I'd settle for happy cohabitation." He twirled a mechanical pencil between his fingers like a windmill, a trick Whitney had never been able to master. "Don't you have any single friends? Someone at work or something?"

"You're that desperate?"

He fidgeted in his chair, looking uncomfortable. "I don't know where to meet anyone. It's not like we're in school anymore, where you run into more people than you can date. And the girls at NASA aren't exactly—well, you know."

"Why don't you meet Gina?"

He rolled his eyes. "Mom's got really questionable taste in women. Seriously, there's no one cute at your firm?"

"There are a bunch of cute girls at work, but most of them are married. And I'm not setting you up with any of the single ones, either."

"Come on, Whitney. Help a brother out."

"Fine," she said. "But if I find a girl for you, you're going to have to get Mom and Dad to back off on me. I can't stand how Mom always pushes me to make partner."

"What's wrong with becoming a partner? I thought it was what you wanted."

She gawked at him, feeling a rush of blood to her face. "When have I *ever* said that I wanted to be a partner?"

"I don't know." He shrugged. "I just assumed."

"Robert, I don't even want to be a *lawyer*. I thought that would've been obvious by now." She sank lower in her seat. "I know that I'm responsible for my own actions, but, God, if I knew back then what I know now . . ."

"Don't do that."

"What?"

"Your spiraling game of regrets. Do you know how lucky you are to have everything that you do?" He frowned, and the crease between his brows deepened into a vertical line. He had inherited their parents' pragmatism, and he shared their inability to separate satisfaction from success, happiness from prestige. "You went to a good school. You're at a good firm. You make a crapload of money. What more do you want?"

"I can't tell you."

His frown grew into a scowl, and his frustration was almost palpable. "Why not?"

"Because I can't." Almost under her breath, she said, "I'm not even sure that I can admit it to myself."

He stared at her, perhaps expecting details, but his severe Big Brother expression only caused her to retreat further into silence. As loose-lipped as he was, she couldn't afford for him to apprise their parents that she spent her weekends at local clubs where she demoed her music in front of sympathetic—or at least nonjudgmental—patrons. She hadn't even told the Valedictorians about her greatest love, even if she shared everything else with them, and while a twinge of guilt nagged at her for her secrecy, she also didn't need the extra attention.

She sighed heavily and closed her eyes. Frankly, had she been living anywhere but Houston, away from her parents' influence, and away from the bubble of mature achievements the Valedictorians inhabited, she might have had the courage to pursue her music full-time. In her dream world, she would have already gone after a recording contract or founded her own label with as much dogged ambition as she had focused on her studies. But here, she was tethered to their rigid expectations, and to her own, acutely bound by the umbilical cord of vicarious and self-driven ambitions. She was exactly what everyone had aspired for her to be, and as much as she recognized and loathed the stunted, boxed-in quality of her own notion of success, she also didn't feel that she had the wherewithal to break out of it.

"Do I need to worry about you?" Robert asked. She blinked quickly, bringing him back into focus.

"No, but I'd appreciate it if you talked to Mom."

"Why can't you just talk to her?"

"Because she doesn't listen to me. She listens to you."

"Fine. If you find me a girl, I'll talk to Mom."

"Deal."

The doorbell rang, and she bounced off the couch and ran to the foyer. After spying Scott through the windows that flanked the mahogany entrance, she flung the door open.

"Hey," he said, and then leaned down to kiss her. "Sorry I'm late. You ready to go?"

"Yeah, let me just get my things. Mom! Dad! I'm leaving!"

"Hi, Dr. Lee. Mrs. Lee," Scott said when they appeared in the foyer. He bowed deeply and let her mother hug him. From the corner of her eye, Whitney saw her father eyeing her with approval. He loved Scott like a son, and she had no doubt that he regarded their relationship as another mark on her belt of accomplishments. She grabbed her bag and headed for the door.

"See y'all later," she said, and then kissed her parents for the third time in a half hour.

"Oh, I'm so glad that you're such a good boy," her mother said, wrapping her arms around Scott.

"So am I," her father said. "Scott, you take good care of her." He was smiling, and Whitney got the distinct feeling that her parents were sending her off on her honeymoon.

"Yes, sir," Scott said, and then bowed again.

"Can we go now?" Whitney complained.

"See y'all later."

After waving all the way to her car, she sank into the passenger seat and sighed. It was time to get the night started.

"Do you have everything?" Scott asked, taking his eyes off the road to watch Whitney shimmy out of her skirt in the tight passenger seat of her BMW. Tate Philips' demo mix pumped through the speakers, and she concentrated on the soulful vocals, preparing herself for the parts that his backup singer couldn't perform tonight.

"Yeah." She slid into a pair of boot-cut Levi's, the faded six-year-old pair that hugged her hips, and tossed her skirt into the backseat. She pulled off her blouse next and exchanged it for a long-sleeved white linen shirt before reaching behind her for her black hand-tooled cowboy boots. She felt like Mr. Hyde now, her alter ego in stark contrast to the Dr. Jekyll familiar to the Valedictorians and her parents, and as they raced to Billy Bob's, she felt her inhibitions evaporate, the veneer of her overeducated pride strip away.

"I don't know why you can't just tell your parents what you do on the weekends," he said, concentrating on the steeply curving overpass. "I really hate that you have to keep everything a secret."

"They're not like your parents," she said. "They'd freakin' *kill* me." She sighed heavily. "You're lucky, you know that? Your parents support you no matter what you do. Mine don't."

"That's because they went to college and grad school. Mine barely finished high school." He turned down the volume a notch.

"What does that have to do with anything?"

"It changes their expectations. Your parents' dreams for you are bigger because theirs were so big to begin with. Mine are just glad that I didn't become a dry cleaner like they did. You should be grateful that your folks are so educated."

"And you should be grateful that yours accept you as you are. In any case, don't tell Robert."

"How does he not know?" He looked at her, amazed. "Y'all live together."

"I use headphones so that I don't make any noise playing the guitar. And he's as oblivious to the obvious as my folks are. Besides, we've got an agreement—I never go into his room, and he never comes into mine. It's the only way we've managed to retain any privacy." She laid her hand on his arm. "Promise me you won't say anything to him."

"Fine." He clenched his jaw, highlighting the taut muscles in his angular face, and under the fleeting flashes of the streetlights, his natural olive skin took on a deep shade of rust. With his rounded eyes, slender nose and curly hair, he looked like no Korean she had ever seen before, and when he had first arrived at her apartment, she had thought him to be at least part Hispanic.

"God, I'm cutting it close," she said. "I hope Tate's not worried."

"Is this a guy from work?" he asked, frowning. "How do you know him again?"

"We were in the same small section at Harvard, and we used to jam at his apartment." She chuckled. "You'd think that everyone at school was obsessed with becoming lawyers or academics, but a good third of my class wanted to be rock stars. Tate's one of the few who actually did something about it." She glanced at Scott, who didn't seem to be listening, and under her breath, she said, "I really admire him for that. I wish that I had the courage to do the same."

Scott swerved across three lanes, almost rear-ending at least one driver as he sped up, and she gripped the dashboard, startled. She was about to comment on his uncharacteristic recklessness when he spoke.

"So—I'm not going to be able to come with you to Billy Bob's anymore."

"Why?" she asked, still clutching for safety.

"The guys want to move our Thursday night Bible study to Friday. It works better for everyone. And I have my correspondence class on Saturdays." He crossed into another lane and then looked at her. "You know, the History of Jerusalem course I'm auditing at Dallas Theological Seminary."

"I know." She finally let go of the dashboard and massaged her stiff fingers, unsure how else to respond. When they had first met, Scott had gone to church as often as she had, which was to say that he attended service whenever he had woken up in time. Over the last several months, however, he had become increasingly involved with an evangelical group he had met on the basketball court, and while she was glad for his spiritual reawakening, she felt that his attitude had shifted, and that his devotion to God had ironically alienated them. His sudden dedication had made him more reserved, too, stoic, in fact, and as uninhibited and fun as he used to be, he now carried himself with a seriousness she hoped would snap soon.

"And I've got a retreat in a couple of weeks at Camp Cradle," he said. "It starts on Thursday before Valentine's Day and goes for a week. Pastor Dave Marsden from Holy Water Bible Church in California is going to be the speaker. We're really blessed to have him." He exited the freeway before turning towards her. "Did I tell you this already?"

"No, you didn't." A pang of disappointment welled in her chest. "So we basically won't see much of each other for, what, a month?"

"Something like that."

"But we've barely spent any time with each other since last Thanksgiving." She took in his impassive face, wounded that he didn't seem bothered that their time together had dwindled to almost nothing. "Sometimes, we don't even see each other all week."

"Well, we would if you went to Bible study with me." Even though he spoke matter-of-factly, she could almost feel the judgment in his voice, like an aggression that was lurking beneath his passive exterior.

"You go to a men's Bible study," she said flatly.

"You know what I mean. The church has a women's Bible study. You could go to that."

"I tried, Scott. Remember? I went at least eight times. I don't have anything in common with those girls."

"You have everything in common with them," he said, as if stating it as fact would make it so.

"No, we don't. We're in completely different stages of our lives. They're all married with kids, and none of them work demanding jobs. I don't know that any of them have ever worked at all." She reached for her bag and pulled out a compact. "No knock on them, and I'm glad that they're settled in life, but they don't understand me. And frankly, I don't understand them. I felt like the odd man out all the time. It was uncomfortable."

"Then find one that fits you better."

"I've gone to at least three. Two of them moved their meetings to the middle of the day, which is absolutely impossible for me. And the third was basically a group of singles looking for spouses." She powdered her now-burning face, catching his disapproving expression in her mirror, and then flung her makeup back into her bag. "Besides, why are you so obsessed that I go to a Bible study? Why isn't it enough that I go to church?"

"Because"—he sighed heavily—"it's like you're not taking your faith seriously, Whitney. You go to church when it's convenient for you, not because it's important. You don't seem to care. It's just killing me the way you take Christ's love for granted." His darkened expression highlighted his reprimand, and coupled with his accusation, he might as well have been challenging her salvation.

"What's wrong with you?" she asked, taken aback by his unfair characterization. "Your relationship with God—my relationship with

God—that's a personal thing. You can't measure it by how often I attend church or by how many Bible studies I go to. You have no idea whether I take my faith seriously—"

"You said that you wouldn't be able to go to service this Sunday because of work, right? Because you had a brief to write or something?"

"What?" she asked, offended by his interruption.

"You're *so* busy, but you have no problem going out tonight." His voice strained, as if he was pleading with her, or perhaps as if he was trying to control himself. Defensiveness stiffened her body.

"I promised Tate. He's paying me."

"Fifty bucks isn't exactly *paying*."

"I wouldn't ruin a friendship—or my reputation—over it, either. And that's so not the point. I'm playing with him tonight because I told him that I would, not because I'm hard up for fifty dollars."

"I don't even get why this is such a big deal to you. Aren't y'all just playing for fun? I thought his parents or cousins owned the place. You told me that most of the audience was his family members."

"They are. What's your point?"

"My point is"—he pulled into the parking lot and sighed again—"if God were a priority in your life, *really* a priority, you'd make the time to go to church every Sunday, not just when you don't have anything better to do. You'd make the time to find a Bible study or to fellowship with people who are edifying and not spend your nights at places like this." He found an empty spot and eased her car into it. "You wouldn't tell me that you had to work, or that you were busy with your music, or that you were going out with your friends, or the hundred other excuses you give."

"Excuses?" Her face burned, and her heart pounded against her chest. "You think I'm giving you *excuses*? I work seventeen hours a day, Scott. I go out with my friends once a month at most, and it's only for a two-hour dinner. And I work on my music when I should be sleeping. I'm doing the best that I can, and you're acting as if I'm missing church because I hang out at the pool all day and party all night."

"There you go again," he said, looking as if she had just proved his argument. "You find a way to justify yourself every time."

"That's really not fair," she said, her voice low. Frustration exacerbated the injustice she felt at his hands. For someone who extolled God's unconditional acceptance, who preached of his welcoming love, she couldn't understand why Scott's brand of evangelism was unreasonably unyielding, or so hypocritically off-putting.

"What's not fair is that you haven't made any kind of effort. . . ."

"You *know* how hard I've tried," she said. "It's not like I would've hunted for a Bible study if I didn't know how important it was to you."

"That's the problem, Whitney. It should be important to you, too. That's what I'm trying to tell you."

"What do you want from me?" she asked, feeling as if he were draining the life out of her.

"You don't want to know." He sounded equally weary.

"Yeah—I do."

He stared at her for a long moment, pensive, and for the next uncomfortable minute, neither spoke.

"Honestly—" He stopped short and looked away.

"Scott, just say it."

"I want you to stop with this nonsense"—he motioned at Billy Bob's—"and get serious about life, Whitney. I want you to focus on the things that matter. I want you to love God and to serve him as if your life depended on it, because it does."

She recoiled, horrified by his condemnation of her greatest love, as if it were nothing more than a frivolous, earthly delight with no relevance or merit to eternity—or to him. Blood gushed between her temples, practically deafening her with its roaring pulse.

"I don't know why everything is suddenly so all-or-nothing with you," she said. "My music is important to me. As important as Bible studies and retreats are to you. You can't ask me to give it up any more than I can ask you to give up your faith."

"I didn't ask you to give it up." He spoke so quietly that she could barely hear him. "You asked what I wanted, and I told you." He sighed and rubbed his forehead. "Forget it. Just forget what I said." He popped the trunk, looking as if he didn't plan on getting out of the car, and she swung her door open.

"You don't really want me to forget," she said, her voice drowned by the boisterous music emanating from the club. "And it's not like I even could."

She stepped onto the graveled parking lot and marched to the back side of her car, hurt and disbelief overwhelming her. Blinking quickly, she gritted her teeth, pulled her guitar case out of the trunk and walked into Billy Bob's. She glanced back, unable to see Scott in the darkness of the room, before heading to a table beside the stage where Tate Philips was chatting with his cousins and pointing at a notebook of lyrics spread on his lap. He looked up, catching her eye, and waved her over. She sat down next to him, and he leaned over and kissed her cheek.

"Hey, sweetheart, I was worried that you might not show. My mom offered to take Heather's parts, but I'd rather gouge my eyes out than sing about how the girl next to me makes me hot and bothered with my *mother*." He laughed, and his throaty cackles blunted the edges of her bad mood. In the dim club, his long dark hair was almost black, and the dilated pupils of his pale blue eyes made them appear darker. He wasn't good-looking, exactly, not with his eerily pale skin and a paunch that belonged on a middle-aged man, but his talent made him incredibly attractive, a variety of personality as appealing as a great sense of humor.

"I'm so sorry that I'm late," she said. "I was having some"—she didn't even know how to describe what had kept her—"troubles."

"Then, you're in the right place, baby." He nudged his cocktail towards her, and she took a sip, feeling the bourbon burn her throat.

"Hey, Whitney," Chris said, reaching out to grab her hand. "You comin' to Mason's next week?"

"Yeah." She nodded, glad that Tate's cousin had given her an open invitation to his bar/BBQ joint/backyard venue in Austin.

"Good deal."

She waved her hellos to another five Philipses, all of them in ad hoc bands composed mostly of members of their unending gene pool. As they chatted, she pulled Tate's lyrics in front of her and double-checked her timing on his lead song while he placed his squat fingers over the fret board, practicing what they were about to perform.

She closed her eyes and sucked in a few deep breaths, trying her best to push her argument with Scott out of her mind. After a second, she opened her eyes and pulled her Fender Strat out of its case, the electric guitar she used once for every dozen times she strummed on her acoustic ones. Tate's music was harder than hers, a gruffer, riff-ridden style in stark contrast with her calm, coffee-shop style, but despite the difference, she loved singing with him, loved how she felt when she harmonized to his strong melody. They had spent too much time in law school writing music when they should have studied for exams, and had fantasized about their singing careers when they should have prepared for moot court. She had filled in for his partner whenever the need arose, and outside of Scott, he was the only one who had ever watched her sing. They had an easy relationship, one of implicit understanding, and even though they saw each other only a handful of times per year, she always felt as if they had been in each other's presence the entire time.

"You ready?" he asked when the ten o'clock set bowed their goodnight.

"Yeah."

They walked onto the stage, he with his drink in tow, and she with a bottle of water. A bright spotlight made it difficult to see her audience, and outside of a few small tables arranged towards the front, the rest of the club was shrouded in a sea of darkness. She searched the small room for a glimpse of Scott, and when she didn't spot him, she sighed and reached down to plug her guitar into the amplifier. Tate glanced over, and when she nodded, he began to strum his guitar, the intoxicating sounds catching everyone's attention.

"Baby, I saw you sittin' there," he drawled into the microphone, his raspy voice echoing against the walls. "You had no idea that I was around. I watched you laughin' with another man. Your charm made me fall to the ground."

"Did I catch your attention?" Whitney joined in.

"Darlin', won't you even notice me—"

" 'Cause you don't know I'm alive—"

"You don't know I'm alive—"

Whitney closed her eyes, losing herself to the song. She imagined that heaven was a grander version of Billy Bob's, where she and God would perch themselves on a stage of clouds, singing with their guitars. A choir of angels would harmonize in the background, jam with them happily instead of criticizing her faults. Such was her paradise, and for the few moments when she leaned into the microphone and strummed the taut strings, she felt as though she were being given a preview.

Three

Hercules walked into her foyer and flung her keys onto the gilded marble table that flanked the wall opposite the spiraling staircase. The brisk, late-afternoon wind swept into the area, chilling the warm air. She waited for Reynaldo Gonzales, her business manager/public relations consultant/personal assistant, to carry his tripod, camera and endless bags of accessories into the house, and from the sound of his grunting and panting, he needed help. Good, she thought, let him struggle.

"Hercules, I'm telling you, you *need* to do this to repair the public's perception of you," he said between ragged breaths. He stumbled through the door and eased two cases of equipment onto the floor, and unmoved by the desperation in his voice, she watched as he straightened his charcoal suit around his boxy frame. "Most Houstonians don't have a clue who you are. For all they know, you're this spoiled brash princess who's never had to work a day in her life. If they knew where you came from, and how hard you and your family worked to get to be where you are, they'd jump all over you. And into your restaurant. You've *got* to do this article for the *Houston Chronicle*. I've already talked to Corrine in the Style section—well, *begged* is probably more accurate—and she's agreed to another article."

"My private life is my private life," she said, feeling her cheeks burn. "I *don't* want the whole city knowing everything about me." Leaving his cases in the hallway, she walked to the family room. He trailed behind, and this being his first time in her home, he gawked at the travertine floors, quadruple crown moldings and twenty-foot ceilings. He dropped his bags when he came upon a thirty-foot wall of windows that looked out on her infinity pool, and stared slack-jawed for a few moments at the magnificent greens of the golf course before swinging around to face her.

"This is what I'm talking about," he said, motioning around him.

"America *loves* a rags-to-riches tale. You're a real Horatio Alger story, you know. I can just see the front page of the Style section. *Hercules Huang—from the Rice Fields of China to the Queen of Texas Cooking.* Doesn't that sound compelling to you?"

"No, it doesn't," she said, irritated by the unflattering title and his unfettered ogling of her house. "I didn't come from rice fields. Beijing's a freakin' city, for God's sake."

"Well, hear me out. . . ."

"No, I will not." Her voice echoed against the faux-finished walls. "I don't want pictures of my house in the newspaper, I don't want my goofy face splashed all over the pages, and I sure as hell don't want the whole city to know that I grew up in a slum in China or the projects of the South. Not everyone wants their Horatio Alger story published, and I'll be damned if I share what my childhood was like with anyone other than you. Not even my closest friends know how screwed up my relationship is with my father, and you're trying to make it sound like we built *my* businesses together."

"We can keep that part out, then," he said, exasperated. "But you said that you were open to damage control."

"It was a stupid article in a shitty paper. What's there even to fix?"

"It was a six-page article in a paper with a circulation of over twenty-five million people, if you're counting Internet subscribers. It's important, Hercules. Did you read the op-eds? People are really upset. They think you consider Texans a bunch of uncultured hicks."

"I never said that," she said angrily.

"You didn't have to. But you *do* have to fix your image. Besides, you agreed to let me do this. You even agreed to let me take pictures of your house. I wouldn't have lugged fifty pounds of equipment in here otherwise." He took off his black square glasses and pinched the bridge of his nose, a sure sign of breaking-point stress.

"Well, I changed my mind. And, to be fair, you never said that you were taking pictures to go along with this—hell, I don't know *what* kind of story you're going after. I thought you were going to take pictures of my kitchen and have some kind of blurb about what chefs really eat when they're not at the restaurant."

"What if you wrote the article yourself?" he pressed, his fatigued eyes beginning to look bloodshot. "I could talk to Corrine and see if she'll let you do that. It'll be about how you became something of a celebrity in Houston, in your own words. I'll just edit it. You know, take out all the F-bombs."

"Maybe," she said, relenting a little as she considered. "Okay." Frankly, a warmer spread in the *Chronicle* would be good for Dragonfly and Dragonfly Deux, and even she knew that she had to endear herself to the city's fickle patrons. Besides, it would be additional promotion for Hercules Cookware, and the folks at Acceleron would likely giggle with glee at the free advertising.

"Terrific. Since I'm here, I might as well take a picture of your kitchen. Just your kitchen. And then, we'll go from there." He looked at her hopefully, his red eyes pleading. She softened at his demeanor.

"Fine."

Reynaldo brightened. "You'll thank me for this." He ran towards the foyer and seconds later, Hercules heard him noisily unloading his camera equipment.

She walked into her family room, sank into the plush Henredon sofa and closed her eyes. The way she and Reynaldo bickered, they might as well have been married. She treated him like a younger brother, even though he was six years older than she, and despite her abusive behavior towards him, she found that she always ended up doing what he said. She opened her eyes and grabbed the remote control. The TV had just fizzed to life when the phone rang, and a series of cacophonous rings echoed throughout the house.

"Hello?" she answered, muting the volume of the TV.

"Is this Her—uh, Hercules Huang?" a voice said.

"Yes. Who's this?"

"This is Calvin Joseph from City Credit USA. You're the cosigner for a Mr.—oh, Lord—Jian Hu Huang?" His voice sounded as though a clothespin had been affixed to his nose, and when he butchered Baba's name, Hercules felt her own nostrils flare.

"Yes, I am."

"I see that Mr. Huang is now three months behind on his Visa bill.

I've called his house, but I've not been able to speak to him. Clearly, at least."

"What does that mean?" She laid the remote on the coffee table, aggravated anew.

"I spoke to him once, and he yelled at me in some kind of gibberish and then hung up," Calvin continued in his nasal voice. The tenor of his whiny drone was made worse by the content of his speech, and Hercules was suddenly overcome by the urge to punch him in the mouth.

"How much does he owe on the account?" she asked, her voice nearly a shout. Her face felt hot, and sweat beaded on her chest.

"Twenty-five hundred dollars."

"What's he buying for twenty-five hundred dollars?" she shrieked.

"Well, most of the purchases are from Albertsons. Some are from a Di—um, Diho Chinese Market. Some are from Shell and Texaco. You can review his purchases online."

"And you're calling for me to pay the bill?" she asked, already knowing the answer.

"Yes, ma'am."

Hercules sighed, letting the rumbles of her exhale rasp against Calvin's ear.

"Fine. I'll write you a check and send it tomorrow."

"Thank you, ma'am."

"Is there anything else?"

"No, ma'am. You have a good night."

Hercules hung up without a return salutation. Motherfucker, she thought, letting the word roll around in her mind. Motherfucking motherfucker. Because her father's credit history essentially precluded him from applying for a credit card, she had to sign on to the account as a guarantor. Two years had passed without incident, and she had all but forgotten that she was the bank's ultimate deep pocket. What was he doing, anyway? It wasn't like him to let his credit card bills slide. The longer she thought about the old man, the angrier, and more worried, she became.

"Is everything okay?" Reynaldo asked. With his Nikon hanging from his neck, he looked like a tourist in her home.

"I've got to go. You can stay here if you want."

"No, I'm finished. I heard your conversation. What's wrong?"

"I need to make sure my father's still alive." She felt her shoulders clench, and she must have pulled a horrendous face, because Reynaldo approached in full counselor mode and took a seat next to her.

"Talk to me. What's going on?"

"My father's the bane of my existence—that's what's going on," she yelled. "I've done everything I can to make him happy. I pay all his bills, his rent, his insurance—I even bought him a car last year. And I've never even gotten so much as a *thank you.* He never says it, but I can just tell that I'm some kind of burden to him. Well, guess what? *He's* the one who's a burden. We all know that if I weren't here, he'd be SOL. And now I think he's got Alzheimer's. Either that or he's refusing to take his medication again. He's forgetting the littlest things—like his Visa bill."

"Calm down. Just go over there and work it out. His bill was probably an oversight. And I doubt he thinks of you as a burden."

She sank deeper into the cushions and groaned loudly, her frustrations fueling her feral growl.

"He's only sixty-nine, but he acts like he's a hundred. Sometimes, I think he's just *waiting* to die. I don't understand. He didn't used to be this way. He used to be pleasant, if you can believe that."

"Calm—"

"Like I even have time for this right now," she seethed.

"Hercules, relax. It's unhealthy to bottle up all this anger." He inhaled slowly, causing his bulbous stomach and rounded shoulders to rise close to his head. "Try breathing deeply." She threw him a caustic look, and he responded with another deep breath. "Breathing deeply helps relieve stress, you know. Or join a karate class, if you want. Maybe you should talk to your girlfriends about him. You need to find some kind of release."

"There's no way I'd ever tell Whitney or Audrey about my dad. You have no idea what kind of perfect families they have. They wouldn't even begin to understand what it's like to have a difficult parent."

"Why do you talk to me about it, then?" He didn't look bothered to serve as her therapist. In fact, he almost seemed pleased to have her confidence.

"Because you *understand* me. You might be the only person who does." She sighed heavily. "God, why do I even care? Things would be so much easier if I just left him to rot."

"I wouldn't be working with you if I didn't think you had at least one compassionate bone in your body."

"I swore that I would be nicer to him," she said, her voice lowering to a normal decibel. "That was my New Year's resolution, by the way, to work on our relationship so that it's halfway decent. I'm already failing at it."

"It's only January," he said. "These things take time."

She glanced at her watch and then jumped off the couch.

"I've got to go. I'll have that article ready for you by the end of next week. You're going to follow me out, right?"

"Yes."

She helped him pack up his belongings, and they walked out of the house together. He patted her arm gently and headed for his used Lexus ES, and she watched him ease into his car as she hopped into her brand-new Porsche. For all her material success, she sometimes wished that she could trade lives with him, if only to understand the source of his serenity and even-keeled temperament. Then again, the exchange would require him to walk in her shoes, and she loved him too much to let that happen.

"Baba? Baba!" Hercules let herself into the shoe box of an apartment. The door caught on something, and she pushed harder before realizing that she had somehow ripped the threadbare carpet.

He looked up from the couch, and if he was startled that someone had just let herself into his home, he didn't look it. His slight frame was draped in a camel-colored rugby shirt and tan pants, and his gauntness accentuated the unnatural largeness of his head, replete with tufts of white hair. If there were such a thing as a living, breathing bobble head, he was it.

"Oh, you're here," he said unenthusiastically.

"Why didn't you answer the door?" She spoke in Mandarin, the only language her father understood, the same language she wished she never had to use in his presence.

"Because you have a key."

"What's going on here?" She surveyed the room, taking in the zigzag pattern of the beige and black couch, the glass top of the ancient coffee table, and the hazy surface of a wooden dining room table that took up most of the back space of the room. From the front door, she could see everything in the apartment save his bedroom, and she already knew that the furniture there was as dilapidated as the mismatched items in the main living area. She didn't even want to guess what his bathroom looked like. The hovel reminded her of the apartment they had shared until she went to New York to attend the Culinary Institute of America, but with none of the charm or sweet reminiscence. It was even in the same Sharpstown neighborhood, the sprawling Chinatown of Houston, where all the street signs were in Hanzi, everyone jabbered in Cantonese or Mandarin, and if you roamed the streets, you might even forget that you were in America.

"Did you eat?" she asked, her voice softer now. Her friends would be astounded to know that she didn't always speak in bellows, or that she could refrain from screeching out *motherfucker* when she chose. Baba couldn't stand yelling, and his ears perked up when she cursed, bringing a glower to his weathered features. It was a facial expression Hercules never wanted to see, and so, though it took all her might, she refrained from using four-letter words in his presence.

"Yes," he said.

"What did you eat?"

"I made some rice."

"That's it?"

He let out an exasperated snort, as if she was disturbing his TV watching with her questions.

"I had some vegetables, too," he said.

"Did you take your medicine?"

He glanced at her from the corners of his slatted eyes, and his leathered features crinkled.

"You don't have to treat me like an invalid."

"If you took your medicine regularly, I wouldn't have to." She searched the dining room table for his pills, the generic prescriptions of thiazolidinediones, meglitinides and phenylalanines, chemicals that jump-started his pancreas and triggered the insulin reaction his body no longer recalled.

"They hurt my stomach," he said, watching as she measured his dosage.

"You need to take them, Baba."

"I already did."

She strode towards the galley kitchen, crinkling her nose at the smell. The apartment always reeked of Chinese herbs, a putrid stench like Ben-Gay mixed with licorice and burning walnuts, and despite having been raised with the odor, the nauseating concoction had never grown on her. It emanated from her father's clothes, from the carpet and from the furniture. The noxious aroma sent her skin crawling, and she searched the cabinets for the source of the scent.

A refrigerator banged to life, drowning out the sounds of the TV. She stepped back, halfway believing that the machine would rattle off into orbit. With a violent jerk, she flung the door open and peered inside. A few eggs and a jar of pickled lotus roots were the only inhabitants of the ancient Whirlpool, and the freezer contained little more than a packet of grocery-store-bought pork dumplings. The rice cooker still hummed with life, and random packages of shrimp crackers lined the sparse counter.

She returned to the living room, careful not to trip over the rubbish that littered the center of the space.

"This TV is worthless," he said, struggling with the remote control. "I can never find my channels."

"Why can't you ever say *thank you* for the gifts I buy you?" She eased the remote control out of his grip and pressed the VCR rubber button. Immediately, his Chinese drama appeared on the screen.

"I never asked you to buy me a TV. This one is so thin." The tone of his voice matched the flatness of the fifty-inch plasma, and his expression revealed no pleasure in what she had considered to be a thoughtful present.

"That's because it's a flat-screen," she said. "You don't have enough room in here for a conventional one. Besides, you'd been complaining about your old TV for months. It was obvious that you needed a new one."

"It was a waste of money for you, then, because I don't even want it. How can anyone figure out how to use it? Why don't you ever think about these things?"

She sucked in a deep breath, willing herself not to flare at his passive-aggressive behavior. She didn't remind him that he had blasted her for his former piece-of-crap television, and she knew that had she not bought the expensive Sony that now dangled from his wall, he would be criticizing her for her failure to care for him.

"With all the videos you watch, I didn't want you to ruin your eyes on that tiny thing," she said. "Besides, I don't want you living like this."

"Like what?"

"Like this, Baba," she repeated, gesturing to the small expanse of his living room/dining room/kitchen. "It's a pigsty."

"With order comes chaos, and chaos, order." She couldn't tell if he was mocking her. "It is only a mess now because I'm in the process of cleaning. You'd better be cleaning out your house, too."

"Why would I? It's always clean. Melinda comes twice a week."

He frowned, and the deep wrinkles that framed his eyes and mouth accentuated the sallowness of his skin.

"Americans have no idea how to clean a house properly. They throw out all the luck and only keep in the bad spirits. The New Year begins in two weeks. You must prepare yourself for it, Xiao-Xiao."

She stirred at the sound of her given name. Her father was the only one who called her Xiao-Xiao. *Hercules* had been her first-grade creation, a response to the butchered attempts of her classmates and teachers to pronounce her grandmother-bestowed designation, and

when she had picked it in honor of her favorite Chinese cartoon character, she had no idea that no American girl would call herself after
a Greco-Roman demigod. Still, despite the teasing she had endured
because of it, she had to admit that she relished the power of the name,
and she took pride in the uniqueness of her identity.

"We're at the end of January," she said, already aware of how fruitless her argument was.

"You will come next Monday to pay your respects to our ances-
tors," he said monotonically. "Even if it is only the two of us."

She didn't respond. Her father waited five weeks after Dick Clark
counted down to the New Year before celebrating the festivity on the
lunar calendar. For weeks before the big day, he dedicated himself to
scrubbing the apartment with choreographed movements, and when he
wasn't cleaning, he was making *mandou*, savory pork dumplings, from
scratch in his tiny kitchen. Perhaps he had forgotten that the Chinese
New Year was a day of thanksgiving and family, hope and expectation
for the future. There was nothing so disheartening as kneeling before
a small wooden table laden with fruit, flowers and candy with a man
who was neither grateful nor hopeful. For that reason, she had refused
to celebrate the Chinese New Year with Baba since her return from
culinary school. Clearly, her behavior was disgraceful, but so was his.
She remained standing where she was and studied the room again.

"How many times do I have to ask you to move in with me?" she
asked. It was a non sequitur question, in line with the non sequitur
conversations they always had. Their dialogues were in keeping with
the rest of their relationship, as incongruous and forced as they were
with each other.

"I don't like your house."

"Why?"

"It has bad chi, Xiao-Xiao. It's so dark with all those north-facing
windows. There's no light or life there. Besides"—he glanced over
quickly—"it's obvious that you don't want me in your home." He
shook his massive head, the shocks of his movements sending his ashen
locks to sway under the dingy lights. "Such an ungrateful child. What
did I ever do to deserve a daughter like you?"

The hairs on her neck bristled, and she gulped down a lump of bitterness. She refused to let him know how deeply his comment stung or how all his comments cut down her self-esteem. Instead, she crossed her arms, as if to protect herself from his criticisms, and clenched her jaw.

"You're being ridiculous," she said. "You think I'd ask you to move in with me if I didn't want you there?"

"Yes."

She twitched her lips, unable to formulate a convincing response. The truth was that she really, *really* didn't want Baba in her house. She asked only because she couldn't stand the guilt of seeing her father in such disarray, and his living in the ghetto while she luxuriated in her mansion ate away at her conscience. He looked sideways at her again, expressionless as usual, and she could almost taste their mutual resentment.

"Are you still working at a restaurant?" he asked.

"I'm not just working there. I own it. I've owned it since day one." Her shoulders clenched further, and she gritted her teeth.

"I didn't come to this country so that you can work like a slave in a kitchen. How many times did I tell you not to do it, to do something more meaningful with your life? How many times do you not listen to me? You have no understanding what the meaning of respect is. You have no idea how much you disappoint me."

"Baba, would you please leave it alone?"

"Your mother would be so terribly disappointed. I know that her spirit is disappointed."

"I said leave it alone," she said sharply.

"So, when are you getting married?" he asked without looking at her.

"When I find a man."

"When are you going to find a man? You're an old maid now."

"Men are not *things*, Baba. You don't just go out and get one." She sank into a tape-bound chair, feeling darker than she had felt all day. There was no way she could share with him how lonely she was or how she likewise longed for a relationship. If people thought that her professional success was inversely related to her desire for marriage and family, they were dead wrong, and her constantly single status was a dilemma she didn't want to share, not even with the Valedictorians. *Especially* not with the Valedictorians.

"In China, your situation would be unacceptable," he said with a grunt.

"What, being single?" She resisted the urge to roll her eyes. "First of all, that's not true, and second, we're not in China. We're in *A-mer-ica*. It would be nice if you could accept that and try to speak English sometime."

"Why do I need to speak English? I don't know anyone who does other than you."

"Do you know how ignorant that sounds?" She caught herself yelling and lowered her voice. "Do you know why I'm here? Guess who just called? The Visa bill collector. They had to call *me* because they couldn't understand what you were saying. *That's* why you need to learn to speak the language."

"I made it this far without having to learn, Xiao-Xiao," he said defensively. "And I'm still alive."

"That's only because you worked in a bunch of Chinese restaurants. I don't know what you would've done if every town in America didn't have a Chinese buffet." She wasn't being sarcastic. Her family had arrived from Beijing in Little Rock, Arkansas, of all places, and they had lived with a host family while her father worked at Super Buffet 8. A year later, they relocated to Natalia, Texas, a town so small that even Dairy Queen refused to set up shop there. Natalia still had Super China Buffet, though, and her father stir-fried to the best of his ability until they moved to Houston.

"We're Chinese, Xiao-Xiao," he said, as if to prove a point of which she wasn't already aware. "We should speak Chinese."

"We're American, too," she shot back. "We live in Texas, which is about as American as it gets. We've been living in this country for twenty-five years." She glared at him, completely at a loss as to why he refused to face reality. Why couldn't he accept his current surroundings and try to fit in? Why couldn't he at least *try* to assimilate?

He stirred in his seat and then returned to his show, apparently finished with their conversation. She checked her watch, dismayed to find that it was already six thirty. She breathed in deeply, putting Reynaldo's advice to practice, and tried again.

"I think it would be best if you moved in with me. It might make things easier for the both of us."

"You treat me like an invalid," he muttered. "Always treating me like an invalid."

"I'm treating you like my father. You can leave all this cra—furniture, and start over at my house. Okay?"

"In Beijing, you'd be married with three children by now. Your husband and you would take care of me. You would respect me and not treat me like an afterthought because you feel guilty about your own selfishness." He spoke with little emotion, but the emotional, exasperated side of Hercules heard nothing but entitlement and self-importance.

"If you're so stuck on how things are done in China, then you should never have moved here. You think I'm being selfish? Watch the news sometime and see how kids are treating their parents these days. You'd be *shocked*. Shocked!"

"Chinese children would never speak to their elders like this."

"Oh, for God's sake. I don't have time for this. I've got to go to work." She snatched her bag off the floor and swung it over her shoulder with a violent jerk. "You stay here by yourself, wishing that you were back in Beijing. I'm leaving."

She walked slowly towards the front door, expecting him to plead with her to return. When she reached the entrance, he didn't say anything, and when she opened the door, he was still silent. With an exasperated groan, she closed the door behind her and waited, still halfway expecting for him to call out to her. After counting to five, she headed towards her car, noticing just how out of place her Porsche Carrera was in the low-income apartment complex. She sighed a final time, knowing full well that she'd be back to try to reason with him soon enough.

Hercules stood in the alley behind Dragonfly, cell phone clutched in one hand, and her leather-bound Filofax secured in her other. Lucas Christensen had left her a voice mail while she had been at her father's apartment, relaying that he had found a perfect location for their San Antonio restaurant. They had dreamed of opening an eatery together since their last days at the CIA, but life had a way of pushing dreams to the outer edges of their priorities. Over the last year, however, their casual conversations had evolved into an almost obsessive brainstorm over the joint venture, and what had been a pastime of fantasy escapism now felt almost real.

She glanced at the restaurant and listened absently to the lively chatter that wafted into the cool darkness of the narrow street. Her four sous chefs could manage without her for half an hour, and if they couldn't, she would fire them all. She located Lucas's number in her agenda, pressed the microscopic numbers of her razor-slim phone with a pudgy thumb and waited. After a few rings, he picked up.

"Dude, Hercules, I had the weirdest feeling that you'd call right now." He still spoke with a laid-back surfer drawl, even though he had left Maui fifteen years ago.

"Did you?"

"Yeah. So, how's it going, man?" he asked. She could tell through the line that he was smiling, and she imagined his brilliant teeth set against his bronzed skin, complete with the seashell necklace he refused to cook without.

"Good enough," she said. "What about you?"

"Great. Hey, check it out. My girlfriend's moving in with me."

"That's fantastic. How's Michelle doing?"

"Actually, it's Tracy. And she's doing fine."

"What happened to Michelle? Y'all were together last month."

"*C'est la vie*, man. When you know, you know. Tracy's the one for me, not Michelle."

Hercules guffawed.

"What about you?" he asked. "You seeing someone special?"

"I don't have time for special. Hell, I don't have time for *not special*, either." She dug the tip of her rubber moccasin into the gravel, uncomfortable with the topic and her pathetic attempt to appear something other than lonely. "Trust me, I've been out with my fair share of *not specials*, and I don't have a time machine to unwaste my time."

"I could set you up with someone, if you're interested," he said. "There's a buddy of mine who I think would be great for you."

"Please," she said, rolling her eyes in the darkness, "spare me the pity. Besides, who said that I was even looking? I've got my restaurants to worry about. Dragonfly is busier than ever, and construction's keeping me up all night at Dragonfly Deux."

"Is that what you're calling it? Dragonfly Deux?"

"Yeah."

"*Man*"—he sighed heavily—"to have your own restaurants. Must be nice."

"Must be nice to be the executive chef at Buccari. I hear rumors of a possible Michelin star. It would be a first for that dump you call a city."

"Even if the rumors were true, what does it matter? It's not mine, you know?" Through the line, she could hear his longing. "There's a difference. I don't own Buccari, Hercules. You own Dragonfly and Dragonfly Deux. Anyway, I've been thinking about that for a while, and I'm totally stoked to get our baby off the ground. I think I found the perfect spot for us."

"Where?"

"There's a vacant space off in old San Antonio. It used to be a restaurant, so all we'd have to do is the finish out. The city's full of general contractors, and we'd be able to hire some folks for next to nothing. Gary knows a few people."

"Who's Gary?"

"He's a friend of mine who works at La Trattoria. He's an awesome cook, and he's interested in teaming up with us. Actually, he's the one who wanted to go the fusion route and lean heavily into Chinese cuisine."

"You talked to someone else about our restaurant?" Hercules asked,

floored by his audacity. She was offended that an outsider had tres-
passed onto her and Lucas's brainchild, and she felt pettily betrayed by
Lucas's having allowed another voice to guide *their* vision.

What sounded like a gunshot blasted from the kitchen, and Hercules jumped at the noise. Through the greasy window that separated
her restaurant from the alley, she saw a ball of fire explode from the
range. Simon Brills, the superstar of her sous chefs, sprinted across the
kitchen with a fire extinguisher. She hurried to the window, wondering
what in the world they were doing.

"We're actually pretty far into the planning process," Lucas said,
oblivious to both her agitation and the deafening noise around her.
"We were thinking of calling the place Zodiac. The theme of the place
would be the twelve signs of the Chinese zodiac. That was Gary's
thought, anyway. I haven't had much time to think about it, but I love
the idea, and it's a pretty safe bet to go with upscale Chinese food.
What do you think?"

Another ball of fire burst on the burner, and she stared, frozen, as
Simon hosed down the flames. The other sous chefs stood by, equally
motionless, and gawked at the spectacle. She headed to the door, her
strides as long as they had ever been.

"Hey, Lucas, hold on a second," she yelled over the whoosh of the
fire extinguisher. "I've got to deal with something." She sprinted into
the kitchen with her phone to her side, and they turned their gaping
stares towards her.

"Something's wrong with the range," Simon said, pointing out the
obvious. "There's a busted gas line or something. Every time we try to
flambé, we get a crazy fireball."

"With all of the burners?" she asked.

"I don't know. We've only tried the far right one."

"Try the others, but only if you can do it without killing yourselves.
When we built this place, we had all the gas lines separated, so hopefully we won't have to shut down the range tonight."

"Yes, Chef," Simon said. The others exchanged wary glances.

She retreated to the alley, keeping an eye on the twelve-burner
range through the filthy window. The grime bothered her, and she re-

solved to clean it, along with the rest of the restaurant, before the Chinese New Year. She was surprised by her automatic reaction, and as her thoughts turned to her father, she tried to squelch the corresponding guilt and fresh irritation.

"Is everything okay?" Lucas asked. "What happened?"

"One of the million things that can go wrong when you own a restaurant."

"Your and Gary's experience will really come in handy, Hercules. You should meet him, and soon. He's really something else. He reminds me of you, actually. Just impressive."

"Is he, now? So, have y'all already discussed staffing?" Even in the face of her sarcasm, it was obvious that Lucas didn't sense that she was upset, and his lack of perception incensed her even more.

"Sort of. We kind of assumed that you'd be too busy with your restaurants in Houston to want to work in the kitchen, so we decided that I'd be the executive chef and Gary would be the executive sous. We still need to hire a saucier and a pastry chef, and probably a few sous chefs, too. I really don't know how you manage your kitchen without an executive sous."

"That's why I've got my business manager. It frees up some time to let me work the menus, and I can still keep up with the daily ops without pulling out my hair." Her stomach knotted as she watched Simon pour brandy into a sauté pan, as nervous as the rest of the gathered chefs. Panic surged through her veins, and she realized how cavalier, and *stupid*, her original solution had been. What was she thinking, asking them to test the other ranges?

"Shit, something's about to blow in the kitchen, and I mean that literally," she said. "I've got to go."

"Okay. Think about what we talked about, though."

"Fine." She hung up and raced into the restaurant. Just as Simon was about to tilt his pan towards the flame, she jerked his arm away.

"Don't," she said, and then turned off the burner. "Let's call the gas company."

The sous chefs exhaled slowly, relieved that they wouldn't be blasted to smithereens tonight. Simon headed towards the phone, and the rest of them scattered around the kitchen to fulfill the patrons' raw orders. Hercules pulled out four portable burners from a shelf under the center island. She had purchased them for such an occasion, and though her peers had lovingly mocked her doomsday worries, her foresight was going to save the evening. She had always been an expert problem solver, a pro planner and strategizer, yet for all her solutions, she had never been able to fix her love life. And she had no idea how to fix her father.

Four

*A*udrey looked up, startled out of her thoughts, when Victor Smith trudged into their open loft with three weeks' worth of dry cleaning slung over his shoulder. Leaves of plastic wrap fluttered about his broad back as he shut the door, and he flung the heavy load onto an oversized leather chair in the living room, grunting with the effort.

"Hey, Auds," he said, massaging his forearm before moving to the kitchen. He returned with two soft drinks to the dining room table, where she had been perched since classes at St. Mark's had let out for the day. She pushed a towering stack of eighteenth-century literature out of the way, giving her an unobstructed view of his hazel eyes and deeply tanned skin, before leaning forward and kissing him on the lips.

"Hey," she said. "Thanks for picking up the laundry."

"Sure. I figured that you were busy with your paper." He leaned over, taking a look at the draft on her computer screen, and then handed her a can of Diet Coke. "You've been working on it nonstop for the last couple of weeks."

"That's because I finally figured out where my dissertation's supposed to go." She popped the top of her drink, glad to discuss her topic with a live human being instead of hashing out ideas within the confines of her mind. "You know how I was stressing about my comparative analysis of the Christian Resurrection story in literature? Well, I've focused my topic to postmodern humanistic approaches to the narrative, and I'm going to concentrate on what I'm calling the Internet Sphere of Literature. I'm psyched that it's finally coming together."

"Well, if you're psyched, I'm psyched, even if I don't know exactly what you're talking about."

"You know more than you pretend to. You were the one who turned me on to the whole idea of the Web as the new medium of discourse."

"That's because it is." He smiled, his braces-straight teeth practically glowing against his bronzed skin, and then plopped another kiss on her lips. "I can't believe my girlfriend's going to be a *doctor*. I'm so proud of you, Auds."

"Are you?" she asked, elated.

"You have no idea. You're going to be a tenured professor before you know it."

"I can't even tell you how great that would be." She let out a deep breath, pondering the desire that had filled her heart over the last year. "Hey, don't tell anyone that I want to be a professor, okay?"

"Your friends don't know?" he asked, surprised.

"No one knows, actually. Other than you."

"Why can't you tell Hercules or Whitney?"

"Because"—she felt slightly foolish for her secrecy—"there's no guarantee that I'll be granted a position, and I couldn't stand their pity if they knew that I had tried and failed."

"You won't fail, sweetheart."

"You never know. Please, don't say anything."

"I won't." He stood up and patted her back, letting his hand linger on her shoulder for a second before he wandered around their apartment. He moved to the coffee table next, stopping to straighten a pile of magazines that had accumulated on the surface, and after fanning them across a corner, he picked up an old copy of *The New Yorker,* sank into the sofa and turned to an article he had dog-eared. Despite his self-deprecation on his own erudition, he was as attuned to intellectual treatments as she, spending most evenings with a copy of the *Christian Science Monitor,* the *Journal of the American Medical Association* or the *Atlantic,* or one of the half-dozen novels he was reading at any given time. After a moment, he looked up.

"We should get ready to leave soon," he said. "We need to be at your parents' house in an hour."

She checked her watch and cringed when she saw that it was already seven in the evening.

"God, I can't believe how fast the time's gone," she said. "I feel like it was just yesterday that I was at my mom's Annual Remission Celebration." She slid off her chair and joined him on the couch, nuzzling up against his chest. "I really appreciate that you're going with me."

"It's important to you, Auds. You don't have to keep thanking me."

"I know. It's just—these things can be absolutely brutal. I mean, I adore my mother, and I love that we're celebrating her good health, but the guest list tends to be a hundred people too long. It can be overwhelming."

"I can't even imagine having so many friends." He stroked her hair, his gentle pats lulling her into an almost sleepy peace. "Hey, I was thinking that we should get her some flowers."

"I'm sure she's already made her florist rich. She can go a little overboard with her parties."

"Even so. We can't show up empty-handed. What do you think of a bouquet of yellow roses?"

She kissed his cheek, touched by his thoughtfulness. "I think that would be lovely."

"Okay." He wiggled out of her grip and stood up. "We'll stop by the flower shop on our way." He pulled his University of Houston sweatshirt over his head, the static electricity raising a veneer of fine dark brown hair to hover over his head. "So, your father's giving a toast tonight. Does he always do that at these Remission Celebrations?"

"He's in town?" she asked, surprised.

"He came in this morning."

"I thought he was going to miss the party." She wondered why no one had told her that her father had flown in from Saudi Arabia or Venezuela or wherever he had traveled this time. If retirement was supposed to relax a man, time had only exacerbated her father's workaholic nature. He spent most of the year abroad, overseeing the operations of Catalyst Petroleum, the independent petroleum-exploration company his forebears had left him, and as scarce as he had become, she could count on one hand how many times she had seen or spoken to him in the last year. She peered at Victor. "How did you know that he came back?"

"I talked to him yesterday."

"You did?"

"I've been talking to him every other week or so. He's been giving me advice on a few investments that I've made." He reached into the dry cleaning and extracted a white dress shirt. Audrey watched, dumbfounded, as he slid his muscular arms into the crisp sleeves. Perhaps sensing her confusion, he flashed a reassuring smile, his cheerful expression highlighting his angular face. "I've been building my portfolio. I don't know how your father knows what's going to hit big so consistently, but he's almost quintupled the amount I started out with. If I keep this up for another couple of years, I won't need to work anymore."

"You wouldn't quit your job, would you? You love teaching."

"Yeah, and I love my kids." His expression turned serious, and he let out a sad sigh. "They're at that age where they'd rather be gangbangers than college students." Affected by his deep attachment to his tenth graders, she watched as he buttoned his shirt. "God, to be fifteen now, especially in their environment. Do you remember what you were like in high school? Sometimes, it feels like a lifetime ago to me."

"Victor, you're only thirty." She shook her head. "I had no idea that my dad was giving you tips."

"He has for a few months, actually. The first time that we met, he told me to call him about financial matters, and I took him up on his offer."

"I knew that you two talked, but I didn't realize that y'all had regular appointments."

He laughed. "Appointments?"

"You know what I mean. He isn't exactly what I'd call *available*."

She continued to gaze at him wondrously. "You might be the first person I know who isn't completely intimidated by him. All of my friends are terrified of him."

"Why? Because he never smiles?"

"That, and the fact that he had a horrible temper when I was younger. He may have yelled at everyone who ever came by the house." She considered. "But he's mellowed out over the years. Actually, I can't remember the last time he raised his voice."

"Well, he's been nothing but gracious to me."

"Then he must really like you."

"I hope so." His eyes darted to the clock. "Seriously, sweetheart, we're going to be late."

"Fine." She got off the couch and moved towards their bedroom. Victor trailed behind, following her to the closet, and she stared at a long row of dresses, unsure what to wear to her mother's annual bash.

"What about this one?" he asked, pulling a flowy black Armani cocktail dress off the rack. He dangled the hanger on the tip of his index finger, and his swinging motion breathed life into the sheer fabric of the outfit.

"That's a little formal, don't you think?"

"The invitation said that the attire was black-tie." He wrapped his free arm around her waist. "Besides, I love you in this dress. You look like a goddess in it."

"What are you going to wear?"

"A tux. I rented one last night."

She sighed. "I can't believe my mother planned her party on a Wednesday. God forbid that anyone should wait until the weekend."

"Why *is* it tonight?"

"Because January twenty-third is the date she found out that her cancer had gone into remission." She wriggled out of her sweats and slipped into the flattering sheath, inspecting herself in the freestanding mirror in the closet. "Hopefully, we can sneak out of there before midnight. I still have to work on tomorrow's lesson plans. I can't show up to class less prepared than a bunch of first graders." She walked to the bathroom and pulled out her makeup bag, spying Victor in the mirror. "You are so good to go with me."

He smiled broadly. "I wouldn't miss tonight for the world."

"Good Lord, what is all this?" Audrey asked as they slowed in front of her parents' house. Several valets were parking cars along the cobblestone driveway that stretched for half a mile, and couples streamed through the front door looking as if they belonged at the White House inauguration gala. The house was ablaze with light and music, and at least three Bentleys idled under the porte cochere.

"Wow, your mother wasn't kidding when she said tonight was going to be black-tie," Victor said.

"It's never been this formal before. Last year, the theme was Honky-tonk Classics, for God's sake."

"Should I be glad that I missed it?"

"Not if you're a sucker for freak shows."

Victor pulled up near the front door, and two valets, both in red suits and black bow ties, rushed to their doors.

"Good evening," one of them said, extending an arm. She took it and slid out of her seat, careful to keep her knees together as she tumbled out of Victor's Honda Accord.

Victor walked around to where she was with a large bouquet of yellow roses, which they had picked up at Flora's Flowers a few minutes ago, and they entered the foyer, she apparently more taken aback by the grandiosity of the party than he. At least half a dozen servers with trays of canapés and caviar milled around the formal living room and occasionally interrupted guests to offer their ware. Another half dozen floated through the salon with champagne flutes and glasses of white wine. An orchestra had set up on the slate-tiled alcove off the ballroom, and Brahms wafted through the open French doors and into the hallways. The house, with its soaring ceilings and marble floors, made quiet conversation impossible, and the voices of what sounded like hundreds of people reverberated against the walls and into Audrey's ears. She could barely hear herself think.

"There you are, darling," her mother said in her drawling Southern accent as she approached. She kissed Audrey on the cheek, her thin lips cool against her skin before she pulled away, and she beamed as she inspected her. "You look absolutely beautiful. Black really does suit you."

"Thanks." She took in her mother's white pantsuit, its sheen catching the light and showing off the dazzling blue of her eyes. "I don't think I've ever seen you wear white or pants to a party."

"White suits are going to be big this year. At least that's what my stylists say." She smoothed her platinum blond hair, perhaps checking for wisps that might ruin her sweeping updo, and as fair as she was, she looked like a business-savvy angel. She turned to Victor next, her hand still on her head. "How are you, Victor?"

"Good," he said, and then handed her the roses. "These are for you."

"Oh, you didn't need to bring anything." She smiled widely, clearly delighted by the colorful blooms, and held them at arm's length while admiring the butter-hued petals before sucking in their fragrant scent. "These deserve to be showcased in the center of the dining room table, but the decorators would kill me for messing with their designs." She cocked her head thoughtfully. "I know. I'll put them in John's study. He could stand to use a little life in there." She patted Victor's arm. "This is very kind of you. Thank you."

"I'm glad you like them," he said with a bright smile.

"Why don't you make yourself at home while I catch up with Audrey? There's champagne and wine, if you'd like. I never see my daughter anymore, what with her working all hours of the night on her paper, and if I don't take advantage of a minute alone with her now, I don't know when I'll get another opportunity."

"Mom, I see you all the time," Audrey said. "We just talked on Monday."

"A glass of wine sounds perfect," he said, glancing at her before turning his attention back to her mother. "I want to tell you 'Congratulations,' but to be honest, I'm not sure if that's the appropriate thing to say."

" 'Congratulations' is just fine, dear. Thank you." She nodded, and he relaxed, relieved.

"I'll bring a glass back for you, too," he said to Audrey, and then wandered into the crowd.

"He's sweet, isn't he?" Audrey asked, watching as he engaged a server in what looked like lively conversation.

"He is, darling." Her mother kept her gaze on him until he headed towards the orchestra, and then turned back to Audrey. "So, has he completely moved in with you now?" Her brows tightened and her smile disappeared, replaced now by concern that aged her face.

"He has a few more boxes in storage, but yeah, pretty much."

"I really wish that y'all wouldn't rush into things," she said quietly. "You've only been seeing each other for a couple of months, and you're already living together. It's too soon."

"I know that it seems soon, but it feels *right*, Mom," she said, hoping that her cheerfulness would allay her apprehension. "Besides, we've known each other for years. It's not like I had a total stranger move in with me."

"But you have, Audrey. It doesn't matter how long you've known him. Two, three months of dating can't possibly give you any idea whether you *are* right for each other, even if you feel like you are." Her lips pursed into a pale pink dot before she let out a deep sigh. "You know that I wouldn't normally intrude in your love life, but you've never lived with a boyfriend before. You've never been this serious with a relationship."

"That's because this is the best relationship I've ever been in. It's the only one that isn't constant drama. Besides, you've been intruding in my love life since middle school." She forced her smile wider, as if her happy countenance alone might assuage her. Her mother frowned, clearly not set at ease.

"I just worry that you're pushing yourself to hurry up and get married. You don't need to. You've got all the time in the world."

"Most mothers would be crushed that their twenty-nine-year-old daughter is still single."

"Well, I'd rather that you take your time and make sure that the person you marry is absolutely right for you."

"Mom, really," she said, wishing that she could impart a satisfying assurance, "you assume too much. I don't feel any pressure to get married. It's not like Victor and I've ever even discussed it. We're just living together."

"But you wouldn't be living together if—"

"Anne, everything is beautiful, as usual," a woman Audrey had never met before said. She had crept up on them, her footsteps drowned out by the cacophony of the room and the sweeping fullness of her gown, and she sidled up to Audrey's mother, looking slightly intoxicated.

"Thanks, Cecile," she said, her disengaged demeanor betraying her preoccupation with Audrey's cohabitation. "You wouldn't believe what a bear it was to organize everything. It seems like everyone's throwing a postholiday bash this week." She laid her hand on Audrey's arm. "I should get back to playing host. Don't stray too far. Dinner starts in a few minutes."

Audrey watched as her mother left with her friend. In a moment, Victor walked up with two glasses of wine and handed one to her, looking around as if for eavesdroppers.

"Is everything okay?" he asked. "That seemed intense."

"Oh, it was fine." She took a swig of her drink. "My mother was just being—protective."

"About what?"

"Us living together. She thinks that we're rushing."

He frowned. "Are we?"

"I don't think so." She sighed. "I *really* wish she didn't worry so much. The more she worries about me, the more I worry about her. She doesn't need to stress herself out. It's not good for her." She stopped short of adding that she feared that constant anxiety might undermine her remission, as if her mother's emotional state might somehow directly correlate with her physical one.

"All parents worry, Auds."

"I know. Even so."

"Hell, if it were our daughter, I'd probably be crazy protective, too. I know that I'd screen all of her boyfriends with a shotgun across my lap."

She guffawed, linked her arm in the crook of his elbow and led him towards the main hall, wondering if he could feel her pleasure through his jacket. They had never talked about marriage before, much less children, and his comment caused her to wonder if her mother's counsel on husbands hadn't been premature.

"Excuse me, everyone," Audrey's mother called from the front of the room, her voice cutting through the noise. The music and buzzing chatter faded, and everyone turned to face her. "I want to thank y'all for taking a few minutes out of your day to relax with us tonight. If you'll join me, we'll be seated for dinner now."

Audrey and Victor walked into the dining room, where the evening's ostentation was on full display. A fifty-foot Baker table spanned the length of the room, draped in chocolate silk and topped with a hundred eggshell-hued place settings. Complementing ivory and sienna silk wrapped each of the guest chairs, the colors perfectly matched with the warm wallpaper that Audrey noticed was new. Gilded fleurs-de-lis peppered the taupe walls, and lights sparkled from the piano-sized crystal chandelier, champagne flutes, wineglasses and votive candles. A dozen arrangements of bloodred orchids towered over the table, having likely cost a florist his entire inventory. In the center of each setting was a golden place card, the overly ornate calligraphy making it almost impossible to decipher the inscribed names.

After a few squints, Audrey located her seat near the front of the table. Victor sat next to her, and for several noisy minutes, her parents' legion of friends wandered around the room in search of their seats with the help of the event planners and Audrey's mother.

Her father strode into the room, his concrete form slicing through the air with pugilistic grace as he moved. He was in a black suit as always, and he seemed to have lost more hair since the last time Audrey saw him.

"Hi, sweetheart," he said, bending down to kiss her cheek before heading to his chair. "Did you just get here?"

"About fifteen minutes ago." Her stomach tightened, and she glanced at him, the way she did every time they were together, to see if he was excited to see her. He nodded at Victor before pulling out his BlackBerry, oblivious to the clamoring around him. His thumbs flew across the keyboard faster than a sixty-four-year-old man's digits should have been able to, and after lingering on his PDA for a few more seconds, he finally looked up and focused on Victor, his expression making clear that his mind was still on business.

"Did you dump Commelast like I told you to?" he asked, his deep voice rumbling through the room like thunder.

"Not yet."

"Sell it now, Victor. That company's about to circle the drain."

He frowned. "But *Fortune* rated the stock as a best value. I heard that the shares are supposed to split soon."

"I've been hearing things, if you get my meaning. Sell it now and put your money into Regerix. That's the little engine that could, if there ever was one. You're not investing more than thirty percent of your portfolio in high-yield stocks, are you?"

"No, sir."

"Good. You want to make money, son, not gamble your life away."

Victor looked at Audrey, and she shrugged in response. She had never cared much for the day-to-day performance of her own investments, and she was content to leave her finances, her half-dozen trust funds included, to the deft handling of her father's financial advisers instead.

"What about you, Audrey?" her father asked. "How are your classes going at St. Mark's? Are you piling your kids up with homework?"

"As much as they're able to handle, which is a lot," she said. "You wouldn't believe how smart they are."

"My grandson is in the eighth grade there," Lois MacDonald said from across the table. "He's going to Loyola next year. Audrey, you should talk to him and give him some tips on how to succeed. He would love to hear from you, especially since you graduated first from both schools."

"I'd be happy to."

Lois gazed around the room. "You know, there are quite a few St. Mark's and Loyola alumni here." Her muddy brown eyes narrowed as she smiled at Audrey's father. "John, you were, what, Loyola's class of 1960?"

" 'Sixty-one," he said, back on his BlackBerry.

"I graduated in 1962." She placed her hand on her husband's arm, and he sipped his Scotch, oblivious to her touch. "Jerry graduated in 1959." She looked at Victor. "Did you attend Loyola, as well?"

"No, ma'am. I went to Martin Luther King High School."

"Oh. I haven't heard of it. Is it in Houston?"

"Pasadena. Actually, I teach there now." He smiled at Audrey. "Funny how we ended up where we started."

"You're an educator, too?" Lois asked with interest.

"Yes, ma'am."

"I'm sorry," Audrey said. "I don't think I've ever introduced y'all. Lois, this is my boyfriend, Victor Smith. Victor, this is Lois MacDonald. She's a friend of my mother's."

"I've known Audrey since she was in diapers," she said with a wide smile. Like Audrey's mother, Lois had smooth, probably Botoxed skin, gleaming veneers and a body made for couture clothing. Unlike her mother, she had wild auburn curls that splayed about her shoulders and a cherubic face, its youthfulness belying her age. She rested her hands on the table, looking as if she were interviewing them. "So, how did you two meet?"

"At a teachers' convention, actually," Audrey said, recalling that Victor had approached her in the fine arts department.

"I followed her around until she noticed me," he said with a laugh. "I couldn't stop staring at her. It only took another five years to get the courage to ask her out."

"She's lovely, isn't she?" Lois asked, looking upon Audrey as if she were her own daughter. "I've always told your mother that she did a wonderful job with you."

"Are your parents here, Victor?" Jerry MacDonald asked suddenly, motioning to a waiter for another drink.

"They're in New Mexico. They moved there after I graduated from high school."

"Oh, I love Taos," Lois said, leaning forward. "We have a summer home there. It's absolutely beautiful." She took a sip of water, careful not to smudge her bright red lipstick. "So, what does your family do?"

"My father's in construction, and my mother works at a day care." He glanced at Audrey, and she placed a reassuring hand on his lap.

"Construction," Jerry said, looking thoughtful. "Does he own Gage Builders? They built our house there."

"No, sir. He was a carpenter for Newman Homes."

"Oh," Lois said, looking confused. "Oh, yes. Of course." Audrey's father tore himself away from his PDA, took one look at her and then rolled his eyes.

"Everyone seems to be having a good time, don't you think?" Audrey's mother said as she walked to her seat. She kissed Lois and Jerry on their cheeks before sitting down, barely glancing at Audrey's father as she settled in. Immediately, he stood up.

"Everyone, if I could have your attention, please," he said. Hundreds of heads turned in his direction. "I'd like to make a toast, if I could. You all are more than guests in our home—y'all are family. You were there for us when Anne got sick with lung cancer nine—no, *ten* years ago, and many of you stood by us when she had breast cancer almost thirty-five years ago. Kinda unfair, if you think about it, considering that she's never smoked a day in her life and eats like an organic monk. But life has a funny way of reminding us what's important, and what's important—the *most* important—is family and friends." His deep baritone lacked any hint of feeling, as if he was simply reciting a speech he had memorized, and Audrey fidgeted uncomfortably, amazed by everyone's ability to accept his performance at face value.

"That's good enough for me," he continued, "but my wife likes to remind herself with parties." A twitter of laughter filled the room. "So, to you, darling"—he bent down and kissed Audrey's mother—"and to you all, thank you for being by our side, and for coming to our Fourth Annual Remission Celebration."

An echoing chime rang through the room as people clinked their glasses together, and couture-clad women approached her mother and told her that she'd better be around next year to throw another great bash. The men leaned over one another and talked about golf, their business excursions and the recent bull market, while servers discreetly placed dishes of endive salad in front of each guest. For the next two hours, the room was abuzz with laughter and conversation, and for much of the meal, Victor answered questions from both sides of the table, listing his educational background, his college degree, his ties to the city and the civic organizations to which he belonged. Audrey held his hand throughout the inquisition, offering explanations when the audience tilted their surgically taut faces, unable to express their confusion with normal human reactions. When the party finally moved from the dining room to the outside pavilion, Victor stayed behind, looking spent.

"Before we go outside," he said, "do you want to see the flowers in your father's study?"

"Why?" she asked, perplexed by the bizarre request.

"Tonight's been a little overwhelming. I could use a little breather."

"Sure. I'm sorry. What did I say about these things being a beating? You did great, by the way."

"Did I?" he asked, distracted.

"Yes." She stood up and followed him to the main hall, and she took his hand and led him to her father's study. With her parents' guests making a commotion in the backyard, the house felt abandoned, and as little time as they had had to themselves all evening, she welcomed the quiet respite.

They walked into the study, and with its dark wood-paneled walls and her father's hunting artifacts displayed prominently, the room felt like a hidden cave. Their yellow roses colored the otherwise dark office, and placed next to a green banker's lamp on the desk, they seemed distinctly out of place. She sat on a sofa underneath two twelve-point-buck heads, feeling the distressed leather chafe against her bare arms. Victor wandered around the space, his discomfort palpable.

"Are you okay?" she asked, worried that the evening had taken its toll on him.

"I'm fine," he said nervously. He stopped pacing and sat next to her. "I wanted to talk to you about something that's been on my mind for a while."

"Okay." She was suddenly anxious, and she crumpled the edge of her dress in her hands, not knowing what else to do with them.

He turned his body so that their knees touched, and he grabbed her hands. "I've been racking my brain for the most creative, the most over-the-top way to do this, and I couldn't come up with anything."

"What are you talking—"

"Wait." He gripped her hands tighter, and she was surprised to find that his palms were clammy. "Okay. I'm going to talk. Just listen, okay?" She stared at him for a moment before nodding, and he sucked in a deep breath. "I realized that it couldn't be over-the-top because that's not how I am. It's not *who* I am. I know that I'll never be able to buy you a house like this, and I'll never be able to give you everything you're accustomed to. You deserve better." She struggled to remain quiet, desperately wanting to blurt out that she didn't need any of those things. "But you also deserve someone who's going to love you every minute of your life, someone who will support your dreams and do everything he can to make them come true. And if you'll let me, I swear to you that I will spend the rest of my days taking care of you the way you should be taken care of." He reached into his coat pocket and extracted a little wooden box, and then knelt down on one knee. Perhaps nerves were impeding his coordination, because he fumbled with the box for a moment before prying it open. A sparkling diamond—cushion cut, Audrey noticed—was set in a platinum band, and pavé diamonds encircled the stone.

"Oh my God," she gasped.

"Audrey, will you marry—"

"Yes," she shouted, even before he finished his question. "Yes, yes, yes, I will marry you." She jumped off the couch and practically smothered him in her embrace, and overcome with joy, she barely noticed when he slipped the ring onto her finger. She held his face in her hands, sure that she was grinning like a jack-o'-lantern, and she gazed at him for a long moment before kissing him. When she pulled away, she saw that he was smiling.

"I'm going to make you so happy," he said. She kissed him again.

"Sweetheart, you already have."

"Yo, miss, you wanna car wash?" a scrawny boy no taller than Audrey asked. He was dressed in a baggy basketball uniform, and his white jersey radiated a red *Heat* and *32* on the front. "Yo' Benz's looking pretty to' up. Tires look shredded, too." He spoke with a strange mix of Texas twang and Ebonics, and considering that he was Asian, his entire accent seemed misplaced.

"I'm okay. Thanks." She slammed her car door shut and headed for Starbucks. She was meeting Jennifer, Amy, and Lindsay, the second-, third-, and fourth-grade teachers at St. Mark's, for dinner at Privé, a trendy new restaurant a few miles from the coffee shop. She was half an hour early, and she was desperate for a few quiet minutes to herself before she had to meet them.

"It's free, though," another similarly dressed boy said. He looked slightly older and darker than the first, but still young enough for Audrey to feel like his mother. He, too, was Asian, and his multiple piercings and tribal tattoos looked like clip-and-press-on versions of the real deal.

"No, thank you. I'm just here to get a drink."

"Come on, sista', don't you want to help a brotha' out?" a third Asian asked. "We only be askin' fo' donations."

"For what cause?" she asked, immediately regretting her question.

"We be raisin' money for vehicular awareness," a fourth baggy-pants-wearing Asian answered.

"Excuse me?"

"We need parts," one of them explained.

"You're asking people for money so that you can buy parts for your car?" she asked, incredulous.

"Yeah."

"You've got to be kidding me," she said under her breath. Loudly, she said, "I don't want a car wash, but thanks for asking." She quickened her pace, anxious to escape their attention. Just then, the heel of her stiletto caught on a crack in the sidewalk, and she flailed about for a moment, trying not to fall or to rip the seam of her narrow skirt. The boys howled, delighted by what they probably considered to be delicious Schadenfreude.

"Damn, uppity girl nearly ate it!"

"Uppity bitch can't even walk and chew gum at the same time!"

Audrey regained her balance and turned around, breathless.

"If I were you, I'd stop harassing people and get *real* jobs to afford your—vehicular awareness." She glared at them with the worst look she had ever cast on her students and then ducked into the frigid air of the coffee shop. Who did they think they were, anyway? Nothing was more irritating, or embarrassing for that matter, than a bunch of scrawny Chinese boys who thought they were black. Even worse were suburban Asian gangsta wannabes who rode their Honda Civics an inch off the asphalt with one too many mufflers in the back and Chinese characters decaled onto the entirety of their souped-up hoopties. *What is it with Asian kids these days?*

She made her way through the packed shop and shuffled closer to the register, an exhausted and uncomfortable cow in the herd of Starbucks-mad Houstonians. Her class had been extra rambunctious today, and when she combined that with two hours of sleep, the left-over effects of six glasses of champagne and a raging headache, it was all she could do not to call her newlywed coworkers and cancel.

"What can I get you?" the cashier asked with a carefree, isn't-Starbucks-great smile.

"Tall nonfat Mocha Frappuccino, please," she said.

"Tall nonfat Mocha Frappuccino," he shouted to the barista, and in a moment, the violent whirring of a blender joined the cacophony of other machines, drowning out the voices of the vehicularly aware thugs. Their comments bothered her, and even though their assessment of her shouldn't have mattered, she didn't appreciate the quickness with which they had pegged her as "uppity."

She took her drink and headed to a table where earlier customers had left a bedraggled stack of newspapers. After settling into the deep cushioned bench, she sipped her Frappuccino and rummaged through the pages until she landed on a copy of the *New York Times*. No sooner had she flipped the paper open than someone touched her hand.

"Gorgeous. Gore-*jess!*"

She looked up to see a slim man bent over with one hand on a Venti coffee cup, and the other on her ring finger. His soot-colored hair had been spiked and pushed towards the crown of his head, like a follicular pyramid, and had he not been in his twenties, he would have looked ridiculous. The towering hairstyle suited him, as did his flat-front khakis and his close-fitting black sweater. He was dark skinned, a darker shade of tan than she, and his watermelon-seed eyes and aquiline nose suggested that he was Amerasian. Audrey couldn't avert her eyes, even though she was fully aware that she was staring at him. He was beautiful.

"Thanks," she said, suddenly self-conscious of her new bauble.

"Is anyone sitting here?" he asked, pointing to a chair across from her.

"Not that I know of."

"Well, I am now." He sat down and crossed his long legs. "Goodness gracious, girl, could your ring *be* any prettier? Who are you marrying, Harry Winston?"

"Better," she said with a laugh.

He recrossed his legs, took her hand again and inspected her diamond. "So, when are you getting married?"

"We haven't set a date yet." She laid down her paper. As much as she had wanted a moment to herself, she didn't mind her new companion. He reminded her of her own students, all unfiltered honesty and enthusiasm.

"Well, I just *love* weddings. Just got back from one, actually." He released her fingers and then sipped his coffee. "It was in India, and, honey, was it *gore-jess*. I love the Hindu people and their traditions. So fanciful. Nothing like these boring American weddings."

"I bet."

"So, have you accomplished everything you ever hoped to? Or will you have time before you get married?"

"I'm sorry?"

"You know, your wish list. Everybody has one. It's kind of like the list of things you want to accomplish before you're thirty, because Lord knows that after you hit the big three-oh, or marriage, in your case, you won't have time to do all the things you wanted to. Me, I want to skydive, travel to South America and have my work displayed at MoMA. Oh, and sleep with Brad Pitt."

Audrey laughed again and said, "I think you can do all those things even after you turn thirty."

"But I won't look *nearly* as good doing it. So, what's on your wish list? Come on, I need a distraction." His face turned dour. "I'm meeting my ex in a few minutes, and I'm just a mess. I talk *way* too much when I'm nervous, and Lordy, am I nervous." He caught himself. "Oh my God. I'm sorry. I hope I'm not bothering you."

"You're fine." She glanced at her watch. "But I'll need to run in a few minutes. I'm meeting some friends for dinner."

"Aren't you a doll? Which is what Kevin is *not*. Honey, we went through the nastiest breakup, and now we've got to divvy up the property." He laid his hand on her arm. "*Never* buy a house with a controlling, psychotic freak. Even if he is *divine* to look at. It'll ruin your life. Ugh, I don't even want to think about it. What were we talking about?" His eyes scanned the air, as if his train of thought were floating in space. "Oh, wish lists. So, what's on yours?" He spoke with a rapid-fire clip, and after a few furtive glances, he focused his attention on her, clearly expecting an answer.

"If I tell you, you promise not to tell?" She leaned in conspiratorially.

"Cross my heart." He scooted forward and gestured on his chest.

"I want to be a professor. An English professor." She didn't add that she would kill for her mother to be as enthusiastic as she was about her engagement, or that her mother's worry-filled disapproval marred her joy.

He straightened up and frowned. "What's so scandalous about that?"

"Nothing, really. I just haven't had the courage to tell anyone about it. Well, my mother knows, and she isn't exactly thrilled by it."

"She prefers illiteracy?"

"She's afraid that I'll turn out to be the workaholic that my dad is." She sighed. "It's one of a dozen reasons why they hate each other, even if they pretend otherwise." She flinched, startled by her own indiscretion. She didn't know why she was speaking so openly with him when she hadn't even told the Valedictorians that she harbored ambitions of a professorship or that her outwardly enviable family had been in tatters for years. Maybe it was because he was a stranger. There was safety in anonymity; he wouldn't judge or pity her, and even if he did, his opinions didn't matter.

"Well, I won't tell a soul." He traced his lips, and then flicked his hand, promising that the vault had been sealed. "So, this wedding of yours. What's it going to be like? Are you going to have doves and swans?"

She considered. "I haven't really thought about it."

"You haven't?" He looked surprised. "I thought all girls dreamed about their big day since kindergarten."

"I wasn't one of those girls. I was the girl who read in the library while everyone played dodgeball."

"You were a *nerd*?" he asked, delighted.

"I don't know that I would've called myself a nerd," she said, unable to stifle a chuckle. "But I wasn't dressing up in white and pretending to be a bride." She sipped her drink and imagined her own affair. "I'm not enamored with a huge Cinderella wedding. I want a small, intimate ceremony with just a few close friends and family."

"Good for you for shirking the gaudy Texas thing. Smaller is always better. It feels more meaningful for some reason." He focused on the mess of papers on the table, looking wistful. "If I were to get married, that's how I would want it. Not that it's an option, but you know." He looked up and then jerked back down. "Oh, shit. There he is."

"Kevin?" She craned her neck towards the entrance.

"Don't look!" He grabbed at her arms. "Keep talking. I don't want him to think that I got here early and waited for him." He fluffed his hair. "How do I look?"

"Great," she answered truthfully.

"Sweet Jesus." He gulped hard. "What were we talking about?"

"Weddings."

"Oh, well, as one who's been to a hundred weddings, let me give you a word of advice." His eyes darted between her face and the door. "You *have* to have something about your heritage incorporated in the ceremony, or it'll be like any other wedding, and you *don't* want something that nobody remembers. Trust me. This last trip to India? It's the only ceremony I can remember, and I wasn't even sober for most of it."

"I'll keep that in mind."

"So, what kinds of tradition does your family have?" It was a nosy question, but given his guilelessness and innocent interest, the inquiry seemed completely natural.

"Well, my family's Irish," she said, giving in to his contagious merrymaking. "We still have family in Dublin. Maybe I'll incorporate something Gaelic into my wedding." She thought about her cousins' Celtic-influenced wedding. "You know, I took traditional Irish dancing for ten years. I actually broke my ankle in practice, and my slip jig's not been the same since. I've always thought that it would be terrific to have a troupe at the wedding. I know my dad would love that." When she looked up, he was gawking at her with a slight crease between his brows. It wasn't until she had thrown away her drink and had walked outside that she realized why.

"Look, it's the uppity bitch!" one of the Lowriders cried. He and his crew were still standing outside with car-wash signs, even though the sun had set since Audrey had been inside Starbucks. "Where's you's gots to be that you can't even look at us?"

"Come on, baby, let us wash your car."

"We'll wash that SL *real* good," another said lewdly.

"Jesus—Christ," Audrey muttered between clenched teeth. She wanted to yell at them again, to tell them to—

"Pull up your pants and shut your mouth," the Amerasian beauty shouted as he burst through the door. He glared at them, and whether it was his terrifying expression or the fact that he was a good foot taller, they fell silent. "Where do you think you are? You're embarrassing yourselves and us with all this pseudo-gangsta shit. It's been raining all day, and no one wants a car wash, you idiots. Now go home before I pull some kung fu on you!"

"You don't know no kung fu," the most heavily tattooed one said.

"You want to find out?"

The tattooed boy glanced back at his friends uncertainly. With a shrug, he slunk off, and Audrey watched, incredulous, as her animated friend approached her.

"That was kind of harsh, don't you think?" she asked. "They're just stupid kids." She spied the boys shuffling into Starbucks, their oversized jeans dusting the floor as they moved.

"Sorry. I guess I took out my aggression on them." He sighed heavily. "It didn't go so well with Kevin. I don't even know why he showed up, because all he did was walk in, tell me to go fuck myself, and then leave." He looked at her wearily. "I think I need a lawyer."

"Do you really? I have a friend who's one."

"You do?" His eyes shone under the streetlight. "Do you think she'd be interested in taking me on?"

"I don't think she specializes in family law, but I'm sure she could help you find the right person." She reached into her bag and fumbled for her planner. "Oh, I don't have my stuff with me, and I don't know her work phone number off the top of my head. Here, take one of my cards."

"Are you a lawyer, too?" he asked, and then perused her information.

"No, I'm a first-grade teacher. But give me a buzz, and I'll give you her contact info."

"Audrey Henley," he read off her card. "You teach at St. Mark's Academy?"

"I do. Oh, I guess I never introduced myself."

"Jimmy Fujimoto," he said, and extended his hand. She shook it, and they smiled at each other. He waved her card. "Thanks for this. I'll call you."

"Hey." She leaned in closer. "Do you really know kung fu?"

"Oh God, no," he said with a laugh.

Five

"*C*ongratulations!" Whitney shrieked into the line. A lawyer in the hallway jumped and glared at her.

"Thanks," Audrey said. "God, Whitney, I've never been so happy in my life."

"So, how did he propose? Was it as romantic as you thought it would be?"

"It was even better than I could've imagined. I don't think I even let him finish asking me before I said *yes*."

The phone beeped, and Whitney's caller ID showed that Will was on the other line.

"Can I call you back? My boss is riding my ass today."

"Sure. Hey, Whitney, thanks again for looking out for a family lawyer. Jimmy's really going to appreciate it."

"No problem. I'll send out an e-mail to the office and let you know what I hear back. Have you told Hercules about your engagement yet?"

"Not yet. I'm going to call her after we hang up."

"Okay. Call me later, okay? I want to hear everything that happened."

"Definitely."

"Bye."

Whitney clicked over. Immediately, Will shouted at her.

"Lee, what the fuck took so long for you to answer?" He didn't wait for a response. "Where are we on those documents? Is the privilege log ready?"

"It will be in a few minutes," she said, fearing permanent hearing damage.

"It needs to go out the door *today*. Bring it to me when you're done." He slammed the phone, sending a shock through her brain.

She turned back to her computer and froze. The screen, filled with her notes a moment ago, was now black. She jiggled her mouse, pressed Ctrl+Alt+Delete a few times, banged on the back of the monitor and then held the power button until she heard the life drain from the machine. A reboot and a desperate prayer later, she was still staring at blackness. In a panic, she called the help desk.

"Karen Lowell, information-technology technician extraordinaire," a nasal voice trilled.

"Karen, it's Whitney Lee."

"Who?"

"Whitney Lee," she repeated slowly. "I'm on the twenty-sixth floor. Something's wrong with my computer, and I've got a serious deadline." For added measure, she said, "It's for Will Strong."

"I'll be right there."

Less than sixty seconds later, Karen appeared at her door.

"That was fast," Whitney said.

"You said it was for Will." She edged her way into the office and began to sit in Whitney's chair, even while she was still seated. Taking her awkward cue, Whitney got up and moved around the desk. *IT techs,* she thought with an audible huff. Whether inspired by Karen's social skills or Audrey's good news, she suddenly thought about her brother and his pleas for her to find him a date, and she wondered if he would be interested in a fellow tech geek. His romantic satisfaction wasn't her concern—she needed him to coax her parents to ease up on her.

"So, what's wrong with my computer?" she asked. "Will you be able to fix it?"

"Yeah. It's going to take a few minutes, though." She shook her head and muttered, "End users. Always blaming others for their screwups." She looked up, and the sun shone through the hallway and onto her face, illuminating her light brown eyes so that they looked like pools of honey. There was a reason why male lawyers loved it when their computers crashed. Karen was gorgeous, personality notwithstanding. "Hey, do you need a laptop? I can check one out for you while I'm working."

"That's okay." She sat in an ergonomically unfit chair in the corner of her tight office. "I'll wait for a bit and see how it goes."

Other than the soft whirring of the computer, the office was silent. Whitney grabbed a draft of the privilege log and thought of how she might broach the subject of a setup. She wasn't even sure if Karen was available. The last she heard, she was seeing someone at a competing law firm. She watched as Karen drummed her long fingers into the keyboard while staring at the screen intently. Her head popped up suddenly, and she faced Whitney, her fingers still dancing over the keyboard.

"Congratulations, by the way. You know, for getting on the firm's diversity committee."

Whitney peered at her, not quite sure what she was talking about. As far as she knew, Boerne & Connelly didn't have a diversity committee, and she had certainly never been notified of her newfound position. Then again, gossip traveled faster than fire in the office, most of it completely untrue.

"Where'd you hear that?"

"I heard Camille talking about it, and she overheard Will bragging about it to the other partners. He's been calling you his prized pig." She laughed, sounding more caustic than amused. "Prized pig. What an ass." She stopped typing. "I don't know how you can work for him. I'd flee for the hills if the firm told me that I had to work with him for the rest of my career."

"I guess I've gotten used to him."

Karen gazed around the office, her eyes greedily taking in the stacks of boxes against the wall, the piles of paper on the floor and several drafts of Will's privilege log on her desk. Whitney had always found the IT tech unnervingly intrusive, and now that she wasn't working her magic on the defective hard drive, she was peering, squinty-eyed, at the series of framed pictures on her desk.

"Is this your boyfriend?" she asked, pointing to the largest photograph.

"Yeah." She didn't add that she had barely seen Scott in the last three weeks, or that palpable discomfort marred their infrequent conversations. The last couple of times they had spoken, he had declined her invitation to listen to her newest roster of songs, and she had turned down his request that they spend a Tuesday evening at the mall to pass out Christian pamphlets to unsaved shoppers. Since then, he hadn't asked her to attend any other church-related event, and she hadn't included him in the progress of her music. She sighed, unwilling to think about their relationship, and she wished that Karen would stare at something else.

"How long have y'all been together?"

"Almost three years."

"Wow." She looked up. "Are y'all going to get married?"

"I don't know." She tried not to cringe at Karen's directness. Construing her bluntness as an open invitation, Whitney decided to venture upon the romantic status of the stranger in her office.

"Are you still with that guy at Fisher and Stevens?"

"No," she said, not at all bothered by the inquiry. "We broke up a few months ago."

"Oh, I'm sorry to hear that."

"Why? It's not your fault. He wasn't ready to get married, and my biological clock's ticking. I told him that, and he took off."

"How long were you dating?"

"Three weeks."

"You told him that your biological clock was ticking after three weeks?"

She looked at Whitney, her expression dead serious.

"I don't have time to waste. It's better to be up front about these things. That's the trouble with the world today. No one's willing to be straight with each other. I've always said that if a boy can't take me for who I am, then to hell with him."

"I guess." She was beginning to have second thoughts about setting Karen up with her brother. Still, just because the information-technology technician extraordinaire didn't sweep her off her feet didn't mean that she wouldn't sweep Robert off his.

"I'm almost finished," Karen muttered. "Give me two seconds."

Whitney took in a deep breath.

"Karen? This is going to sound strange, but I might know someone who's attuned to—uh, your biological clock."

She perked up. "Really?"

"Yeah. He's actually—"

"Lee, there you are," Will shouted, causing Whitney to jump. She had been so focused on a setup that she hadn't heard him come in. In his uniform of a navy pin-striped suit and crocodile boots, he was as blustery as ever.

"I'm having technical issues," she said.

"Did you get this?" He flung an oversized postcard at her, and it spun in the air before landing on her desk. If he was worried about the privilege log, he didn't look it. She picked it up and read quickly. It was the first time she had seen the invitation, and considering that it was about, and for, VIP members of the Houston Minority Business Association, she wasn't sure why Will was sharing the placard with her.

"No, sir," she said, and handed the card back to him.

"You need to go." He crossed his arms, his broad frame torturing the fabric of his suit. "We've got a table for ten, and there aren't enough attorneys that—well, we'd like for our minorities to get first dibs at the table. It's in May, so you've got plenty of time to rearrange your schedule to fit the event in." He looked at her expectantly.

"Does it matter that I'm not a member of the MBA?"

"What kind of question is that? You're a minority. That should be good enough for admission."

Karen gasped and gawked at Will. Whitney simply sighed.

"Will, I'm not sure—"

"We need to make a good showing at this thing," he bellowed. His cheeks were instantly red. "Did you read the latest issue of *Texas Lawyer*? It gave us an 'F' rating on diversity. I told you that we need to change the public's perception of us, and I expect that there will be enough press at this event to shut those boys at *TL* up for a while."

"Can I make a suggestion?" she asked, convinced that he had forgotten about their previous discussion on the topic of diversity.

He frowned, perhaps confused that she hadn't accepted his demand with a burst of gratitude.

"Instead of focusing solely on perception, why doesn't the firm make a concerted effort to hire more minorities?" she asked. "I don't understand why everyone is so reluctant to do so. Why can't we re- cruit at the Sunbelt Minority Conference or have lawyers get involved with Junior Achievement? Or have all of the minority lawyers recruit instead of breaking us up by offices? I ran all of those ideas by Martin Krieger, and he shot them down." She already knew the futility of her question. "I mean, perception is important, too, but what good does it do if there's nothing to back it up?"

"Who has time to get involved in those things?" His scowl deep- ened, and she could almost feel his aggravation. "Billable hours, Lee. I'm not wasting time on things that don't bring in money. This isn't a charity we're running here. It's a business."

"But getting our face out into the minority community would bring in—"

"You're going, and that's final. Why are you even arguing with me about this?"

She placed her head in her hands and rubbed her temples. Either she could go willingly and be marginally remembered for having been a team player, or she could protest his assumptions and be crucified in front of the powers-that-be for her failure to promote the firm. There was no use fighting his request.

"Fine," she said. "I'll be there."

"Of course you'll be there. Get me those documents by the end of the day. That reminds me. You're billing the Goolsby matter by the tenth of the hour, right? The client's cheaper than my grandmother, so I'm going to need your itemized time every Friday." He blinked rapidly, apparently noticing Karen for the first time. "What the hell are you doing here?"

"Whitney had some—"

"Come to my office. I spilled coffee on my keyboard, and now my computer's fried to shit." With that, he turned on his heel and stomped out of her office.

"I can't believe he did that," Karen said, her eyes still bulging.

"If you stick around long enough, he'll pimp you out, too."

"I wouldn't do it, strictly out of principle." She pursed her lips, indignant, and peered at Whitney. "Why aren't you offended? Don't you think what he did was racist?"

"In a way, I do, but he won't sit still long enough to hear me out. I don't know if you've noticed, but Will isn't much of a listener. Besides, he pulls that crap on everyone. Do you know Chris Anderson?" Karen nodded. "He was on the track team in high school, and Will makes him run the Houston Marathon every year with the firm's logo on it, even though Chris has a metal screw in his knee and can barely walk. At least Will doesn't think I'm athletic."

"That's ridiculous. All of it." Karen crossed her arms and huffed. "And being athletic isn't the same thing as being called out for being a minority. You could sue for this."

"I'd never win." Whitney shrugged, slightly amused that the white IT tech should be more outraged by what she, the Asian, had experienced. She was right, of course, and Whitney had long known that Will had problems with sensitivity, but other than prodding him towards the right direction, what could she do? She wasn't his mother, and she wasn't a civil rights activist. She was a nobody associate who didn't care enough about the firm to make a difference.

"Well, your computer's fine now." Karen popped out of the chair and headed for the door. Suddenly, she spun around. "Wait. Didn't you say that there might be someone who was interested in my biological clock?"

"Yeah," she said, glad that Karen remembered.

"Who is he? Does he work here?"

"Uh—no. Actually, this is him." She pointed to a framed picture of her and Robert at the beach. It was unfortunate that he looked mildly inebriated with halfway-closed eyes and a crooked smile. She had brought the photo to work because she found his expression hysterical. And because she looked fabulous in it.

"Huh. He's kind of funny-looking." She didn't look excited. "Does he always look like this?"

"Of course not." She smiled as widely as she could, as if she could convince Karen with her sunshiny happiness. "That's a terrible picture of him. He's actually very attractive in real life. He's an aeronautics engineer at NASA. Sends rovers to Mars and stuff."

"Oh," she said, instantly more enthused. "I guess one date wouldn't hurt."

"Great." She felt cheery, despite the nagging feeling that she was setting her brother up with a loon. "I'll have him call you."

"Okay." She glanced at her watch. "I've got to go. Will's probably upset that his computer's down. God, spilling coffee on his computer. Why do I have to clean up everyone's mess?"

Karen scurried out of her office, leaving Whitney to bang out the privilege log. She spied the invitation that Will had dropped on her desk. A dozen professionals of varying shades, the board of directors for the minority council, she gathered, huddled together in the picture, apparently thrilled to be recognized for their efforts in the business community. It was ridiculous that Will believed her presence would impact the firm's ostensible estimation of diversity, a simplistic lightbulb moment of someone who refused to give the problem more than two seconds of his attention. It was another notch on the belt of issues she had with the firm, and as she studied the plastic smiles on the card stock, she wondered if they felt used, too.

"*Whit-ney!* Pass the kimchee, will you?" Robert asked. "God, what's wrong with you?"

Whitney stirred. She was sitting at the dinner table at her parents' house, having accepted her mother's offer for a home-cooked meal, and when she looked up, her brother was scowling at her. She located the little bowl of bright red cabbage among the two dozen saucer-sized plates of pickled root vegetables and pushed it towards him.

"Sorry. Here. Since when does that sensitive little stomach of yours handle spicy food?"

"Since I discovered Tagamet," he said, looking at her as if she had lost her mind. "If you'd been paying attention, you would've heard me talk about it thirty seconds ago."

"Is everything okay?" her father asked. His brows creased with worry, and he pushed up his glasses with an index finger.

"Yeah, I'm just tired, and maybe a little distracted with work. I have to go back to the office after dinner." Truth was, she had been preoccupied with her latest compilation of lyrics, and in between moments of musical inspiration, she was thinking about Karen Lowell. Her brother was going to be thrilled with the beauty she had dragged back to the lair, and she had even gone so far as to print off Karen's picture from the firm's intranet. She couldn't wait to see his reaction.

"You work so hard," her mother said proudly. "You are going to become a law partner in four years, I predict. I can already imagine."

"Mom, *please*. How many times do I have to tell you to lay off?" Blood rushed to her head, and she glared at her mother, who, completely unaffected by the reprimand, gazed back happily.

"I can't be excited for you? We've never had a lawyer in the family before."

"The chicken's really good," Robert interrupted, graciously allaying the tension.

Her mother beamed, and her bulbous cheeks rose, squashing her glasses against them.

"You like it? Oh, I'm so glad." She clapped her hands together, thrilled.

"Yes, it's good," her father said.

"Isn't it? I spent all day marinating the legs. It's very easy, really. You just use a little bit of soy sauce, sesame oil, sesame seeds and black pepper. Oh, and ginger and garlic, of course. And some green onions. You can add sugar if you want, but I don't like it too sweet. Soak that for about four hours, and then grill the chicken. You can do it at the same time that you're making the other *ban chan*." She was always quick to blurt out a recipe, oven temperature and all, as if everyone would forget her long hours in the kitchen otherwise. If she had one talent, cooking Korean food to perfection was it, and even if they spoke English to one another and celebrated the Fourth of July with as much gusto as the Stewarts next door, her mother never prepared anything that didn't originate in their homeland.

"Well, it's delicious," Whitney said.

"Thank you, honey." She shoved her glasses up again and faced Robert. "Oh, before I forget, Mrs. Hahn said that Gina's coming to visit from Philadelphia this weekend."

"Really?" He didn't seem interested.

"Don't make any plans for Friday night. I'm going to invite her to dinner."

"Gina's a lovely girl," her father said with a mischievous grin.

"She's very smart. She's specializing in orthopedic surgery." Her mother nudged Robert, as if to congratulate him for winning the dating-game lottery.

"She's a little older than you, though," her father said. "What is she? Thirty-five? Thirty-six?"

"No, she's maybe—thirty-eight," her mother said. "She started medical school late because she was getting her Ph.D." She brightened and patted Robert's shoulder. "Like you."

"What does she look like?" he asked.

"She's—ah, well, she's very smart," she said, reaching for the large bowl of rice.

"You said that already." He looked dismayed, already realizing that they had set him up with a troll. "What—does—she—look—like?"

"How would you describe her?" she asked Whitney's father.

"Well, she definitely doesn't look Korean."

"She's a little dark."

"Kind of skinny."

"Have you noticed that one of her eyes is bigger than the other?" her mother asked in a loud whisper.

"So you're setting me up with a butt-ass-ugly chick," Robert said, clearly insulted.

"Not *ugly*," her mother said. "We would never try to set you up with someone we thought was ugly. She's, oh, how would I describe . . . ?"

"She's just not classically beautiful like your sister," her father said, regarding Whitney with pride. "That doesn't mean she's not attractive in her own way."

Robert sank his head into his hands. "I can't believe that I'm actually considering meeting her. Christ, I've hit rock bottom, haven't I?"

"Gina's very nice," her mother said, still trying to sell the poor girl to him. "Very polite."

"I'm sure she is." He threw Whitney a beseeching look, and she prickled, feeling defensive on behalf of a girl she had never met.

"Robert, either go and see what she's like, or don't go and stop complaining. You're being a jerk."

He rolled his eyes, and she figured that now was as good a time as any to introduce Karen. She reached into her bag, located the printout and set it on the table. Her parents leaned over and squinted at the picture, moving their glasses up and down over their aging eyes as they tried to examine her.

"Who's that?" her mother asked.

"Isn't she pretty?" Whitney asked. "She's a friend of mine from work."

"She's very cute," her father said. "Let me see."

"Is she a movie star?" her mother asked.

"Mom, I just said that she's a friend of mine from work. She's in our IT department."

"Very lovely," her father said, and then passed her mother the picture.

"Let me see that." Robert ripped the photo out of her hands.

"She saw your picture in my office, and she *still* agreed to go out with you," Whitney said. She expected her brother to glare at her, or to retort with an insulting comeback. Instead, he just nodded, and his silent self-deprecation surprised her. "Hey, I'm just kidding."

"I—"

"But she's white," her mother interrupted.

"So?"

"So Robert's not going to marry her. What's the point of asking her out?" She grabbed the bowl of picked seaweed and shoveled the greenish black slivers onto her plate.

"Why can't he marry her?" Whitney asked, surprised by her mother's sudden interest in ethnicity.

"Because he should marry a Korean girl," she said matter-of-factly. It was the first time she had ever placed parameters on their future spouses, and considering that Whitney had dated a Colombian boy in high school and a Filipino in college, she imagined that the issue should have arisen sooner.

"You never said anything about this before."

"I'm saying it now. We're Korean, and Koreans marry other Koreans."

"It's for the best," her father said through a mouthful of rice. "Your marriage will last longer this way."

"Dad, Jeannie and Mark are getting divorced," Whitney said, referring to her Korean-married-Korean cousins.

"Well, that's a complicated situation."

"I'm sure all divorces are complicated situations."

"What your father is trying to say is that we understand each other better," her mother said. "Children of the same generation and the same culture will always understand each other better than if they were different." She frowned, unsatisfied with her explanation.

"We don't have much left of ourselves here," her father said. "Your mother and I have been talking about this issue more recently."

"Why?" Robert asked.

"It's the main theme of *Poppies in the Field.* You know, second-generation children and the misunderstandings between them and their parents. It's a very good miniseries. You can get it at the Korean grocery store. Three for ten dollars if you go on Wednesdays."

"God," Robert said, rolling his eyes again.

"Anyway, my point is, yes, we are American, but we don't have the same customs that they do. We have our own culture and our own language, and we should be proud of it."

"You used to say America was a melting pot, Dad," Robert said.

"It *is* a melting pot. But you should marry a Korean anyway."

"I don't think *melting pot*'s the right way to describe it," her mother said. "The only people who use the term *melting pot* are people who don't have a culture of their own. We are Korean, we have our own culture, and we don't want to mix it with every other culture. There would be nothing of us left that way. How would you know where you came from?"

Whitney regarded her parents. They were articulating as best they could what she appreciated innately. Maybe she couldn't express it any clearer than they, but she understood the desire to retain her history, to know what it meant to be Korean. Still, in her parents' attempt to assimilate into a foreign culture, they hadn't introduced her to any of the customs with which they were raised other than their cuisine, and now that they were insisting that she and Robert marry someone of their own kind, the cafeteria-style culture-retention plan felt incongruous. In fact, it only highlighted what she had long ago realized— that she wasn't fully Korean, wasn't fully American and wasn't sure what Korean-American even meant. She was like so many others, the Valedictorians included—a unique breed of nationality. They weren't between cultures, as she had heard someone describe them. They were their own culture, a mishmashed patchwork of ideas and habits from their disparate worlds, strung together to form whatever the hell she had turned out to be.

"We didn't do a very good job of passing our traditions to our children," her mother said, looking regretful. "We thought it would be easier that way." She patted Robert's arm. "Marry a Korean girl."

"Find me one that's not butt-ass ugly and maybe I will." He gazed at the picture of Karen.

"You know," Whitney said, "you can do better than her. She's a little, uh, strange."

"Jesus," he muttered, "how is it that the only single girls left are weirdos or she-beasts? Am I really this hopeless?"

"No. You just have a terrible attitude, that's all."

"Depending on how it goes with Gina, I might still give that IT friend of yours a call." He spoke under his breath and glanced at his parents, who were chatting animatedly between themselves, oblivious to his refusal to heed their advice. "At least you have Scott. Congrats on bagging yourself a Korean boy."

Her mother caught Scott's name and looked up.

"Honey," she said, "I was planning on making *hae-mul-pah-jahn* this Saturday." Her father murmured with pleasure, looking as if he could already taste the thin, savory pancakes. "Can you and Scott come for dinner? I haven't seen him in weeks."

"He's going to be out of town this weekend, actually." She felt her stomach tighten, a reflex of unease and dissatisfaction that plagued her whenever she thought of him.

"Oh, that's too bad. Where's he going?"

"Dallas." She didn't want to say any more, but her mother's quizzical expression demanded further explanation. "He's meeting a professor who teaches the class he's auditing." Even though she was aware of the improbability of a rescheduled dinner, she said, "Maybe next weekend, Mom."

"You can still make *hae-mul-pah-jahn* for me," her father said before launching into an overlong list of fillings he most craved. Delighted by his enthusiasm for her cooking, her mother began to rattle off instructions on how to make one of his favorite dishes.

"So, do I have the apartment to myself this weekend?" Robert asked Whitney with a grin.

"No more than usual," she said, shrugging.

"You're not going with Scott to Dallas?" She shook her head, and he frowned. "Why not?"

"He didn't invite me."

"He didn't? But y'all do everything together."

"No couple does everything together, Robert. He's got his own life, too."

"Oh." He was quiet for a moment, and she wondered if he was contemplating her relationship with Scott. After twitching his lips thoughtfully, he asked, "Well, do you care if a few guys come over on Saturday to play poker?"

"Be my guest. I'll probably need to work anyway."

"Cool."

She returned to her plate and picked at her rice with her chopsticks, her appetite gone. The fact was, until recently, she and Scott *did* do everything together, spent every free moment as if it might be their last. They may not have shared their disparate interests with matching enthusiasm, but neither had they ever excluded each other from their pursuits, or left each other out of their plans and decisions. That he was no longer asking her to attend church every Sunday or to find a Bible study was almost worse than his earlier relentless persistence, and his silence was infinitely more deafening than his nagging pleas that she take up his deepest love with equal vigor. She imagined that he had stopped trying because he felt that his attempts were futile, or perhaps because he no longer wished to force her into a role he knew that she couldn't fulfill. She had stopped trying, too, had relinquished her efforts to weave him into the most important aspects of her life, and as she toyed with the *ban chan* on her plate, she knew it was because she refused to share her most precious passion with someone who didn't want to appreciate it, with someone who couldn't even pretend to support her. Unhappy with the realization, she wondered if Scott had likewise retreated and was now guarding his consuming Christianity against her for the same reasons.

"Honey," her mother said suddenly, jarring Whitney out of her thoughts, "don't forget to take the kimchee when you leave. I packed two jars for you. If you want, I can pack some *ban chan*, too. I know that you like the—oh, what do you call it in English? You know, *ggaen-eep*."

"I think they're called perilla leaves."

"Pe-ril-la," she repeated slowly, folding the word into her memory. "Okay, take some perilla leaves with you, too." She twitched her lips for a moment. "No, I cannot call them perilla leaves. Take some *ggaen-eep* with you."

"Pack some *gal bi,* too," Robert added. "Maybe Whitney will start cooking at home."

"Or you can," she shot back.

"You've got to be the most undomesticated person I've ever met," he said, shaking his head. "I guess Mom's recipes are going to die with her."

"No, I wrote them all down for you," her mother said. "You should try it sometime. Impress Gina with it. Oh, I can't wait for you to finally meet her."

"Mom, for God's sake, I don't need you to set me up with this girl."

"Robert, she's a Ph.D., you're a Ph.D. She's Korean, you're Korean. She's from a good family, you're from a good family." Her smile practically split her face. "Trust me, you're going to love her."

If relationships were only so easy, Whitney thought.

Six

"Xiao-Xiao, I want you to have a beautiful life," Hercules' mother said as she lay in a hospital bed. The thin covers were folded at her waist, and a thousand tubes plugged into her body, like a medical experiment on the living. "I want you to work hard and make me proud."

"You talk as if you're going to die," Hercules whispered. She wanted to assure her that there was no reason to speak so melodramatically, but her throat closed, and she couldn't choke out the admonition.

"I want you to marry a man who loves you, and I want you to be a good wife. Promise me that you'll do this."

"Mommy," she said, afraid to blink for fear that her tears would spill, "I'm only fifteen."

"I know," she said, her words barely audible. "But promise me anyway." Her eyes closed, and her breathing slowed, and in the sterility of Hercules' memories, her mother was beautiful.

"Okay. I promise."

Her mother nodded weakly, and at the time, Hercules had believed that she had acknowledged the promise. Perhaps the superficial observation had been her emotional and psychological defense, because in hindsight, it was clear that she had been quaking with pain.

Hercules had stood up from the chair in which she had spent the last twenty-four hours and placed her hand on her mother's shoulder. Her eyes didn't open, and her chest didn't move. Hercules shuddered. This wasn't her time. It couldn't be. She was only forty-five years old, and until six months ago, she had been the picture of vibrant health.

Her father sat on the other side of the bed, his thin lips pursed into a line, his complexion as sallow as her mother's. He cast his gaze down, unable to watch her expire, and as he hunched over in the aluminum chair, he looked as though he had just been disemboweled.

After the doctor had noted her time of death, he left them alone, and she sank next to her mother in a stupor. Her senses had been deadened, as if God knew that the loss was too much for her to bear, and she recalled feeling strangely numb and apathetic. Her father, on the other hand, acted perhaps in the only way he knew how, and instead of hovering close by her mother, or even taking her hand into his own, he went to the farthest edge of the room, tucked his head into the corner and wept until midnight.

"Hercules, what do you think?" Reynaldo Gonzales asked. He flipped through a series of photographs of prototype cookware and held one up. "This is a good start, don't you think?"

Hercules blinked hard. Her vision cleared, and she saw that she was sitting at a booth at Dragonfly. Her black-suited business partner was looking at her, searching her face for approval. She hadn't let herself think about her mother's death, not since the cancer had robbed her of muscle and bone and had turned her olive skin green. Yet Hercules' dreams of late had lingered on little else, and as she gazed at Reynaldo without really seeing him, all she could think about was her teenage promise to her dying mother.

"Are you listening to me? Hercules—*hell-o!*"

"What, motherfucker?" she snapped.

Reynaldo frowned. "God, sometimes I feel like your grandma, you know that?" His voice turned squeaky and high-pitched, his falsetto impression of a woman. "Quit daydreaming. Work hard. Be nice to people. Pay attention to your business manager." His voice reclaimed his deep bass. "*Stop cursing.*"

"Sorry." She knew that she and Reynaldo had more bases to cover than they had time that afternoon, yet she couldn't focus for the life of her. She had spent the last forty-eight hours at the restaurant, and when she wasn't racking her brain for creative new ways to prepare venison, or standing over a stove searing pork tenderloins while a hundred patrons waited impatiently, she was poring over the balance sheets of Dragonfly, dealing with her produce vendors, working on the interior plans of Dragonfly Deux, writing articles for *Texas Mag* and the *Houston Observer* or designing a range of cookware. She desperately needed a break, if even for a few hours, to give her a chance to feel like a human being instead of a workaholic troll who had hit her limit. When she looked up, he was still scowling at her like an angry parent.

"That reminds me," he said, "the article you wrote for the *Houston Chronicle* was perfect. Have you been reading the op-eds lately? People are starting to love you again, and our receipts are proof of that. I sent a draft to *National Spectator*, and they want to run it in their March issue. We retained the copyright, so we don't have any legal issues with a reprint."

"That's good." She was barely paying attention to him, and as if she were caught in mental quicksand, her thoughts returned to her mother.

"It's a big deal." He reached into his briefcase and pulled out a copy of the periodical.

"Yeah."

"*National Spectator*, Hercules. Anyone who subscribes to the *Robb Report* or *Fine Living* reads it. Hell, anyone who reads *Vogue* reads it. It's got a circulation almost as big as *Vogue*."

"I *know* what *National Spectator* is, for God's sake," she said, exasperated. "You don't have to talk to me like I'm a moron."

"What's going on?" He laid down the magazine. "You're being a bigger bitch than usual."

"Nothing." She sighed deeply and leaned her head against the banquette. "I've just got a lot on my mind."

"Your father?"

"You don't even want to know," she muttered.

"Well, whatever it is, you need to focus on this." He waved a picture of steel cookware in front of her face. "What do you think? Acceleron wants to know by *tomorrow* which of these you prefer. If you ask me, I'd say to go with the fully anodized line."

"Let me see that." She snatched the catalog from the table and stared at the pictures. Pots and pans. Spatulas and colanders. Saucepans and double boilers. Hercules Cookware was finally coming to life, and she could barely concentrate.

"You can fork the metal like this," he said, leaning over so that his pink tie draped over the table. "The handles remain cool even on the range. I know chefs don't care about that at all, but consumers do. We really need to push cool-to-the-touch products."

"Yeah," she murmured as she studied the catalog.

"If you're not happy with these, I'll bring the other set of sketches." His round face shone as he grabbed a napkin and doodled. "We can curve the bases more like this, see?" Just as he pushed the drawing towards her, her cell phone rang.

"I've got to get this," she said, glad for the interruption.

"Make it quick." He tapped on his watch. "Deadlines." She edged out of the booth and moved closer to the entrance.

"What's up?" she answered.

"Hey, so did you talk to Audrey about her engagement?" Whitney asked. She sounded far away, and her voice was muffled as if she were calling from a cave.

"Yeah, she called me a couple of weeks ago." She thought about her friend, felt genuinely happy for her and tried not to let the good news highlight her own nonexistent love life.

"We should start thinking about throwing her an engagement party. I don't know if they've picked a date yet, but that doesn't mean that you and I can't plan in the next couple of months."

"Sure. Maybe we'll do something in Austin." The thought of a lazy day on a patio chair cheered her, and the stress that was screwing up her shoulders eased a notch. Through static, she heard clicking noises and laughter. "Where are you? I can barely hear you." She glanced at Reynaldo, who was scribbling furiously on a napkin. He looked up and tapped on his watch again.

"I'm in a warehouse. My boss is having me review some off-site documents."

"Jesus, Whitney, I thought you were a freakin' lawyer."

"Well, this is what freakin' lawyers do. Don't worry about me, though. It's delightful out here, what with the rats and bugs and six thousand boxes to get through." Hercules heard something shatter and several high-pitched shrieks before Whitney returned to the line. "Hey, let me call you later. I've got to go."

"See ya." She returned to the table where Reynaldo was wringing his hands, as close to anxious as she had ever seen him.

"Hercules, I swear to God. You know how I feel about procrastinating. We have to make a decision now."

"I've already decided," she said authoritatively. "We'll start out with a ten-piece set, and if Acceleron gives the green light, we'll upgrade to a twelve-piece set. Maybe roll that out a season after the initial set. Let's go with a ten- and twelve-inch fry pan, a three and a four and a half saucepan, an eleven-inch skillet, and an eight-quart stockpot. Curve the handles like you've got on your napkin so that consumers don't get their fingers too close to the metal. I want my signature stamped to the bottom of every piece and also on the handle so that no one forgets the product. Hercules is a brand, so we need to make my stamp as ubiquitous as the Nike swoosh."

"Great," he said. She could tell that he was excited, and his concentration and the open catalogs of kitchenware snapped her into business mode.

"I want to trademark the name Hercules, as well. Can you look into that?"

"I already have," he said, pleased with her sudden focus. "I've applied for your full name with the PTO as well as the name of your restaurants. Intellectual property is part of the deal with the cookware, and we're still in negotiations as to who will own what percentage of everything. I don't want you to get your hopes up, though. Acceleron's got a lot more leverage on the intangibles of the deal right now."

"I figured as much. And since branding's so important to you, I've decided that Dragonfly Deux's also going to be comfort food. Same concept, slightly different name. We can play on the Dragonfly name as we open more restaurants. Where are we on the build-out of Dragonfly Deux?" He looked up. "Please tell me that the contractors are finished. I don't know how many screaming conversations I need to have with them to make this happen on time."

"Well, the construction's almost—"

"When's it going to be *completely* finished?" she interrupted. Heat rose against the back of her neck. There was nothing so maddening as contractors, and she refused to understand why it was the one industry that couldn't keep time.

"They say it'll be another month," he said calmly, and then gathered the pile of prototype catalogs.

"That's what they said last month."

"You know how these things go." He motioned around him. "This place was a year behind, remember? You should be grateful that Dragonfly Deux's been delayed by only two months."

"God," she said with a rumbling sigh. "From now on, always, *always* put a 'time of the essence' clause in our GC contracts. With liquidated-damages provisions."

Reynaldo checked his watch. "Well, we've got more clout now to get away with those," he said. "I've got to go, but we need to square off some of the details on the Acceleron line. Are you going to be here tonight?"

"Yeah."

They both hopped out of the booth, and she was about to walk through the swinging door to the kitchen when Reynaldo reached out and touched her arm.

"Really, are things okay with you?"

"Yeah, they are. Or they will be."

He continued to peer at her, and his roving inspection made her antsy.

"You know, my father brought my family to this country from Cuba when I was four, kind of like you," he said. The abrupt tone of his business mode was gone, and the hardness of his eyes melted into friendly pools of molasses brown. "My parents never tried to assimilate when we got here, even though me and my brothers learned to blend in with the rest of the country. I never understood why."

"Why are you——?" Hercules began to ask. Reynaldo put up a hand to silence her.

"Maybe it was because they were too busy working, or maybe it was because they had their Spanish-speaking friends, or maybe it was because they thought Castro would be run out soon. I don't know. They're in their seventies now, and they still talk about Cuba as if it's where Jesus sleeps at night. I used to feel so ashamed of them. I tried to make them into something they weren't and something they didn't want to be. It wasn't my place to change them. I know that now, and I accept them for who they are."

"Why are you telling me this?" In the eighteen months that they had worked together, he had never shared his family's history, and she couldn't imagine what had sparked his sudden openness.

"You need to understand that you're not the only person with a difficult parent. Or an immigrant parent. Maybe then you'll stop feeling sorry for yourself, stop being so angry with your father and just get on with life. You're an adult with a successful career. Be happy with that." He bent over and picked up his briefcase. "I'll send you the final draft of the article before *National Spectator* goes to print."

"Thanks." She watched as he left the restaurant and wondered if her moods were really so transparent. She appreciated his empathy, even if he didn't know that she had been preoccupied with a matter that wasn't Baba-centric. Still, his advice on simply letting her father be—she wasn't ready to take a give-up approach to the issue. With a heavy sigh, she pushed through the swinging door and stepped into the kitchen. What she would do with her father would have to wait until the evening. The restaurant would open in five hours, and she had a menu to set.

"It ain't no thang but a chicken wing," Chris Stone drawled with a grin. He swirled his pan over an open flame, letting the oil sizzle as sliced peppers and onions twirled in the pizza-sized skillet, before he cocked his wrist. A rainbow of julienne vegetables shot into the air. The rest of the chefs cheered at the seven-foot catapult, and Hercules looked up from the corner desk where she had been putting together the evening's menu.

"You even trying, man?" Simon Brills asked, cracking his knuckles in anticipation.

"Simon, you're up," Hercules said. The five chefs were in the kitchen, dressed in white pants and undershirts, oblivious to the heat radiating from the half-dozen ovens and steamers. The back door was

opened to the alleyway, and the humidity of the early February air permeated the kitchen, settling on her skin like sweat. Dragonfly wouldn't
open for several hours, and the time between lunch and the mad rush
before dinner was Hercules' favorite time of day. The languid afternoon was the chefs' playtime, and at the moment, they were competing for the title of the highest tosser of vegetables.

"Take that," Simon shouted, and with a full body jerk, he blasted a
wave of sliced onions at least ten feet into the air. The crew whooped
and hollered, banging their palms against the aluminum table.

"Simon takes it," he said, referring to himself in the third person, as
he always did at their kitchen competitions. He clasped his hands and
shook them over his head, already celebrating.

"Chef hasn't gone yet," Jenna Morgan said, "so quit your cheerin'."

"Yes, Chef, it's your turn," Chris said. "You can't let Simon think
that he's got any skills."

"Watch and learn." Hercules felt her earlier stress and fatigue drain
as she concentrated on the task at hand. She cracked her knuckles
dramatically and then stretched, leaning side to side with exagger-
ated motions. She was about to grab at a container of thickly sliced
green peppers when the phone rang. Simon trotted to the corner of
the kitchen and scrunched his face as he listened to the caller.

"What? Who is this?" His voice rose until he was nearly shouting.
"I think you've got the wrong number. No, this—Chow? There's no
Chow here."

Hercules looked up. "I'll take it."

He handed the cordless to her and then returned to the gaggle of
merrymakers.

"Hello," she said into the line.

"Xiao-Xiao, they're trying to cheat me! These—these cheaters,"
her father shrieked, his Mandarin cutting like blades in her ear.

"Baba, calm down. Who's trying to cheat you?"

"These people. These cheaters." He was hysterical, and man-child
that he was, he could barely speak between heaving breaths.

"Where are you?" She moved into the dark space of the dining
room, away from the rowdiness of the kitchen, and away from perked

ears. Everyone knew that she was top dog of the place, and that at twenty-nine, she was a business savant on top of a culinary ace, but her father's call shattered the veneer of hard perfection she had built, and his helpless shouts dragged her into the past like quicksand. It wasn't something she wanted to be reminded of, and she definitely didn't want the others to know that she was ruled by a sixty-nine-year-old man in between a raging bout of hypoglycemia and insanity.

"The Lexus dealership," he said, his breaths still ragged. "I was trying to get an oil change, and they're trying to charge me for it."

"Were you expecting it for free?" Hercules rubbed her temples. She didn't want to deal with this. She just wanted to toss vegetables and relax with the rest of the idyllic chefs.

"You said that oil changes for the first sixty thousand miles were free."

"I don't remember what I said, Baba. How much is it, anyway?"

"I don't know."

She sighed. The LS 430 had been a gift, a response to his constant complaints about his beat-up Toyota Camry. In his typical Baba style, he had never asked her to buy him a new car, but from the vociferousness of his criticisms, she had understood that he expected her to lavish him with an expensive ride. On most occasions, he refused to drive it for fear of being robbed. When he did drive, all of Houston was at risk or was otherwise frustrated at his terrified, and terrifying, driving. And then, of course, there was this, his inability to care for the gift because of his refusal to learn English. She sighed again.

"I'll be right there," she said, and then hung up the phone. It was almost three o'clock, and she imagined that they had plenty of time to straighten out the misunderstanding. Lord willing, they would be able to settle the matter without a humiliating episode at the dealership. She swung the door open and stomped into the kitchen. Eight expectant eyes bored into her.

"Is everything okay?" Simon asked. His eyes were glassy, and he swayed slightly, as though he were too relaxed to stand.

"I've got to take care of something." She peered at Simon. "You all right?"

"*Mucho bueno*, Chef."

"You're going to have to be my number one until I get back. If anything gets fucked up, I'm holding you responsible."

"Yes, Chef."

Hercules eyed him and the rest of the staff one last time before heaving yet another sigh. She barreled her way out the back door, jumped into her car and eased her way into the alley. In a moment, she was cruising down the highway, grateful that at least the roads weren't clogged bumper to bumper with imbecilic drivers. The longer she thought about Baba, the faster she drove, her frustration burning like fuel.

It wasn't fair. How could they even be related? Where were the similarities? After all, she was full of purpose and ambition, and he was listless and uninterested. She was gregarious and sociable. He was a reclusive hermit. She was competent and assimilated, and after twenty-five years, he was still a total foreigner. Her cell phone rang suddenly, rattling her out of her thoughts, and she grabbed it out of the cup holder without looking at the caller ID.

"Hello?"

"Hey, it's Lucas. Why haven't you been returning my calls?"

"Because I'm mad at you," she said bluntly, aware of how immaturely petulant she sounded.

"Why?"

"Because the restaurant in San Antonio was supposed to be *our* deal. We were supposed to make decisions together, and you went out and found that Gary guy to take my place."

"Hercules, no one's taking your place, and I didn't go out and try to find someone else. He and I were just talking, and when I mentioned that I was going into business with you, he begged to be included. He's majorly starstruck by you. Hell, I'd be, too, if we hadn't been friends since school."

"I'm still pissed," she said, her irritation melting a little at the compliment. "I wouldn't have done that to you."

"You would have if the situation were reversed. Think about it. What would you have done if I had two restaurants going and didn't have any plans on moving to Houston? You would've found someone competent to add to the staff, and you'd be ticked off if you had to discuss every detail with me before going forward. This is what I'm talking about, Hercules. You've got serious control issues. I don't know how to get that through to you."

She didn't respond. He was right, of course, both from a business perspective and probably from a personal one, too. Obviously, his having stumbled upon Gary would save them time in the future, and even she knew that her irritation with Lucas was nothing more than psychological transference of her feelings for the other man in her life. She bit her lower lip, wishing that, for once, she could shake the annoyance that burrowed into her psyche like a plague.

"I swear, you're going to love Gary," he said. "And if you don't, we'll ditch him."

"Fine," she said through clenched jaws.

"You're still coming out on March sixteenth, right?"

"Yeah."

"Have a drink with me and Gary. Or meet me at the restaurant, and Gary will show you how great he is in the kitchen. See for yourself that he's an awesome cook. He's got incredible business sense, too. He sold his restaurants to the Romanesco Group for an enormous amount of money before he opened La Trattoria."

She let out a rumbling groan. "Fine. I'll meet y'all on Friday night."

"Cool. I'll see you then."

She snapped her phone shut just as she was pulling into the Lexus dealership, and she spotted her father as soon as she drove to the service department. He was sitting on a concrete bench with his legs crossed, making him appear even slighter than he was. The sight of him, powerless like some kind of wounded animal, roused pity in her, and a surge of protectiveness, too.

"Baba," she shouted through a crack in her window.

He looked up, his paper-thin eyes squinting in the sunlight as he peered at her, and he rose from the bench and walked over.

"You said that the oil change was free," he said. "They keep saying I have to pay." He mumbled, using words that Hercules had never heard before, and then groaned. "Why did you ever buy me a car full of troubles? I never asked you to waste your money on such an expensive clunker that keeps breaking down."

"Really, Baba, would it kill you to be thankful for once in your life?"

"Show me something to be thankful for, and I will." He talked in his usual monotone voice, and the indifference with which he spoke made his words that much more provocative.

"A huge part of me just wants to leave you right now and let you figure it out," she muttered under her breath. "Like you even could." She knew what an agoraphobe he was, knew that for a Chinese man who lived in Chinatown and was surrounded by Chinese neighbors, he didn't have any friends. He didn't even have acquaintances as far as Hercules was aware, and despite her palpable frustration, she found herself feeling sorry for him. She threw the gearshift into park, turned off the engine and stepped out of the car. "Come on, Baba. Let's figure out what's going on."

They headed to the entrance without speaking to each other. She sighed again, her tenth in as many minutes, and tried to gulp in deep breaths. When she glanced at him, his usually sallow face had gone white, and he blinked quickly, as if he was on the verge of blacking out. She reached out and steadied him.

"Did you take your medicine today?" she asked.

"What?"

"Your diabetes medicine, Baba," she said, placing the back of her hand onto his perspiring forehead. "Did you take it today?"

"I don't remember," he said, looking confused.

"Do you still have the pack that I left in your glove compartment?" He stared at her blankly, and she wrapped his frail arm around hers. "God, I hope so. Let's go look."

He didn't say anything as she led him towards his car, and her shoulders clenched as she realized that she couldn't postpone moving him in with her much longer. There was simply no way around it. As his only relative in the States, and perhaps the only person in his life, she was going to have to care for him. He was already completely dependent on her, and whether or not a dutiful daughter would have willingly taken in an ailing, miserable, intolerable father because of the customs of her heritage, Hercules was going to have to become his parent because no one else would.

Seven

"Chiaroscuro," Audrey said slowly. In the dimmed room, she was able to make out ten pairs of eyes focusing on a print of Baglione's *Sacred Love Versus Profane Love*. How her students would react to a lesson about Renaissance artists was anyone's guess, and considering that they had just returned from a boisterous half hour of lacrosse, she hoped that they would be receptive to the lecture.

"What's chiaroscuro?" Matthew Tobias, one of her students, asked.

"It's Italian for 'light and dark.' You see how the background is dark, and the two subjects here are light?" She motioned to the extended figures at the center of the work. "It's a study in contrast, and if done correctly, it gives the piece a three-dimensional quality, and it trains your eyes to what the artist considers to be important."

Matthew nodded slowly, clearly understanding. With hair so blond that it looked white, and pale skin balanced against his navy blazer and sand-colored pants, he was a study in chiaroscuro himself. The other children relaxed on the floor where they were sitting Indian-style, all in navy St. Mark's blazers and tan skirts and slacks. It was obvious that they, too, comprehended the dramatic juxtaposition of color and texture, and Audrey's heart leaped when their eyes flitted from Baglione's work to the print of Caravaggio's *Crucifixion of St. Peter*.

"Caravaggio also uses chiaroscuro," Alexandra Gilton said.

"But it's not as obvious as Baglione's," Carlton Lexington said.

To say that her students were gifted was an understatement. They weren't merely gifted; they were *brilliant*. So were the other two sections of first graders, and the school prided itself on the quality of its kindergarten-through-eighth-grade students, which was to say that they only accepted certified and documented geniuses. Whether the result of rigorous courses or an innate propensity towards the cerebral, her kids soaked up a curriculum of junior high school levels of math, English, science, Spanish, French, anthropology and art like six-year-old sponges. They even seemed to relish long lectures on the various subject matters, and when Audrey was in front of them, equally immersed in the philosophies of Plato or Socrates, she felt more connected to them than she did with her friends and family.

She turned the lights on, and the children squinted, struggling to adjust to the brightness. She motioned for them to return to their desks, and they scrambled into their seats.

"All right, now—"

"Miss Henley," a voice said from the intercom. Everyone's eyes zoomed in on the small speaker near her desk. Crackles emanated from the system, sounding as if the connection was shorting. Audrey waited for a few seconds, and when the interruption quieted, she turned back to her class.

"Okay, now that we know what chiaroscuro is, we're going to make our own pieces."

"What was that noise?" Alexandra asked.

"Nothing, I'm sure," Audrey said. "It's probably just a wiring problem from all the renovations."

"For the chapel?" Alton Peterson asked.

"I bet it's for the new gymnasium," Jennifer Crawford said.

"My mom said that we're getting a new aquatic center," Rosemary Chilton said.

"Get back to the lesson, Miss Henley," Matthew said impatiently. She felt herself smile. There was no question who was her favorite student.

"Everyone, forget about the renovations. If you'll look over there, you'll see that we've set up a little studio where you're going to make your own masterpieces." She pointed to the side of the classroom where her assistant had set up ten canvases on easels with a smock hanging from each one. Sixty-five shades of childproof watercolors rested on a counter nearby, as did massive prints of the Italian greats and modern versions of the artistic technique. She had even brought stills of Frank Miller's *Sin City* as further examples to inspire her students.

"Miss Henley, would you please respond," someone called from the intercom again. Judging from her almost incomprehensible Texas twang, the voice belonged to Doris Bateman, the school's administrator. Audrey walked over and pressed the TALK button.

"I'm in the middle of class, Doris."

"I understand, but you need to come to Mr. Kennedy's office. You have a few visitors."

"Miss Henley's being called to the principal's office," Barron Phillips said in a singsong voice.

"Y'all keep it down in there," Audrey said, and put a silencing finger to her lips. She turned back to the speaker. "Is everything okay? Who is it?"

"Everything's fine," the voice said. "Your mother's here, and she's got a couple of gentlemen with her. She says that she needs to speak with you." Doris sounded somewhere between exasperated and awed.

"Tell her I'll be right there," Audrey said, unwilling to guess why her mother had decided to visit her at work. She walked to the front of the classroom and placed her hands on her hips.

"You have one hour to work on the assignment. I'm going to step out for a minute, but if you have any questions, Jeannette will help you." She motioned to her teaching assistant. "Don't worry about finishing today. We're going to work on the project all week."

"Ooh," they said happily, their eyes going wide. They glanced at one another and again at the posters hanging on the chalkboard, before sprinting to their easels. She watched with affection as they found their names on the easels and examined their miniature studio.

"What are we supposed to draw?" Matthew asked.

"Whatever you want, so long as you can show me how you've used chiaroscuro. You can draw people, like Baglione and Caravaggio did, or you can create something from nature, the media or anything else. This is art, which means that you can be as free or restricted as you'd like." She helped Sarah Saunders with her smock, and then leaned against the counter as ten kids bustled about, manically fetching cartons of paint to begin their work.

"So, chiaroscuro is about putting different things next to each other?" Samantha Carrington asked. She looked hesitant, as though daunted by the fact that she was to turn a white space into something resembling the exemplars.

Audrey crouched next to her. "Yes, it's about placing opposites against each other. Light and dark."

"Different," Samantha said.

"Why different?" Audrey asked, goading Samantha into understanding the philosophy of contrast.

"Because different is beautiful," Matthew shouted from his easel.

Audrey pulled her ivory cardigan closer around her and headed towards the administrative building. The grounds of the twenty-acre school were blissfully tranquil, and other than the low whir of newborn crickets and her own kitten heels clacking against the cobblestone walkway, the tucked-away campus was silent. She could only imagine what her mother wanted or whom she had dragged along to the school. *This is why everyone needs a job,* she thought. *So that sixty-two-year-old women with too much time on their hands don't disrupt those who do.*

"Darling," her mother cried as soon as she stepped into Carlton Kennedy's office. "I haven't been in the principal's office since you were in the eighth grade." She kissed her cheek, her thin lips barely touching Audrey's skin. "I hope this isn't a bad time."

"Mother, this is a *school*, and I'm in the middle of class. Unless someone's dying, yes, this is a bad time." From her periphery, she spied Doris studying her mother, her eyes greedily taking in her Chanel box jacket, eggshell-hued silk pants and just-highlighted platinum blond hair. A moment later, she slunk off into her office, leaving Audrey alone with her mother and two strangers.

"Well, I've got great news," her mother said, her cheeks flushed to a delicate pink, "and you weren't answering your phone."

"I never turn on my cell during school hours."

"You really should."

"It's against the rules."

"Is it?" She cocked her head. "They really need to change that."

"Mom, please," she said impatiently, "what's your great news?"

"Oh, well, Lois MacDonald, Fiona Bellington, Dixie Susman and I are cofounding a new philanthropic trust. We're calling it the Houston Cultural Exchange Center for Children." Her face flushed a shade darker, the way it did when she was thrilled. "Your father's already agreed to underwrite the inaugural gala we're planning to host in the fall." She must have noticed Audrey's surprise by her parents' sudden cooperation, because she shook her head. "Well, he didn't really *agree*. I just decided. He'll find out later." She smiled brightly, clearly captivated by her own ideas, and then motioned to her companions. "Anyway, I was able to get Houston's most desired coordinators to plan the event. Carlos"—the thin planner waved—"and Gianfranco"—the chubbier one smiled—"are booked to the hilt right now, but they agreed to do the gala as a favor to me."

"How can we say no to *Mee-sus Heen-ley?*" Carlos said. He looked like a Hedi Slimane groupie, lanky, bowl-cut and dressed in a black suit complete with a skinny black tie. Gianfranco, apparently a Versace enthusiast, nodded excitedly.

"The Cultural Exchange is going to focus on international exchange programs so that underprivileged children will have an opportunity to be exposed to other cultures. There isn't a program like it in Texas, and it's about time that we had one." She laid a French-manicured hand on one of the event planner's arms and leaned in. "I just thought of something. The fall gala should play up on an international theme. I'm not sure how, exactly, but I think that would be fabulous."

"But of course," Gianfranco said, enunciating every vowel of his words. "We already have many grand visions in mind. It will be the most beautiful celebration Houston has seen in years."

"*This* is why you called me out of class?" Audrey asked, unable to keep her exasperation in check. "You couldn't wait until after school let out to tell me this? What in the world does this even have to do with me?"

"Well"—her mother looked even cheerier—"since we're cofounding the Cultural Exchange, we have the ability to choose junior committee members. Everyone's daughters have already agreed to head one of the committees, and we thought that you would be perfect to chair the fund-raising committee. It would give you a lot of exposure to the community."

"Since when have I expressed interest in chairing a committee?" She stared at her mother, who was still clearly taken with her budding charity. "It's been years since I've even attended one of these functions."

"Darling, that's exactly my point. You *haven't* been involved in worthwhile causes in ages, and I think this organization is right up your alley." She crossed her arms, displaying her long fingers. "It may be nonstop until the gala, though. There's so much to be done, and with the event on November fifteenth—"

"Mom, stop. I appreciate your thinking that I would be a good fund-raiser, but I don't have time. I've got my kids to attend to, and the school's Fall Fair's coming up. That takes an enormous amount of planning. Besides, I really need to concentrate on my dissertation. I'm basically staying up all night as it is to work on it."

"But it's not due for another year, Audrey," she said, perplexed. "And you can always ask for more time if a year isn't enough, can't you? I know that Jennifer Latham's daughter received an extension after she had a baby."

"I'm turning it in early," she said, feeling her shoulders clench. The very idea of waiting to finish her paper flooded her with panic. She was so close to the finish line, and she was anxious to move forward, to interview for professorship positions. There were only so many opportunities available, and with each passing day, she felt as if the already limited field were narrowing, even if she knew that her fears were statistically unfounded. As if she could sense Audrey's anxiety, her mother's face wrinkled with concern.

"Sweetheart, you don't have to push yourself so hard all the time. Your program gives you six years to complete your degree because you *need* six years. And you're working a demanding job on top of that. I'm sure your professors would understand if you needed extra time to finish your paper."

"I don't need extra time." She noticed Carlos and Gianfranco watching them, their heads turning to whoever was speaking as if they were observing a tennis match, and she found their overly attentive gazes unnerving. "It might be a little rough for the next few months, but I can handle it. Besides, it's not like I'll have an easier schedule postsubmission. If I'm lucky, I'll have dozens of interviews for positions at colleges."

Her mother sighed, looking pained. "I really wish you would slow down. Sometimes you act as if everything has to be done by tomorrow. You remind me so much of your father in that respect." Almost under her breath, she said, "I don't know how that happened. You barely ever saw him, and yet you somehow took after him completely." She sighed again. "I just don't want you to wake up twenty years from now and regret having had so much on your plate all the time. I don't want you to have missed out on the present because you were too busy planning for the future."

"Mom, really, you don't have to worry about me. Besides, if you think I already have too much on my plate, why do you want me to chair one of the Cultural Exchange's committees?"

"Because it's something different from your world of academics." She smiled. "Plus, these charities are *fun*, darling, and you could stand to use a little more of it. And they're for such great causes, too." She laid her hand on Audrey's arm and leaned in. "It would also give us a reason to spend more time with each other."

"You want to spend more time with me than we already do?" she asked, managing to smile back. "I don't think I can commit to it this year. Besides, the gala conflicts with the date Victor and I were thinking about for our wedding."

"Audrey is getting married?" Carlos asked, his hand fluttering to his chest.

"*Mee-sus Heen-ley*, why you not tell us?" Gianfranco asked. "Oh, I can already imagine what kind of beautiful ceremony it will be." He tugged on Audrey's mother's sleeve. "You have to let us do Audrey's wedding. It will be magnificent."

"Wedding is our specialty," Carlos practically shouted.

"And Audrey is such a beauty. An *exotic* beauty." He gazed at her dreamily. "I am having beautiful vision of Japanese feast. It is so traditional, but so *avant-garde*."

"Or maybe we do Hong Kong banquet."

"Oh, yes. That would be stupendous!"

"We must start to plan now!"

"Stop," her mother said, looking as if she had been impaled. She held up her hand, her obscenely large diamond ring catching the light, silencing them. "Audrey, may I speak to you for a moment, please?"

"You'll have to make it quick. I really need to get back to class."

She pulled Audrey to the side of the room, leaving Carlos and Gianfranco to chatter enthusiastically about a Far East–themed wedding, each interrupting the other with another shouted suggestion. Doris poked her head into the room again, looking as if she was about to say something, before retreating silently.

"Audrey," her mother said, her cheeks burning a strange reddish color, "you cannot *possibly* be thinking of a November wedding."

"Why not?" she asked, trying not to get defensive.

"Why not?" Her expertly arched brows rose high. "Why *not*? Because you hardly know the boy. You don't know what his family's like. You don't—"

"I've met them, actually." She dropped her voice, dismayed that they were arguing in the middle of the principal's office. "Last month when we went to New Mexico. They're lovely people."

"Three months with Victor and one visit to his parents—is that supposed to be enough? Am I the only one who sees what a huge mistake you're making?" Audrey shrank back. "What on earth is wrong with you? Why are you so desperate to rush into marriage?"

"We were just *thinking* of November, Mom. And that's nine months away. It's not like we're going to Vegas tomorrow." She regretted having said anything at all about specific dates. Had she known that her mother would attach to it as if it were written in stone, she would've kept her mouth shut. "I don't know why you're getting so bent out of shape over this. We love each other. We *get* each other. How is our wedding—our relationship—a mistake?" Her words only seemed to upset her mother further.

"This is absurd. A marriage doesn't work just because you love or get each other. You two have nothing in common. Your father and I don't know anything about his family. We barely know anything about Victor."

"You know that he teaches tenth-grade biology at MLK High." She recognized the superficiality of the statement, knew that the résumé-like fact wouldn't undermine the truth of her mother's comment. "You know that—"

"I know that he's a teacher." She looked as if she was trying to control herself. "That's *all* I know about him. That may be well and good if you two were just friends, or if . . ." She trailed off, unwilling to finish her sentence. Instead, she pinched the bridge of her nose with her delicate fingers and sucked in a deep breath. "What about his plans for the future? How is he going to take care of you? Please tell me that he's attending graduate school of some kind. Please tell me that Victor intends to become a doctor or a lawyer, or that he will get his MBA and find a job that pays more than thirty thousand dollars a year."

"I can't tell you that," she said, feeling awful for the way her mother was presenting his professional ambitions. "He's happy where he is."

Her mother continued to press her lips together until they were almost invisible.

"You don't have to worry about money," Audrey said, wishing that she could assuage her mother. "Victor and I do just fine on our salaries. And even if all of that went to hell, you know that Dad's made sure that I'll always be taken care of financially."

"Darling, I'm not—I know that." If possible, she looked even more troubled, and when she saw that Carlos and Gianfranco were heading their way, she shooed them away.

"If you're not concerned about Victor's ability to support me, then why do you care what he does for a living?"

"Because—everything about this relationship is wrong. It just is." She grasped Audrey's wrist. "Darling, he's not the one for you. I hate to say it, but that's how I feel. I don't want you to find that out after you marry him. Open your eyes now."

"Mom, stop." She eased her hand out of her grip. "I appreciate your concern. Really, I do. I know that three months doesn't seem like a lot of time because—well, it isn't. But Victor and me—it just feels right.

It *is* right. I feel it in my bones. I can't explain myself any better than that." Her mother looked horrified. "If you're freaking out because November is too soon, then we'll prolong the engagement. Make it a year. Maybe two. You have to know that we're not in any rush." Her mother continued to stare at her, clearly unconvinced. "And if you're worried because you don't know anything about him, then spend some time with him. You'll see for yourself that he's perfect for me."

"Darling, I don't—"

"Please, Mom. For me."

Her mother didn't respond, and Audrey checked her watch, sure that her kids, energetic geniuses that they were, had demolished the classroom by now.

"I've got to go," she said. "If you care about me at all, please try to be supportive. Please try to understand."

"Get back to your class, Audrey." Consternation still masked her face. "We'll talk later."

"Fine." She leaned closer, and her mother kissed her on the cheek. With a halfhearted smile, she left the principal's office, feeling worse than she had ever felt in Mr. Kennedy's presence twenty years ago.

"Mother, please, I can't talk about this right now," Audrey said as soon as she picked up the phone. She had less than two minutes before her students returned from classical-music appreciation class, and her mother's incessant calls were treading on her last overtaxed nerve.

"Uh—I'm looking for Audrey Henley," a male voice replied.

"I'm sorry. I—this is Audrey. With whom am I speaking?" She wished that the school phones had caller ID. Screening her calls would be so much easier.

"Audrey? It's Jimmy Fujimoto. Do you remember me? You gave me your card at Starbucks a few weeks ago. I was talking about my psycho ex, and you were talking about your wedding."

"Of course I remember," she said, feeling out of sorts.

"Is this a bad time?"

"No, you're fine. I'm sorry, I thought you were my mother. She's been calling me all day and driving me absolutely insane with—" She stopped herself short. "Well, it's a long story."

"Is it wedding related?"

"Sort of."

"Honey, *all* mothers go nuts with their daughters' weddings. Oh, speaking of weddings, may I make a suggestion?"

"Sure."

"I know I said that all ceremonies should incorporate something from one's heritage, but I—well, I'm not sure that Irish jigs are quite the thing. I'm sure you'll be beautiful in your Irish costume, but I can't imagine all those legs flying about at a reception. *Lord of the Dance* gives me the heebie-jeebies, to be honest with you. I feel I owe you that much, since I was the one to turn you on to all of this."

"Relax," Audrey said with a laugh. "I doubt there'll be any Irish jigs, and given the way everything's been going, we may just elope." She rummaged through her agenda and found her notes. "I guess you're calling about my law-firm friend?"

"I am, indeed."

"Her name's Whitney Lee, and she's with Boerne and Connelly. She talked to a couple of the lawyers there, and none of them handle property disputes. But she's asking for referrals, and I should be able to get you a name in the next couple of days."

"You are just the nicest girl in the world to do this for me," he said emotionally. "I'm going to repay you somehow. Whitney, too."

"Really, it's not a big deal. Whitney gets requests for referrals all the time."

"It's a big deal to me. I don't know any lawyers or anyone who knows lawyers other than you. I'd be sunk without you."

"Seriously, Jimmy, I'm happy to help."

"Do you know what I'm going through right now? It's become a war of attrition at my house. Kevin refuses to divide the property, and I refuse to leave my home. So we're both still there, trying to make each other crazy. He brought all these man whores home, like *that's* going to make me jealous."

"How immat—"

"So *I'm* bringing all of these gorgeous, sexy boys home, too. He's not the only one who's still got it, and if he thinks he can run me off, then he can just kiss my ass."

The warning bell sounded, three gonglike blasts that signaled that her students would be strolling through the doors any minute.

"Hey, do you like art?" Jimmy asked.

"Of course," she said, remembering that one of his wish-list goals was to show at MoMA.

"Even postmodern art?"

"Sure. Why?"

"I have a friend who's going to show his collection at the Nesbitt Gallery. Do you know the place?"

She knew the Nesbitt well, having spent at least half a dozen Saturdays perusing the walls of the tiny hall. It was barely the size of her parents' master bathroom, a diminutive treasure trove of visual goodies of which nobody seemed to be aware.

"I've been there a bunch of times," she said, watching the door. Six-year-olds, fresh from an hour of Rachmaninoff, began to stream through her door.

"Have you?" he cried. "Then you know how great it is. Will you come to my friend's showing? It's going to be on March second, and his stuff's really incredible. There'll be lots of food and wine, and I hear it's almost impossible to get your name on the guest list."

"Ooh, Miss Henley's on the phone," Gemma Hollingsworth sang, characteristically about to launch into recitations of school violations.

"March second?" She spoke quickly and hunched lower, as if her students wouldn't be able to see her hovering above her desk. "Jimmy, I've got to go, but the second sounds fine."

"It starts at seven thirty. Bring Whitney, too. You won't regret it."

"March second, seven thirty, with Whitney in tow. I'll see you then."

"You are just an angel, Audrey. Gorgeous. Just *gore-jess!*"

Eight

"Lee! Lee!" Will Strong screamed from the hallway. "Get your ass over here!"

"I've got to go," Whitney said calmly into the receiver. Will had called an emergency meeting, which wasn't really a qualified kind of gathering. All his assemblies were certified exigencies in his book.

"So, you'll go to the gallery with me?" Audrey asked. "I think it'll be fun, and it's not like we go to art showings every day."

"Yeah, that's fine. I guess I could use a little culture. Oh, before I forget, let me give you a name for a family/property-division lawyer. Several people recommended him to me, and I think he'll be good for Jimmy. He's got a reputation for being an asshole, which sounds like just what he needs."

"Okay, go ahead."

"Lee, goddammit! Where the fuck are you?"

"Hey, let me call you later," she whispered. She could hear Will's steps ring against the marble floor. "I don't know what my boss's problem is today, but he's going ape shit right now."

"Thanks so much, Whitney," Audrey said quickly. "I think you'll like Jimmy. He's kind of—well, he's really great."

"I'm sure."

"See ya."

Whitney gathered a notepad and pen and hurried into the conference room next door. The expansive space, marbled from floor to ceiling in a cold shade of eggshell, felt like a mausoleum. James Carothers, the fifth-year unslept associate, was already seated in one of the twelve leather chairs that flanked the black granite table, his face white with fear.

"I need one of y'all to explain this," Will shouted. He was waving a sheet of paper as he paced the room, and his crimson cheeks burned brighter against the ivory walls. "Who the *fuck* let this happen?"

Whitney sat down next to James and watched Will thunder about. He was in a worse mood than usual, and while his actions were always brusque, his movements were now carrying a certain violence. At last, he stopped and let his charcoal suit settle on his broad form before he slammed the document onto the table, and his heavy fist caused the surface to quiver. He glared at James for what seemed like an eternity before shooting a scathing look at Whitney.

"Opposing counsel called," he seethed, letting the words sink in, "and he couldn't have been happier. And do you know *why*? Because *someone* went through our documents like a blind man, or, better yet, like a fucking *retarded* man and decided that it would be just peachy to produce this little gem."

Whitney leaned forward and studied the paper. It had been marked *Confidential, Work-Product Privileged* and *Attorneys' Eyes Only*. Although most lawsuits were built on circumstantial evidence and innuendos pieced together through multiple documents and bits of testimony, this case had a bona fide smoking gun. And she was staring at it. She distinctly remembered flagging the client's mea culpa transcribed into written form, and had made a notation for the paralegals not to produce it. There was no way that she was responsible for this screwup, and she sighed with relief that she wouldn't be the one to suffer the brunt of Will's wrath.

"I'm going to do my damnedest not to kill one of you, or both even," Will said between gritted teeth, "but I can't promise that you'll still have jobs at the end of the day."

Brenda, his secretary, appeared at the door. Her eyes took in the situation before she knocked on the wall.

"What?" he shrieked, whizzing around.

"Mr. Strong, Amy's on line one."

"Tell her I'll call her back."

"She says it's important."

"Does it look like I'm doing something *unimportant*?" His face darkened and his eyes seemed to turn instantly bloodshot. "Jesus Christ, tell her that I'm at *work*, making *money* so that she can spend it all on her fucking handbags."

"Fine. I'll just tell her that you've got more important things to do," she said, her disinterest on par with his fury. "By the way, this is the sixth time she's called." After fifteen years with him, she was accustomed to his mentally unstable hissing bravado. She might have been the only person brave enough to speak to him without fearing a slap in the face.

"Goddammit, this had better not be about the fucking drapes again." He turned to his underlings. "Don't move." He followed his secretary out the door, his pounding steps threatening to crack the expensive stone under him.

James glanced over at Whitney, his face even paler than before. His hazel eyes were glazed over, making him appear as if he had been crying all morning, and she noticed a loose thread on the seam of his gray suit.

"Whitney, I know that we've only been working together for a few months, and we don't know each other really well, but I'm a really nice person." His words tumbled out, and he inched closer to her, his jerky movements making her nervous.

"I know you're a nice person," she said unconvincingly.

He leaned on the edge of his seat, and his long legs bent towards the floor so that he was practically genuflecting before her. His face contorted with panic, and his voice was shrill.

"I'm a good lawyer, and I can't lose my job. I wouldn't normally ask something like this, but I swear, I'll do anything to make it up to you." He stared at her, unblinking, for a few unnerving moments, and she recalled that he likely kept firearms in his desk. "I need you to take the blame on this."

"What?" She felt her eyes go wide. "Are you insane?"

"Please!" He lurched forward and grasped her arm. "I need this job. We've got three kids at home, a mortgage and two car payments. My wife hasn't worked in five years. Whitney, please, I'm begging you."

"Did you produce that document?" she asked, nodding to the center of the table. "Because I know I didn't."

"I don't remember," he said, and finally let go of her suit jacket. "But I'm the only one reviewing the files, other than you. If you didn't produce it, then I'm sure I did. But if I tell Will I'm responsible, he's going to fire me."

"How do you know that?" She crossed her arms and rolled her chair out of his reach. "The firm hasn't fired a lawyer since I've been here."

"Because this would be my third strike." He moved closer to her. She scooted farther away, and to her dismay, James followed. "Strong's got a three-strike rule. Screw up three times, and you're out. This would be my third. I'm not incompetent, believe me, but with the baby up all night, I haven't slept in two—"

"What the fuck are y'all doing?" Will exploded as he swept into the conference room. Trying to avert another beseeching clutch, Whitney had backed her chair halfway across the room. Desperate to convince her, James had traveled with her, and the two were now twenty feet from where they had first sat down.

"Sorry, sir," Whitney said, and pushed herself into place. James stood up and moved his chair to its original spot and sat down. His hands trembled as he took his seat.

"My wife has just informed me that the renovations are taking longer than expected," Will yelled, "which is her way of telling me that she's going to need more money. Now, I can't make money if I have to waste my time trying to get y'all to act like fucking professionals, can I? So let's make this easy. Which one of you produced this document?"

They sat silently, hoping that Will was speaking rhetorically. A miracle was still possible, another interruption from Brenda perhaps, and maybe he would calm down enough to talk about solutions instead of proceeding with his witch hunt of blame.

"Answer me, goddammit! Which one of you little fuckers turned over this document?"

"Sir, I didn't . . . ," Whitney began to say. She glanced over at James. His lips were quivering and his hands were convulsing in his lap. She thought she saw tears in his eyes. A mortgage, she thought. Two car payments. Three kids. Hasn't slept in, what? Two days? Two months? Two years? Two strikes. Versus her none.

"I didn't look through the documents carefully," she finally said slowly, making eye contact with her boss. "I'm sorry. I must have produced the document." Her face stung as though someone had thrown acid on her, and she averted her eyes, fully expecting Will to scream until the windows shattered.

"You—didn't—look—carefully," he repeated, his words escaping in slow motion. "You—must—have—produced—the—document." A demonic trace in his voice sent shudders down her spine, and she suddenly worried that she had made a terrible mistake. "Get up," he commanded, "and pack your shit. You're out of here, Lee."

Whitney and James both gasped, the horror on James's face outexpressing hers. She had expected Will to unleash his psychotic fury on her, perhaps strike at her with his squat fist, but to be fired? She was being *fired*?

"You've got until"—he checked his watch—"noon to get your things in order. Security will escort you out the door." He yanked the paper off the table and stormed out, cursing down the hall as he rushed towards his office.

Whitney stood up and steadied herself against the table, convinced that she was going to faint.

"Oh my God, I don't know what to say," James said. "I'm sorry." He was still frozen in his chair, looking as if he had forgotten how to move. She stood still, unable to restrain the madness that was rising through her body like a plague.

"I've never been fired from anything in my life," she said. "*Ever!* I was the valedictorian at Loyola, and Will's kids can barely keep a C average over there. I graduated summa cum laude from Duke *and* Harvard. I do a damned good job here. I'm not someone you just fire!" Her body was shaking, and she blinked hard, trying to stave off temporary insanity.

"I'm really sorry." He stood up and shoved his hands into his pockets.

"You've got to tell Will that you produced that document," she said, glaring at him. "Actually, I don't care if you say that—just tell him that *I* didn't produce it. You can't let me take the fall for this."

"I'm sorry," he repeated, his words barely audible. "I—I can't do that."

Whitney gaped at him, too shocked to react.

"I'm really sorry for this," he mumbled. "I'm really, really, really sorry." He raised a hand, as if to pat her on the back, but then lowered it before he could touch her. Quietly, he left the room, his loafers barely making a sound.

"What do you mean, he fired you?" Robert asked.

"He fired me," Whitney slurred. She looked up from her bottle of Jack Daniel's to see her brother gaping at her as if she had just announced that she could fly. "*Fired*. Terminated. Given her walking papers. What part of the word don't you understand?"

"But I don't get it. What's the big deal, anyway? So you produced a bad document. Wasn't your client at fault to begin with?" He glanced at the balcony, where two packs' worth of Marlboro Lights butts crammed an ashtray, and then sat on the coffee table across from the couch where she had curled up into a ball.

"That's so not the point," she muttered. "Clients don't pay seven hundred dollars an hour to admit that they're wrong. Besides, the document was work-product privileged. We had no business producing it."

"Can't you ask the other side to give it back?"

"You don't think Will's already tried? This is really bad, Robert. The client could sue the firm for malpractice." She exhaled deeply, and her sigh turned into a rumbling groan. "I'm sure Will thinks I'm beyond stupid to have let this happen. God, I don't even want to think about it." She sighed again, unable to figure out another way to breathe.

"It's probably nowhere near as bad as you think," he said gently, his concerned expression confirming that her situation was, in fact, as bad as she imagined.

"This is unbelievable. I have *never* been so humiliated in all my life." She didn't want to dwell on her graceless exit from the firm, but her mind refused to consider anything else. As all of Houston had watched with varying expressions of pity and suspicion, she had walked out of downtown's tallest building with her effects in a single cardboard box, complete with two security officers at her side. As if the trip to the gilded doors wasn't enough, she had spotted Will's secretary spying in the corner of the lobby, apparently present to confirm that the problem employee was properly banished. Just then, the contents of her flimsy container broke through the bottom and onto the marble floors, rendering her shattered picture frames and hornbooks exposed for all to see. It was all she could do not to burst into tears.

"How long have you been sitting on the couch?" Robert leaned over and inspected items from her tattered "Good-bye, Boerne & Connelly" box.

"I don't know. Since around one, I guess." The monotony of her voice must have concerned him, because he sat on the couch next to her and tried to hug her, but the stench of whiskey and cigarettes stopped him. With a big-brother frown, he eased the whiskey bottle from her clutches and stood up.

"Do you want to go over to Mom and Dad's?" He walked to their little kitchen and returned the bottle to the cabinet.

"No."

"Do you want to order Chinese?" She noticed that he was staring at a dark stain on her Loyola sweatshirt. He probably couldn't believe that after ten years, she was still wearing it.

"No."

"What do you want to do?"

"Nothing. Sit here and wallow in self-pity for another hour. Give me that much."

"Is there any way you can explain the situation to your boss?"

"He's not what you'd call a listener. Besides, I don't know if I even want to work with him anymore. I don't know what I should do. Maybe I'll look for another job, although I can't imagine who's going to hire a third-year associate who was fired from her last firm." She buried her head in her arms. "I don't know. Maybe I'll take a break for a while. For a couple of months, at least. Lord knows I could use it."

"Maybe you should call your boss," he said. "He might understand. He's probably not as mad as you think he is."

Whitney lifted her head. She was grateful that her brother, who tended to be as analytical as the data he studied, was trying to encourage her, and as feckless as his words were, she still appreciated his uncharacteristic optimism.

"It's not like I even *wanted* to work there, you know? But to be fired? I took the hit for James because I felt bad for him, and look where it got me. I can't *believe* the way I was treated, and after giving five thousand hours of my time each year that I was there. God, talk about not having any loyalty to its employees. You would've thought that I was stealing from the partnership or something."

"Did you ever think that everything happens for a reason?" He returned to the coffee table and sat down so that his face was level with hers. "Maybe this is God's way of telling you something."

"What on earth could he possibly be telling me? To be more self-preserving?" Even as she spoke, she had to admit that she had been thinking the same thing. She had been spending seventeen hours per day at the office and another five on her music. Her taxing schedule had been the result of her job's mandates and her personal obsession, and it had become clear that both ends of the spectrum were suffering as a result of her split attention. She hadn't felt like she could give up either, and she wondered if her termination was perhaps God's way of making the decision easy.

"I'm just trying to look on the bright side," he said. "Maybe this happened for a reason that we don't understand yet."

"Maybe." She let her head fall back against the cushion.

"So I guess my chances with that IT chick are over." He spoke lightly, and his teasing, however ill timed, made Whitney feel a smidgen better.

"Really, Robert, it's no loss on your part." She straightened. "What ever happened to Gina? Did y'all hook up?"

"It—uh, it didn't go so well."

"Oh, so you already went out?"

"Not really," he said, his cheeks an inky red. "She came to visit her parents, and Mom had them all over. I don't know where she got the idea that Gina was single or interested in me, because she showed up engaged to some guy in Philadelphia. Towards the end of dinner, she finally blew up and said that I wasn't her type."

"How did that conversation even come about?"

He rolled his eyes. "Mom kept asking what she thought of me, even after we had all heard how her boyfriend popped the question, and after two hours of Mom being Mom, Gina finally said that she wasn't at all attracted to me."

"Really?"

"*Ugly enough to work for the space program* is what she really said."

Whitney laughed hard. Robert looked hurt, which, in her disheveled state, only made her laugh harder.

"I'm sorry. You're not ugly. I hope you know that." She rubbed her eyes and blinked rapidly. "At least you found out that she's a bitch before you got yourself involved."

"Yeah." Whitney's stomach growled, and the grinding noises caused Robert to flinch. "What the—you haven't eaten today, have you?"

"No. And you can't blame me for not having much of an appetite." She finally sat up straight for the first time all afternoon and brought her knees close to her chest.

"It's almost eight o'clock." He scowled, pulling his best worried-brother look. "Whitney, you've got to eat something. You're going to make yourself sick. This is why Mom and Dad worry about you all the time." He stood up. "I'll order something."

"You don't have to do that."

"You have to eat. You're too thin as it is."

"Stop. Sometimes I wish we weren't roommates, you know that?"

"Whitney," he said in a warning voice.

"Scott's coming over in an hour," she said. "We're going to dinner."

He sat back down on the coffee table. "Did you tell him that you were fired?"

She cringed. "No, and I don't plan to, either. At least not until I process it first. Besides, I don't think that's why we're going to dinner tonight."

"Is it a special occasion?"

Not if you consider a breakup a special occasion, she thought. She felt her face screw up again as she shook her head, and then closed her eyes. Given the day she had already had, she considered postponing their date, unsure how much more stress she could handle. On the other hand, she knew that tonight had been a long time coming, and when Scott had called to invite her to a dinner they hadn't shared in ages, she understood that this meeting would be their last, even if neither had said so. She sighed heavily. If they were going to end their relationship, it might as well be today. She opened her eyes and eased herself off the sofa, light-headed from hunger and exhaustion.

"I'm going to take a shower."

"Good, because you stink." He grinned, and she tried to return the expression, enormously thankful for his attempts to cheer her up.

She went to her bedroom and shut the door before traipsing into her bathroom. Everything—her hair, her clothes, even her skin—reeked of smoke, and as filthy as she was, both inside and out, she wished that she could purge her disgust. She stepped into the shower and let the scalding water pound the toxins out of her body, and for a few long moments, she was still, content to allow the steady stream to breathe new life into her traumatized soul. When she could no longer stand the blistering liquid against her back, she stepped to the side and lathered her hair furiously, as if she could wash out the misery of the day.

I need to talk to you, Scott had said on the phone. It was strange that as disconnected as they had become, as incomprehensible and alien as they now seemed to each other, she should have immediately understood what he had meant. She had agreed to his request that they take a two-week break to "think about things," and they hadn't spoken since he had returned from his Christian retreat at Camp Cradle, not that she would've even known how to converse with him anymore. She pondered the fact that their relationship had been slowly dying over the last three months, moving from dissonance to disengagement to neglect and then practically abandonment, and she wondered why neither had simply ended what clearly wasn't meant to be. Perhaps it was because colossal blowups hadn't marred their union, hadn't forced them to choose between continued misery and separation. Instead, their universes had spiraled farther apart, had succumbed to inertia, so much so that she realized that an actual breakup might not be much more than a formality. The idea depressed her, highlighted just how little she and Scott had left of each other.

With a heavy sigh, she wrapped a towel around her chest and then stepped out onto the tile floor. Her jeans and silk top waited for her on the counter, and she dressed herself as if on autopilot, her thoughts practically audible in her head. Just as she finished blow-drying her hair, three knocks rasped against the door. She hurried into a pair of high-heeled wedges and made her way to the living room, surprisingly sober despite an afternoon of wanton boozing. Scott and Robert stopped talking when they saw her.

"Hey," she said, giving Scott a small wave.

"Hey. You look really nice." He seemed nervous, and his visible anxiety stoked her rising discomfort.

"Thanks," she said, taking in his tan box-checked oxford shirt and black slacks. "So do you."

"Are you ready?"

"Yeah."

"I'll see y'all later," Robert said, and then opened the front door for them. He patted Whitney's back as she walked out, and the gesture felt strangely like a benediction.

"Were you planning on talking at all tonight?" Whitney asked Scott, finally breaking the silence that had settled between them since they had left her apartment. They had been mute all the way to Limón, an upscale Mexican restaurant they had frequented at the beginning of their relationship, and other than the few words they had directed to the waiter, they had hovered over their dinners completely quiet. Scott stopped picking at his pork enchiladas and looked up.

"I'm sorry," he said uneasily. "I was just thinking. I've been thinking a lot these days."

"So have I." Nerves deadened her hunger, and as sick as she felt, she wasn't sure that she could manage another halfhearted bite of her spicy red snapper.

"I keep asking myself, how did we get here?" He spoke quietly, looking as if he hadn't yet discovered the answer to his question. "We used to talk all night, remember?" She nodded, and a pang of sadness stung her as she recalled their better times. "We used to understand each other so completely. But now—everything feels so off. Like we both changed in too many ways to bridge the gap."

"You think that I changed that much?" His statement surprised her. She knew that she wasn't the same person that she might have been three years ago, but she felt that her differences had been minor, akin perhaps to the effects of aging. And in comparison with his total transformation, she may as well have been preserved in amber.

"Yeah," he said. "You did."

"How?"

"You were a lot more supportive when we first started going out. Even when you weren't interested in whatever it was that I did, you were still supportive." He wiped his hands on his napkin and placed it on the table. "Like, I knew that you didn't care about softball at all, but you went to every single one of my league games. I mean, you even played shortstop for a while. And you hated running, but you still went to the track with me three times a week just so that we could spend more time together." His lips curled into a sad smile, and he leaned forward, the edge of the table jutting against his stomach. "But now I don't know. Church, Bible studies, my retreats—sometimes I think that if I had gotten involved in those things a few years ago, you would've been a lot more enthusiastic about it."

"Scott, you can't even compare softball and running to your interest in everything church related." Her heartbeat quickened, and she realized that she was talking too fast. "You didn't obsess about softball or running. Not the way you do with church. And you had never criticized me, or made me feel bad if I didn't have time to run with you, or if I just didn't want to. You never demanded that I take up your interests. You were just encouraging. About everything. *Especially* with my music. Hell, you were my biggest fan. And that made me want to be your biggest fan, too." Her chest ached with longing, and judging from his pained expression, she imagined that he felt it, as well.

"I know that I——" He broke off, looking even more troubled.

"And I don't know that I would've been a lot more supportive of your interest in church a few years ago. I would've done exactly what I did these last few months. I would've attended church more regularly. I would've gone to as many Bible study classes as I could. I probably would've even listened to Dr. Tony Evans in the car on the nights when I came home really late from work. The difference is that three years ago, that would've been enough for you." She poked at the remains of her fish with her oversized fork before pushing her plate away. "But with your church activities—it's like you want me to be something that I'm not. It's not fair. I never put those kinds of pressure on you. I never even asked you to enjoy music."

He propped his elbows on the table and sank his face into his hands. After rubbing his temples, he looked at her, his worn expression revealing his obvious distress.

"I know that I wasn't being fair," he said. "I wasn't blaming you when I said that you'd changed. I changed, too. Some of it was good, I think. A lot of it wasn't." He sighed heavily. "I never meant to criticize you, or to make you feel bad. You have to know that."

"I know," she said, unconvinced.

"I only wanted for you to be as excited about God as I was." He rubbed his forehead, clearly upset. "I don't even know what happened. Somewhere along the way, I became infatuated with being this Super Christian, this person who walked the walk and talked the talk, and somehow, I ended up driving everyone away. Honestly, it didn't even occur to me until I went on this retreat that I hadn't opened up to you and shared my faith experience. The most important thing in the world to me, and I never included you." He frowned, looking unsure of himself. "There's no excuse for it, but everything was such a mess in my head that I'm not sure how I would've been able to explain it so that it made any kind of sense. Sometimes, it still doesn't."

She leaned into the narrow table so that their heads almost touched.

"Try anyway," she said.

"What?"

"Try to explain it to me. I want to hear about your faith experience. It's important to you, and I want to understand it."

He regarded her for a long moment before his features relaxed, and his earlier tense expression melted into the smallest of smiles. As slight as the alteration was, coupled with an openness they hadn't had in months, it was enough to remind Whitney of their earlier, happier rapport.

"You know the Road to Damascus story," he said, "where Saul is blinded by Jesus's voice and is so affected by it that he renounces his old life and then changes his name to Paul?"

"Yes."

"Have you ever experienced anything like that? An event that rocked your world and transformed you in every way?"

"Not like that, no."

"Even with your music?"

She shook her head. "No."

He frowned slightly, perhaps discouraged by her response, and when he continued to stare at her, she realized that he was expecting some kind of explanation for the impetus of her consuming passion.

"Did I ever tell you how I started fantasizing about becoming a musician?"

"You didn't, actually."

"At the end of my freshman year in college, I woke up late to register for the next semester. By the time I got down to the registrar's office, the only elective still available was an Introduction to Guitar course. I didn't want to take it, because what was I going to do with an Intro to Guitar class? But I did, and I liked it, but I didn't love it. I still practiced the guitar after the semester was over, though, probably because I had a lot of free time."

"How did you have free time?" he asked. "I thought you were an engineering major."

She shrugged. "Engineering was easy. Boring, but easy. Anyway, the same thing happened my junior year. I woke up late, *again*, and the only class left was a music-composition class. I took it and loved it. By that time, I was good enough at the guitar to put the class to use. I'd always hummed random melodies that popped into my head, but after I took that class, I found myself doodling lyrics when I should've been paying attention to vectors and velocities. My first year in law school, I saw Alison Krauss and Susan Tedeschi perform, and Jonny Lang, J. D. Crowe, Rhonda Vincent, Hem—"

"Did you study at all at Harvard?"

She smiled. "Only when I absolutely needed to. I wasn't really interested in the law, other than to debate theoretically, and honestly, I was barely even interested in that. I wanted to sing. I wanted to work on my music. I wanted to be onstage like everyone I saw."

"So you had three epiphanies."

She shook her head. "They weren't epiphanies. They were a bunch of mundane things that I didn't think anything of at the time. But, in hindsight, I'm convinced that they happened exactly the way they were meant to happen." She fiddled with the corner of her napkin. "You might think that I don't have faith, or that I don't take it seriously, but I do believe that God has a plan for me, even if he doesn't strike me with lightning to reveal what it is."

"I don't—" The anguished expression returned. "I shouldn't have said that you don't take your faith seriously. I know that you do." He focused on his water glass and traced the rim of it, deep in thought. "Maybe you didn't have the Road to Damascus experience because you paid attention to what was going on around you. You remembered what you were supposed to remember, and God didn't need to strike you with lightning to catch your attention." He looked up. "But he did with me, and it happened at the retreat. It was actually why I had asked that we take a break. I needed to process it and figure out what I was supposed to do."

"Did you?" She reached for her glass and took a sip of water, calmer than she had felt all evening.

"Yes." If he had been distressed before, he was now almost serene. "I've been called to the ministry, Whitney. Without a doubt, one hundred percent, I've been called."

"What?" She frowned. "What does that mean?"

"I've been praying about this for a long time now, and at the retreat, God made it crystal clear. I don't know how to explain it, but I believe in my heart of hearts that I was put on this earth to minister to others." He leaned forward, and the sleeve of his shirt fell onto his plate. "I've been called to be a pastor, Whitney. And maybe a missionary after that."

"Are you serious?" Perhaps she shouldn't have been surprised, given his all-consuming passion for Christ, but she was nonetheless.

"Yes." He smiled. "I resigned from NASA today, and I've already enrolled at Dallas Theological Seminary for fall classes. I leave in a couple of weeks."

"But it's only March."

"I'm going to audit a few summer courses, and I have to find an apartment, get settled in—you know, all the mundane things that come with a move." His lips were still curled into a smile, but the rest of his expression was practically shouting what they both had to know.

"You're not going to ask me to try to make a long-distance relationship work, are you?" she asked, her voice so low that she wondered if he could hear her.

"It's not an issue of distance. Would you be willing to support me if I became a pastor? Or a missionary? Would you be willing to give up your whole life—your job, whatever musical career you could have— so that you could play the guitar to a bunch of children in Uganda? Or risk your life to save those who've never heard of Jesus in Tibet?"

She remained mute, unwilling to vocalize her answer.

"I wouldn't ask that of you," he said, reaching out to touch her hand. "And I don't expect you to follow me, either. I already know that you can't go where I need to go. I don't mean that you're not capable, but you just can't. As much as I love you—and I do—you're not the one I'm supposed to be with."

Her stomach dropped, and she tore her gaze away from him, feeling as if he had just impaled her. She had known all along that they couldn't move forward together, that a breakup was inevitable—hell, she had even imagined that the actual split might have the painless quality of a formality—but his words still ripped her heart in two. A lump lodged in her throat, tightening her airway so that she couldn't speak.

"I'm really sorry," he said. "I really am. But I need to do this. I hope you can understand."

She nodded, unable to give him any semblance of articulation.

"I told you a few months ago that I wished that you'd give up your music." He spoke softly, looking rueful. "I shouldn't have said that. I didn't mean it. I have no doubt that you're going to be successful as a singer. You've got the talent for it."

"You don't have to say that." Her words trembled, and her hands were shaking.

"Yes, I do. You need to hear it, because it's true. I can't walk away and have you think that I don't like your music, and I wouldn't be able to live with myself if I gave you the impression that what you want to do was somehow not good enough."

She kept her focus trained on the floor. It was obvious that Scott was exorcising his sins, and that he was trying to right his past wrongs so that he could end their relationship with a clean conscience. Clearly, he needed closure, and after a few minutes of painful silence, she nodded, giving him the peace he sought. He gave her a toothless smile, thanking her for her forgiveness.

"So, this is our good-bye, then," she said, her words barely audible.

He sighed softly. "I guess it is."

They sat quietly for another interminable moment, and for as many emotions as were overwhelming her, she couldn't discern what she was feeling. She watched, numb, as he eased out of his seat, walked around the table and slid into her side of the booth, and she didn't move when he nudged closer to her, his arm almost touching hers. Cold blasts from the air conditioner carried the scent of his cologne, and she could almost taste the fruity trace of his shampoo. She sighed heavily, and he wrapped his arms around her, practically smothering her with his muscular limbs. Until the restaurant closed and the busboys began to vacuum the floors, they remained where they were, as reticent as when they had first arrived. For the next hour and a half, disappointment, hope, sadness, depression and joy flooded her, both in succession and in combination, and after those had taxed her psyche and frayed her nerves, a final sensation edged into the mix, its effect assuring her that they would be just fine. With a final sigh, she leaned her head against his shoulder, wondering if he also felt the peace—and the twinge of relief—that had finally settled upon her.

Nine

"Mom, I cannot believe that you made Victor meet you at *Neiman's*," Audrey said. She was sitting in a chair in one of the store's oversized dressing rooms, wiggling a foot and trying to tune out Carlos and Gianfranco. They were seated next to her, chatting loudly in Italian as they rifled through the Polaroids they had taken of her mother's various outfits, and an emaciated sales associate hovered near the closed door, looking bored with all of them.

"Darling, I'm going to be in Gstaad with Eleanor and Bea for the next six weeks, and after that, I've got at least three events to prepare for. If we didn't spend time tonight, we wouldn't have another chance for who knows how long. This was the best that I could do." She gazed at herself in the 360-degree mirror, inspecting her teal blue evening gown for flaws.

"I hardly think that he was hoping to spend the afternoon with you while you tried to figure out what you were wearing to some charity event." Audrey sighed, almost glad that he had to excuse himself so that he could begin his long drive to school and preside over a parent-teacher night.

"Well, I thought we had a lovely time nonetheless."

"So, do you like him any better?" She leaned forward, propped an elbow onto her knee and rested her chin on her hand. She felt strangely nervous, as if she were hoping that Victor's three hours with her mother would be enough to ease her apprehension. The notion was preposterous, and she wondered why she was treating their meeting as the ultimate test rather than the first of many encounters. Her mother looked up.

"Audrey, I never said that I *don't* like him. That's not the issue. I'm concerned that you two are rushing your relationship. And after talking to Victor, I'm concerned about a few other things, too."

"Like what?" she asked, feeling her heart pound out of her body.

"I *theenk* the Carolina Herrera looks best," Gianfranco said suddenly, looking up from his stack of pictures. "It looks the divine on you, *Mee-sus Heen-ley*."

"The Vera Wang is beautiful, too," Carlos said.

"If you like, we can arrange for you to be fitted at Alberta Ferretti's studio."

"Or perhaps we can have Roberto Cavalli make something for you."

"I don't think that will be necessary. I'm meeting Stefania de la Guardia tomorrow morning before my flight. Everyone's raving about her designs, and she's promised to show me something spectacular." She seemed preoccupied, perhaps pondering her bullet-point list of issues with Victor, and Audrey watched as the skinny salesgirl helped her mother with the unending eye-and-hook closures, then glanced at her watch.

"I've got to leave soon." She tugged at her jeans and readjusted the laces on her knee-high boots. "I promised a friend that I'd go to an art showing at the Nesbitt Gallery, and I still have to pick up Whitney."

"Are you talking about Johanssen Frasier?" She slipped out of the teal creation and into the pink bouclé skirt suit she had arrived in, managing to extract her BlackBerry while changing.

"Who's that?"

"He's one of the up-and-comers in a series we're doing at Junior League in conjunction with the Children's Education Fund. He's a distant relation to Wilhelm and Candace Frasier." She scrolled through her PDA and then placed it in her bag. "That reminds me. Morgan Appleton asked me if you were interested in joining the League. I know you're busy, but I told her that I'd check anyway."

"It's not just that I'm busy." She considered her words, searching for a way to state her disinterest without sounding as if she was dismissing her mother's greatest passions. "I just don't think I'm League material." Her mother looked up, evidently surprised by the statement.

"Of *course* you're League material. Everything about you—your poise and maturity, your ambitions, your kindheartedness—that's exactly what the Junior League's about. We'd be thrilled if you joined."

Audrey sighed. Since she had returned to Houston, her mother had encouraged—begged, in fact—her to join the Junior League, or the Houston Philharmonic Orchestra Trust, or the M. D. Anderson Benefit, or the Muscular Dystrophy Association Crystal Charity Ball, or the dozen other charities to which she lent her name and checkbook. As much as Audrey had grown accustomed to her mother's incessant talk of philanthropy, she was beginning to tire of her unending invitations to join the catty popularity contest of the city's wealthy. She had attended enough benefits to know that the ostensibly charitable organizations brought out the worst kind of human behavior, and she was mystified that for all her mother's years in that environment, the woman hadn't been affected by its repulsive narcissism and self-importance.

"Well, think about it," she said when Audrey didn't respond, "and let me know if you change your mind."

"Okay." She watched as her mother slipped into her high-heeled slingbacks, and wondered if she planned on expounding on her earlier comment about Victor's shortcomings. When she reached for her slim alligator bag without saying a word, Audrey spoke. "You said that you had other concerns about Victor."

She tucked her purse under her arm. "I do."

"Like what?"

Her mother twitched her lips, looking ill at ease. "Audrey, I know that you don't want to hear this, but I really do think that if you marry Victor, you'll regret it. Your relationship—it'll never work. I don't see how it could."

"Why not?"

"Because"—she seemed strained, and her eyes were suddenly weary—"he said that he's happy being a teacher. He doesn't feel the need to pursue a career beyond that."

"So?" Her heart was beating with the intensity of a jackhammer, and she felt fiercely defensive on his behalf.

"You, on the other hand, have ambitions that would terrify most men. I don't doubt that Victor's secretly intimidated by you."

"Mom, he's not like most men. He doesn't have to compare himself to me or to anyone else." Her mother let out a muffled guffaw, as if her disbelief had forced the reflexive reaction. "Why is it so hard to believe that there are people who are content with what they have? Not everyone's trying to claw their way to the top."

"If that's true, then it only makes the matter worse. He's not motivated beyond what he has. Doesn't that worry you?"

"Why would it?" she asked, feeling her face crush under her frown.

Her mother sighed deeply, her troubled expression bordering on what Audrey thought was frustrated despair.

"Has it never occurred to you that Victor might be marrying you because of the family you come from? Or because he knows that you're set to inherit nine figures?"

"Oh my God." She rolled her eyes, insulted by the suggestion. "He's not like that."

"You don't know for sure."

"He didn't know that I had a dime to my name until the second month of our relationship. We were friends for almost five years before that, and we never talked about money."

"He saw that you drive a Mercedes, darling. He saw that your apartment's in one of the most expensive neighborhoods in Houston. He's not stupid. He *had* to know that you had—"

"A lot of women drive nice cars and live in West U. That doesn't mean that their family owns a petroleum company." Her mother looked as if she was about to speak, but Audrey continued. "Victor's a good person. He's kind and sincere. He cares about me. You said so yourself. I can't even imagine Victor as a gold digger, and frankly, I don't think you really believe it, either."

"Audrey, all boyfriends are kind and sincere at the beginning. Of course they're caring and reasonable and faithful and everything else you hope for. Even your father was that way when we were first married." She scowled and stopped herself short, clearly unwilling to veer their discussion towards the one relationship that she refused to discuss. "You've put yourself in a lose-lose situation. Either he's a gold digger—"

"Please stop—"

"Or eventually, he's going to feel emasculated by you. No man wants his wife to be more ambitious than he is, and he certainly doesn't want to be making far less than she does. Even if Victor says that he's okay with it, he doesn't mean it. He *can't* mean it."

"You're wrong." She felt less sure of herself, as if her mother's insistence had chipped away at her thick wall of certainty. "You just are."

"Darling, I've seen this so many times before." She spoke quietly, no longer looking as if she was trying to persuade, but as if she was simply recounting what was fact. "With my friends, with family, with people at the country club. I'm not trying to be a dark cloud over your happiness. I'm trying to protect you from the inevitable. Maybe you don't believe it now because you're young and idealistic. I don't have those luxuries anymore. I don't have those delusions."

"Maybe that's your reality, Mom. But it doesn't have to be mine."

"Reality doesn't pick and choose. It just *is*."

"So, you're not even going to try to support me?" she asked, psychological exhaustion causing her to feel as if her voice had left her body.

Her mother sighed for the fifth time in as many minutes. "Darling, do you think I'd be so concerned if I *didn't* support you?"

"I can't talk about this anymore. I have to go." She gave a halfhearted wave to her mother, and then to Carlos and Gianfranco, whose presence she had forgotten until she moved to leave the room. She bolted from the dressing area and scurried down sections of Chanel and Yves Saint Laurent before bursting out of Neiman's. After a sprint across the parking lot, she found her car and piled into it, starting the engine before she had even closed the door.

As she zipped down I-10 towards Whitney's apartment building, she thought about her mother. Maybe she had witnessed dozens of her friends mired in protracted divorce proceedings, had seen bitterness fuel greed and an insatiable desire to ruin their soon-to-be exes. Maybe she had observed firsthand the repulsive quality of gold diggers, had gossiped with her vacation mates about the nefarious goings-on of their circle of acquaintances. And maybe she was right that ambitious women terrified most men. But those reasons hadn't brought on the death of her own marriage, hadn't ravaged a union that should have ended in divorce years ago but never did. There were relationships that couldn't be salvaged by money, or spared by the lack of it, and there were those, like her and Victor's, that wouldn't be ruined by either. She couldn't explain her conviction that Victor was the one for her any more than her mother could persuade her that he wasn't, and the more she tried to rationalize what felt so sure to her, the more circular her argument became. She loved him because she loved him, and he was right for her because he was.

She pulled up to the curb where Whitney was standing and tried to straighten her face. She didn't want to drag Whitney down with her problems, and doubted that she'd even understand. There were certain things her friends might never fully grasp, namely adoption into an old Texas family that lived behind carefully crafted walls of pretense, instead of childhood from birth in a normal one. She imagined that they must have envied her financial position, and she figured that her ostensibly lucky situation wouldn't encourage sympathetic, or empathetic, ears.

Whitney opened the passenger door and fell into her seat, looking like death. Dark circles rimmed her eyes, and her normally flushed cheeks were colorless. In fact, her entire face was the shade of triple-bleached flour, and in head-to-toe black, she seemed to be wearing her emotions literally.

"Are you okay?" Audrey asked.

Whitney leaned against the headrest and closed her eyes.

"Do you ever feel like you're in a bad dream and can't figure out a way to wake up?"

"What happened?" Audrey asked, startled. She tried to look at her without rear-ending a vehicle.

Whitney opened her eyes and blinked a few times before gazing about in a daze. "Well, let's see. Yesterday, I tried to be nice to someone at work and ended up getting fired for it. And then I spent the rest of the day watching bad movies on Lifetime."

"Oh, my God. I'm so sorry. . . ."

"Then, Scott and I went out to dinner—" She scowled and stared out the window for a long moment. "Anyway, we broke up."

"What?" she gasped. "Why? I didn't even know that y'all were having problems."

"We've been having problems for a long time." She was quiet again, pensive. "I guess when it boils down to it, we wanted different things. He wanted to be a pastor. Or a missionary. Or both. I don't know." She sighed, her exhale turning into a full groan. "You know what's crazy? I was completely fine last night. I know that we weren't meant to be. If he hadn't done the actual dumping, I would have eventually. But I still spent the entire day in bed feeling ridiculously depressed. I don't even know why."

"You dated him for a long time, Whitney," she said, still shocked by the news. "It's not like you can cut off your feelings for him entirely. At least not the next day."

"Maybe."

"Wow, this is just—I'm so sorry." She didn't know what to say, and she watched as Whitney leaned back again and placed an arm over her eyes. "Do you still want to go to the showing tonight? I mean, I really want you there, but I don't want to push you into something that you don't feel like doing."

"No, we're already on our way." She lowered her arm and tried to smile, managing a dismal grimace instead. "Besides, you told Jimmy that we'd go, and it would be rude not to show up. I'll try to put on a happy face when we get there."

"Thanks, Whitney. I think it'll be fun. If nothing else, maybe being around people will get your mind off of Scott. But if you want to leave early, just grab me and we'll go." She turned into the parking lot, which was already full, and as she navigated the gravel-paved site for an empty spot, Whitney spoke.

"Are *you* okay? You looked kind of funny when you picked me up."

"Yeah. Just—my mother's been—well, everything's a bit of a mess right now."

"Good God, I don't even want to think of my mom's reaction when she finds out that Scott and I are through. Maybe I won't even have to. Robert will tell my parents. I don't know what else he and my dad have to talk about all day at work."

"I'm sure she'll be fine. It's you that I'm worried about." She glanced at Whitney, who seemed to be wincing, scowling and trying to smile all at once.

"Hey, don't tell Hercules that I got fired or that Scott and I broke up. I'll tell her soon, but I just—I can't even think about it right now."

"I won't say a word." She eased the car into a tight spot, and they sucked in their breath and wriggled out. A few steps later, they were inside the gallery, a small house that had been gutted so that the entire space resembled an ultramodern living room. Scandinavian-style couches formed a rectangle around a barricade of work near the center of the room so that patrons could discuss the pieces while sipping cocktails comfortably.

At least a dozen people walked around them, as mismatched as the art showcased. A woman in a black cocktail dress and matching stilettos walked arm in arm with a shorter man dressed in a suit. A young girl in ripped jeans and Converse sneakers sat on a bench and fingered her dreadlocks. There were a few who wore their tattoos as clothing, and they stood side by side with aristocratically aired people as naturally as though they had arrived together. The dimmed light of the gallery cast shadows on their profiles, and trancelike industrial music played on the overhead speakers. The Nesbitt resembled an Ecstasy-filled rave more than Sotheby's, and from a distance, Audrey imagined themselves the subjects of a moving David LaChapelle photograph.

"I don't understand modern art," Whitney said, frowning at the pieces on the wall. "I mean, I get abstracts like Kandinsky and Jasper Johns. I actually like those, but—"

"I don't mean to sound like an elitist know-it-all," Audrey interrupted, "but Johns wasn't so much abstract as he was part of the neo-Dadaist movement."

"Well, that shows how much I know about anything." She motioned at a wall of neon-painted pay phones and approached them skeptically. "Okay, Miss Elitist Know-it-all. What the hell is this?"

"I have no clue," Audrey said, scanning the room for Jimmy.

"And there's another one over there. Is that supposed to go with these? Is the artist trying to say something about society's disengagement? To show how disconnected we are from each other? This one phone apart from all the others—is that a statement of America's isolationist stance? God, that sounds like a bunch of bullshit even to me."

They strolled slowly through the small space, frowning quizzically at most things in the room. When they reached the center of the gallery, Whitney tugged at Audrey's arm.

"This one's nice. *This* I get. Is this what Jimmy's friend did?"

"I'm not sure."

"It must be. It's in the center of the room."

Audrey studied the series of lithographs hung on the wall, six blocks of reds and oranges stacked on top of one another. From afar, the colors seemed distinct and sharp, like a simple array of bright hues, with one block leading naturally to the next. Close-up, however, she couldn't discern where one shade started and the other ended, and though the piece had seemed so elementary from a distance, a closer inspection revealed chaotic touches, as though the artist had been furious while creating it. She, too, didn't know much about twenty-first-century art, but she knew what she liked, and she loved what she was seeing.

"So—what do you think?" a voice asked behind her.

She turned around and saw Jimmy. He was dressed much like he had been at Starbucks, in slim-fitting khakis and a cream-colored sweater. His hair was spiked up into the same youthful pyramid, and his bright smile was infectious.

"I love it."

"Do you really?" he asked self-consciously.

"I like it, too," Whitney said. "It kind of feels like a techno Rothko."

"Techno Rothko," he said, looking pleased. He grasped her hands. "You must be Whitney. I can't tell you how much I appreciate your helping me out with"—he scrunched his nose as if he smelled something distasteful—"Kevin and the house."

"It's not a problem at all. I hope it was helpful."

"It was. This lawyer friend of yours is a bit pricey, but I like his style. Something of a pit bull, this guy. Even looks like one." He studied her, his eyes roving up and down her body like a sentient price scanner.

"I guess pretty girls *do* travel in packs, because you are just *gore-jess*." He reached out and touched her hair before turning to Audrey. "Y'all could be sisters! One a little *Town & Country*, the other a little Goth."

"I've had a rough couple of days," Whitney said. "I haven't done Goth since Audrey's Halloween party in high school."

"Man troubles?" he asked.

Audrey felt herself tense. She appreciated his unfiltered candor, and she reveled in his unsolicited, too-honest opinions, but she wasn't sure how Whitney, still emotionally raw and unaccustomed to him, might take his bluntness.

"Something like that," Whitney muttered.

"Take it from me, honey, men are creatures of the devil. Look at what's happening to me. Hopefully, your situation doesn't call for an attorney." He chuckled, and his laugh turned from mirthful to slightly sour. Whitney smiled politely.

"So, where's your friend?" Audrey asked. "I take it this is his collection?"

"Oh—well." He placed his hands on his hips and giggled nervously. "Yeah, this is it. Uh—I feel a little foolish about this now, but there's, uh, hmm." His cheeks were a drunkard's red, and he fidgeted wildly, swaying back and forth, like a discombobulated pendulum. Finally, he threw up his hands and sighed. "Okay, there's no friend. It's just me. I know that sounds unbelievably stupid, but I wanted to hear your honest opinion, and if you hated it, I didn't want you to act like you didn't just because you wanted to spare my feelings."

"I would have been honest regardless," Audrey said. "Really, Jimmy, this is wonderful."

"Really?" He looked at her, still skeptical.

"Really."

"Really," Whitney echoed when he looked at her expectantly. He eyed them both, as if to make sure they weren't lying, before relaxing completely.

"I'm so glad." He wiped his brow theatrically and then looked around. "I hope other people like it, too. I'm hoping to attract a wealthy buyer."

"I'm going to step outside for a minute," Whitney said. "If I see any wealthy buyers, I'll send them your way." Audrey watched as she headed out the door. She worried about her, and she was about to follow her when Jimmy touched her arm.

"Is she okay?" he asked.

"Yeah, she's been going through a rough time. You know. Work. Boyfriend." She saw the faintest of glows through the windows. "I figured. She's just having a smoke."

"Poor thing." He shook his head and sighed deeply, as concerned for her as if he had known her from the cradle. "Nothing like stress to get me back on the sin sticks."

"You smoke?"

"*Used* to. Now I only do it socially, like on the weekends, or at these kinds of functions or whatever. So, yeah, basically every day." He chuckled. "Whatever gets you through the day, right?"

"Well, hopefully, our trip will help mellow her out a little. Get her mind off of things."

"Ooh, what trip?" He hooked his arm through hers and led her around the gallery.

"Whitney, me and another one of our friends are going to Austin in two weekends."

"Get out!" He pushed her arm, the way her girlfriends did in college. "*I'm* going to be in Austin then, too."

"You are?"

"Girl, Austin's my town." He smiled widely and moved his shoulders to the synthetic beats of the music. "My parents are still there. So are my grandparents. It's my grandpa's ninety-sixth birthday, and the entire extended family's coming to see him."

"When are you going up?"

"I haven't figured that out yet. The actual party's on Friday night, but I might have to go a little earlier, depending on what flights are still available." He stopped dancing and groaned. "I *hate* flying. I know it's supposed to be the safest way to travel, but I just can't get used to the fact that we're in the *air* in a freakin' fifty-ton piece of metal." He cringed, and a flash of worry crossed his face. "I always think I'm going to die. And with all of the security and everything—" He sighed. "God."

"Why don't you drive, then?" Audrey asked. "It takes the same amount of time to drive to Austin as it does to fly."

"The hooptie that drags my ass around town won't make it three hundred miles. And if I missed my grandpa's birthday—his *ninety-sixth* birthday—I can't even imagine what my family would say." He crinkled his nose, clearly unhappy.

"Why don't you just come up with us? I've got plenty of room, and we're driving up on Friday afternoon anyway. I could drop you off at your grandfather's house."

"I couldn't ask you to do that." His hazel eyes grew larger, and as small a gesture as Audrey had offered, he seemed taken aback by her generosity.

"Why not?"

"Because—I mean . . . ," he trailed, looking uncertain.

"It's not a big deal, Jimmy. And I'm sure the girls would be glad to have you." He still looked hesitant, and she patted his arm. "I've decided. You're coming with us. Meet me at my apartment on Friday at two thirty."

"Only if you're sure that they won't mind. I don't want to barge in on what sounds like a girls' trip."

"I'm sure." She smiled at him, excited for the extra company.

"Girl, what would I do without you?" He picked up his moves where he left off, and he began to bop his shoulders to the vibrating beats. "I'm going to make this up to you—again. We should meet up sometime during the weekend. I can show you where all the cool kids hang out."

"Okay," she said with a laugh.

"Oh, wait." He frowned suddenly. "Shit. I just remembered that my lawyer scheduled a meeting with Kevin and his lawyer on Friday for something called a mediation." He stopped dancing and crossed his arms, looking disgusted. "God, both of them are such pieces of shit. It's so obvious that Kevin's trying to irritate me until I go crazy and just give him the house. And his lawyer's just as bad. You know what he calls me?" He didn't wait for Audrey to guess at an answer. "Not Jimmy. Not Kevin's ex. Not the rightful owner of half of the house." He rolled his eyes. "He's been referring to me as *that Chinese guy.* Like he's so clever."

"You don't look Chinese," Whitney said suddenly, startling Audrey. She turned to see that her friend had sneaked up behind her.

"I'm not," he said, shaking his head. "Try explaining that to Kevin's asshole lawyer."

"What are you really?" Whitney asked.

"Japanese-Filipino-English-French." He studied her for a moment. "You're not Chinese, are you?"

"Korean," Whitney said.

"I knew it," he said with an authoritative nod. "I can always tell." He turned to Audrey. "From the looks of you, I'd say you were, too. Where are you from? Besides Ireland, I mean."

"Well," she said, feeling all nine liters of blood flood her face, "you're right. I'm originally from Korea, too. But I don't remember anything about it. I came here when I was two months old." She felt as if all the lighting had focused on her, and she glanced at Whitney, who was smiling kindly at her. She wondered if she pitied her, or if she was simply being courteous.

"Mmph, isn't it confusing as shit?" Jimmy asked.

"What is?"

"You know. Being Korean with the last name *Henley.* Am I Korean? Am I Irish? Should I act more English, since I look it, or should I act more Japanese, because I'm more Japanese than anything else? *Girl,* I feel your pain."

"I've actually never really thought about it much." Truth was, until she had reconnected with the Valedictorians, she had never thought about it at all. Race was an almost taboo topic at home, and whenever she had raised the issue about her origins, her mother had immediately changed the subject, her palpable fluster training Audrey never to discuss the subject.

"You've never wondered where you fit in this world?" he asked, incredulous.

"I mean, I have, but—I guess not as much as you."

"I think about it all the time," he said. "Sometimes, I wonder how I might have turned out if I weren't such a mutt."

"Trust me, it's no better being straight-up Korean in Texas," Whitney said. "And it's hard to bust stereotypes when everyone in your family is an engineer, is great at math, drives like they're blind and works at NASA. I bet most people think that all I care about is Hello Kitty and brand names, and I could give two shits about either."

"Girl, don't even get me started on stereotypes," Jimmy said, rolling his eyes. "I can't tell you how sick I am of being called *exotic.*"

"No one really tells me any of that," Audrey said quietly. "I mean, I've never had anyone talk about my race." Even Whitney and Hercules, who tended to babble about racism and culture in general, rarely spoke of their own heritage, leaving Audrey with no one to talk to about the one aspect of her life that confused her most.

Jimmy and Whitney didn't say anything, but the way they looked at her, it was obvious that they were stumped by her statement.

"No one?" he asked. "Seriously?"

"Seriously," Audrey said, her face on fire again. "I don't know why. Maybe my circle of friends hasn't expanded much since college. Maybe people figure that I'm adopted and don't want to talk about it. I don't know what the reason is, but people don't approach me wanting to talk about race."

"You're the first person I've ever met who's said that," he said, looking at her wondrously. "People ask me questions all the time, like what I am, or what I consider myself to be, or where they can get good Chinese food. I get asked idiot questions every day."

"I don't get asked *every* day," Whitney said, looking at Jimmy curiously. "You're not one of those supersensitive people, are you? Where everything's about race all the time and no amount of political correctness is enough?"

"Honey, please. So long as people treat me right, I don't care *what* they call me. Call me *oriental* if you want, so long as you're nice about it."

"You don't look oriental at all," Whitney said. "I think mixed kids are the best-looking human beings on the planet."

"This coming from a *gore-jess* goddess!"

Audrey watched as Jimmy and Whitney bantered about what nationality they most resembled and what actor should play them in a film. She thought about her own appearance and wondered how her friends and colleagues regarded her. Most times, she considered herself an amorphous American, a woman without any color at all, and when she was surrounded by her Waspy family members and their Waspy friends, it was hard not to think of herself as anything other than white, too. It was a ridiculous self-perception, or nonperception as it were, and now that Jimmy and Whitney were chatting loudly about the size of their eyes and the exact hue of their skin, she felt as if she had spent the last twenty-nine years deluding herself as to what she really was.

A cell phone rang, interrupting their conversation, and Whitney fumbled in her bag to retrieve it.

"I've got to take this." She strode out the door, and in a moment, Audrey saw another little glow of her burning cigarette.

"Well, help me find a rich patron," Jimmy said, linking arms again. "Let's bag me a modern Medici."

"I'm not sure there are any here tonight." She took small steps on the slick pine floor. "Do you find it strange that I know so little about Korea?"

"Honey, I don't find *anything* strange."

"Well, are you disappointed, then?"

He stopped and looked at her, surprised. "Why would you say that? You are who you are, and I adore you as is. We could all do with a little more culture in our lives, whether it has to do with different customs and nationalities or something that doesn't need an explanation." He motioned at the wall of paintings. "Why do you think I do what I do?"

"Yeah." She felt herself smile. "You know, I'm really glad that you're going to Austin with us."

"I'm glad you're driving me," he said merrily.

They meandered about the small space, occasionally chatting with other guests. For the most part, they stuck to themselves and talked about Jimmy's domestic troubles, his family in Austin and his unfettered passion for his work. She talked about her thesis, and he listened with rapt attention as she described the redemptive power in the Resurrection and how it was apparent even in his own lithographs. By the time Whitney returned, they had circumnavigated the gallery a dozen times, still without a buyer, and Audrey decided that if he didn't find someone in the next few months, she would buy his entire body of work.

Ten

"Auds, I take back all the crap I've ever given you for your having two cars," Hercules said, making herself comfortable in the backseat of Audrey's Lexus GX. "This ride's freakin' awesome. Maybe I should get an SUV for my road trips."

"You don't take road trips," Whitney said, turning around in the passenger seat so that she had a better view of Hercules and Jimmy. Jimmy was still staring at Hercules, perhaps awed by her booming voice and the tank top that revealed her massive cleavage.

"That's because I don't have an SUV." She opened the moon roof, allowing the bright sunlight to overwhelm the cabin before she squinted and closed it halfway.

"Considering how much luggage you brought," Audrey said, taking her eyes off the road to look in the rearview mirror, "I should've gotten a van. Or a bus."

"You realize that we're only going away for the weekend, right?" Whitney shook her head, amazed that Hercules had shown up at Audrey's apartment with an oversized suitcase, a small roller, a party-sized Igloo and a duffel bag stuffed to explosion. Whitney hadn't brought much more than two outfits and her toiletries, and considering that she planned on spending her days by the pool, she doubted that she would even need her paltry carry-on.

"I like to be prepared." Hercules pulled her ankle to her knee, and in a pair of tattered khaki shorts, her white thighs were on full display, likely exposed to sunshine for the first time in years. "There's nothing worse than going somewhere and then realizing that you're not dressed for it. Besides, a lot of what I brought is spices and cooking utensils."

"The house already has everything," Audrey said. "And you really didn't need to bring an entire cooler of food. I don't know what you've heard, but Austin *does* have grocery stores."

"We're not getting in until close to seven, and I still have to meet Gary and Lucas tonight. I don't have time to run all over town looking for a freakin' grocery store." Her cheeks reddened, and she shook her head. "You should be thanking me for making dinner instead of giving me endless shit. I'm trying out a few recipes tonight, and it's going to be *delicious*." She jabbed an elbow into Jimmy's side. "Have you ever been to my restaurant?"

"No, I haven't. Even if I could afford it, I'd never make it through the waiting list." He smiled without parting his lips, looking like a nervous schoolboy with a raging crush. "I hear you're amazing."

"Who told you that?" She grew in her seat, clearly enthused by the flattery.

"Audrey. Whitney. The *Houston Chronicle. Texas Monthly.* Everyone, actually." He turned his body so that he was fully facing Hercules, as preppy in his pink and green polo shirt as she was dressed down. "I can't believe I'm in the same car with you. I'm like, *so* starstruck right now." He giggled. "Everyone I know thinks you're the bomb. You're like an icon in the gay community. I *love, love, love* that you called Houston a city full of right-wing Nazis, because it is. Girl, if my ex knew that I was traveling with you, he'd lose his mind." He pulled his cell phone out of his pocket and flipped the screen open. "I might text him, just to hack him off. Can I get a picture of us together? Kevin will never believe this." He stopped suddenly, and his hand flew to his mouth. "Lordy, I'm doing it again, aren't I? I babble when I'm nervous or excited, and I'm a little of both right now." He giggled again, and his excitement reminded Whitney of a teenage girl in the presence of a boy band.

Hercules smiled widely, her teeth on full display, before leaning forward and poking Audrey's shoulder. "You were right. I *do* like this guy."

Audrey chuckled. "I told you that you would."

"So, how do y'all know each other?" Jimmy asked. "Do you take trips like this all the time?"

"We went to the same high school," Hercules said. "These overachievers ended up graduating as covaledictorians with me."

"You guys have known each other since high school?"

Whitney settled into her seat and gazed out the window, barely listening as Audrey and Hercules chatted about their orientation at Loyola, their having taken two dozen AP classes together, Audrey and Whitney's prom-committee days and their identical GPAs. She was exhausted, having slept even less in the last two weeks than usual, and while Jimmy spoke excitedly about his first encounter with Audrey at Starbucks, she took in the tall grass that bordered both sides of the two-lane road, the random wood-sided houses that dotted the otherwise uninhabited countryside and the unending pastures of sleepy longhorns. The scenery was soul-refreshingly idyllic, and as Audrey raced down Highway 71, Whitney could almost feel her stress melt.

"Y'all, I can't even tell you how glad I am that we're getting away," she said. "As much as I've been through in the last couple of weeks, I thought for sure that I'd have a nervous breakdown by now." She caught herself, immediately regretting having said anything at all.

"Why? What happened?" Hercules asked.

"Just"—she couldn't bring herself to say any more—"you know." She hadn't yet told Hercules that she had been fired from Boerne & Connelly, or that she and Scott had ended their relationship. Come to think of it, other than the pithy explanation she had given Audrey on their way to the Nesbitt, she hadn't talked about either incident at all. She had refused to dwell on them, as if they had been nothing more than a ghastly dream of gross injustice and disappointment, and if she had hoped that fourteen days of solitude would bring peace and acceptance, she realized that her feckless repression had only caused her to fall into a deeper funk. Audrey glanced at her, clearly understanding that Hercules was still in the dark, and Whitney shook her head, unwilling to sully their happy travels with the miring impetuses of her depression.

"Honey, you're not the nervous-breakdown type," Jimmy said. "You're stronger than that. I can see it in your energy rays."

"What are you talking about?" Hercules asked. Whitney turned around and peered at him.

"I'm kind of psychic, you know," he said, as merry as ever. "Always have been. I can read people's energies, and the minute I meet someone, I know what he's like." He shrugged. "I don't know why no one else can see them, because they're really clear to me."

"You read energies," Whitney said flatly, convinced that he was joking.

He nodded vigorously. "I've never been wrong, too. Even with Kevin." He placed a hand on Hercules' leg and shook his head. "He was this gorgeous human being, and then he turned into a monster. I should've seen it coming, because at the end, his aura was nothing but gray."

Hercules leaned closer, obviously interested in what he had to say, and Whitney squelched the urge to roll her eyes. For someone who championed self-driven success and meticulously planned achievements, Hercules had always harbored a strange affinity towards anything resembling a horoscope, and as closely as she was inspecting Jimmy, Whitney knew that his parlor trick appealed to her like an epicurean shop.

"Read my energy," Hercules said, straightening up as if he were about to take her picture. "What am I like?"

"Oh, Lord," Audrey said, grinning. "This ought to be good."

"I want to hear what you're like, too," Hercules said, poking Whitney's shoulder.

"H., you already know what I'm like. No offense, Jimmy, but I'm not into—well, whatever it is that you see." She turned back around, feeling dread tense her shoulders. As silly and irrational as her fear may have been, the narcissistic exercise still made her uneasy. Perhaps a lifetime of her mother's apprehension towards the "devil's work" had ingrained a mistrust of the ostensibly innocent New Age contemplation, and despite Jimmy's insouciance, an uncomfortable case of the heebie-jeebies was overtaking her. She sank lower in her seat, hoping that he couldn't see her aura above her headrest.

"So?" Hercules asked. Whitney heard her wriggle around in her seat. "What do you see?"

"Well," Jimmy said, sounding too excited, "you've got tremendous energy, which is what I would've expected from someone as awesome as you."

"I do?" she asked happily.

"Girl, you're almost all oranges and reds. Those are powerful colors. Most leaders have those colors. It means that you need to control your environment and the people in it, and you're really interested in the finer things of life. You have this drive to show people how successful you are."

"I could've told you that without looking at her head," Audrey said.

"But there's also something else," he said, ignoring Audrey. "Kind of a brownish fuzz behind all that brightness. Like—you're not settled. You're still expecting something that hasn't happened yet, but I can tell you that it's right around the corner." He murmured inaudibly. "Something amazing is waiting for you, maybe in Austin. Or maybe in Houston. Yes—definitely in Houston."

"What is it?" Hercules asked with unabashed fervor. Whitney let out a little snort, astounded by Hercules' engrossment, and she turned around to watch the freak show in the backseat.

"I think it's a person, actually." He was quiet for a moment, and he placed two slender fingers on Hercules' forehead. "Yeah, that's right." He perked up, apparently delighted by what he saw. "Someone special is waiting for you. You've seen him a thousand times before, but you've never looked at him the way you were supposed to. If you let him, he could really surprise you."

Hercules leaned against her seat, pensive for a moment. Her brows furrowed, and she peered at Jimmy with narrowed eyes.

"You're being serious? You're not screwing around?"

"Of course not." He shook his head, and his spiky hair wiggled with the frantic effort. "I wouldn't do that to you."

"Because if you're wrong, I'm going to pound your freakin' 'nads in."

"Hercules," Whitney said, embarrassed by her outburst.

"Jimmy, don't listen to her." Audrey turned around and shot Hercules a warning look. "She doesn't mean that."

"I do, too," Hercules said indignantly. "He just said that something incredible is going to happen, and if I get my hopes up only to be disappointed, I'm going to be pissed."

"He's only saying it to be optimistic," Audrey said. "You don't have to threaten his manhood because he gave you good news."

Jimmy regarded Hercules, apparently not put off by her brash behavior. "You know what? You're totally a turtle."

"A turtle," Hercules repeated, clearly unimpressed by the comparison.

"Or a piece of French bread. You know—all hard and crusty on the outside, but soft and tender on the inside. You remind me of this *gore-jess* boy I once knew—he acted like a crazy bitch because he was so insecure, kind of like you." She winced and pulled back, and he patted her thigh. "You don't fool me, honey. You're nothing but heart, and I know that you pretend you're all harsh because you think it'll keep people away. You're terrified of getting hurt, but because of it, you're missing out on the best things in life."

"You're freaking me out," she said, looking enchanted and anxious at the same time. She poked Whitney's shoulder, her eyes still glued to Jimmy. "Read Whitney's aura."

"I said that I don't believe in psychics," she said, annoyed by Hercules' persistence and jabbing finger.

"Then, don't listen to what he says. *I* want to hear it." Whitney didn't respond, and Hercules' prodding turned into a slap on her upper arm. "Come *on*. I've always wanted to go to a fortune-teller with y'all, and we're in a car with one. We can't let him go to waste."

"I swear to God, Hercules, Jimmy's right about your needing to control people." She swatted Hercules' hand away, already aware that she wouldn't let the matter go until she had driven Whitney bat-shit crazy with her insistence. She twitched her lips, realizing that she had little choice but to give in to Jimmy's prognostication. The sooner she could choke down his readings, the sooner they could talk about something else.

"You want me to read you?" he asked, still cheerful.

"Fine," she said, determined not to read anything into his augury. "What do you see?"

"A lot of gray," he said, gently taking her hand into his. "A lot of a mustardy color. There's a lot of smokiness in your halo, but I'm also picking up a really strong yellow vibe."

"What does that mean?" Hercules asked. Audrey glanced at them in the mirror, her lips pursed tightly.

"It means that you've been through a lot, and you're still upset by it." He nodded. "Honey, I sympathize with you. I know exactly what you're feeling."

Whitney sighed. Even without his prescient ability, she knew that he empathized with her. After all, his relationship had fallen apart, albeit in a much more dramatic way, and she imagined that as a fellow artist, he was likewise stuck between his grandiose dreams and the stifling borders of reality. Clearly, he understood her, even if his life differed vastly from hers, and even if he didn't know that she dreamed of becoming a singer, and his compassion—whether from true clairvoyance or sensitive body-language perception—dulled the edges of her recent distress.

He pressed the pads of his thumbs into her palm and concentrated on the lines in her hand. After another moment of inspection, he kissed her fingers, and she stirred, touched by his sudden tenderness.

"You'll be better than fine, and you know it," he said. "That's what I meant when I said that you're strong. You're going to come out of this mess soon, and what you've been dreaming about—it's going to happen." He nodded emphatically, and his lips parted into a brilliant smile, his bleached teeth practically glowing in the shade. "I promise you that."

"What the hell are you talking about?" Hercules asked. "What mess? What dream?"

"I can't tell you," he said.

"Why not?"

"Because she won't let me."

"What do you mean, she won't *let* you?" Hercules asked, frowning severely.

"It's not my place to say what she doesn't want me to say."

Whitney pulled her arm away, suddenly unsure of herself. When Jimmy had spouted generalities about Hercules, she had halfway believed that he was fabricating statements simply to appease the overly eager chef. But his vague statements about her own strength and dreams felt strangely personal and frightfully specific, and as lightly as he carried himself, his words had intoned a gravity she didn't associate with him. Goose-bumped from scalp to heel, she continued to stare at him, and if she had initially thought that he had refused Hercules an explanation because he didn't know what Whitney's dreams were, she was beginning to wonder if he had actually refused disclosure because he respected her discretion.

"What's he talking about?" Hercules asked, staring at Whitney.

"I don't know," she said, too taken aback to produce a more coherent response. They continued to look at each other, Hercules clearly disconcerted, and Whitney still befuddled by the entire ordeal. After a few wordless moments, Hercules shook her head, let out a little snort and then craned her neck against the window, shielding her eyes as she squinted at passing signs.

"I don't get y'all," Jimmy said after an uncomfortable pause.

"Why?" Whitney asked.

"Because—it's like you don't have the first clue about each other, and you've known each other since high school. I wish you could see what I see. All three of you have amazing energies about you, and from where I'm sitting, y'all might as well be a bunch of rainbows." He shook his head. "You're just *gore-jess*. All of you. But when Hercules gets close to Whitney, the energies don't blend. They stop short, like there's a wall between you. There are walls between all three of you, and I don't get why you can't open up to each other."

"We're completely open to each other," Audrey said nervously.

"No, you're not. And it's a damned shame, too, because whatever color's missing from one of you shows up in another. You could totally help each other with whatever you're going through instead of bottling it all up inside." He sighed. "It makes me sad."

"What makes me sad is that there isn't a freakin' bathroom for the next fifty miles," Hercules said, apparently no longer interested in the vehicular therapy session. "I'm about to piss my pants."

"You're joking," Whitney said, glad to be finally off topic. "We've only been on the road for forty-five minutes."

"I had a Venti latte from Starbucks before we left. I didn't think it would kick in so soon." She tapped Audrey's shoulder. "Drive faster. If we don't find a gas station soon, I might make you pull over at the next bush."

"Hercules, I swear to God. I asked you before if you needed to use the bathroom."

"I didn't have to go then," she said. Whitney stifled a laugh, amused by the parent-child road-trip banter.

"Well, I don't know where the next rest stop is," Audrey said.

"Just find me a bathroom, will you?"

Eleven

"I can't believe that your parents don't come here more often," Whitney said, swirling her wineglass. "This view is unreal." She gazed at the sparkling lights of the city, and from her vantage point of the slate-tiled patio high over Lake Travis, Austin's twinkling skyline was breathtaking. She sucked in the cool evening air, and whether the result of the Hill Country scenery, the fact that Jimmy was at his grandfather's house instead of offering additional psychic observations at Audrey's mansion, or the unending glasses of wine, she almost felt content.

"I forget how much I love this place," Audrey said, reaching over the table to refill their glasses with Chianti. "God, I needed this. I could just sit out here all night and drink until I pass out."

"You and me both."

They were quiet for a moment, perhaps incapacitated from the unending array of Hercules' wood-roasted buffalo tenderloin, Parmesan gnocchi, pickled Cipolini onions, warm chocolate pudding cake and two bottles of wine, and Whitney watched silky sheets of water flow from an eight-foot stone waterfall into the lit pool below, mesmerized by its rhythmic ripples. The adjoining spa was calling to her, tempting her aching muscles with its healing bubbles, and she glanced at Hercules, wondering how much longer she had to wait until she left. With her typical bluster, she had insisted that they christen the Jacuzzi together, and rather than argue over the ridiculous request, Whitney and Audrey had secretly agreed to soak themselves after the most demanding of the group departed.

"Well, tell your father not to sell the house, because it's freakin' beautiful," Hercules slurred suddenly, barely able to remain upright in her seat. "I feel like I'm in the Hollywood Hills or something, like"— she burped quietly—"some kind of celebrity."

Whitney and Audrey exchanged amused glances. Hercules had imbibed more than her usual half-glass limit, and judging from her blood-shot eyes and loopy smile, Whitney imagined that she was completely drunk.

"You *are* a celebrity," Audrey said, reaching out to steady her. "I read your article in *National Spectator*. That's a huge deal, Hercules. And to think that we've known you since high school."

"You read that?" Hercules' flushed cheeks lifted as she smiled.

"I did, too," Whitney said. "It was a great article."

"It was, wasn't it? It must have caused a stir, because *Texas Monthly* wants me to be a regular contributor. I don't know if I'll do it, though, because I'm pretty much tapped out." She took another sip of her drink. "I don't even know what the hell they expect me to write about on a continuing basis."

"Why don't you talk about what you were like as a kid?" Whitney asked. "What or who your influences were, how you became interested in cooking, that kind of thing. You never talk about your childhood or any part of your life before you went to the CIA, and I think it would be nice to open up to your readership."

"Come to think of it, you hardly ever talk about anything personal," Audrey said. "Even with us."

"How's that relevant?" Hercules asked. "What does my personal life have to do with *Texas Monthly*?"

"It's interesting to the readers," Whitney said with a shrug. "Gives them some context as to why you cook the way you do, what drives you. I always like to read about the human aspect of success. It makes the achievement seem more immediate."

Hercules frowned. "Well, if you must know, I cook because I'm brilliant at it. . . ."

"Not to brag or anything," Audrey said with a snort.

"Of course not," she said matter-of-factly. "And as for how I became interested in becoming a cook—I don't know. I just always was. It's in my soul. It's the only thing I ever thought about. I can't explain it any better than that."

"You should include that in your article," Whitney said. Hercules didn't respond. She seemed to be daydreaming. More likely, she had lost control of her faculties, and she gazed at the pool, apparently trans-fixed by its underwater lights. She drained her glass and then turned to them, as out of it as Whitney had ever seen.

"It's crazy how far we've come since high school, don't you think?" she mumbled, her face as red as her drink. "I'm the world's greatest chef"—she pointed clumsily at herself, burst into a gale of laughter and then pointed at Audrey—"and you're getting your freakin' Ph.D." Her gaze landed on Whitney next, and she narrowed her eyes as if inspecting her. "And you're a freakin' phenomenal lawyer. Or you're going to be once they actually let you do something at that firm of yours."

Whitney tensed. She'd known that the subject of her job would come up eventually, but as much as she wanted to share her troubles with Hercules, she certainly didn't want to apprise the drunken chef now of her unemployed status.

"I've got to be honest with you," Hercules said, her eyelids falling halfway. "I always thought you'd do something more than work at a mongo law firm. I don't know why, but I did. Out of the three of us, I always thought you were the smartest, you know? I imagined that out of our class, you'd be the one to do something incredible with your life rather than work for some giant corporate machine where you were just another cog." She shrugged clumsily. "It's not what I would've expected from you at all."

"What *would* you have expected?" Whitney asked.

"I don't know." She blinked slowly. "Something *amazing*. Something that no one would've ever expected."

Whitney didn't say anything. She was startled, and deeply flattered, by Hercules' remark, and desperate for affirmation that she was destined to sing professionally, she wondered if her friend's rumination wasn't yet another confirming sign of her future.

Hercules rocked back and forth like a chubby pendulum, looking as if she was trying to coordinate an upright position.

"We should take her inside." Whitney caught her as she swung too far to the left.

"Are you going to be okay to meet your friends?" Audrey asked.

"Lucas is my friend. I haven't made up my mind about Gary yet." She rested her elbow on the table and cradled her chin in her palm. "What time is it?"

"Almost eleven."

"Shit. They'll be here any minute."

"You can't go like this," Whitney said, concerned. "You can barely stand up."

"Then I'll take the meeting lying down. It took freakin' forever to get this date lined up." She pushed her chair back a few inches, and the iron leg scratched against the tiles with a skull-tingling screech. "Ugh. I don't feel so good."

"Jesus Christ, H.," Whitney said. "Come on. Let's get some water into you."

"What are y'all going to do when I'm gone?" She leaned heavily against Whitney's shoulder, practically crumpling her, and they hobbled slowly towards the house.

"I don't know. Maybe we'll go for a swim. Or just hang out here for a while."

"You're not going to hit the hot tub without me, right?"

"Of course not," Audrey said, trailing them with their glasses. Whitney looked back, and Audrey shot her a mischievous grin. "We'll probably just drink the rest of the wine that you brought."

"Well, don't overdo it." She shook her head. "Y'all are freakin' lushes."

"Auds, are you almost ready?" Whitney called from the hallway, her voice echoing against the walls and the soaring ceiling. She was standing in a pair of flip-flops and a zebra-print bikini, fluffing a beach towel around her shoulders as if it were a cape. She couldn't wait to soak in the Jacuzzi, to relieve the tension that had contorted her twenty-eight-year-old body into that of a centenarian. Hercules had stumbled into Lucas's car an hour ago, leaving the others to scrub away the explosion of a mess she had left in the kitchen, and after forty-five minutes of intense cleaning, Whitney felt as if her muscles had succumbed to rigor mortis.

"The strap of my suit broke," Audrey said through the closed door. "Why don't you head on down while I fix it?"

"Do you need help?"

"No, I'm almost finished. I'll be there in a couple of minutes. I'll bring the wine."

"Is it okay if I explore a bit?"

"Be my guest."

Whitney took small steps down the hall, stopping every twenty feet to gawk at one enormous room after another. She pulled her towel closer around her body and stepped into what looked like Audrey's father's hunting-trophy room. Two twelve-point-buck heads flanked opposite sides of the wall, and at least a dozen stuffed wildcats leered at her from within the cavernous space. The bust of an antelope rested in a corner, gazing gently upon the zebra and lion skins that carpeted the parquet wood floor. She glanced at a shelf of photographs, all of them boasting a handful of people crowded around an unsmiling Mr. Henley, and from the squat trees, the draped cheetah around his neck and the felled elephant, she gathered that he spent some time in Africa.

She left the eerie menagerie and made her way to the next room, barely glancing at the honky-tonk-styled ballroom, where she imagined the Henleys had two-stepped. As strange as a dance hall was in a residential building, it fit the rest of the Hill Country architecture of the home, what with its muddy-colored oak beams and Texas-stone floors. She moved on to the movie room, complete with six rows of leather seats, a twenty-foot projection screen and an antique popcorn maker. A few more steps provided jaw-dropping views of the two-story library and an exercise room that could have doubled as a warehouse, and after she closed the door of the wood-paneled steam room, she headed towards the backyard, overwhelmed by the extravagant, if rustic, abode. A final room caught her eye, as if the house had saved the best for last, and she wandered in, feeling for the first time as if she were trespassing.

"Good God," she muttered under her breath as she peered at an orchestra's worth of instruments. Violins, violas, a cello and a bass hung from their stands, exposed to oily fingers and oxidizing air. Why they weren't housed in their protective cases was beyond her, and if no one inhabited the house, then certainly a hidden staff must have tended to these delicate pieces. Brass and wind instruments took up another partition of the space, as naked and dust free as the rest of the collection. She took in the grand piano that rested on an elevated platform, the Corinthian leather benches that formed an open rectangle in the center of the room, and the unending walls of packed bookcases, unable to keep from ogling at them all.

She tiptoed to a final corner of the room, feeling as if she were bumbling about in a cathedral. Several guitars, all acoustic, lined themselves against the wall, and before she realized what she was doing, she picked one up, sat on a tufted ottoman and began to strum on the stiff strings. Her fingers roved over the fret board, her calloused tips finding their place as she picked Isaac Albéniz's *Leyenda*, the Spanish ode in E minor that she loved even more than the popular bullfighting *Malagueña*. Music echoed through the acoustically favorable hall, bouncing against the walls and into her ears, and the clarity of the noise mesmerized her, lulled her into a trancelike oblivion. She was so absorbed in the melody that she didn't notice Audrey standing at the doorway until her fingers had come to a rest on the strings. The sight of her friend stopped her heart, and they stared at each other, one clearly as shocked as the other.

"I had no idea that you could play like that," Audrey finally said. She wandered into the room, clad in her mended black bikini, and she was clutching a bottle of red wine, two glasses, a towel and her sandals. Still in a daze, she sat on the bench opposite Whitney.

"I started to play in college," she said, her face on fire. Her heart was pounding out of her chest, and her hands were suddenly clammy. "I'm sorry. I shouldn't have touched anything. This place is like a museum."

"My dad's crazy about collecting things." Audrey lowered the bottle onto the floor. "You should see the garage." Whitney stood to return the guitar, but Audrey reached out and held her arm. "Don't put it away."

"Auds, your father's really scary. I think he'd kill me and add me to his hunting collection if he knew that I was touching his stuff."

"Trust me, he doesn't care. Hell, if he knew that you could play like *that*"—she shook her head—"he'd *give* you the guitar." Sliding her flip-flops onto her feet, she didn't take her eyes off Whitney, and if Audrey had noticed that the towel she'd been carrying had fallen to the ground, she didn't bother to pick it up. "You never told me that you were so good."

Whitney sat back down, feeling out of sorts. "No, I guess I haven't."

"Is that your dream?" she asked, looking lost in her thoughts.

"What do you mean?" If possible, her heart beat even faster.

"I keep thinking about what Jimmy said in the car. About how your dream would come to fruition. You probably think that he's full of shit, and maybe he is, but"—she stopped, her face screwed up with uncertainty—"I don't know. What he said about you, me and Hercules—that we put up walls between us—it's kind of true, isn't it?"

Whitney regarded her. Her immediate reaction was to brush aside the comment, to assure Audrey, and herself, that their relationship was as open as Jimmy had declared it wasn't. There was a perverse pleasure in keeping secrets, in internalizing her desire to sing professionally so that she alone could handle it, like an inanimate toy. At the same time, she knew that it was the one area in which she had no outside perspective, no reprieve from her own obsessions, and the tension she felt as a result was slowly gnawing away at her. Audrey was right, and whether it was because they were in a bizarre emporium of instruments, that they were exhausted and still slightly drunk or that a denial was obviously disingenuous, she nodded. Maybe it was time that they opened up to each other. Actually, she couldn't think of anything more appropriate.

"There are a few things that I've never told y'all," she said.

Audrey pulled the cork out of the bottle and poured two glasses. "If I started on all the things I've never told you, we'd be here all night."

"Well, we've got all night."

Audrey nodded, and her lips curled into a small smile as she handed her a glass of wine. Whitney took a long sip of it, letting the alcohol soothe her nerves.

"So?" Audrey asked. "Is playing the guitar your dream?"

"It's the soundtrack to my dream, actually. *Fantasy's* probably a better word for it." She placed her glass on the floor, contemplating how to explain her deepest desire. "I've wanted to be a singer since law school. And not just the kind that screeches in the shower, but a recording artist. With an album and an audience." She looked at Audrey hesitantly. "I'm sure that sounds incredibly flaky to you."

"It doesn't sound flaky at all." She smiled kindly, and her simple expression encouraged Whitney to continue.

"I've written a lot of music over the years, and I've performed at Billy Bob's in Houston a few times. I've played at Mason's here, too. I actually have a standing invitation to come back whenever I want."

"Whitney, that's awesome," she said, clearly impressed. "Why didn't you say anything before? I would've loved to watch you play."

"Because . . . ," she trailed, uncertain how to articulate the self-conscious, insecure reasons she had kept quiet. "I'm not sure that I'd ever make it as a recording artist, and I was too embarrassed to let y'all know that I was desperate for a career where success isn't the usual outcome. I mean—the only thing worse than failure is *public* failure, and I would rather die than have y'all pity me. Does that make sense?"

"Absolutely."

She sighed. "Besides, it's not like there was anything to say. I haven't really done anything about my music, other than write lyrics in my bedroom and sing at a few local joints. People who are serious about making it in this business put together a demo and send it anywhere they can in order to get their foot in the door. Or they find an independent label to represent them. Or they make their own CDs and sell it out of the back of their car. Or they try out for *American Idol*. They do *something*, is my point."

"So why can't you make a demo and send it out?" Audrey grinned. "Or sell homemade CDs out of your trunk? I'd buy one."

"There are so many reasons." She finished her drink. Immediately, Audrey refilled it. "I haven't put myself out there because I'm not sure how I even feel about a singing career. Don't get me wrong. I want it more than anything. But, wanting something, daydreaming about it—

that's a world away from actually going after it. There's safety in fantasies. The real world comes with my family's expectations, unstable finances, an uncertain future, what y'all think about me, what I think about myself." She sighed again. "I haven't been able to get past any of that, and jacking around at Billy Bob's is as much as I've been able to handle."

Audrey's brows furrowed. "You shouldn't have worried what Hercules or I think. What you want to do is wonderful. I'd totally support you. I'm sure Hercules would feel the same way."

Whitney reached across the divide and grasped Audrey's hand. "I know. But still."

"So what are you going to do?" She was practically radiating sympathy, and when Whitney examined her expression, she thought she detected empathy, too.

"I have no idea." She laid the guitar on the bench next to her and sank onto the floor. Audrey joined her, and in the middle of their fort-like encampment, the gargantuan room shrank into the coziest of spaces. "A part of me thinks, *Screw it all. I'm going to give this music gig a real try.* Another part of me thinks that I need to grow up and be a responsible adult. Get another job. It's what everyone expects. Sometimes, it's what *I* expect."

"Why don't you work on your music full-time, at least for a year or two?" She folded her legs underneath her and peered into the wine bottle, which had long since gone dry, before reaching for Whitney's glass. "You can always get another job if your singing doesn't pan out, but at least this way, you won't spend the rest of your life wondering, *What if?*"

"Maybe," she said, not at all convinced.

"Seriously, Whitney. What you can do"—her eyes roamed the guitar—"that's a gift. And if you can sing half as well as you play, I don't know how you'd fail." Her mouth set, making her appear almost stern. "It would be a damned shame if you didn't try to make something of your music because you felt beholden to this incomplete image everyone has of you."

"Yeah," she murmured, pondering Audrey's counsel.

"I really want to hear you play. Show me how awesome I know you are." She reached for the guitar and stopped midmovement. "Actually, you said that you've got a standing invitation at Mason's, right?"

"Yeah."

"Can you call up your friend and see if you can squeeze in a set tomorrow?"

"You're serious?"

"I'm dead serious. Call your friend."

"I could just play something right now, Auds."

She shook her head. "I've got to hear you play live in front of an audience." Before Whitney could respond, Audrey said, "Consider it your engagement present to me." She grinned, and from her bloodshot eyes, Whitney realized that Audrey was completely inebriated, too. "I'm going to embarrass you with how much I cheer."

"Okay." She felt herself smile, and she picked up their now-communal glass of wine. "You know, I really envy you," she said. "Hercules, too."

"Why?"

"Because y'all have your lives put together. She's doing what she loves and making a really good life for herself. How many twenty-nine-year-olds do you know have a little empire going? And you—you've got a great job, you're getting your Ph.D., and you're getting married to a wonderful man. I feel like I'm the only one who's still trying to figure out what I'm supposed to do in life."

Audrey frowned. "I wish my mother saw things the way you do."

"Does she not?"

She groaned, the guttural rumble echoing against the walls. "This is going to take more booze. Come on, let's go hunt for some." She stood and pulled Whitney up before leading her down the hallway and into a wine cellar. At least ten thousand bottles rested in the zigzagging honeycomb that extended from floor to ceiling, and the slightly chilly room brought goose bumps to Whitney's scantily clad skin.

"Which one looks good to you?" Audrey asked.

"Jesus Christ, Auds. This is all amazing." She couldn't stop goggling at the treasure trove. "If your parents decide not to sell the house, I'll house-sit for free."

She chuckled and extracted a purple-labeled bottle, clutching it to her chest as if it were a baby. They left the cellar and walked into the backyard, and as high as they were above the city, the stars seemed to hover inches above their heads.

"It is so gorgeous tonight," Whitney said before sucking in a lung-cleansing breath. "Do you want to go for a swim? Or are we really waiting for Hercules to come back to—how did she say it?—*christen* the Jacuzzi?"

Audrey laughed while gazing at the pool. "You know what? I might just lie down on a chaise. After the way we've been drinking, I'm afraid that I'll drown."

"Well, if you're going to drown, I'm not going in, either. I don't think I have enough coordination right now to save you." She plopped onto a thickly cushioned chaise that bordered the pool, and pulled her towel over her. Audrey sat down next to her on the wide chair and set the bottle of wine on the table beside her. That they were in their swimsuits by the pool—in the dark—struck Whitney as ridiculous and wonderful, and she allowed herself a delicious sigh, feeling as serene as she had felt in a long time. She was astonished that her drunken blab-all had been so therapeutic, and she regretted not having told Audrey earlier about her deepest desires. She leaned against the tufted back and turned to her, grateful for their nascent openness. "So, how *does* your mother see things?"

"Well, she's not exactly thrilled about my engagement. She thinks we rushed into it." She looked at Whitney. "Do you think we got engaged too fast?" Whitney hesitated, and Audrey reached out and touched her arm. "Honestly."

"Honestly"—she weighed her words—"I was a little surprised when you told me that you were getting married. I mean, y'all have only been dating for, what, five months?" Audrey nodded. "And you got engaged after three. It seemed fast to me, but only because your last few boyfriends were long-termers."

"I know." She stared at the pool, deep in thought. "It's the strangest thing, Whitney. I never really thought one way or the other about marriage. I figured that if it happened, great. If not, fine. But then I met

Victor, and everything just clicked. It's like I knew on our first date that he was the one. I told my mom that we could have a superlong engagement so that she wouldn't worry so much, but frankly, I just want to be married. I'd elope right now if I didn't know that it would give her a heart attack."

Whitney peered at her, bewildered. "Why the immediacy? What's the difference between what y'all have now and what you'll have once you're married?"

"Practically, nothing. Emotionally, though, psychologically—I guess I'm craving permanence. Or stability. Something solid. Maybe I see marriage as a way to move on with life." She shrugged. "Or maybe I found the person I want to be with forever, and I don't want to wait. I don't know why I want it so bad. I just do." She sighed, looking unsatisfied with her explanation, and Whitney, at a loss for helpful words, patted her leg.

"I guess I can understand that." Frankly, she couldn't. The idea of marriage had never consumed her, had never been a goal that demanded immediate attention. She imagined that she'd be just as happy if she was single for the rest of her life as she would if she found someone to call her husband, and given her recent romantic disappointment, she couldn't even fathom that a man might transform her outlook on marriage the way Victor had Audrey's.

"Well, my mother doesn't understand," Audrey said quietly. She grabbed the wine and fumbled in the table's lone drawer before extracting a bottle opener. With startling dexterity, she managed to yank out the cork with one hand. She glanced about, apparently realizing that they had left their glasses in the house, and then took a swig straight from the bottle before handing it to Whitney.

"Give it time, Auds. A long engagement might not be such a bad thing. At the very least, your mom won't be able to say that you rushed into marriage."

"No, but she'd still believe that Victor's a gold digger." Whitney reacted, taken aback by the characterization, and Audrey, noticing her surprise, sighed again. "I don't know why she insists on expecting the worst of him. Maybe it's because my parents' marriage is such a wreck.

I have to believe that she's projecting her own issues onto my relationship."

"Your parents?" Whitney asked, confused. "But every time I see them, they seem so happy."

"When's the last time you saw them together?" Audrey curled her legs underneath her and stared at the sky. "They don't even live in the same house. My dad travels all year so that he doesn't have to run into my mom, and when he's actually in Houston, he stays at the Shalimar downtown. The only time they're ever in the same room is at my mom's Remission Celebration, and my dad just gives the same toast he gives every year and then leaves before the party's over."

"I had no idea," she said, stunned.

"They probably haven't had a real conversation in ten years. Honestly, I don't know why they're even married. The entire thing's such a farce. It's humiliating, actually." She laid her arm over her eyes, as if she could block out the cause of her distress.

"Have you ever talked to your mom about it?" Whitney asked, still taken aback by the Henleys' expertly hidden dysfunction.

"There are two things that we never, *ever* discuss—my parents' relationship and the fact that I'm biologically Korean." Audrey lowered her arm and looked at Whitney. "Those are big-ticket items, don't you think? Things people *should* talk about?"

"Does it bother you that y'all don't?"

"Frankly, it's been easier not having to deal with either. I just ignore them, like they're not real issues. I think I'd be a basket case if my mother insisted on talking about her relationship with Dad constantly, and I wouldn't even know how I'd react if she started to talk about race." She was quiet for a moment. "But every once in a while—I don't know—I feel like we're living this fiction."

"Audrey, it's not fiction. There are no rules how you're supposed to behave. She's your mother, and you're her daughter. Period."

"I know, but there are a lot of spaces between those two points. Look how I turned out." She pointed at herself for emphasis. "Hell, half the time, I think I'm white. I mean, I told Jimmy that I was Irish, for God's sake." She snorted, and even in the dimness of the night, Whitney could see her cheeks flame. "He must have thought I was delusional." She gazed at the sky pensively. "Maybe it wouldn't be such a bad thing to know where I come from. I could audit a few classes at Rice on Korean history." She considered. "I might throw in a beginning language course, too."

"I'll join you on the language course. It would be nice to understand it as well as a kindergartner."

"Deal." She turned her head and looked at Whitney. "Oh, speaking of Rice—I want to be an English professor."

"Well, I think that would be marvelous." She rested her head against the back of the chaise and took in the star-studded sky. She didn't need to ask why Audrey hadn't previously told her any more than Audrey had to repeat Whitney's explanation of her fear of public failure, and their silent understanding encouraged her, made their relationship feel stronger than it had felt hours ago. Their evening-long openness contented her, released the tension that repression had built. She closed her eyes, realizing that she was drowsy, and she welcomed the intoxicating sensation that had eluded her for the last two weeks. She was drifting to sleep when Audrey spoke.

"We should've talked a long time ago."

"At least we're talking now."

They smiled at each other, the kind of empathetic smile third graders and mature women alike gave when they felt bonded to each other. They didn't have any answers, and they hadn't experienced any epiphanies, yet Whitney felt as though her yoke had been lifted. If anything, Audrey was bracing the other end, and for now, that was good enough.

Twelve

"Remind me why we're going to some dive of a club when we could still be in the pool," Hercules said from the passenger seat of Audrey's car.

"Because Whitney's singing at Mason's tonight," Audrey said, shooting her a frown. "We just talked about this two hours ago."

"Are you okay?" Whitney asked, trying to quell her nerves in the backseat. She had told Hercules about her music while they had skimmed across Lake Travis in Audrey's sharp-nosed boat, and if she had expected a barrage of questions about her singing abilities or the genesis of her interest, she had been surprised by her reticence instead. Hercules had been uncommonly quiet, saving her harangues for the two dozen phone calls she had fielded throughout the afternoon, and as preoccupied as she was, Whitney wondered if she had listened to a single thing she had said all day.

"I'm fine," Hercules said tensely, her obvious stress exacerbating Whitney's thundering heartbeat.

"How'd it go last night with Lucas and Gary?" she asked, gripping the guitar case tighter. "I didn't hear you come in."

"That's because y'all were sprawled out on a lawn chair like a pair of winos. I tried to get you to come inside the house, but you were too hammered to move. I finally went to bed around six in the morning."

"Well, thanks for putting a blanket over us," Audrey said. "I was so out of it this morning that I thought that the lawn gnomes had brought us a down comforter."

"If you know of a group of gnomes for hire," Hercules said, "let me know. I could use them."

"Are y'all going to open a restaurant in San Antonio?" Audrey pulled into the rear parking lot of the tiny club, which had served as a one-story house decades ago. Several other clubs dotted the cramped street on the edge of downtown Austin, each as charmingly run-down as Mason's.

"Not with those sons of bitches, no. But I have another contact, and we're supposed to talk about a possible venture in Austin."

"I thought you were interested in San Antonio," Whitney said.

"That place is a *dump*." She didn't say any more, and given that she was still clearly smarting over whatever had happened with Gary and Lucas, Whitney didn't press her for particulars. "God, my stomach doesn't feel right. Maybe a drink will make it feel better. Or maybe that's what screwed me up in the first place."

"I have some Tums if you need it," Whitney said.

"I've built up an unfortunate immunity to them. I could be eating a fistful of Tic Tacs, and my body wouldn't know the difference."

"We're here," Audrey said, and then turned off the engine. "Hey, Whitney, I hope it's okay that I invited Jimmy. When I told him that you were performing tonight, he lost his mind. You should see how proud he is."

"He is?" she asked, touched by his excitement. She tumbled out of the car with the guitar and closed the door, catching the pained look on Hercules' face as she did so.

"You'll see for yourself," Audrey said, focused on the edge of the parking lot. "He's right there."

Whitney turned to see Jimmy practically sprinting towards them, his face lit up with an ear-reaching smile. He was dressed casually, in jeans and a fitted T-shirt, and he caught up with them in a few long-legged hops before swallowing Whitney in his hug.

"Girl, I can't believe that you're performing," he said. "You're going to be so awesome. You're going to be a star!"

"Calm down," Whitney said with a laugh. "You haven't even seen me play."

"I have such a good feeling about this. When Audrey told me that you were going to do a set, I had, like, a vision or something." He finally released her, still jovial. "Oh, and your energy is so right on, too. Trust me, you gorgeous thing, you're going to be amazing."

"I just want to have fun tonight. Good music, great barbecue—that's heaven, my friend." She patted his back. "Come on. Let's go in."

He carried her guitar for her, chatting happily with Audrey as they entered the club. Hercules trailed behind them, and Whitney behind her, and they made their way through the main area, the inside of the house as dim as the dusky evening outdoors. Scattered about the wide-planked wooden floors were less than a dozen tables, where college students and native Austinites were gnawing on pork ribs, and a bar took up an entire wall, complete with a neon margarita sign. Whitney led her friends outside to the patio, where a large stage faced long rows of picnic tables. Some fifty people were sprawled throughout, family-style, and the vibe of the place was less of a performance hall than that of a friend's backyard party. She spotted Chris Philips, Tate's cousin, and he approached her, beer in hand.

"Hey, darlin', it's good to see you," he said, wrapping a sausage-like arm around her shoulders. His beer-hard gut pressed against her side, and as tall as he was, she felt as though she were embracing the Michelin Man.

"Hey, thanks for squeezing me in."

"I should be thanking you. The band that was supposed to play tonight canceled, and until you called, I thought we'd have to torture everyone with our music." He leaned in. "Honestly, everyone's glad that you're playing instead of the band. They're terrible. Nothing short of screeching baboons."

"You're too kind."

"I'm too honest. Baby girl, I don't know why you won't put out a demo tape already."

"That's a long conversation." She eased out of his grip and motioned to her friends. "Chris, these are my friends. We're up here for the weekend."

"Nice to meet y'all," he said, raising his beer to them. "The bar's inside if you want anything to drink." He patted Whitney's back. "I've got to take care of a few things. Make yourself at home."

"Thanks." She watched him retreat into the building. Audrey and

Jimmy found space at a table in the middle of the backyard and waved Whitney over, and given their varying outfits of jeans, shorts, espadrilles and flip-flops, they fit in with the rest of the casual twenty- and thirty-somethings that patronized Mason's. Hercules took a phone call in the corner of the patio, and Whitney sat down next to her friends, feeling at ease in the relaxed environment.

"So, how do you know that guy?" Jimmy asked.

"He's a friend's cousin. I've known him for"—she considered—"I guess almost five years now. His whole family's great. They're all musicians, too."

"Like the Partridge Family," he said, brightening.

"Nothing like them, actually," Whitney said with a chuckle.

"What time do you go on?" Audrey asked.

"Nine." She rested her back against the edge of the wooden table and placed her elbows on its surface. "I'll probably perform for half an hour. Chris's fifty million family members usually take up the rest of the night." She shook her head. "I don't know why they even bother with guest acts. I think they'd prefer just to have the whole place to themselves."

"Well, you're going to be marvelous," Jimmy said, practically exploding with pride. "No, you *are* marvelous!"

"I hope you still think so after I'm done." She glanced at her watch and then stood up. "I'm going to set up. You sure you don't want anything to drink?"

"I don't think I can handle it," Audrey said with a grimace. "I'm still hungover from last night." She peered at Whitney. "You're okay?"

"Amazingly, yeah."

Audrey shook her head and turned to Jimmy. "I don't know how many bottles of wine we went through. I feel sick now, and spending all day in the sun didn't help."

"Why don't y'all order some food?" Whitney said. "This place has some fantastic barbecue."

"Ooh, I haven't had good barbecue in ages," Jimmy said, gazing around. "Where's our waitress?"

"There are no waiters," Whitney said. "You have to order from the bar."

"Okay." He stood up. "I might have to sneak some back to my grandparents. My mother won't let them eat meat or salt or anything spicy because she's afraid that tasty food's going to ruin their health. But, my God, they're in their *nineties*. I think she can stop worrying about what they eat."

Hercules walked to them and then plopped down on the bench.

"I'm *starving*," she said. "Where's our waiter?"

"I'll hook us up," Jimmy said before trotting inside.

"I'll see you in a bit," Whitney said. "Y'all, don't make fun of me, even if I suck."

"I would never," Audrey said.

"You're not going to suck," Hercules said at the same time.

Whitney smiled, grateful for the vote of confidence. She walked to the stage with her guitar case, and for the next few minutes, she tested the microphone, pulled her hair into a ponytail, took a sip of water from the bottle Chris had set aside for her and tuned her guitar. She settled on the wooden stool from where she would perform six of her songs and gazed into the audience, her previous nerves gone now. She had never been an anxious performer, even if she had to concentrate on keeping her food down for hours beforehand, and the happy audience did much to relax her. Familiar faces, most of them belonging to Chris's family, smiled at her reassuringly in between bites of smoked sausage and brisket. Votive candles lined the rustic tables, giving the backyard a romantic glow, and the breezy March air carried the din of conversations and the melodious croaks of toads. Her friends were laughing over a story Jimmy was telling, complete with wild gesticulations, and when Hercules cracked a smile, Whitney felt ready to sing.

"Good evening, y'all," she said into the microphone. "I want to thank my good friend Chris Philips for letting me sing tonight, and I thank all of you in advance for suffering through it." A twitter of laughter echoed through the night air, and several people shouted out their encouragements.

"Baby girl, let those pipes rip," Chris yelled before sticking his fingers into his mouth for a sharp whistle.

Her fingers moved over the strings, plucking chords—A, F-sharp minor, A—and she began to sing.

"Whoever said that you were easy," she cooed into the microphone, "didn't know you like I do—you told me that you wouldn't love me—I couldn't believe that it was true." She heard her voice resonate against the back of the stage, appreciated its throaty reediness and, when she peered into the audience, knew that they did, as well. Chris was swaying to her melody, his elephantine body astonishingly pliant. Those who knew her music lip-synched along silently, their heads nodding with each beat of her song. A handful of people looked as if they had been arrested midmovement and were staring at her, and a covey of what appeared to be fraternity members were taking pictures of her with their cell phones. Jimmy was gazing at her like an adoring pet, and the Valedictorians gawked, their expressions in between awed and incredulous.

"Why couldn't you let me go?" she belted, her fingers moving furiously over the strings. "Why couldn't you let me go?" She felt so alive, experienced every second as if it were an eternity of the present. The vitality was in stark contrast with her days at Boerne & Connelly, where she had wished her days away—wished for the weekend, wished for a psychological respite that had never come, wished for a current assignment to end. She had spent so much time pining for an indeterminate future that she didn't realize that three years had passed, none of them worth remembering.

For the next half hour, she strummed and sang until she reached her final chord and rested her fingers on the body of her guitar. Chris whistled again, rousing the rest of the audience to cheer. Her friends made the most noise, their applause almost embarrassing, and when she walked down the stage and towards them, they clamored around her as if she had just won a Grammy.

"That was awesome," Audrey said, beaming.

"I told you that you were marvelous," Jimmy said.

"What the hell?" Hercules asked, her hands on her stomach. "Why didn't you tell us that you had crazy talent?"

"She just did," Jimmy said, his smile practically splitting his face.

Audrey nudged her chin in Whitney's direction, leaned in and whispered loudly, "I think you've got a groupie. He's been staring at you all night."

"Hey, darlin', let me buy you a drink," the blue-polo-shirt-wearing groupie said, and then shoved a beer into Whitney's hand.

"Thanks." She raised it to him in thanks before taking a sip. Audrey flashed her a mischievous look before joining the rest of the chatty group, leaving her with the generous stranger. He eyed her, inspecting her every feature, and after a moment, he grinned, the expression somehow highlighting the blueness of his eyes.

"I hope you don't mind me saying," he said, "but you are smokin' *hot*."

"I don't mind you saying," she said, still too pumped by adrenaline to mind his unfettered ogling. "Although it doesn't mean quite as much coming from someone who's clearly drunk."

"I'm not drunk." He considered. "Maybe I am just a little. But it's not affecting my vision." He smiled again. "Trust me, I don't have beer goggles. I'm a lot more honest when I've been drinking."

She sat on a bench next to Hercules, and her admirer took a seat too close to her. Hercules groaned, gripping her belly, and her face contorted as if she had just ingested poison.

"I'll be right back," she said. "I think I'm going to puke."

"Are you okay?" Whitney asked.

"Who the hell knows?"

"Do you want me to go with you?"

"No—I—" Her eyes widened with panic, and she jerked up and stumbled through the tables, her steps quickening as she bolted into the building.

"I'm Kyle, by the way," the polo wearer said, apparently unaffected by Hercules' quick departure.

"Whitney." She shook his extended hand. Close-up, he was even better-looking than he had been from a distance, what with his dark hair and tanned skin, and she took a long sip of her Shiner Bock, wondering why, in her dozens of trips to Mason's, she hadn't noticed him before.

"Whitney?" he repeated. "Like Whitney Houston?"

"Yeah. Before she thought crack was wack." She grinned, deciding not to explain that her father had named her after Eli Whitney, the cotton gin inventor, whom he, for whatever reason, adored.

Kyle whooped with laughter. "So, where you from?"

"Houston."

"Houston! I love that town. I've got a lot of family there."

"Is that where you're from?"

"Atlanta, actually. We're just here for spring break to see a few buddies. We don't have class until Tuesday."

"You're in college?" Whitney asked, dismayed that she was being hit on by a frat boy. Or even worse, a teenager.

"Law school," Kyle corrected. "We graduate in May."

"You keep saying *we*."

"Oh, my boys are here somewhere. I just peeled off to talk to you. I had to find out who you were."

Her cheeks warmed, and she glanced at Audrey and Jimmy, wondering if they were witnessing Kyle's unsolicited adulation. Unfortunately, they were at the edge of the next table, clearly deep in conversation, and they seemed oblivious to what was happening on her side of the bench.

"So, I recorded your performance on my phone," Kyle said, leaning into her so that his lips were almost touching her ear.

"How creepy," she said, not at all unnerved.

"That didn't come out right. I was trying to say that I thought you were unbelievably phenomenal, and I couldn't help myself. I had to get a video shot of you."

"Thanks." She felt herself flush, and she was glad that the place was dark enough to conceal her pleasure.

"I'm going to send it to my uncle. Actually, I'll do it right now." He fumbled with his phone. "He owns a record label here, and I'd bet money that he's going to fall absolutely in love with you." He looked up and grinned, showing off his perfect teeth. "I'm already halfway there."

She laughed. "Seriously, Kyle, is that the best you can do? I've heard better pickup lines from my girlfriends."

"Is it working?" he asked, looking amused.

"Not really." She laughed again, feeling lighthearted from their banter. As many smitten—or, more accurately, drunk—men had tried to feel her up with false promises of a recording contract, she knew better than to believe that Kyle had any real connections to the music industry. Still, she loved his attention, cheesy as it was. If anything, it was lifting her out of the depressed, and depressing, funk that had mired her for the last two weeks.

"So," he said, leaning closer to her, "my boys are throwing a party at the hotel. We've got a suite, and the view's amazing. It would be great if you came. Maybe I could—"

Just then, Whitney heard someone clear her throat, loud enough to sound as if she were choking. Kyle glanced up, recoiling immediately, and Whitney followed his horrified stare, flinching when she saw what had caught his attention.

Hercules loomed over them. Her frizzy hair, which had been pulled into a tight ponytail earlier, had unraveled, and the kinky do splayed around her head like a cartoon of someone being electrocuted. Whitney caught the paleness of Hercules' face, and the soft glow of the tabletop candles highlighted the pallor of her cheeks. Hovering over them, she looked like a monster awoken from a Mary Shelley dream.

"I feel like shit."

"What the—what happened to you?"

"I think I got food poisoning. Maybe it was from the garbage I ate last night." She held her stomach, and her face contorted. "Are you going onstage again, or can we go?"

"We can go." Whitney reached over Kyle to tap Audrey's arm. "Audrey, we need to leave." Kyle was still staring at Hercules, as if encountering an apparition from a nightmare.

"What in the world?" Audrey asked, her eyes wide. "You were fine a second ago."

"That's how food poisoning works," she said, her expression mottled with distress and crankiness. "It sneaks the fuck up on you. Either that or Lucas poisoned me. I wouldn't put it past Gary to have slipped me arsenic."

"Hercules," Jimmy began.

"Are you Hercules Huang?" Kyle interrupted. "From Dragonfly in Houston?" He looked awed again. "I *thought* you looked familiar. My folks are big fans of yours. They've seen you on *Good Morning, Texas* a bunch of times." He extended his hand. "I'm Kyle Brett, by the way."

"Good for you." Her face was turning an unnatural shade of green, and she rested her hands on the table, looking as if she was about to vomit on them. Her cheeks puffed out, and she shut her eyes before shooting Whitney and Audrey a beseeching look. "Can we *please* go now so that I can die in private?"

"Yeah, come on," Audrey said. "We'll take you home." She turned to Jimmy, and they spoke for another moment while Hercules glared at them, tapping her foot impatiently.

"Thank you," Whitney said to Kyle.

"For what?" he asked, surprised.

"For making me feel alive for the first time in weeks." She patted his arm and turned around just as he opened his mouth, perhaps about to ask for her number. Unwilling to turn their chance meeting into something more, she stood and joined her friends.

With Audrey on the other side, Whitney helped Hercules out of the club, down the parking lot and into Audrey's car. Hercules dry-heaved for the duration of the drive, and as soon as they entered the house, she ran to the guest bathroom, moving faster than Whitney had ever seen her, before vomiting into the toilet. Whitney hurried to the kitchen and brought back a large bottle of water, returning in time to catch the last of Hercules' retching. Audrey was standing beside her, patting her back, and after a few more miserable moments, Hercules slumped against the side of a cabinet with tears in her eyes.

"Oh my God, I'm going to die," she said, looking uncharacteristically vulnerable.

"Come on, H.," Whitney said. "Let's get you to bed."

They heaved Hercules up the spiral staircase and into an enormous guest bedroom, where two king-sized beds flanked opposite sides of a stone fireplace. With a few grunts and yanks, they helped her out of her soiled shirt and skintight jeans, and after another vomiting session in the adjoining bathroom, Hercules returned to the room. Scrubbed clean, and in a fresh T-shirt and a pair of sweatpants, she looked much younger than her twenty-nine years.

"Seriously, I think this is it," she said as she crawled into the bed on all fours. She plopped onto her back and brought the covers up to her chin. Audrey sat next to her, and Whitney placed the bottle of water on the nightstand.

"Here," she said. "Drink this. You're probably dehydrated."

"I'm really sorry." Hercules wiped her eyes roughly with her forearm. "I ruined your night."

"No, you didn't." Whitney stroked Hercules' frizzy hair.

"What are y'all going to do?" she asked. "Are you going to go back downtown?"

"I wasn't planning on it." Whitney turned to Audrey. "What's Jimmy doing?"

"Hanging out with his family. It's just the three of us tonight. I was thinking that we could hang out here."

"Y'all should go out," Hercules said. "I don't want you to catch my disease."

"For God's sake, H.," Whitney said, "you're not diseased."

"I'm just saying—if I die tonight, I want you two to know that I love you. You really were the best friends I've ever had."

"Lord, Hercules." Audrey stood up and pointed to the wall. "The intercom's right there, if you need us. Get some rest."

Hercules nodded. "Good night."

"Good night."

"Good night," Whitney said, leading Audrey out of the bedroom. She turned off the light and closed the door before heading down the stairs with Audrey, and halfway down the grand spiral, she turned to her. "What do you want to do?"

"Well," Audrey said with a grin, "we never did christen that Jacuzzi."

Whitney laughed. "Let's do it."

Thirteen

"I'd better lose weight at least," Hercules muttered as she tried to control her trembling. "This is bullshit." She had slept maybe two good hours before an oppressive nausea had woken her up. After a rapid succession of violent hurls, she had decided to stay in the bathroom, and too wasted to bring bedding into the space, she had wrapped herself in a robe, laid down a few towels and slept on the freezing marble floor. When Audrey and Whitney had come in from their jolly jaunt, she had no clue, but the last time she checked, they were both asleep, huddled together like children in the adjoining bed. Why they hadn't sprawled out in one of the six other bedrooms was beyond her, and just as she wondered if they had stayed close to her side out of concern, she felt bile climb her throat. In a moment, she was over the porcelain bowl again, retching with a stomach-cramping force.

"Hercules?" Audrey called. "Are you okay?"

"No, I'm not okay," she said, sure that Audrey couldn't hear her hoarse, muffled voice. She dragged herself off her knees and hobbled into the room. "What are you doing up?"

"I can't sleep. My ankle's killing me."

"From what?"

"I sprained it last night when I slipped on the floor," she said, screwing up her face. "I haven't done that since the eighth grade."

Whitney stirred, and a second later, her eyes opened. She reached for her neck, winced and then looked at Hercules.

"How are you feeling?"

"Worse than last night," Hercules said, a lurching sensation causing her to salivate as she spoke.

"She's still puking," Audrey explained.

"Did you drink some water?"

"Yeah, and I threw it back up. At this point, I can barely keep air down." She noticed Whitney cringing again. "Are you okay?"

"I must've slept funny," she said, grasping her neck. "It hurts to move my head."

"This is sad," Audrey said with a laugh. "I've twisted my ankle, you've cricked your neck, and Hercules is sick to her stomach. I didn't think we'd be spending our trip laid up."

"That's what happens when you get old," Hercules said miserably, letting her body fall against the doorframe.

"We're not old."

"When your digestive system shuts down for no reason at all, you're old." She held her belly and grimaced. "God, my stomach has *never* felt so bad, *ever*, and I've eaten a lot of shit in my life. I've eaten worse than shit and have been fine."

"Do you think it might have been something that we ate yesterday?" Whitney asked.

"No. Y'all are both okay." She climbed onto the empty bed, fluffed a feather pillow and eased her head onto it. After having survived eleven bouts of violent vomiting and having slept less than six hours during the entire weekend, she was physically demolished. Her throat was raw and probably bleeding, her legs shook when she stood, and the room was so cold that her bones ached. Her eyes scratched under each blink, and every touch felt like she was being electrocuted. Her body was caving in on the outside, and she felt the weight of her world, compounded by an inexplicable frustration, bloat her on the inside.

"Did you eat anything when you went out with Lucas?" Audrey asked.

Hercules groaned. "We went to a Mexican dive and ate Mexican dive food. Nachos. Tacos. Nothing that would do this to my stomach." Another wave of nausea washed over her, and she choked down the acidic mucus that crept up her throat.

"Maybe it's not the food," Audrey said. "Maybe you're overstressed."

"You probably made yourself sick from working to death," Whitney said. "Sometimes I worry about you, Hercules. You work all the time.

Even people at the firm don't work twenty hours a day every day. It's not healthy."

"I have to," Hercules said, burrowing deeper under the covers. "I've got a lot going on."

"But you never give yourself a break. I doubt that you even sleep anymore. One person isn't meant to do everything that you do. Hell, *three* people aren't meant to do it."

"I know, but . . ." Hercules trailed, and tightened the comforter over her shoulders, as if it would smother the rush of panic that was beginning to overwhelm her. If Whitney had intended to chastise gently as a concerned friend, she had instead forced a spotlight on the enormity of Hercules' to-do list, on the unattainability of meeting everyone else's deadlines and expectations. As much as she had viewed her unending activities as nothing more than a lofty challenge, she now felt that everything in her life—her restaurants, her planning for new ones, her line of cookware, the ceaseless interviews and articles, her father—was suddenly impossible, and the longer she thought about them, the more upset she became. She propped herself upright, trying fecklessly to stave off the rising hysteria that clutched her, and blinked quickly, desperate to push back the tears that were demanding to be unleashed. She turned around so that the girls couldn't see her cry, something she hadn't allowed herself to do since she had emigrated to America, all the while cursing herself for succumbing to what she had to believe was a food-poisoning-induced nervous breakdown.

"Hercules?" Whitney asked. "Are you okay? What's wrong?"

She couldn't speak for the acidic lump that was blocking her throat, and she turned further, hoping to move out of their sight.

"Are you crying?" Audrey asked, the concern clear in her voice.

"Of course not," she managed to say. "I've just got a feather or something in my eye."

"Okay, that's the worst lie I've heard in a long time," Whitney said. Hercules heard her get out of bed, and in a moment, she found herself face-to-face with her. Close-up, she saw how worried Whitney was, and her anxious expression somehow exacerbated Hercules' rising inability to control her emotions. When Audrey sat down on the other side of her, as alarmed as Whitney, she lost it completely. Tears streamed faster than she could wipe them away.

"Jesus Christ," she said, horrified, "what the hell is wrong with me?" She held her palms to her eyes. "What is this?"

"What's going on?" Audrey asked, handing her a few tissues. "H., talk to us."

Hercules pressed the soft tissues against her face, immediately soaking them. "This is ridiculous. I don't cry. I *never* cry. My eyes must be broken. My entire body's revolting against me."

"Did something happen on Friday?" Whitney asked, reaching for the box of Kleenex on the nightstand.

"What do you mean?"

"Ever since your meeting with Lucas and Gary, you've been really tense, like something's been on your mind. Well, more than usual, anyway. And now, you're—" She stopped, looking unsure of herself.

Hercules sighed heavily. Through her blurred vision, she was able to make out how troubled they were, how distressed her uncharacteristic bawling had rendered them, and she stared at them for a minute, momentarily confused by what she was seeing. In the hazy dimness of the room, the outlines of their faces reminded Hercules of her mother, and the ephemeral quality of their profiles somehow aggrandized the vulnerability that had already left her feeling exposed. She shuddered as she sucked in a deep breath, and whether it was the result of a sleepless night, her devastated digestive tract, both or something else altogether, she felt as if she were in another world, a shrouded space that felt like a safe confessional. And as carefully as she had guarded her problems from her friends, had presented herself as one who always achieved her goals, she now felt a compulsion to unload her tribulations, as if holding them in for another second might crush her completely.

"They dropped me," she finally said. "Seven years, Lucas and I had been dreaming about opening a restaurant together, and after talking about concepts, space, price points, everything, he went off with Gary and broke ground on the place we'd planned."

"They stole your idea?" Audrey asked, frowning.

"Stole it and made it real," she said quietly. "They'd already hired all the chefs. Put together the menu. I don't even know why Lucas asked me to meet with them. The whole thing was a freakin' disaster."

"I'm sorry," Whitney said. "I can understand why you're so upset."

"I'm not upset about it." She sighed again and dabbed the last of her tears with her tattered tissues. "Well, I am, but not really. Honestly, I expected it. It's why I'd already lined up other contacts here. That's business, shitty as it is. People will railroad you, backstab. It happens all the time."

"If you're not upset about that, then why—?" Audrey began.

"Because it's another disappointment that I can add to my list of disappointments," she blurted. "Because it reminds me so much of my dad the way that they just took and took and took and then left me with nothing in the end."

"Your dad?" Audrey asked, looking bewildered.

"I've tried to understand that he's old," she said before she could stop herself, "and that he doesn't want to learn to speak English, even though he's been here for twenty-five years. I've tried to accept that he's never going to assimilate. Fine. But if he's so stubborn about being who he is, why can't he accept me for the way I am? Why can't he even try to have my back? I've done everything that I could to make him happy, and he still hates me."

"Your father doesn't hate you," Whitney said, looking even more perturbed.

"The way he talks to me, I'm pretty sure that he does."

"No father hates his child. I don't think it's possible."

"I know that I shouldn't let him get to me, but I can't help it." She sighed again, as if she had forgotten how to breathe otherwise. "He affects everything that I do. It's like I have this cloud over me all the time, and it ruins everything good in my life. I don't know how to shake that feeling. It's making me crazy." She wiped her face roughly. "It's making me freakin' *cry*."

"Maybe y'all are too close," Audrey said. "You go over to his apartment all the time. You're constantly running after him. Maybe a little distance would do you some good."

She shook her head. "I can't do that, Auds. There's no one else to take care of him." She crumpled the tissues in her hand and dabbed her eyes. "I don't understand. We used to have a decent relationship. When my mom died, he changed completely. It's like he's a totally different person now. The Criticizer is what he is. *Be Chinese. Do something other than be a chef. Get married and have kids,* for Christ's sake. Does he think that I don't want that? Does he not know that I'd give my right arm to have someone who adores me the way Victor loves you"—she turned to Whitney—"or the way Scott does you?"

"I had no idea that you were even interested in marriage," Whitney said, squirming uncomfortably. "I don't think I've ever heard you talk about it."

"You never even talk about guys," Audrey said.

"I don't talk about them because I haven't been on a date in forever," Hercules said. "I haven't had the time to meet them, and it's not like they're stopping me on the street to ask me out." She let out a rumbling groan. "Trust me, I know how pathetic that sounds."

"Why haven't you ever told us about this before?" Whitney asked. "You shouldn't have to keep everything bottled up."

"Because"—she considered the question, unsure how to articulate her response—"I didn't think you'd understand. Y'all have perfect families. You have great relationships with your parents. They actually listen to what you say, and they're open to what you want. They support you. How could you even relate to the mess that my father and I have?"

"Because I can," Whitney said, averting her gaze. "I do understand what it's like not to have parents who support what you really want."

"How?"

She fidgeted, as if she suddenly couldn't find a comfortable position on the bed. "What you saw last night—that's what I want to do full-time." Hercules felt herself frown. "Maybe it sounds stupid, but there it is. That's my life's worth, H., and the way you're looking at me now is exactly the way my parents will look at me, except they'd follow that look up with a disownment, and I'm not even exaggerating. Maybe I shouldn't care so much, but I do."

Hercules was speechless. She had seen for herself how talented

Whitney was, but she would never have dreamed that she would treat her musical ability as anything more than a hobby, a pastime to impress her family and friends. She was a Harvard grad, for God's sake. A lawyer at an international firm. Hercules couldn't imagine giving up the prestige of her degrees and job for a life of certain destitution. And yet—

"My family's the farthest thing from perfect," Audrey said suddenly. "And my mom's convinced that Victor and I are going to have as messed up of a marriage as they do. You're not the only one who's got issues at home."

Hercules stared at them. "Why didn't y'all ever say anything before?"

"For the same reasons you never shared what was going on with you," Whitney said. "I didn't think you'd understand, and a huge part of me was terrified that you'd judge or criticize. I already get enough of that at home. And I got a huge dose of it from Scott, who, by the way, I'm no longer seeing."

"What?" Hercules felt her eyes widen. "Why not?"

"Because he couldn't understand what I wanted to do, and I couldn't support him the way he needed to be supported." She shrugged. "We couldn't make it work, so we had to go our separate ways."

"Well, I can't do that with my father," Hercules said. "Sometimes I wish I could, but I can't."

"So what are you going to do?"

"What *can* I do? I have to move him in with me," she said, unhappy with the inevitability.

"You don't *have* to," Audrey said. "There has to be some alternative."

"I've thought about it every which way," she said, grateful for her attempt to appease. "He'd never forgive me if I stuck him in a nursing home or if I found a home-health-care provider for him, and this living-apart shit's not working. I can't go to his apartment ten times a week to make sure he's taking his meds, and I don't trust him to take care of himself anymore. Why do you think I've been so cranky the last few months?" She leaned her head against the headboard and groaned. "I don't even want to think about how much he's going to complain that I'm still single."

They were all quiet for a moment, perhaps pondering Hercules' predicament, or perhaps digesting the truth that, until now, they had never fully opened up to one another even though they had considered themselves to be best friends. The thought both saddened and encouraged Hercules, as if she could take comfort in their shared fear of rejection or their mutual desire to impress one another. Yet, the same fears and desires underscored their admiration for one another, highlighted the importance they placed on one another's opinions and judgments. She closed her eyes, mulling over her thoughts, when she realized that a whole half hour had passed without a desperate lurch to the bathroom, and when she opened them, she saw that Whitney was looking at her with a bemused expression.

"You know," she said, "I'm not sure how I can help you with your father, other than to be the proverbial supportive shoulder for you, but maybe I can do something in the romance department. Tell me what you're looking for in a man, and I'll see what I can do."

"We're not in high school," she said, even as she felt a strange rush of excitement. "I can't just give you a list and then have you set me up with someone."

"Why not? Indulge me."

Hercules peered at her, feeling inordinately foolish, and Whitney stared back at her expectantly. *What the hell,* she thought.

"Well, it would be great if he were tall, dark and handsome."

"Of course."

"I'm just kidding. I don't care what he looks like so long as he's kind and funny."

"That's it?" Whitney asked, looking as though she was taking mental notes. "Because if I find you kind and funny, and then he turns out to be dumb as rocks, you can't complain."

"What are you, a genie?" She considered. "Yeah, he's got to be smart. And different. I don't think I could date someone in the food industry."

"Smart, kind and funny. No chefs. Got it." Whitney smiled widely, looking almost impish.

Audrey stood up and stretched. "What time is it?"

"Seven in the morning."

Audrey climbed back into bed. "Oh, good. We've got a lot of time. I was thinking that we'd leave around three or four this afternoon."

For the next two hours, they lay curled up and chatted about Audrey's relationships with Victor and her mother, Whitney's six-year obsession with music, and Hercules' frustrations over her father. Until today, they had never spoken so frankly about what they wanted to do, or what really bothered them, and having unloaded her troubles onto her friends, Hercules couldn't believe that the subjects hadn't arisen earlier. Kept inside, her relationship with her father had taken on a grandiosity that Audrey and Whitney apparently didn't perceive, and now that it was in the open, her troubles somehow seemed slighter. As they packed slowly, all while limping and craning and vomiting, she wished that they had taken this trip a long time ago.

Fourteen

$\mathcal{W}$hitney rolled over and squinted at her clock. It was six fifteen, and in the darkness of her room, she had no idea if she had slept for twelve hours or twenty-four. After spending their last day in Austin on the boat and in the water, the girls had driven back to Houston, and Audrey had dropped Whitney off at her apartment last night, where she had wordlessly stumbled to her bedroom and fallen onto her bed. Sleep came before her head had even hit the pillow. She was in the same Duke blue sweatshirt that she had traveled in, and her hair was streaked with lake residue, the specific content of which she didn't want to imagine. Unable to stand her own filth, she pushed herself off the bed, padded to the bathroom and turned on the shower. As she lathered her hair, she could hear her brother in the kitchen, grinding coffee beans noisily the way he did every Monday morning. Poor NASA cog, she thought. Thank God she didn't have a job to mess with. As soon as she was clean, she planned on popping in a pair of earplugs, slipping an eye mask over her face and returning to bed.

She tossed a towel over her hair and walked around the bedroom. Pictures of her and Scott still decorated her dresser, and memories of happier days drifted through her mind. She turned the frames around, unwilling to remove them altogether, even though there was no hope that they'd reconcile. Their breakup was for the best, she thought with a heavy sigh. The phone's sharp trills shook her from her thoughts, and she rubbed her scalp vigorously with the towel to drown out the noise.

"Whitney!" Robert yelled. "It's for you."

"Who is it?" she called, livid that telemarketers were calling at the crack of dawn.

"Someone named Will Strong," he said through her closed door. "He says he's from Boerne and Connelly."

She froze. Will was calling? Why? It had been more than two weeks since she had been gracelessly fired, and his call felt unnatural and unnervingly invasive. She threw the towel onto the bed and pulled her robe tighter around her body. With her long hair lank and sopping about her shoulders, she cracked the door open and grabbed the receiver from her brother. This had better be about a severance package, she thought, her boldness belied by the butterflies in her stomach. And he'd better apologize for calling so early.

"Hi, Will," she said as cheerfully as she could. *What the fuck do you want?* she wanted to add.

"Whitney, thank God you're awake." His voice grated harshly through the line. "Are you coming in this morning? We haven't seen you in a while, and we were beginning to worry."

A stabbing pain shot between her eyes, a warning blast of an impending migraine. Was Will calling to make fun of her? Did he think this was funny?

"Will," she said slowly, "you *fired* me, remember? I assumed that meant that I wouldn't be showing up to the office anymore, especially since security now has my ID." She couldn't remember the last time she was so angry, and it was all she could do not to hang up and hurl the phone out the window.

"What?" he gasped. She imagined that he was reeling at her words. "I didn't *fire* you. I was just hacked off about the document review."

"Yes, you did," she said evenly. "You told me, if I recall correctly, to pack my shit, and that I was no longer, and that I would never be, an employee at Boerne and Connelly." She walked into her bathroom, still gripping the receiver. The heat of her fury burned through her scalp, and she was astonished to find that the crown of her head was almost dry.

"Oh, *that*." He chuckled as though she had fallen victim to a prank. "No, I was just mad. *Of course* I didn't fire you. How could I? You're my prized pig." A pause hung on the line for a moment. "Well, not *pig*, you know. Anyway, I'm trying to say that you're a valuable employee."

Whitney stood still and wondered if her ex-boss was on drugs.

"If I'm still employed, then why has no one contacted me in the last two weeks?"

Will coughed, and miles away, she thought she detected uncharacteristic discomfort.

"I'm going to be honest with you," he finally said, his voice controlled and deep. "I need your assistance in the same matter that you were working on when you left. James is no longer with the firm, and you're the only one who knows those documents well. Hell, you're the only one who's even talked to the witnesses. I'm asking you if you would come back."

"I don't think so." Her having been fired, humiliating as it might have been, had released her from his tyranny, and it had freed her to follow her convictions. It was simply too late now to throw pathetic compliments her way in the hopes of luring her back to the firm's cage.

"What?" Will exploded, apparently convinced that his charm would have won her over. "Why not? Are you working somewhere else?"

"No."

"For God's sake, Lee, I need you to help me on this. What do you want? A raise? Done! A bigger office? You can have James's."

"Is there really no one else that can take my place?" She shifted uncomfortably in her bathrobe. Why did he want her to return so badly? Third-year associates were as replaceable as batteries, and for every one of her, there were legions of unhappy replacements willing to whore themselves out for the obscenely large salary.

"We would like to have you back. That's all."

"If you want me to return, I'd like to be paid for the lost time," she said, the words escaping before she had even had a chance to think. Something in his voice had caused her to pity him, and she wondered if he had already tested a host of other associates. They had probably fled after a day, citing his temperament as proof of a hostile working environment.

"Of course. Lost time," he quickly assured her.

"Since you mentioned a raise, I'd like to be paid thirty thousand dollars more this fiscal year. I work an inordinate number of hours, and I don't think my current salary reflects my efforts."

"Done."

His quick response surprised her, and her confidence swelled. They both knew that she had him by his nether region, and given the amount of grief he had caused over the years, she felt that she was simply asking for past remuneration.

"And, because I've been with the firm for a while, I think it's only fair that I get an extra two weeks of vacation."

"How much did you have before?" he asked.

"Two weeks."

"Fine. You'll have a month."

"And I have to leave by seven on the first Friday of each month."

"Didn't you always?"

"No."

"Okay. Okay. You've got it. So, you'll come back?" His words regained some of the confident swagger that had dropped off a moment ago.

"Yes, I'll come back." She felt strangely out of control, as if a part of her brain had short-circuited and was operating without consulting the rest of her gray matter. It was foolish to return to the place that had made her so miserable, yet she couldn't help but think that she was being offered a second chance with the firm for a reason, even if she had no earthly idea what that reason could be.

"I'll see you at eight," Will said.

"*Today?*"

"Yes, *to-day*. My God, how long of a vacation did you need? That'll count against your four weeks, by the way. See you soon." He hung up, leaving Whitney speechless. She clicked off the phone, and as she shuffled into the kitchen in a daze, she wondered what in the world she had just done.

"Whitney? How are you?" Amber Tenney asked gingerly. Her pale blue eyes darted around Whitney's face, as though she were inspecting the prodigal employee for traces of disease.

"I'm fine," she answered, suddenly self-conscious. She was in Amber's office to pick up her security badge and her building identification. When she had first been employed with the firm, Amber had simply grunted and flung the two cards at her. She had more important things on her mind, like the solitaire game on her monitor and the slice of pecan pie on her desk. Now the hefty administrative director—which was a fancy title for the keeper of the ID cards—was peering at her with the interest of a celebrity stalker.

"Here's your ID badge and your security card," she said, her voice so low that Whitney could barely hear her. She didn't understand why the admin was handling her like a combustible bomb. "You'll need to swipe these through the—"

"Amber, I've been here for three years," she interrupted. "I don't need a primer on card swipes."

"Oh! I know, it's just . . ." She looked away, obviously contemplating how to query her. She fidgeted in her seat, and Whitney wondered if the administrative director's eight-hour shifts of electronic solitaire had caused her to go mad.

"I'll see you later," Whitney said, about to stand.

"You know, Will didn't mean to fire you," Amber said suddenly.

"Excuse me?"

"He told me that he only wanted to scare you and make you *think* that you got fired. But he was going to chase you down and tell you that you had another chance. I mean, you didn't have any strikes with him. Whatever you did to make Will so upset would've been your first, and he always gives his lawyers three chances."

Whitney stared at her. She didn't know why she was explaining Will's thought process, and she was slightly disturbed that the administrative employee, whose sole function was to pass out building badges, knew the details of her employment history.

"Anyway, he got on a phone call and couldn't get off, and by the time he tried to reach you, you had already left the building."

"You make it sound like I left voluntarily," Whitney said, trying to keep the aggravation out of her voice.

If possible, Amber looked even more uncomfortable.

"Well, I just wanted to let you know that you were never meant to be fired."

"Why are you telling me this?"

"Why? I—uh—we didn't want you to think that you were being treated unfairly for being—uh—well, anyway, I heard that you refused to go to the, um, diversity dinner, or wherever it was that Will wanted you to go to."

A shock of electricity shot through Whitney's spine.

"*Excuse me?* Who told you that I refused? I told Will on the spot that I'd go."

"You did? Well—I just heard . . ."

"This is insane. I don't care what you heard. I *never* said no, and I didn't do anything wrong." She bit her lip, unwilling to push the matter further. She wanted to blurt out that James Carothers had brought this calamity on her, and that he should have been the focus of the staff's gossip. She couldn't believe that after two weeks, people were still talking about her, and she toyed with the idea of throwing the ID cards back at her and leaving. Deciding instead to calm down, she breathed deeply and turned to walk out of the office. Before she was out the door, Amber called after her.

"Whitney? You're not going to sue the firm, are you?"

She turned around slowly, convinced that she was mired in a terrible dream.

"Why in the world would you think that?"

"No reason." Amber blushed, and her round face resembled a tomato. "It's just—you know how it is here. People talk nonsense all the time, and one of the things I'd heard was that you were going to sue for discrimination." She dropped her voice to a whisper and looked around as though she were gossiping about someone else. "You know, because you were fired, and because you're a—minority."

Whitney gawked at her as though she had just announced that she was Jesus Christ. Was that what people thought? Was that why Will had rehired her? Because the firm was afraid that she might sue it otherwise? The notion was ludicrous.

"I never thought about suing," she said sharply. She stomped out of Amber's office and continued to fume all the way down the hall. That she would extort the firm with a frivolous suit simply because the opportunity had ostensibly presented itself offended her. She wondered if the elitist River Oaks Country Club partners assumed that she carried herself with a chip on her shoulder and was on the constant lookout for a way to gouge them. It occurred to her that despite what she believed to be an astute perceptiveness, she had never picked up on the fact that people regarded her as an "other." Until today, she hadn't thought they could have, and in the recesses of her mind, she still didn't believe that anyone, save a few gossipy admins, did.

"So, how's it going?" Robert asked. He laid his tray on the patio table and transferred his plate, glass of iced tea and brownie to the surface, all while trying to keep the collar of his Windbreaker from flapping into his face in the breeze. Whitney placed her salad on the tiled top and handed her tray to him.

"About as well as I could expect, I guess," she said, and then spread her napkin over her lap. "Thanks for taking me to lunch. I know you had to drive from BFE to get here."

"No problem," he said with a charitable smile. "We just finished a project, so I don't have a whole lot going on this week."

"I really could use a break from my boss. It's only been a few hours, but I'm starting to remember what it's like to be Will's donkey. When I left HR, I had fourteen e-mails waiting for me." She took in a deep breath, and the air, unusually crisp for Houston's normally muggy March, filled her lungs.

"I guess he doesn't waste time," he said, looking around at the crepe myrtle and magnolia trees that lined the restaurant's deck. "I've never been here. Is the food good?"

"I like it." She watched as her brother took apart his sandwich and inspected each layer of it. It was an obnoxious habit, another notch on the stereotypical Enginerd belt, but he had a weaker digestive system than those of most octogenarians. When he was sure that he could eat the turkey, avocado, bacon and sprouts without suffering system failure, he reassembled his lunch and took a bite.

"You're right," he said through a full mouth. "This is delicious."

"I'm glad you like it." His meticulous handling of food reminded her of Hercules, and of her desire to land a man, and Whitney toyed with the idea of setting her up with Robert. After all, they were both single, smart and desperate to marry. She was thinking of how to broach the subject when he spoke.

"Mom and Dad are really worried about you, you know."

"They are? Why?"

"Because you got fired from your firm a couple of weeks ago. They think something's going on that they don't know about. Like drugs or alcohol or something."

"You're joking, right?" she asked slowly, dismayed by his disloyal tattling and their unreasonable reaction.

"No. They've been bugging me about it." He shook his head. "They keep asking if we need to stage an intervention."

"Why can't they just ask me what's wrong?" She laid down her fork and stared at him. "We don't need you to serve as an intermediary."

"Because they don't think that you'd be straight with them," he said as he poked at his fruit salad. "You know how they are."

She felt her face burn in the cool air, and his matter-of-factness did nothing to allay her irritation.

"I swear to God, Robert, why would you do something so stupid as to tell them that I was fired? How did you *expect* them to react?" She felt her throat tighten, and she could hear her voice squeak a full octave higher. "Besides, it's none of your business, and it's not your place to tell them that I got fired. How many times do we have to go through this? I can't *stand* that you're such a blabbermouth."

He regarded her in full Big Brother mode, but she could tell that he was also slightly worried that he had done wrong by her.

"They asked, Whitney. What was I supposed to say?"

"They asked specifically if I was fired?"

He frowned and busied himself with his tea. "Well, no . . ."

"Did you tell them that I was rehired? Or do they think that I'm lying in a ditch somewhere with a needle hanging out of my arm?"

"Of *course* I told them that you were rehired," he said, rolling his eyes. "I explained that it was all a big misunderstanding. You know how melodramatic Mom gets about everything, and how she lives through you. You'd think *she* had been fired, the way she's been acting. Give it a couple of days. Things will be back to normal, and they'll only be worried about you in a general sense."

She glared at him while he munched noisily on his salt and vinegar chips. He looked up casually and then blanched.

"Why are you looking at me like that?"

"I just want to make sure that we get something straight," she said as calmly as she could. "I know you mean well, but I need you to promise that from now on, you won't tell Mom and Dad everything that happens to me. They worry enough as it is, and the way they react to every small bit of news really stresses me out. If you can't swear that our confidences will remain in confidence, I won't have any choice but to keep you out of the loop."

He gawked at her, his fair skin taking on a hue of strawberry. "I can't believe you'd talk to your older brother that way."

"Promise me."

He scowled at her and then nodded. They both knew that for a thirty-two-year-old double-Ph.D. NASA engineer, he was a terrible gossip, worse than any secretary at Boerne & Connelly. They had discussed the problem at least three times before, and even though she never planned on making good on her threat to strand him, she couldn't afford to have him blabbing about every aspect of her life to her parents. Thank God he had no clue what she did in her free time.

They ate silently for a few minutes, and Whitney watched a table of women in tracksuits pick at their salads. They didn't seem at all hurried, and she wondered what they did all day. She checked her watch and realized that she had to mush.

"So," Robert said suddenly, "now that you're back at the firm, do you think you'll run into that IT girl you were talking about? Karen Lowell, I think her name is. Is she still single?"

"You're not concerned that she's not Korean?"

"Not really. I know Mom and Dad want us to marry Koreans, but frankly, I don't see why. If they're worried about fundamental under-standings, well, I'd probably understand a fellow engineer or scientist over a Korean girl who reads *Us Weekly* all day. And I'd choose a white, black, Hispanic, whatever *ambitious* girl over a vapid Korean in a heart-beat." He sipped his water and tapped her arm. "So, you'll check out Karen?"

"I guess." She took a bite of her salad and considered his options. In comparison with the beautiful, albeit socially inept, IT tech, Hercules seemed like a frightening alternative. Still, she had high hopes for them, and the more she considered them as a couple, the better matched they seemed. "Hey, I was thinking of setting you up with another friend of mine. I think you'd like her even better than Karen."

"Who?"

"Before I tell you, can I get a firm commitment that you'll say yes?"

"Why would I do that? I have no idea who you're talking about."

"I wouldn't set you up with a troll, Robert. She's a nice person. Smart, interesting, successful, an overall great package."

"Then why's she single?" He looked at her skeptically.

"Why are *you* single?"

He narrowed his eyes, still wary. "She's a good person?"

"Do you think I'd try to set you up with a *bad* person?" She smiled as brightly as she could, hoping to encourage, and he crossed his arms and sighed.

"Fine, you've got my commitment. What do I have to lose, right?"

"Exactly. Let me square things away with her. I'll let you know re-ally soon who it is."

"*What?*" His brows shot up. "You won't even tell me who the girl is?"

"Not until I get a yes from her." She patted his arm, and he looked as if he were about to strike her. "Don't worry. I'll tell you really soon."

He pursed his lips, still clearly unhappy. "Fine."

She glanced at her watch again and groaned.

"I have to be back in ten minutes. God, today's been so bizarre. Everyone's saying that Will rehired me because he's afraid of a racial-discrimination lawsuit. Isn't that just beyond ridiculous?"

"I don't know that I'd say it's ridiculous," he said, stabbing a red grape with his fork. "I think it's kind of surprising, though."

"Why?"

"Because you never see Asians suing their employers. At least, that's been my perception. I figure that most people think of Asians as nonthreats, even if they *have* been wronged and have legal recourse. Maybe we worry too much about fitting in to sabotage our careers with lawsuits." He shrugged. "I wouldn't think that employers worry much about Asian employees."

"Maybe." Whitney considered. "Except for me, apparently. Do they not think of me as being the typical Asian? Am I the loudmouthed exception?"

"I don't know. Maybe they've gotten so used to you that they don't think of you in terms of color."

"They do when they need something." She let out a rumbling sigh. "I hope the firm doesn't see me only in shades of liability. I can't think of anything more insulting, actually."

"You work at a law firm, Whitney. I'm sure that's exactly how they see you." He wiped his mouth and smirked. "So, they're worried you're going to sue, huh? Are you going to take advantage of it?"

"Why would I do that?" She thought about her earlier demands of a pay raise and additional vacation time, and she worried that she *had* taken advantage of the situation. "I don't want everyone to hate me."

"There you go." He looked smug, as if he had made his point. "*That's* why you don't see Asian plaintiffs. They're too worried that people won't approve."

"It has nothing to do with that," she said, knowing full well that he was right, at least with respect to her. She was nothing if not an approval seeker, or, more accurately, a disapproval shunner. "I don't have a meritorious case, Robert. There's no blame to be assigned, other than to a nut of a partner who has problems following through with his kooked-up plans. Besides, not all Asians worry about approval. Can you imagine Hercules in my situation? She'd probably be yelling in the hallways about how she was wronged."

"God," he said, rolling his eyes. "*That* would be a sight to see. Then again, I can't imagine a company actually hiring her."

His reaction troubled her, and she hoped that he didn't find her friend unappealing.

"Why not?"

"Because I think there's some value in being perceived as submissive, although I believe the operative word is *team player*." He pushed his plate away. "Let me give you some advice as someone who's been working for ten years. Don't take it personally if they start a sensitivity training program, or if everything's about cultural awareness and diversity for the next few weeks. That's just how companies respond."

"I guess it's a good thing, but that kind of corporate response seems so disingenuous." She couldn't imagine Will bothering with any kind of sensitivity training. He'd likely explode in a vitriolic rage five minutes into the program. She glanced at her watch.

"Do you want me to wait for you?" she asked. "I can probably sit for another few minutes."

"No, you go. I brought some work with me."

"Okay." She stood up and kissed his cheek before bolting to the parking lot. She wasn't looking forward to an afternoon of hushed whispers and darting eyes, and she could only imagine the rumors that were swirling in the hallways. She hoped that Will wasn't likewise discussing the subject of a "problem employee" with the executive board. If he was, she would pack her bags for good.

Whitney was poring through documents when she heard the tile-splitting rings. God, she thought, Will was coming to see her. It would be his first visit since her return, and she was suddenly nervous at how he might approach her.

"Lee," he shouted even before he got to her door.

"Hi, Will."

"We've got depositions rolling in the next few weeks, and I'll be relying heavily on the documents we got from plaintiff's counsel. There are over a hundred boxes in Conference Room A, so you'd better get your ass over there."

"Okay."

"Also, we decided that we're not going to worry about the Minority Business Association dinner. The executive committee thought the minimum amount of donation was too much, so we're scrapping the whole thing." He stared at her, and she didn't get the impression that he was waiting for a response. In fact, judging from his concentration, he was likely trying to recall what else was on his bullet list of action items. His scowl disappeared, and he almost smiled at her. "Oh, welcome back."

"Tha—"

Before she could finish thanking him for his quasikind words, he bolted out of her office. His boots thundered against the marble floors, and she could hear his distinct shouting at passersby.

She leaned back and sighed. She didn't know what she had expected from him. Certainly not an apology. Will probably didn't even know what one sounded like. Perhaps she had hoped that he'd assure her that she hadn't been hired to fulfill a diversity quotient, or rehired to stave off an imaginary lawsuit. It would have been nice to know that he intended to follow through with his plans to revamp the firm's image, and she chided herself for feeling disappointed by his thoughtless, and apparently forgotten, strategy to attract minorities. She was disheartened by his inability to carry a promise to fruition, and after picking up a notepad and a pen, she walked down the hallway, wondering why in the world she had agreed to return.

Fifteen

"Lord, grant me the serenity to accept the things I cannot change, the courage to change the things I can and the wisdom to know the difference," Hercules muttered under her breath. She wasn't paying attention to the words of the prayer, and the soothing meter of the verse wasn't calming her down. Today was moving day, and she was standing in Baba's ratty apartment, where she had announced two nights ago that he was to pack his belongings and move into her house. He had acquiesced without a fight, perhaps because he expected his only daughter to care for him, but more likely because he knew that resistance would have been futile. Now she was surveying his boxes and praying that she'd be able to keep her frustration under control.

"I said I want all of it," Baba said defiantly.

"You want to move all of this?" she asked, motioning to the expanse of the room. "You don't need it. Just get new stuff when you move in. Actually, you don't even need to do that. All the rooms are already furnished. You can just pick the one you like best."

"I want my furniture. I've had it for over thirty years."

She looked at the couch with disdain. The wretchedness of the mustard yellow piece was accentuated by a shit-colored zigzag, like Charlie Brown's shirt stretched too tightly across a sagging, support-less bench. A second couch in a burgundy paisley took up another wall, and with the chaotic amoeba-laden pattern across from the acid-trip Charlie Brown sofa, Hercules wanted to set them both on fire. There was no way that this dreadful furniture, if she could even call it that, was coming to her home, her gracious manor worthy of a spread in *Architectural Digest*, yet she knew that there was no stopping it, either.

Her cell phone rang, and she answered it, still glaring at Baba's furniture.

"Hercules Huang."

"Chef, it's Cecil," Cecil Johnson, one of her sous chefs, said. "I know this is really short notice, but my kid's got strep throat. I've got it, too, the way I'm feeling. I wouldn't ask for the night off, except that I'm probably contagious."

"Shit, that's terrible," Hercules said, barely paying attention. "Thank God Wednesdays are our slowest nights. Make sure that you come in tomorrow, though."

"I will. Thanks, Chef." She could hear a baby crying in the background, and its anguished wails sent chills down her spine. As soon as she shut her phone, George, one of the movers, approached.

"Ma'am, you want us to move everything?" He surveyed the room, his side to her, and she stared at him, glad that he couldn't see her unfettered ogling. Tall and muscular, he had the physique of one who moved TVs and refrigerators all day. His ebony skin glistened in the warm humidity of the apartment, and it occurred to her that he resembled a Nubian Mr. Clean. All her father saw was a black man in his home, and he shrank back, visibly distraught.

"He's not going to hurt me, is he?" He regarded George with such overt suspicion that Hercules pulled him to the side.

"For God's sake, stop it."

"He's going to steal my things." He clutched at a bag of clothes while eyeing the rest of his belongings, and to her horror, he began to shout at them. "You go! You go!"

"Baba!" she snapped, and then in Mandarin, so that George wouldn't understand, "No one in his right mind would steal this furniture. Cut it out."

"Xiao-Xiao, you don't know about those kinds of people. They'd kill us if they could." His voice was shrill, and he appeared to be on the verge of hysteria.

"What's wrong with you? I know them. They moved me a couple of times before. Quit acting like a baby." She let her voice sharpen, and when her father saw that she wasn't budging on the choice of movers, he stopped talking, although he didn't let them out of his sight.

She watched as he scowled at the intruders, and sighed. Had he been racist for the sake of being racist, or if he thought that a natural hatred towards a group of people was the Chinese way, she would have let her temper fly. But he had been held up at gunpoint in one of his restaurants while she had visited as a child, and the ordeal had scarred him much deeper than it had her. To him, there was no dark-skinned person who wasn't about to attack him, no descendant of Africa who didn't belong in jail. Like all prejudice, his fears were irrational, but nothing she had ever said had convinced him otherwise.

George wandered about, apparently oblivious to Baba's palpable bigotry. So long as the movers didn't understand Mandarin, she wouldn't have to worry about their taking offense, and for once, she was glad her father spoke no English.

"Where should we start?" Eddie, the second mover, asked.

"Start with the kitchen while I try to talk some sense to my father," she said, watching as they hustled into the narrow space. She turned to Baba and was about to speak when her phone rang again.

"What is it?" she answered, barely paying attention to the caller.

"Hercules, it's Chris," another one of her sous chefs said. "I just found out that my mother was in a car wreck."

"Jesus Christ. Is she okay?"

"I think so, but I'm flying out to Toronto in two hours, and I won't be able to come in tonight. I'm really sorry, Chef. I'll work six days next week to make it up."

"Don't worry about that now. We'll figure something out. Let me know how she is."

"Thanks so much, Chef," he said, his voice breaking slightly.

She glanced around her, slightly unnerved. Frightening familial situations notwithstanding, two of her chefs had now canceled. She hadn't planned on working tonight, but it seemed that she didn't have much choice but to go in. Her father coughed, catching her attention, and she looked up to see him struggling with a chair.

"Oh, no, you're not taking the recliner," she said. The faux-leather monstrosity seemed to be leering at her, and with a mess of silver duct tape holding together the little stuffing left inside, it looked more like an experiment in Dr. Frankenstein's lab than a chair.

"I *am* taking the recliner. And I don't want to hear any more of your criticism. If you won't let me take my recliner, my rug, my coffee table, *everything* in this apartment, I won't go. You can tell your monkey friends to leave." His small chin jutted up, and he set his jaw firmly. He wasn't kidding, and the determination with which he spoke infuriated Hercules.

"You won't go? You think you can live here? You haven't paid rent in two months, Baba. You were in the process of being *evicted*. You get that? There's no one to take care of you. There's no one who can even *understand* you. You should be so lucky that you have a daughter like me, and it wouldn't hurt if you said thank you every now and then. If you can't bring yourself to do at least that, then please, just stop talking." Her words spilled out before she could catch them, and as soon as she finished, she was horrified. She hadn't meant to insult him, and she certainly didn't want to start off the day like this. Today was supposed to be a celebration, or as much of a celebration as two enormously resentful people could share. It was supposed to be the first day of his new life.

"I'm sorry. I shouldn't have said that," she said. Her face was on fire, and she could feel sweat trickle down her neck. Her phone rang again, and she was about to turn it off when she saw that Jenna Morgan was calling.

"Please tell me that you're coming in tonight," she said to her pastry chef. "I'm starting to think that all of you are conspiring to piss me off."

"What? Oh—I'm so sorry," she said, "but I can't. I twisted my ankle this morning, and the doctor said to stay off of it for a few days."

"You can't cook with a sprained ankle?"

"I can't walk, Chef."

Annoyance spread through her body like a virus, and she breathed slowly, trying to control her agitation.

"I'm really sorry, Chef," Jenna said. "I'll be back in two days, I promise."

"Fine," she seethed, and then snapped her phone shut. What were the chances that her entire crew would become sick, hurt or grieved on the same night? At least Simon Brills hadn't yet canceled, although in the past few months, he had gone from her number one to the most unreliable of them all.

"Who do you keep talking to?" her father asked.

"The incompetents at the restaurant. I've got to go in tonight, but George and Eddie will take care of you."

"You're leaving me with these—these Georges and Eddies?" he asked, eyes wide.

"They're fine. They'll be nice to you so long as you're nice to them, okay? I'll be home as soon as I can." She collected her overstuffed bag and walked towards the door. When she turned back, her father was struggling with a coffee table, apparently set on dragging the mirror-topped homage to the seventies to her house. She moaned and stepped outside. She would have to deal with his crap later.

Hercules stood akimbo and scowled. Simon Brills, her executive sous chef, was late again. If he was hopped up on dope right now, she thought, he'd be finished. From the sous chefs' discreet whispers, she had gathered that he liked to spend his free time holed up in his little apartment, snorting anything smaller than his nostrils. But he had never let it affect his work, and until recently, he had been her always-on-time star. Now she was lucky if he showed up at all. She was about to phone him when someone walked into the kitchen.

"Hello," he said, as easily as if he had worked at Dragonfly for years. She watched as the stranger took an apron from the wall and tucked his head into the loop.

"Who the hell are you?" she asked, feeling her eyes go wide.

"Peter Murphy. Simon hired me to do the prep work." He clasped his hands and stretched upwards. Twisting from side to side, he let out a satisfied sigh as his back cracked with a whir.

"Simon *hired* you?" Hercules asked, incredulous.

"Yeah. Are you Hercules Huang?" He extended a hand. She grasped it and shook, restraining the urge to crush it in her paw. "It's just incredible to meet you," he said with a smile that could have advertised for a dental practice. "I'm a big fan of yours. This is such an honor."

She softened at the compliment. At least Peter had initiative. She stood quietly and observed as he picked up a knife and slowly eased it into a tomato. The longer she watched, the clearer it became that he had no idea what he was doing. She shuddered a few times as he nicked his fingers.

"Peter." She placed a hand on his forearm, and he put the knife down. "Have you ever worked in a restaurant before?"

"No, ma'am, this is my first time." He flashed his brilliant smile again, visibly proud of his inexperience.

"Then why did Simon hire you?" She crossed her arms and leaned against the counter. She could kill both of them for their audacity. This was *her* kitchen, and *she* was going to decide whether someone had a job.

"Well, he's a friend of mine," he said. "Actually, we're roommates. See, I just got out of college, and I don't really know what I want to do with my life. I'm not really employed right now, and Simon thought that I might be helpful around here. You know, my parents always said that being a classical-studies major wouldn't land me a job, and they were right. Who—"

"Stop." Hercules didn't want to hear his entire life story, and she wasn't running a charity. She needed a chef, a chopper, someone who could slice tomatoes without requiring a trip to the ER. It was obvious this arrangement wasn't going to work, regardless of how much help Simon wanted. He wouldn't need the assistance if he actually showed up when he was scheduled to appear, she thought, growing more indignant by the moment.

"Do you know if your roommate intends to put in an appearance tonight?" She tried to rein in her frustration.

"I don't know," he said with a shrug. "He wasn't in the apartment when I left."

"I see." Her face felt hot, and she walked into the refrigerator to cool down. The walk-in commercial beauty had been the latest addition to the kitchen, and though it had cost her an arm and a leg, she found the cost worth it. At the very least, her head wouldn't overheat and explode tonight. She walked out in time to see Peter sucking on his middle finger.

"What the hell are you doing?" she asked, afraid to hear the answer.

"I cut my finger, ma'am," he answered with his hand still in his mouth. "I guess this knife stuff's harder than I thought it would be."

Hercules wanted to cry. Dragonfly was set to open in two hours, and she alone couldn't prepare meals for the hundred-top restaurant. With the usual five chefs down to one, she contemplated closing for the night. She cursed Simon under her breath and debated whether to release Peter. She decided against it. He might not be much help in the kitchen, but he could very well be an effective courier. Watching him suck his finger like a man-child, she picked up the phone and dialed.

"Hello," Whitney answered, her voice stretched into song.

"It's me. I've got a situation in the kitchen. You cook a lot, don't you? You know how to chop vegetables?"

"Um—I've chopped vegetables before. Why? What's going on?"

"My chefs have all bailed tonight. Will you come to the restaurant?" She turned her back to Peter, unwilling to witness the harm he was bound to inflict on himself.

"Okay. Sure. I'll be over in a few minutes."

"Thank you," Hercules gasped. "Thank you, thank you, thank you."

"Hey, Hercules? Don't expect a whole lot. I mean, I'm not a professional."

"I know. Just get your ass over here. And bring Audrey, too."

Whitney arrived at the kitchen with Robert in tow, and the sight of both Lees brought tears to Hercules' eyes.

"Thank you," she gushed, and rushed towards them. She hugged Whitney first and then moved on to Robert. He returned her embrace before wandering around the room, marveling at how such a small space could produce so many dinners.

"I don't know if Audrey can make it," Whitney said.

"What?" Hercules cried.

"I couldn't get ahold of her," she said apologetically. "I left her a voice mail, though."

Hercules clenched her jaw, unwilling to imagine what kind of disaster the night would yield.

"What do you want us to do?" Whitney grabbed an apron and tossed another to Robert.

"Jesus, where do I even start?" Hercules ran from station to station with a surprising lightness that always took over when she was panicked. "Okay, for desserts, we're going to have to do with leftovers or offer complimentary wine. I can do a lot of the cooking, but I'll absolutely need the prep stations ready. Can you fix the *mise en place?*"

"What's that?" Whitney asked.

"It's a fancy word for setup," Robert explained. He had already made himself at home, and was scanning the trays of colorful vegetables with an analytic eye. "I've taken a lot of classes, Hercules, if you don't mind teaching a novice."

"You've taken classes?" she asked, impressed.

"I mean, just at Central Market," he clarified, his cheeks burning bright pink. "But I know most of the basic terms and techniques."

"That's good enough," she said, and patted his arm. "If you could get Whitney started on the *mise en place*, I'll show you the rest of the kitchen and what we're going to need."

Whitney grabbed a knife from a wall magnet and imitated Robert's movements. Tucking her knuckles under like he instructed, she soon found a rhythm. She looked up, and Hercules was astonished to see that she was still chopping.

"I'm a really quick learner, Herc. Show me what else you need."

Hercules ran to her with an armful of produce, and they proceeded to prepare the fish, meat and poultry. Whitney and Hercules moved on to the salads while Robert made hollandaise and béchamel sauces, using only her oral recitation as a guide. As if God had flown them to their own Fantasy Island, both Lees whipped, stirred and sliced like culinary savants. How it had even been possible, Hercules didn't care, and if she was viewing them through a forgiving lens of gratitude, that was fine, too. They were angels to her, and had she had the time, she would have smothered them both with kisses.

Hercules stepped into the foyer, as battle weary as if she had single-handedly manned the restaurant tonight. The adrenaline that had kept her going in the kitchen was quickly wearing off, leaving her wasted and shaking with fatigue. Tonight had been the most stressful night she had ever faced. Thank the good sweet Lord that Whitney and Robert had come to the rescue. Thank God that her chefs had bailed on a surprisingly slow Wednesday and not a furiously paced Saturday. She would have been in ruins otherwise.

She walked into the living room, where her father sat motionless in a beige outfit of a rugby shirt and slacks. He was watching a Chinese talk show, and several commentators spoke in rapid-fire Mandarin. How he had managed to find a Chinese network in her ten-thousand-channel satellite guide was beyond her. Until now, she didn't even know that her package included international options. She sank next to him on the couch, and despite her exhaustion and frayed nerves, despite her desperation for sleep, she resolved that they were going to have a nice conversation if it killed her.

"You're home," he said woodenly. He barely looked up before turning his attention back to the TV, but his slight glance was enough for her to catch the scowl on his face.

"Yeah, I'm home." She lifted her aching calves and rested them gently on the coffee table. "Did you get everything moved in okay?"

"No. One of those monkeys broke a family heirloom."

"Please don't call them 'monkeys.' They're people. They have names." She breathed in deeply and imagined blue oceans and white sandy beaches. "What did they break?"

"A figurine that your mother loved. It's priceless. That's what you get for using monkeys."

"What did I just say?" she asked, hearing the strain in her voice. "Show me what they broke and I'll square up the account with George."

"It doesn't matter. There's no amount of money that will bring it back."

"Where'd you get it?"

"Hallmark." He looked at her, as if he was anticipating exasperation. "I didn't say it was expensive. I said it was priceless."

She took in his pitiful expression, reminded again that after almost fifteen years, he was still grieving the loss of her mother. Maybe his lingering pain should have tempered her animus towards him, but instead, his refusal to move forward, his inability to get past his heartache, only highlighted his selfishness. She had lost a loved one, too, and she hadn't abandoned life or its responsibilities. She had tried her best to be a decent daughter, and she resented the fact that he had used her mother's death as a crutch to cease being a decent father.

"I'll talk to George," she said through gritted teeth.

He looked about the living room and grunted. "Your house feels like a museum. There's no character. No history. It's like you're living someone's life, playing make-believe."

"It's custom, so I don't know why you'd feel that way. I picked everything out myself." She followed his gaze, and as she studied the furniture her interior decorator had chosen and the faux-finished walls, she had to admit that she didn't disagree with his observation. It had been almost a year since she had moved in, and she still felt as though the McMansion didn't belong to her.

"Such a big house for one person. So unnecessary. What are you trying to prove? That you're better than everyone else? It's unattractive to be so showy."

"It's not a sin to have nice things," she said defensively. She curled her feet underneath her and stared at the TV, unwilling to look at her father. "I work really hard, and I deserve what I've got. That's not showy. That's pride."

"When are you getting married?" he asked, the non sequitur question perfectly appropriate in his eyes.

"At the rate I'm going, never." She sighed wearily, trying to stave off her irritation.

He recoiled slightly, and his eyebrows arched. "I hope you're not trying to be American by becoming an old maid. You need to get married, Xiao-Xiao. All Chinese women do, and you're practically a spinster, while everyone else is having children."

"You'll stop criticizing if I have a child?" she asked mirthlessly.

"That's not funny. By the time you have a child, I'll be dead." He shook his head, and the tufts of white hair that billowed from his scalp swayed. "I don't know why you care so little for marriage. Your mother would find it so unacceptable. She wouldn't understand why you feel like you have to abandon your culture and adopt this horrible American mentality."

"What do you expect me to do, Baba? We're in America." She rubbed her forehead, trying to massage away the tension that knotted her temples.

"We may be in America," he said, "but we're Chinese. If I go to the grocery store, or to the bank, or anywhere else, people don't think I'm American. Nobody treats me like my name is Tom."

"No one treats you like an American because you don't speak English," she said flatly, unable to understand why he refused to acknowledge this simple, glaringly evident fact.

"That's not my problem." He jutted his small chin upwards indignantly.

"It *is* your problem, Baba. You're *here*. Like it or not, the national language isn't Chinese. People speak English, they drive Chevrolets, they eat hamburgers, they celebrate the Fourth of July. Why do you refuse to accept that? Why can't you learn to assimilate, even just a little?" She was shaking from fatigue and frustration, and from the exertion required to keep her voice calm.

"Why should I assimilate?" he asked, perplexed. "I just told you. We are Chinese."

She stared at him, at a loss as to how to respond. After a moment, she said, "I don't get you. If you are so stuck on the fact that we're Chinese—if you refuse to engage in the country you've lived in for two decades—why did you even bring us to America in the first place?"

He frowned at her, looking as if he couldn't believe she hadn't yet grasped the obvious.

"Why do you think, Xiao-Xiao?" he asked. "We came here so that you could have all of this." He waved his outstretched arm around him. "We came here so that you could be happy and have a life that was your own."

"If that's true, then why do you insist on making everything so *un*happy for me? Why do you constantly criticize the life that I have?"

"I never . . ."

"I don't understand you at all." She stood up, feeling as if she might collapse, and her voice was so low she could barely hear it. "I've done everything I can to make you happy, to make you think that I'm a good daughter. I did well in school. I made something of myself. And I've done the best that I know how to make sure that you're taken care of. But you don't seem to notice those things. You only see the negatives." She saw that her hands, as steady as they had always been, were now trembling. "Do you know how hard it is for me to listen to you criticize? Do you have any idea how much you hurt my feelings?" He blanched, and his bushy brows knit together. "Maybe life didn't turn out the way you'd hoped it would, Baba. Maybe you wished that you weren't where you are now. But you are. And as much as you think that life cheated you, you still have a roof over your head and a daughter who looks after you. I don't know why you can't appreciate that. I don't know why that isn't good enough."

"Xiao-Xiao, I—it's—" He stopped short, looking unsure of himself, and for a few moments, they were quiet. After another minute of painful silence, it became clear that he didn't plan on speaking, and she sighed, realizing that there was nothing more she could say.

"I'm going to bed," she said wearily. "Your room has a down comforter on the bed, but if you get cold, there are extra blankets in the closet."

She walked out of the living room, her scalp tingling from the disappointing night. As soon as she got to her bathroom, she reached into the shower and yanked at the knobs until hot water poured out. She felt horrendous inside and out, and she had barely stripped out of her chef's pants before she pushed herself into the stall, hoping to scrub away the misery that clung to her skin.

As hot water streamed over her shoulders, she felt the knots along her back relax, and as much as she tried to focus on unemotional, unhurtful matters such as Dragonfly's gross receipts for the night, her mind insisted on wandering back to her father. Surely, it wasn't strange that she should look to him for approval and encouragement, but perhaps it was unreasonable to continue to search for them when the previous ten million attempts had been rebuffed. Maybe she had kept trying because she had achieved all her other desires, or maybe it was because what should have been the most simple, the most natural, was also the most heartbreakingly unattainable to her. She turned off the water and stepped into her robe, feeling dazed from the rigor of the day. Somewhere in the distance, her phone rang, and she answered it, still feeling as if she were in a trance.

"Hello?"

"Hey, it's Whitney. Did you get home okay?"

"Yeah."

"Hey, I wanted to ask you something. I'm not kidding, so don't laugh, okay?"

"Okay."

"What do you think of Robert?"

"Who?"

"My brother," she said, sounding too cheerful. "Robert Grant Lee, space cadet at NASA."

"What about him?"

"I was thinking about what you said in Austin, about wanting someone who was tall, dark, handsome, funny, kind and a nonchef, and he's all of those things. I think he's got a crush on you, not that he'd ever admit it, and I thought y'all might be good together."

"What?" She could barely understand what Whitney was talking about, and in her stupor, she felt as though she were dreaming.

"Would it be the worst thing in the world to go out with him?" Whitney's voice suddenly sounded far away. "It would be just one date."

"Is this the guy who's waiting for me?"

"What are you talking about?"

"When we were going to Austin, Jimmy said that someone was waiting for me at home."

"I don't know. Maybe." There was a pause, and Hercules was about to place the phone back on the receiver when she heard Whitney's voice. "So? Will you go out with him?"

"Sure. Whatever. Yeah."

"Awesome. I'll have him call you."

Hercules hung up and wobbled back to her bathroom. As soon as she wrapped her hair in a towel, she turned off the lights and crawled into bed. Her body ached, and she closed her eyes, grateful that she had three hours to rest before she had to meet with her business manager. As she drifted off to sleep, she thought about Robert, still unsure whether she hadn't just imagined that he was going to ask her out.

Sixteen

"Oh, come *on*," Audrey muttered, glaring at the orange LED that was flashing on the printer. "What's wrong with you?" She pressed the green button again before returning to the other side of the dining room table, where her laptop was flashing an error message, and after squinting at it through bleary eyes, she called out to Victor, who was sitting on the couch surrounded by the heap of biology exams he was grading. "Hey, hon, something's wrong with the printer."

"Let me see." He rested his red pen on the coffee table and walked to where she was.

She rubbed her eyes and sank into a chair, feeling panicked. "If I can't print my dissertation after I stayed up all night to finish it, I'm going to scream. And then I'm going to throw the bloody thing out of the window."

He inspected the troublesome machinery for a moment before pulling out the bottom tray, and with a cocked grin, he went to the hallway closet that doubled as an office-supply room and returned with a ream of paper.

"Auds, you're just out of paper." He filled the tray and pressed the green button again. In an instant, paper spit out of the printer as if it, too, couldn't wait to expel her assertions on the Internet Sphere of Literature's influence on the biblical Resurrection story. "See? Easy peasy."

"Oh." She felt slightly foolish, too exhausted to appreciate the inanity of her threats to punish the high-speed Hewlett-Packard. She watched paper flow from the top of it, and when she was satisfied that it was behaving properly, she trudged to the couch and plopped into its soft folds. Victor joined her, careful not to sit on his students' exams, and she rested her head on his shoulder.

"You really should get some rest, sweetheart," he said. "You didn't sleep at all last night, and you've been working like a maniac for three months straight."

"I couldn't help it." She closed her eyes, feeling her heavy lids sting with fatigue. "The ideas were coming so fast, and I had to get them down on paper before they disappeared."

"I can't even imagine trying to write a three-hundred-page paper. On one subject, no less. I don't know how you do it." He shook his head, and his movements jiggled her out of her repose. She opened her eyes and straightened.

"Have you ever seen that movie *Amadeus?*" she asked.

"A long time ago."

"You know how Mozart could hear an entire symphony in his head even before he jotted down the first measure?" He nodded. "That's how I felt with the last two chapters of my thesis. I felt like I was just transcribing these thoughts that came to me."

"That's because you're a genius." He smiled widely, his admiration almost palpable.

"I wouldn't call myself a genius. But I do feel as if a part of me was on autopilot, if that makes sense. I mean, I worked my ass off, but I've never felt so inspired before." She patted his thigh. "You must be my muse."

"I didn't realize muses came packaged as biology teachers."

"Now you do. I got more done in the six months we've been together than all the previous years combined."

He kissed the top of her head. "I can't tell you how proud I am of you. There aren't enough ways for me to say it." He kissed her again. "So, what now? I mean, after you turn your paper in."

"I wait. Hopefully, my dissertation director will like it. If he does, I get my degree. And then hopefully, a college will offer me a position."

"You'll have more offers than you'll know what to do with."

She felt herself smile, his encouragement lifting the fatigue from her body. "I wish I were as optimistic as you are. It's really, *really* tough to break into academia. Hell, if the University of Alaska extended me an offer, I'd take it, and you know how much I hate cold weather."

"I wouldn't mind Alaska, actually. I've always loved snow. Maybe it's because we never get it here."

She chuckled. "Us in Anchorage. Can you imagine what my mom would say?"

"I don't know, but it wouldn't be good. And I don't doubt that she'd blame me for it." His response came immediately, answering a question she had asked rhetorically, and she stared at him, fearing what might have compelled his uncharacteristically negative reaction.

"Did she say something to you?" she asked carefully, feeling her heart pound. For all of her mother's concerns about their engagement, Audrey couldn't remember a time when she hadn't been pleasant towards him, but his ruminative expression confirmed his understanding that his relationship with his future mother-in-law was less than perfect.

"Not specifically, no. But I don't have to hear her say that she disapproves of us getting married to know that it's true." He sighed. "I wish she could see that I'm not a bad guy." He held her gaze, and his almost pleading expression broke her heart. "I wish she could see that I love you, and that I'll spend my life trying to make you happy. I'd do anything to make her believe that."

"She will. We just have to give her some time." She tried to smile reassuringly, as if she could convince him, and herself, that her mother would come around. His desire to do right by her mother endeared him even more to her, if such a thing were possible, and it reaffirmed the good qualities she found blaringly obvious. She imagined that most men would have dismissed the difficult-to-please mother-in-law, regarded her as some kind of stereotypical, noxious burden they were destined to tolerate until she was ripe for a nursing home. Not that Audrey would ever present the hypothetical alternative in defense of Victor. She couldn't even fathom placing her mother in a home, and she knew that she'd never marry a man who was keen on stashing the elder Henley away.

The printer beeped, alerting that it was hungry for more paper, and he stood to feed it. He stayed at its side, shepherding her dissertation's slow birth into the apartment, and other than the groaning noises the overtaxed machine was making, the house was silent. After another moment, it, too, quieted, and she gazed at the thick tome that Victor was carefully laying on the dining room table, aware that he was handling the culmination of her six years at Rice, the progeny of her obsessions and arduous work. The sight of her doctoral achievement stirred a surge of energy out of her fatigued body, and she was suddenly compelled to bring the rest of her plans into fruition.

"Hey, Victor," she said, "what do you think of a beach wedding in the Bahamas? One of my dad's friends owns the Ocean Club on Paradise Island, and he said that he'd hold all of March next year for us, but I have to let him know pretty soon if we're going to take it." She moved his biology exams to the coffee table and lay down on a stack of pillows.

"I thought you wanted to have a small ceremony here." She heard his footsteps against the wooden floor. In a second, he was standing by her head, and she scooted over as he sprawled out next to her.

"I keep thinking about what Jimmy said about weddings." She propped her head up on her hand and rested her free arm across his stomach. "I don't want to have an ordinary one that no one will remember. Plus, it'll give our friends a reason to take a vacation. I know that Hercules and Whitney have been working themselves ragged, and they won't take a break unless I give them a reason to." She smiled, thinking about the Valedictorians. "I'm going to ask Whitney to sing at the reception."

"You've got some incredible friends, you know that? A professor, a chef and a musician lawyer. There's got to be a joke in there somewhere." He smiled, causing little wrinkles to frame the outer edges of his hazel eyes. "I think a beach wedding would be great. I'm sure my parents would appreciate getting out of the States."

"Plus we wouldn't have to make ourselves crazy with the planning. The resort's got an entire staff to take care of everything. One of my sorority sisters got married at the Ocean Club several years ago, and it was absolute perfection." She recalled the lavish party, the all-night reception, the fourteen bridesmaids and ten groomsmen. "You know, out of all of my friends, I thought Emily would've been the mother of

Bridezillas, but because all she had to do was pick out a wedding gown, she turned out to be only a semimonster."

Victor laughed. "Well, let's definitely go that route, then. I'd hate to see you morph into a—what did you call it?"

"Bridezilla."

"Yeah." He laughed again before pulling his arm out from under her and checking his watch. "Why don't you get some rest? I need to go to the office for a bit."

"Oh, I was hoping that we could take a nap together." She nuzzled closer to him and closed her eyes.

"I have to grade my kids' lab assignments. They're due on Monday." He kissed her on the mouth, his warm lips still sweet from the Coke he had been nursing all morning, and then slowly untangled himself out of her grip. "Do you want to go to bed?"

"I'm good right here," she murmured, already halfway asleep. Exhaustion was rendering her senseless, and she was barely conscious of the fleece blanket that he was pulling over her.

"I'll be back in a few hours," he said, his voice sounding far away. "I tell you what. I'll take care of dinner tonight. We've got to celebrate you finishing your paper." He kissed her cheek again, and by the time she heard the front door open and close, she was sure that she was dreaming. What felt like an instant passed before someone began to knock, and when the rhythmic pounding turned aggressive, she pushed herself off the couch and shuffled to the entrance. In a flash, Whitney was in the apartment, and after eyeing Audrey, she frowned.

"You're not going out like that, are you?"

"Where are we going?" she asked, trying to shake the grogginess from her interrupted slumber.

"We're supposed to be at Central Market in fifteen minutes." Audrey didn't respond, and Whitney's frown deepened. "For the cooking class, remember?"

"That's today?" She blinked quickly, feeling out of sorts. "Oh, Lord. I totally forgot. Give me five minutes."

"After nagging me about it all week, I can't believe you forgot."

Whitney sat on the couch and continued to examine the room, her brows knit together.

Audrey ran into the bedroom, flung open the closet door and grabbed a faded gray T-shirt and a pair of jeans. Seconds later, she was in the bathroom, brushing her teeth while trying to squeeze into her clothes. In the midst of finishing her dissertation, she had forgotten that she had all but demanded that Whitney join her for a cooking class. Central Market, being the hoity-toity grocery store that it was, offered courses every Saturday morning, and today, the entire two-hour session would focus on Korean cuisine. When Audrey had heard about it on the radio, she had immediately signed both of them up.

"I'm ready," she said, bounding out of the bedroom. "God, I hope we don't see anyone we know. I haven't showered yet."

"Neither have I. I haven't even slept yet." Whitney was still on the couch, and in a pair of inky-blue jeans and a white tank top, with her hair in a ponytail, she looked much younger than her twenty-eight years. And, for having stayed up all night, she looked like a million bucks.

"Why haven't you slept?" Audrey smashed her feet into a pair of flip-flops and then grabbed her bag.

"I played at Billy Bob's last night and stayed out later than I should have. And then I went back to the office and worked on a brief until"— she checked her watch—"thirty minutes ago."

"God, Whitney, you push yourself way too hard."

"Says the woman who stayed up all night working on her paper," she said, looking at Audrey's completed dissertation on the dining room table.

"How'd you know?"

"Am I wrong?"

"No." She smiled, tickled that her friend knew her so well, grabbed her keys and then opened the door. "Are you ready?"

"I can't believe I agreed to do this." Whitney grimaced. "You know how much I hate cooking."

"Don't ever let Hercules hear you say that."

Whitney drove as though she were racing laps at Talladega, and Audrey gripped on to the dashboard as she weaved her BMW between SUVs and eighteen-wheelers. Too scared to speak, she clenched her jaw and closed her eyes as Whitney whizzed to the grocery store. In half the time it should have taken a conscientious driver, they were in the parking lot of Central Market, and she fell out of the car with a sigh of relief. The closer they got to the entrance, the more excited she felt. It would be the first time that she had ever taken a cooking class, the first time that she attempted anything remotely related to her culture, and the course, as simple as it might have seemed to a stranger, represented a new level of growth for her. She couldn't wait to reconnect with her culinary and ethnic roots.

"Where's the class?" Whitney asked.

"Upstairs."

"I didn't know this place had an upstairs."

They walked through rows of organic produce, and Audrey stopped for a moment to admire a section of white peaches, papayas and kumquats. As busy as the last few months had been, she hadn't had the time to stroll through aisles of fresh produce, and the unending rows of nature's brilliant colors rivaled the beauty of precious jewels. When she looked up, she thought for sure that she was dreaming. Her mother was a couple of aisles over, perusing cantaloupes. What was she doing here? She usually sent her staff to pick up groceries, and judging from the bewildered look on her face, she may as well have been shopping for gorillas. As if sensing Audrey's presence, her head popped up suddenly, her clear blue eyes locking with Audrey's, and she reacted, looking as surprised as Audrey felt.

"Darling, what are you doing here?" she asked. In a charcoal pencil skirt, a white silk blouse, black stilettos and obscenely large diamond earrings, she seemed starkly out of place even in the luxury grocery store.

"Whitney and I are taking a cooking class. What are *you* doing here?"

"Ever since I got back from Switzerland, my body's been a mess. My circadian rhythm is completely off, and I'm craving fruit constantly."

She reached for the greenest of the pack and touched it tentatively before turning to face Audrey. "It's so strange that I ran into you. I was going to call you today."

"Why?"

"I wanted to talk to you about Victor."

"Mom, please. If you're going to try again to talk me out of marrying him, I really don't want to hear it." She sighed deeply, unsure how much more motherly dissuasion she could handle, before glancing about for Whitney, who was nowhere to be seen.

"I'm not going to try to talk you out of it," she said, stunning Audrey. Her expression carried no joy, and if she had experienced a change of heart, she was apparently still struggling to deal with the transformation. "I've been thinking about this for a while now. I can only tell you so many times how I feel about your engagement before you tune me out, and I don't want that. You've made it clear that you're going to spend the rest of your life with Victor, and I'm not arguing with you about it anymore."

"You're not?" She felt strange, and for as long as her mother had expressed her disapproval of their engagement, her sudden retreat roused a nagging suspicion. "But you've spent the last six months telling me that we're making a mistake."

"Well"—she frowned, looking as if she was gauging her words—"honestly, I still feel that you are, but what can I do? Either I learn to accept it, or I don't, and I'm not willing to ruin our relationship because of who you chose to marry."

"Oh my God, you have no idea how happy you just made me." A flood of emotions overpowered her, combined with an exhaustion-created vulnerability, and she had to fight back tears. "Victor and I were actually talking about you this morning. You should see how much he wants to convince you that all he wants is for me to be happy. He'd do anything to prove it to you."

"I'm glad to hear that." She eased out of Audrey's grip and then checked her watch. "Are either of you going to be home later today?"

"We should be. Why?" Through the corner of her eye, she spied Whitney, who was facing a staggering shelf of crackers, and if Audrey had been shocked by her mother's change of heart, she was doubly surprised to see her friend with a basket in the crook of her arm and an array of condiments in the bin.

"We're having a document sent to you."

"What document?"

"Your father and I had our lawyers draft a prenuptial agreement." She gazed at Audrey, her features taut with businesslike determination. "Since Victor's so keen on proving that he's only interested in your happiness, he shouldn't have any problem signing it."

Audrey gawked at her, thunderstruck. "What did you just say?"

Her mother continued to peer at her, and her brows furrowed together. "Really, Audrey, is this such a surprise? Surely you expected it."

"I didn't." Her voice seemed to emanate from outside her body, sounding hollow in her ears. "Why in the world would you ask Victor to sign a prenup?"

"Why do you think? If your marriage falls apart, I will not allow you to get stuck in court for who knows how long, fighting over money." She darted her eyes about Audrey's face, as if trying to read her thoughts, before letting out an exhausted sigh. "Sweetheart, I hope you and Victor are happy for the rest of your lives. I really do. But I can't guarantee that. No one can. And if your marriage doesn't turn out the way you'd hoped, the prenup will give you a clean way out."

"I don't need a clean out, Mother. I don't need an out at all." Whatever exhilaration she had felt a moment ago was gone, and defensiveness and an overwhelming panic caused her voice to shake. "This prenup—it's just—it's unnecessary. And insulting."

"We are not debating whether it's necessary for Victor to sign the agreement. If he wants to marry you, he's going to sign it. Period." She pursed her lips, her expression twisting with both protectiveness and frustration. "I wish you weren't so stubborn, darling. This is for your own good. Why can't you see that?"

Audrey didn't respond. Frankly, she didn't know what to say. Had she been a bystander, an objective observer estimating someone else's financially disparate relationship, maybe she would have appreciated the financial wall erected for self-preservation. Hell, maybe she would have insisted upon it. But she wasn't a bystander, and she wasn't an objective observer. She was the unfortunate subject of the dilemma, and she was unable to see the situation through anything other than indignant lenses.

"He doesn't have to sign it right away," her mother said, her voice cutting through Audrey's thoughts. "But he does need to return it before y'all get your marriage license." She sighed again. "Darling, please try to understand." She laid her hand on Audrey's arm, looking pained. "I have to go, but I will call you later."

Audrey watched as her mother picked up a cantaloupe and a bag of red grapes, and until her mother left the produce section, she didn't move. A moment later, Whitney approached gingerly, her basket laden with random condiments.

"I figured that y'all needed a moment," she said. "Auds, are you okay?"

"I"—she felt her face screw up—"I have no idea."

"What happened?"

"My mother wants Victor to sign a prenup."

"Oh." She readjusted her grip on her basket, her expression impossible to read.

"Would you sign one if you were in Victor's situation?" she asked, unsure what she wanted to hear. She could barely figure out what to think. A million thoughts, smashed together with a thousand emotions, obfuscated reason, and with fatigue perhaps compounding that, she felt paralyzed to process her run-in with her mother.

"I can't answer that." Whitney frowned, looking disconcerted. "I wouldn't even be able to imagine."

"How would you feel if you were in my shoes, then?"

She considered for a moment and then shook her head. "I really don't know. But—I guess the question is—how do *you* feel?"

She was silent for a minute, trying fecklessly to summon a response. Finally, she shook her head.

"I don't know. Numb, actually. I think I felt every emotion at once, and it short-circuited my system. I can't even think it through rationally." She leaned against a stand of apples, feeling as if she was about to faint. Whitney reached out and steadied her.

"Do you still want to go to the cooking class? We're not that late, and I doubt that anyone would notice us. We don't have to, though. We could go somewhere and talk. Or we could have lunch. There are a bunch of great restaurants on this street." She was babbling nervously, evidently unsure how else to react to Audrey's sudden catatonic state.

"Do you mind if we bail? I don't think I can stay here." As much as she needed to escape the store, she was still sorry to miss a cultural diversion, and she looked up to where the class was being held, unhappy that her first foray into her heritage had been ruined. Whitney glanced over, perhaps sensing her loss.

"Hey, why don't you come over to my parents' house tomorrow? My mother's cooking would blow this stuff away. You can't get much more authentic than that."

Audrey nodded, and they shuffled silently to the parking lot, the bright sun momentarily blinding them. She heard Whitney's voice, but in her funk, she was unable to grasp anything she was saying. Horror had deadened her senses, and dread had deafened her to all else, and as they drove aimlessly around the city, all she could think of was how Victor would react to the prenup. God, she didn't want to find out.

"Victor?" Audrey called as she walked through the door. "I'm home." She dropped her bag and keys onto the small table by the entrance before moving into the open expanse of their loft. The dining room table, which had served as her makeshift office for the last year, was now clear of her computer, printer and fifty pounds of books, and in their place was a ruby runner she had never seen before, a half-dozen white lit candles, a nosegay of red roses and two place settings. The lights in the rest of the apartment had been dimmed, and a bubbling pot joined the soft whir of the convection oven in the kitchen. She stood still for a moment, gaping at the beautiful arrangement, when Victor emerged from their bedroom in worn jeans and a plain blue T-shirt. He was smiling, and the mesmerizing expression, aided by his having thoughtfully transformed their home, rendered him breathtaking.

"Hey, sweetheart." He bent down and kissed her, the flicker of the candles catching the green in his eyes.

"What is all this?" she asked, still floored by the setting.

"I told you that I was going to take care of dinner."

"I know, but I figured that you would've called for takeout."

"It isn't every day that you finish your dissertation. That calls for a celebration, and I plan on celebrating by pampering you tonight." He was still cheerful, and she wondered if her mother had refrained from delivering the prenuptial agreement, process-server-style. "You should see what I did with the bathroom. After dinner, I'm going to draw you a bath."

"I thought you had labs to grade. When did you do all this?" She sat down at the dining table, feeling as if she had walked into a dream.

"A few hours ago. Don't worry. I put your stuff in the bedroom, and your paper's safe in a folder on your nightstand." He went to the kitchen, opened the oven and extracted a casserole dish. She couldn't see what he was doing behind the raised counter, but she heard the clanking of dishes, and she smelled the aroma of garlic and rosemary. "Where'd you go, Auds? You were dead asleep when I left this afternoon."

"Whitney came by, and we—we caught a movie." Nerves washed through her body. She didn't want to inform him that she had run into her mother at Central Market, or that she had expected someone to have delivered prenup papers. If no one had dropped off the offending document, she certainly didn't want to ruin the evening with the issue.

"Well, I hope you're hungry, because I spent all afternoon cooking." He returned with two plates and set them on the table before dashing back to the kitchen. Audrey stared at her dish, taken aback that Victor had managed to prepare beef Wellington, much less cook it to perfection. Accompanying the main feature were grilled root vegetables and a cake of potatoes, and she inspected her meal like a gaping monkey for another moment before she broke out laughing.

"You know that Hercules is one of my best friends, right? I've been to Dragonfly at least fifty times."

"It's that obvious, huh?" He returned with a bottle of wine, looking triumphant, and then sat down and poured her a glass. "Hercules owes me ten bucks."

"Did y'all bet whether I'd notice that you had picked up stuff from her restaurant?"

"She didn't think you would. In fact, she's the one who told me to say that I'd made dinner from scratch." He chuckled. "I guess she wanted me to impress you with my culinary abilities."

"You *do* impress me"—she leaned forward and kissed him on the lips—"but not because of your cooking skills."

He raised his wineglass. "Well, sweetheart, here's to your having a chef for a friend, and to your having finished your paper. I am so proud of you." He grinned. "On both counts."

She clinked his glass and took a sip, doing her damnedest to repress the misery that was overwhelming her. His kindness was killing her, and his lovely words, and even lovelier gestures, were rousing a defensive anger in her. Of all the people in the world to ask to sign a prenuptial agreement, she would have placed him last on her list, and the idea that he should consent to a prophylactic relinquishment of any part of her struck her as egregious and unfair. She was trying to stuff down the fumes of her aggravation along with her sautéed squash when Victor spoke.

"Is it not good?" He laid his hand on hers. "I heated everything like Hercules instructed."

"It's fine," she said, unable to repress a guffaw. "I'm sorry. I guess I'm just a little tired."

"You haven't slept in almost two days. I'd be out of my mind by now."

"I'm fine." He looked unconvinced. "Really. This is wonderful." She smiled as brightly as she could, and he seemed to relax.

"What movie did you and Whitney watch?" he asked.

"Have you heard of *The Host*? It's a Korean movie about a monster that's chasing a dysfunctional family. Whitney's brother had a DVD of it, and for whatever reason, we both wanted to watch it. It's pretty good, actually. If you want, I can borrow it from her."

"Sure." He considered. "I think I read about it in the *New York Times*. It was well received, wasn't it?"

"Yeah."

They were quiet again. Audrey thought about *The Host*, about the young girl swallowed by a chemically mutated river creature. As much as the movie had been an action-packed thriller, it had also struck her with its rich symbolism, and throughout the tension-filled scenes, Audrey had felt as if the director were speaking to her. Its visceral images still haunted her, and they replayed in her mind until Victor spoke.

"So, someone came by the house today," he said.

She stared at him, sure that he could hear her heart thunder.

"Your parents say that if I want to marry you, I have to sign a prenup."

"Where is it?" she asked, feeling as if they were moving in slow motion.

"In the bedroom." His features relaxed, and in the dimness of the room, he appeared to be smiling. "I signed it, by the way."

"What?" She jumped out of her chair and rushed into their room. A manila envelope lay on the small writing desk she had tucked in the corner, and she ripped the document out, cutting her fingers in the process. She scanned the five-page contract, growing more upset as she read each provision, and when she saw Victor's signature on the last page, she wanted to vomit.

"Auds, it's no big deal," he said, standing at the doorway.

She whipped around and gawked at him. "How can you say that? It's a *huge* deal. Why did you sign this? Why didn't you talk to me about it first?"

"Because I knew that you wouldn't let me sign it. I had to do it before you tried to talk me out of it." He spoke as calmly as she felt out of control, and his obvious peace stoked her rising hysteria.

"This is—I can't *believe* my parents. How could they—how . . . ?"

"Audrey, calm down."

"Why aren't you angry? How can you just stand there and say that this isn't a big deal?" She shook the legal-sized paper, practically crumpling it in her hand. "This totally dicks you over, Victor. It says that I have the sole discretion to end the marriage, and if I do, you get nothing."

"I know."

"That's it?" she cried, hearing the shrillness in her voice. "That's the extent of your reaction?"

He sighed. "Sweetheart, I know that you're trying to look out for me, and I love you for it, but you don't have to worry. That"—he pointed to the prenup—"that's just a piece of paper. It doesn't have anything to do with how I feel about you. We're going to live happily ever after, which means that the prenup will never come into play." He smiled, the expression somehow highlighting his sadness. "And if we don't work out—if you decide to leave me—well, I wouldn't want anything from you anyway." He rubbed his temples with one hand before letting out a sigh. "I'm not explaining myself very well. What I'm trying to say is that I never asked you out because I thought you were a gold mine. And I definitely didn't ask you to marry me because I thought I would benefit financially. If I need to sign a prenuptial agreement to prove that to your parents, I'd do it a thousand times." She continued to gape at him, and he frowned. "Really, what did you expect? You and your family are worth more than I can even imagine. Why would you think that your parents *wouldn't* try to safeguard their money? Why are you getting so bent out of shape over it?"

"I'm getting bent out of shape because"—she sucked in a deep breath and tried to collect her thoughts—"I'm marrying you for better or for worse, in sickness and in health, until death do us part. You and I are family, the same way that my parents and I are family. What they're asking you to do—it's like they're giving you a warning that if you screw up, or if you somehow don't live up to the expectations they had for you—they have the right to disown you. They can pretend that you were never their son, and they were never your parents. They're asking that you assent to a way out of the family even before you've had a chance to be in it." She was shrieking, yelling at him for the first time in their relationship, and as rational and restrained as she had always imagined herself to be, she now felt completely out of control. Victor peered at her, and what he was thinking, she had no idea.

"Are you talking about me, Auds?" he finally asked. "Or are you talking about yourself?"

"What?"

He walked into the room and sat on the bed, looking pensive, and she fell into the chair by the table, shocked into silence by her outburst. Clearly, she had confused the defensiveness she felt on his behalf with her own tucked-away insecurity, and she considered the latter, perhaps for the first time in her life. She knew that she was responding so poorly to the ostensibly well-intentioned prenup, not because she was an idealist blind to reality, but because it highlighted that which she had refused to fathom—her parents had chosen her, had plucked her from the lowest of backgrounds and, if they so chose, could release her into the blurred world of the forgotten.

"Your parents are your parents," Victor said. "They're always going to want the best for you, and they're always going to protect you. That's the nature of parents, Auds. Nothing's ever going to change that."

She got out of her chair, took two long steps to where he was and planted a deep kiss on his lips. He pulled her into his lap, cradling her in his strong arms, and after a moment, she wriggled out of his grip and headed back to the desk, where the carefully drafted document lay. She picked it up, unable to stomach the sight of it, and before she had a chance to think about what she was doing, she tore it in two. She shredded the two fragments into four, and the four into sixteen, and while Victor stared on in horror, she ripped the prenup into as many pieces as she could.

Seventeen

Whitney walked into her parents' kitchen and dropped her purse into a chair. It was Friday evening, her designated day to hang out with her family and enjoy her mother's cooking. Tonight, she was craving her mother's *gal bi*, the sweet and savory deliciousness of braised short ribs that outdid those of any restaurant in Houston. More importantly, however, she was keen on discussing Robert's dating life. Specifically, his dating life vis-à-vis Hercules Huang. He was already sitting at the kitchen table, grazing on chicken wings, when she walked up to her mother and kissed her cheek.

"Hi, honey," her mother said, rubbing minced garlic off her hands. "Why are you in a suit?"

"I just came from the office." She turned to her brother. "Hey."

"Hey." In a navy polo shirt and khakis, he looked as though he, too, had just returned from work. She imagined him at a bar with Hercules, laughing perhaps over a cosmonaut joke, and she was about to broach the subject when her mother spoke.

"Well, I'd like to see you in more suits. You look very pretty." She turned on the faucet and rubbed her hands under a stream of water.

"Thanks." Whitney perked up at the compliment. It wasn't like her mother to praise her for anything unrelated to a career, and she of all people wasn't one to notice flattering attire.

"I read an article in *USA Today* about appearances," she said. "Did you know that an attractive woman gets paid more than an unattractive one?"

"Mom, that's so random," Robert said through a full mouth.

"Whitney's outfit reminded me of it."

"Well, I'm sure it's not *just* because she's attractive." Whitney pulled out a Coke from the refrigerator and walked back to the counter. "She's probably got more self-confidence, and employers pick up on that."

"Maybe." Her mother dried her hands on a dish towel and picked up a knife. "Well, the article was actually about women who gave up their careers to become stay-at-home mothers. I don't know why they mentioned attractiveness."

"Did the article continue on another page?" Whitney already knew the answer. Her mother would begin to read a piece that began on A1, and when she turned to A6 to finish the story, she often read the wrong continuation column. It no longer surprised her when a horrifying report about a pit bull mauling ended with the declining fish population in Alaska.

"Yes. Anyway, there's a backwards trend of professionalism. It's so strange. When I was in school, we thought that we could handle it all—families, careers, everything."

"And now?" Whitney asked, wondering why she was focused on the subject. Surely, she had read similar articles before, but she had never once mentioned the possibility that a full family life and a satisfying career weren't possible. Considering that she was the unsolicited champion of all things profession oriented, Whitney couldn't even imagine that she would have finished the article.

"Now the workplace is so different. It's more difficult, I think. Raising children is more difficult. Everything just seems so much tougher now." She was chopping vegetables with a mechanical precision even as she was facing her, and Whitney watched carefully, terrified that she might cut herself.

"I know a lot of women who have left the firm to raise their kids."

"Well, that's understandable. You have to pick what's important in life, honey." She laid down the knife, and her eyes glazed over as she looked into the family room. A heavy sigh escaped her, bringing her back into the present. "Everything just seems too much these days." She pursed her lips and shook her head. "Hyun-Mi Cha, one of our classmates, died last week. It was in our alumni newsletter. She was a judge in Korea, and we all thought that she was incredible. A woman judge in Korea, can you even imagine? But the article barely mentioned that. Instead, it focused on how miserable she was, how discriminated against she felt and how she was living a life she didn't want to live. It's just beyond imagination."

"That's—," Whitney said.

"It's unbelievable," she interrupted. "What kind of article would talk about the regrets in someone's life, especially when she just died? It's just—just unbelievable. Your father already sent an e-mail complaining about it."

"Maybe she felt really strongly about her situation."

"Yes. It's very important to be happy." She was quiet for a moment, more pensive than Whitney had ever seen her. "There are lots of things that are more important than career. Or money."

Whitney stirred. She felt as though she was just given an opening. Until today, her mother had never even hinted that a woman could choose a path that didn't involve an advanced-degreed job, and even though she had only edged the door open to an amorphous notion of happiness, Whitney still felt hopeful. Was it possible that she valued satisfaction over a congratulatory article in an alumni newspaper? Could Whitney throw out a hypothetical about her musical career without causing her mother to retreat into her shell of ostentatious achievements?

"Hi, honey," her father said as he entered the room. He pecked her cheek and then looked at Robert. "What's that?"

"Wings," he replied, still looking taken aback by their mother's sudden stroke of reasonableness. "I got three dozen from Wings-N-Things."

"Oh, spicy food." He grasped his belly and then plopped into a chair next to Robert.

"It's not spicy at all, Dad," Robert said. "I asked that they hold off on the seasoning."

"That's why there's no taste," he said, scrunching his face as he chewed on the beige-colored flesh. He turned to Robert. "How can you live like this?"

"I can't upset my ulcer."

"Don't eat too much," her mother said, and placed a slab of marinated meat onto the indoor grill. "Dinner's almost ready."

The family gathered at the table to a meal of *gal bi*, a simmering cauldron of bean-curd soup, two dozen bowls of various *ban chan* made up of mostly red-pepper-soaked roots and cabbages, rice and chicken wings. Whitney piled a small portion from each bowl onto her plate, and she wondered how she could best ease into a conversation regarding her passion for music without sending her parents into cardiac arrest. Perhaps constant reference to their deceased classmate's profession-induced misery was the way to go. She was forming a speech when her mother spoke.

"So, Scott's mother told me that he went to seminary."

"Where did he go?" her father asked.

"DTS."

Whitney looked up, surprised that his name had come up. They hadn't mentioned him in almost two months, not since he had quit his job and left for holier pastures.

"Long-distance relationships can be so difficult," her father said.

"Excuse me?" Whitney stared at him.

"Excuse me, what?"

"Why are you talking about long-distance relationships? You know Scott and I aren't together, right? We broke up in March."

"What?" her mother gasped. Her father choked on a chicken wing. "What do you mean, you broke up?"

"We broke up," she repeated slowly, feeling her face burn as her parents gawked at her.

"What did you do?" Her mother's face wrinkled with concern, and the color drained from her cheeks.

"God, Mom, I didn't do anything," she said, irritated by the implication. "We both grew out of the relationship." She turned to Robert. "I thought you told them."

He looked at her, his initial surprise turning into indignation. "You told me not to."

"Why didn't you try counseling?" Her father had stopped eating and was studying her for answers. "A lot of couples have a trial separation before they end their relationship. Didn't you guys at least *try*?"

"We weren't married." She shrugged helplessly. "We were just dating."

"But you were *going* to get married," her father argued. "We all talked about it."

"Well, sometimes things just don't work out that way." She felt awful. She knew how much her parents loved him, how much they had already considered him family, and as she regarded their anguished faces, it was clear that they felt dumped, too.

"Oh my goodness," her mother said. "This is terrible. How could this have happened?"

"Y'all, I'm sure Whitney already feels bad," Robert said, his shirt dipping into a bowl of red-pepper paste as he reached for yet another piece of chicken. "You don't need to make her feel worse."

"Thank you." She threw her brother a grateful smile and looked at her parents. They didn't say anything, and she wondered if, in their despair, they even felt sympathy for her. She cleared her throat. "Well, I've been thinking about your friend from college, the female judge who was so miserable in her career. It's actually very similar to what I've been going through. I realized that I don't need Scott to make me whole. I don't even need my job to make me complete. I'm my own person with my own desires and dreams, you know?"

Her parents peered at her, puzzled.

"Well," her father said simply.

"And just so you know," she continued, "I think that I've found my true calling. What *God* wants me to do. It's like he revealed it when we were in Austin, which I'm sure you think is a strange place for an epiphany." Good, she thought, framing a singing career as God's insistence might be the most effective argument. "I know y'all don't—"

"Did you and Scott pray about the situation?" her mother interrupted. "Did you talk to Reverend Lee about your relationship?"

"What?" she asked, dismayed that her mother was still on the subject. "Why would we talk to Reverend Lee about it? I barely know him."

"He offers couples counseling," she said. "You should have seen him."

"Mom," she said sternly, "our breakup was for the best. Why can't you let it go?"

"Because it isn't worth letting go, honey. You two were perfect for each other."

"Oh," her father moaned. "I feel like—who is that?" He focused on the ceiling for inspiration. "That little chicken who thought the sky was falling."

"Chicken Little?" Robert suggested.

"Yes. I feel like Chicken Little."

"Because of *this?*" Whitney asked incredulously.

"Because of this, and because of other things," he said, lowering his fork.

"What other things?" Whitney asked. Her parents concentrated on their dinner in response.

"Mom and Dad put a lot of their retirement savings into this one stock," Robert said. Her parents scowled. "Commelast. Is that right?"

"Commelast," her father muttered.

"Anyway, the stock hasn't been doing so well."

"How not well?" Whitney asked.

"It was delisted from NASDAQ yesterday," Robert said, his face registering the stomach-lurching sensation Whitney now felt.

"So it's basically worthless?"

"Yeah."

"How much of their retirement did they invest?"

"All of it," her mother said flatly. She sighed with such despondency that Whitney felt her anxiety. "Well, thank the good Lord that at least your father still has a job." She stood up, walked to the stove and put on a kettle. Crossing her arms, she watched the water boil.

"Were you about to say something?" her father asked.

"What?"

"You were talking about what God revealed to you while you were in Austin. Do you feel called to the ministry, too?" Concern masked his face, and at the same time, he looked genuinely interested in what she had to say. His earnestness crushed her.

"It was nothing," she said. "I don't even remember what it is."

He leaned over and kissed the top of Whitney's head, rose from the table and silently walked out of the room. Her mother poured herself a cup of tea and also bussed her children before joining him in the family room, leaving Whitney and Robert alone in the kitchen.

"Why didn't you tell me about this earlier?" Whitney asked, poking Robert's arm.

"They didn't want me to say anything."

"Why not?"

"Whitney," he said with an older-brother sigh, "they didn't want to worry you, okay? They *never* want to worry you. You know that."

She gazed out the windows, digesting the news of her parents' financial situation. It was just like them to keep her in the dark. They had always shielded her from their problems, as if their younger female child wouldn't be able to handle, or help, their ordeals. Instead, they apprised Robert of every issue that faced the family, expecting him to safeguard the information or provide a solution. It was unfair to ask one child to shoulder their burdens to the exclusion of the other, but she knew that her parents had grown up in Seoul under the same expectations. Korean parents didn't ask their younger daughters for anything except for a good education, a reputable job and a Korean husband. From their firstborn sons they demanded the moon, and usually threw in a request for the sun.

"Are Mom and Dad going to be all right financially?" she asked.

"They should be," he said, the doubt on his face belying his words. "I mean, they won't be taking any fancy vacations, but they should be able to make ends meet with what Dad's making now." He rested his elbows on the table and rubbed his temples. "Mom's right. At least Dad's got a job."

"We should pitch in and help."

"I don't know how much I can," he said, his face falling. "I've been saving and trying to make a dent in their mortgage and bills, but I still have a lot of school debt." He groaned. "God, I don't even want to think about how much I owe in school loans."

"I make money, too. Let me help you."

"Fine." He sighed heavily. "I've got some of their paperwork at home. We can go over it tonight."

"Good." She gazed into the family room, where her parents were watching a Korean drama. They had moved into the house only a year ago, and she knew that they had sunk every penny available to them on the down payment. They still owed an enormous amount on the mortgage, and given that they had just tanked their life savings in a foolhardy investment, she wasn't sure how her father's paycheck would cover their present expenses, let alone their future.

"We're really lucky, you know that?" she asked before standing to clear the table.

"How so?"

"Mom and Dad gave us everything, and even if we were never rich, we never lacked anything." Indeed, until recently, they had lavished their children with everything their hearts could have desired, and had somehow scrounged up enough money to send both of them to Loyola Academy, Duke, Harvard and MIT, not to mention funding swimming, tennis, piano and ballet lessons, as well as a short-lived equestrian obsession. Whitney suddenly felt an anguishing guilt, and an overwhelming gratitude.

"Yeah. I guess you're right."

"You guess?"

"I never really thought about it. I think I spent so much time worrying about everything that I never stopped to think about all the good things they've done."

"That's really unattractive, Robert."

"What is?"

"Your small-mindedness." He frowned, and she planted her hands on her hips. "I really wish y'all had told me about Commelast before they invested. Didn't you do any research on the company beforehand?"

"Of course we did," he said wearily. "Look, Whitney, you know that we're not stupid, and I really don't want to get into a game of regrets. It's done. Let's just move on." He went to the kitchen and picked at the plates of leftovers while she cleaned.

"I just don't understand why they'd put their entire nest egg into one stock."

"Whitney, drop it."

"Why didn't they—"

"Jesus Christ, I said drop it," he snapped, his face mottled with restrained anger. "Talk about something else or stop talking."

"Fine."

Neither of them spoke, and she listened to the Korean drama playing in the living room while she loaded the dishwasher.

"Hey, Scott asked how you're doing," he said suddenly.

"He did?" She looked up, surprised. "I didn't know that y'all still kept in touch."

"I probably talk to him just as much now as I did before he moved to Dallas." She frowned at him, puzzled. "He's consulting on a few projects until we can find someone to replace him."

"What'd you say when he asked how I was doing?"

"I told him that you were fine."

"Oh." She shoved a fistful of chopsticks into a compartment in the dishwasher, hovering over them for a moment before returning to the sink. "How's he doing?"

He jumped up on the counter and watched her rinse off the dishes. "Good. He's happy in Dallas."

"I'm glad." She realized that she meant it. Time had done much to buff away the unpleasantness of their last few months together, so that she recalled their relationship with fondness. She had never been one to keep up with her exes, but she considered sending Scott an e-mail, if only to wish him well in seminary.

"God, I can't even imagine how Mom's going to try to set you up with someone," he said with a chuckle. "Ten bucks says that she'll have a list ready by the end of the night."

"I don't want to think about it." She ran her hands under the water, and Robert handed her a towel. "Thanks. Hey, do you remember what we were talking about the last time we had lunch?"

"You mean when I had to make a pact to go out with whatever monster you dragged back to the lair?" He rolled his eyes. "So, who is it?"

"Just keep an open mind, okay?"

He frowned, and she worried that he wasn't warming to her flattering presentation of his prospective wife. "You know what, Whitney? Call me a loser if you want, but it is *hard* to find someone once you're out of school. Why do you think so many people sign up for Internet dating sites? Half the guys in my class at work are members, and I've even considered giving it a try, so don't worry about my having an open mind. It's about as open as it's ever going to get."

"Okay," Whitney said, and sucked in her breath. "I thought you might be interested in Hercules."

"Hercules?" He didn't hide his surprise, but he didn't seem disgusted, either. She remembered how boys in high school had recoiled at the idea of dating an overweight, slightly unkempt woman, and she still felt a roaring protectiveness when she caught men doing unflattering double takes at the chef.

"She's a really good person." She didn't know why she was trying to sell her friend to her brother. They had known each other long enough to make their own judgments, and he already knew that she was a terrible matchmaker.

"I know." His entire face flushed, and being as fair as the rest of her family, his diaphanous skin seemed to glow. She couldn't tell if he was excited or offended, and perhaps he wasn't sure, either. "What made you think of her?"

"Y'all are really similar, even if you don't think so. I think you'd complement each other."

He blushed even deeper and turned his back to her, and Whitney watched as her brother bumbled about the kitchen, clumsily tidying up the mess.

"So, you'll think about it?" she asked. He didn't respond. "Robert?"

Finally, he nodded, uncharacteristically pleased, or at least not viscerally irritated, that someone was going to intervene in his romantic endeavors.

"When are you going to call her?" she pressed.

"I don't know. God, it's been so long since I've asked anyone out."

"Call her soon. There's nothing more flattering than a guy who takes the initiative."

He nodded again, looking contemplative, and she thought of her own Mr. Right. She had no idea what kind of man he would be, and she didn't have a requirements list to speak of. But she was sure that she'd know when she saw him. Something would register in her heart like a blip on a radar screen, an inexplicable charge that only she would understand.

"Hercules, huh?" Robert was still red as he wandered out of the kitchen.

Whitney soaked a sponge under the faucet and proceeded to wipe down the table. She was glad to have taken Robert's mind off their parents' financial woes, if only temporarily, and she glanced at them in the family room, feeling anxiety bubble in her veins. If she had been certain about her destiny before dinner, she now felt doubly doubtful of what she was supposed to do. It was clear that the roles of parent and child were slowly reversing, with Robert and her succeeding to the task of provider and caregiver, and her parents evolving to the part of the provided and cared for. The shift was frightening, and while Whitney was able and willing to fulfill her new position, she didn't quite feel ready.

Eighteen

"It's freakin' depressing at our house," Hercules said, placing her forearm over her eyes. She leaned against her usual booth at Dragonfly, her ad hoc office, and the plump leather backing cushioned her aching shoulders. "It's not like I'd expected my dad to turn into Little Miss Sunshine when he moved in, but honestly, I really hoped that he'd change, even just a little. I thought that he'd at least try to tone down how much he criticizes me." She sighed heavily and then lowered her arm. Reynaldo was sitting across from her, a sad, empathetic smile spanning his moonlike face.

"Some people just never change, Chef. You can't let him keep getting to you."

"You know that we haven't spoken in over a week? I couldn't listen to all the shit he said, so I just stopped talking to him." She cringed, embarrassed by her childish defense mechanism. "I guess he got tired of being the only person in the conversation, because he stopped talking, too." She leaned her head against the banquette and sighed again. "Honestly, I don't know what's worse—his constant barbs or complete silence."

"Maybe you should talk to someone about it," he said, sounding concerned. "A professional counselor might help you."

She looked up at him. He wasn't joking, and in a camel-colored sweater and matching sport coat, he looked like her ignorant impression of a professional counselor. She let out a groan.

"I don't know." She checked her watch and craned her neck towards the entrance. "Where the hell is this guy? His interview was supposed to start fifteen minutes ago."

"I'm glad you finally got rid of Simon," he said, likewise twisting to look at the front of the restaurant. "I told you that he was a short-termer with real attention problems."

"I didn't get rid of him. I told him to get off the smack. He's in re-hab now, and he knows that if he sobers up, he's welcome back here."

"I wouldn't have expected you to be so patient," he said, his bushy brows raised high.

"He's talented, and that's all there is to it. Besides, I don't know if a guy with a drug problem is any worse than a person who can't show up on time. God, what's with kids these days?" She glared at the front door, willing the interviewee to walk through. The longer it remained unmoved, the more irritated she became.

"He'll show." He reached into his bag and pulled out a copy of this month's *National Spectator.*

"This is crazy," she said, watching as he flipped through the maga-zine. "When I got out of school, I might not have been the most talented saucier or the best pastry chef, but I always made sure that I was never late to anything. And I *never* talked back to a prospective employer. That's all I'm getting today—a bunch of sniveling shitheads who think they're entitled to everything the world has to offer. It makes me want to knock their heads together."

"That's what my generation thought of yours, actually," he said, still poring over the pages.

"You're only six years older than I am."

"In any case," he said, turning another page, "we've only inter-viewed three people so far, and we've still got all day."

"One more minute," she said. "If this foolio doesn't show up in the next sixty seconds, it'll be curtains for him."

Just then, the door opened, and a large man lumbered through. He was as young as the rest of today's interviewees had been, and with his *University of South Carolina COCKS*—inscribed red cap and bulging belly, he looked like the token fat fraternity boy on his way to a kegger. Unfixed hair matted against his forehead, and in jeans and a faded gray T-shirt, he didn't resemble someone hoping for a job. He looked like a bum, and once he'd made an initial impression that he didn't care about the position, or her restaurant, his existence flared Hercules' temper.

"Are you Hercules Huang?" he asked. "I'm Bob Teller. I'm here for the sous chef position for this restaurant or Dragonfly Deux. You said to come at two o'clock?"

"It's two nineteen, Bob," Hercules said in a low, almost baritone voice, certain that he could feel her displeasure.

"Sorry," he said, not sorry at all. His cell phone rang, and he reached into his pocket.

"Let it go," she said. "Sit down and let's get this started."

"But it might be another restaurant," he said, looking affronted. "I'm trying to line up all my interviews this week."

"You answer your cell phone, and you can kiss this job good-bye," she snapped. "I might also put in a word to my friends at Sans Souci, Oliphant, Baudelaire's, Cormick's, Jeffrey's and Butter about you. There are a hundred more phone calls I can make, and you're on really thin ice right now."

He glared at her, turned off his phone and sat down. Reynaldo scooted to make room, and Hercules ripped a sheet of paper off her notepad. She felt her neck burn, and she took in deep breaths to calm down.

"Did you bring your résumé?" she asked.

He pulled a piece of paper out of a folder and placed it on the table close to him, so that it was almost out of her reach. When he didn't hand it to her, she leaned across the surface and snatched it, all the while contemplating shutting down the interview right then. Had she not been hard up for staffing, she would have.

"Art Institute of Dallas, the Green Grape," she muttered as she studied the document. "This is good. You just get out of school?"

"In December."

"How long did you work at the Green Grape?"

"About five months."

"Why'd you leave Dallas?"

"My parents live here." He straightened and crossed his arms. "My mother had a stroke, and my father couldn't take care of her by himself."

She looked up, surprised. She hadn't expected him to be conscientious, and the explanation made her hate him just a little less.

"How much vacation will I be allowed?" He leaned forward and rested his hairy arms on the table. "Given my situation, I'm going to have to be able to take off if my mom needs me. That's a nonnegotiable part of my deal."

"Two weeks," she said, barely paying attention to him as she worked her way down his credentials. "You'll understand if I ask you for proof of your mother's condition. It's not that I don't trust you, but the information would be helpful in creating some kind of alternative work schedule."

"And holidays?"

"What?" She looked up.

"Do I get holidays off?"

"Have you ever worked in a restaurant that closed on holidays?" She laid his résumé on the surface and stared at him.

"No, but I was hoping . . ." He stopped and leaned forward, the edge of the table practically splitting his belly in two. "Let's just cut to the chase, Hercules. I'm the best there is, and you'll see that I can do twice as much in half the time as anyone you'll interview. Everyone at the culinary institute knew it, which is why I made them call me 'Chef.' I plan on opening my own restaurant one day." He brought a fat arm close to his face and checked his watch. "This is just a pit stop, and you'd be a fool to pass up someone as creative as I am. But, hey, it's your decision."

Hercules felt her mouth drop. She couldn't believe the balls on this boy, and she wanted to slap him for referring to himself as "Chef." The word literally meant "chief," or "head," and it was a title that was bestowed on someone, not a designation up for self-proclamation. That her sous chefs called her "Chef" instead of "Hercules," "Huang" or "Hey, you" was a continual sign of respect, and she was offended by Bob's instant, and ignorant, presumption when he hadn't proved himself worthy of the honor.

"Stand up," she commanded. "I'm no fool, Bob, and I won't let you go if you're as creative as you say. But it's a small community, and if you can't prove yourself right now, then that means you're a liar. There's nothing more useless to me than a liar, and if I find out that you've been anything less than one hundred percent honest with me, I'll make it my personal mission to ensure that you don't get the chance to prove yourself anywhere else."

His eyes bulged, and he rose slowly. Reynaldo sighed quietly and scooted out of the booth. They walked into the kitchen, and she surveyed the room before pulling out leftover swordfish, crabmeat and sirloin from the refrigerator. She dropped them onto the steel center island and pointed to a station of chopped herbs.

"Impress me," she said, and then crossed her arms.

"Excuse me?" He frowned, and his already ruddy cheeks burned brighter. "What do you want me to make?"

"Whatever you want, so long as it's good and in keeping with the restaurant."

"But I don't know what kind of food you serve."

"You didn't do any research at all before you got here?"

"Not really. I mean, I figured that I'd—"

"Cook, Bob."

He bit onto a nearly invisible lower lip and glared at her. If he was flummoxed a moment earlier, he was now furious.

"You don't get to talk to me that way, Hercules."

"Yeah, I do. I own this place. Cook." She was livid, and his standing up to her only incensed her more.

He stared at her for another moment, and his already flared face turned a darker shade of mango.

"Fuck you. I don't need this shit." He turned and stormed out of the kitchen.

She let him go without a return curse. There was no reason to waste her breath. He had waltzed in here, arrogant as the rest of the morning wannabes, without any understanding of, or any desire to understand, what Dragonfly and she were about. They hadn't studied up on the cuisine, and they didn't even have basic manners. They had no respect for those who had paved the way for them, and she was offended by their cavalier attitudes. She was glad to be rid of him, and in the middle of a muttered rant about the unappreciative and entitled youth of today, she stopped short. She sounded just like Baba.

"Jesus, Hercules, was all that necessary?" Reynaldo asked.

She jumped at the sound of his voice and turned around. "You wouldn't believe how rough some of the interviews were when I was on the other side of the table, and I *always* had my shit together. Now no one seems to give a flip, and it's a huge waste of my time to have to go through this process every time someone leaves. I'd rather find someone now than have to repeat this process next month."

"I agree, but there are ways to interview without losing your cool. It's not healthy, and honestly, it's not really professional."

"Professional?" she asked, agog. "Half the cooks I know are freakin' savages. I'm about as professional as you're ever going to see." She considered. "Well, I'm the most civilized, anyway." He guffawed and folded his arms, looking amused and parental at the same time, and she understood that he wasn't backing down on his reprimand. She sighed. "How do you stay so calm? You're just as busy as I am, and you're probably surrounded by more idiots, but I've never seen you lose your cool."

"I try to accept people for who they are." He shrugged and smiled placidly. "I accept life for what it is. I can change what I can change, and everything else, I just have to let it be."

"You sound like one of those AA members. The Serenity Prayer and all that."

"That's where I got it, actually. I was in AA. I still am." He was barely whispering, but as shocked as Hercules was, he might as well have been shouting.

"I had no idea."

"I'm ten years sober."

"How could we have worked together all this time, and I've never known that you were an alcoholic?" She felt her eyes protrude from her head, and she wondered what other life-changing news he hadn't yet shared.

"You never ask about me." He uncrossed his arms and sat on one of the stools in the kitchen. "It's not a criticism against you, Chef. Business is business, and life is life. But you have a harder time than most separating the two, which is why half the time, I feel like your therapist. And since I'm playing that role right now, listen to me when I say that sometimes, you just have to let things go. You have to let them be what they are without expecting more. Funny thing is, you might be surprised by what the universe gives you back in return."

A ring sounded in the front of the restaurant, interrupting their session. She headed to the dining room, and an enormously busty woman in a power suit was standing at the doorway, smiling widely and looking like she was selling Avon products.

"You're Hercules Huang," she said, clearly starstruck. "It's such an honor to meet you. I read your articles in the *National Spectator, Texas Mag*, and the *Houston Chronicle*. Actually, I've read everything I could find about you." She pulled out a sheet of paper from her bag and handed it to Hercules. "I brought a copy of my résumé. Oh, I'm Sasha Sunshine." She giggled. "I'm sorry, I'm a little nervous."

"Come sit down," Hercules said, and led her to the same banquette where Bob had pissed her off. She glanced around for Reynaldo, who hadn't joined them. "What kind of name is Sasha Sunshine?" She was conscious of her tone, and she tried to speak as kindly as possible. Reynaldo's advice was still swirling in her mind, and she was determined to follow it.

"It's my real name," she said, blushing at the question.

"No kidding."

"Actually, I changed the spelling of it," Sasha said. "It was originally spelled s-o-n-n-e-s-c-h-e-i-n."

"Oh."

Hercules read through the remainder of the résumé.

"I see you spent four years at Laurent," she said. "That's a great restaurant. I did my internship there."

"Did you really?" Sasha appeared genuinely interested. "It was such an incredible learning experience. I understand that your menu is really similar. I just moved to Houston last week and haven't had a chance to eat here, but I read everything I could about Dragonfly and basically memorized the Web site."

"Did you?" Hercules brightened as she took in the chef hopeful. "Tell me, what do you think about working on holidays?"

"Holidays?"

"Yes, holidays," she repeated, worried that all her interviewees were going to request those days off. "You know, Christmas, Easter, Thanksgiving, Hanukkah—why are you looking at me like that?"

Sasha straightened her face. "I guess I'm surprised that you're asking about it. I always assumed that we'd be working holidays. We did our best business on holidays."

"Exactly," Hercules said, relieved. She was ready to hire the woman. "Your résumé looks great, and I like you. I just have a couple of questions to ask. Formalities, really."

"Shoot," Sasha said with a rock-star smile.

"I'll need you to take a drug test. You don't take any drugs, do you? Cocaine, marijuana, heroin, et cetera?"

"No, no," she said, still beaming at her.

"Cool. You've never shown up to work drunk, have you?"

"Of course not."

"Ever been arrested for a felony? Served time for a felony?" Hercules scribbled on Sasha's résumé. As far as she was concerned, this woman was going to suit up today. Hell, with Dragonfly Deux set to open in a few months, she might let her take on more responsibility there. Hercules couldn't be the executive chef in both places, and if Sasha was as good as she was hoping, she might promote her to the post.

"Yes," Sasha said. Hercules stirred and looked up.

"Excuse me?"

"I've served time for a felony," she said matter-of-factly, though her cheeks were now flaming.

Hercules was at a loss. No one had ever answered the question in the affirmative, and she certainly hadn't expected Sasha Sunshine to.

"What were you convicted of?" As a policy, convicted felons were out of the question, and the interview should have stopped there, but she was curious. And hopeful. If the infraction hadn't been violent, maybe she would make an exception.

"Armed robbery."

"What?"

"I was convicted of armed robbery," Sasha repeated.

"I heard you the first time," Hercules said, astonished by the answer. "I'm asking you for details."

"Well, I don't do drugs now," she said sheepishly, "but I did a few years ago. I was high, and I robbed a couple at gunpoint. I'm obviously not proud of it, and I've changed since then." She lurched forward and grabbed Hercules' hand. "Please don't hold that against me, Chef. I'm a really great cook, and I'll do whatever you want to prove it to you."

Hercules sighed and released Sasha's grasp. "I'm sorry, but I have a policy not to hire felons." Sasha's face fell, her expression breaking Hercules' heart. "But I tell you what. I'm going to keep your résumé and think about it. I'm calling back a dozen or so people to show me their skills in the kitchen. If you really impress me, I'll consider you, okay?"

"Thank you," she cried. She clasped Hercules' hands again. "You won't be disappointed. I promise!"

"I'll call you." Hercules got up from her seat.

"Thank you," Sasha repeated, and left the restaurant, nearly crashing into the wall on her way out.

Hercules watched as the interviewee stumbled to her car. She already knew that Sasha had a place at Dragonfly Deux. Her past didn't matter. For the first time all day, a person with a respect for her, and her restaurant, had done everything to impress her, and her attitude alone was worthy of a position. There simply was no need to test her in the kitchen. And if Sasha faltered, Hercules would train her herself.

"Well, that wasn't so bad, was it?" Reynaldo asked. He had come out of hiding from the kitchen and walked up to the table.

"Where've you been?"

"I made a few calls while you were in here." He motioned at the door. "Sasha seems perfect, felony conviction notwithstanding."

"You've got fox ears," Hercules said, happy about the new chef. "Any calls for me?"

"Actually, yes." He pulled out a slip of paper from his jacket and placed it on the table. "I talked to Dr. Larry Kushner over at Rice. He teaches behavioral psychology, and he's got a few degrees in counseling.

If you ever want to talk to someone about your dad, you might want to give him a ring."

"You really think I need professional help?" Hercules picked up the contact information and studied it.

"It wouldn't hurt. I doubt that you're talking to your friends about anything personal, and I don't want you to have a meltdown at an Acceleron meeting." He tapped the paper. "Give him a call or go visit his office. I've already told him about you."

"How do you even know the guy?" she asked suspiciously. "Are you a patient?"

"He was my roommate in college. Funny how differently we turned out, huh?" He glanced at his watch and then picked up his things. "I've got to go. Don't forget. Our final meeting with Acceleron's design team is tomorrow. I also spoke to your guy in Austin, and things are looking really good for a third restaurant." He patted her back affectionately. "We'll talk tomorrow."

She watched as he pushed open the front door, and felt as cared for as she had in ages. In a way, he was her brother, father and wise aunt, all rolled into a chubby Cuban package, and she realized that on top of being a friend and business manager, he was her personal counselor and yogi, as well. She felt herself smile, grateful that she had him in her life, and she was about to head to the kitchen when the phone rang.

"Dragonfly, Hercules speaking."

"Uh—Hercules? It's Robert Lee, Whitney's brother."

"I know who you are. What's up?" It was strange that he was calling the restaurant. Actually, it was unlike him to call her at all. In the fifteen years that they had known each other, he had never once phoned, and as he paused, coughed and cleared his throat, she thought about Whitney's call a few days prior. Slowly, she realized that she hadn't dreamed that Whitney had advised that Robert was interested in her, and while Robert was struggling to find his voice, she suddenly became nervous.

"Are you okay?" she asked, interrupting his cackling fit.

"Yeah. I'm fine. Sorry about that. I had something in my throat. Hey, listen, what are you doing this Friday?"

"You mean, other than working? Nothing, really."

"You're working? Oh, well, we could schedule it around you."

"Schedule what?"

"Oh—uh, I was thinking that it would be nice to grab dinner. Go watch a movie or something. Maybe coffee. Or a drink." He sounded uncomfortable, and she wondered if he approached all women with such bumbling grace.

"Actually, I'm free Saturday. Do you want to do dinner on Saturday?"

"Saturday's perfect," he shouted. He cleared his throat again. "Yeah. I'll pick you up around, say, seven?"

"Great," she said, feeling a Joker-like smile stretch her face.

"Great."

"Great," she repeated, unable to conjure a wittier response.

"Gre—okay. I'll see you then."

She hung up, sure that she was grinning like a loon. She remained where she was, listening to her thumping heartbeat return to normal, and a thousand thoughts whirled in her mind until Reynaldo's counsel edged its way into the forefront. *Sometimes, you have to let things go. You might be surprised by what the universe gives you back in return.* A part of her wanted to mock the platitude, to deride its hippie lackadaisical-ness. His attitude of acquiescence went against everything she knew, against her dogged determination to force her dreams into reality. Yet, Robert's call reminded her that if there had been one area in her life that she had never pushed with her characteristic ferocity, it was her love life. And now, despite having given up on her romantic desires ages ago, she had a date. The thought encouraged her, gave her hope for the matters that plagued her still. Of course it was naive, simplistic and foolish in fact, to believe that the universe might somehow compensate for the tattered relationship she shared with her father. Even so, she allowed herself to wonder if one day she might be surprised by what the future had in store for them both, if she might be met with the kind of father-daughter relationship she had always dreamed of, or at least one that didn't break her heart. Possible or not, it was a lovely notion.

Nineteen

*A*udrey stood outside Dr. Eric Rymer's office, about to knock on his door. He, the head of the graduate English department at Rice University, had called her at eight in the morning, and when he had asked that she come by shortly before lunch to chat about her dissertation, she knew that he had found it either extraordinary or worthy of being defecated on. He didn't typically meet with students to discuss work in between the two extremes, and her excellence or failure had apparently affected him such that he was compelled to deal with her before his favorite meal of the day. As she thought about what he might have to say, anxiety crawled through her body like ice. She knocked three times and prayed that he hadn't found her work shit-tastic.

"Come in," he shouted through the door.

She entered and scanned his paper-strewn office. Sunlight streamed through a wall of dirty windowpanes, highlighting the disarray of his space. He was hunched over his desk, pudgy hands clasped together on a stack of papers, and his massive argyle-sweatered form threatened to swallow his chair.

"I'm not sure whether to be excited or terrified," she said, closing the door behind her. He looked up.

"Take a seat, Miss Henley. And, no, there's no need to be terrified. Imagine that, a student scared of me." His deep voice rumbled against the shelves and hardwood floor, and he smiled, looking thoughtful, as if he was imagining a class full of petrified pupils. He was oblivious to his own gravitas, unaware that all thirty-six doctoral candidates mentally genuflected in his wake. She had always considered him genius incarnate, a master of the written word, which was why she had chosen him as her dissertation director. He regarded her, his slate-hued eyes sunken in his deeply lined face.

"Sir?"

"I have a lunch meeting in a few minutes, so I'll get right to the point." He unfolded his hands and flipped through her paper before returning his gaze to her. "I see that you created a dossier with Career Services."

"I did."

"So I take it that you're interested in a teaching position at a university after you graduate?" He was staring at her so intently that she tucked her hair behind her ear self-consciously, a nervous tic that she hadn't been able to break since high school.

"I think most students dream of tenure," she said carefully, tucking her hair again.

"You know that I'm leaving Rice at the end of this semester." He leaned back in his chair and swiveled to the right, and then to the left, like a meditative gyroscope.

"Yes, sir. I heard that you're going to chair the English department at Amherst." She felt out of sorts, still halfway expecting Dr. Rymer to raise the merits or flaws of her dissertation, and his unexpected comments about both of their careers stoked her already pounding heartbeat.

"That's correct. The department and I have been working on arranging seminars for next fall and the spring semester after that, and the faculty at Amherst is really attracted to interdisciplinary courses." He stopped rocking. "I sent your dissertation to the sitting chair of the college, and he was quite taken with you. Apparently, he has some thoughts on what you had to say about the varying shades of deity and God's frailty evidenced in prose. He was particularly impressed with your extrapolation of Christ's redemption in modern media, or what you call the Internet Sphere of Literature."

"He was?" Her stomach lurched at the flattering remark.

"We've discussed adding a course for next spring on the intersection of religion, literature and twenty-first-century media, and after reading your paper, we think you'd be the perfect person to lead the class." He tapped on her thick thesis. "You've already got the materials at your ready. I know it's a bit out of left field, and it's probably not the way Amherst normally decides what courses to offer, but that's one of the perks of heading up a department, I suppose." He chuckled, baring a full range of oversized, coffee-stained teeth. "In any case, you've got a few weeks to think about it, although I hope you tell me sooner rather than later."

"You're asking me to move to Massachusetts?" she asked dumbly, shocked by the invitation. She couldn't believe that Dr. Rymer was asking her to teach at *Amherst*, a bastion of lovers of literature, full of like-minded individuals with a similar passion for the written word. She gaped at him, fully aware that she was staring at him like a moron, yet she couldn't tear away her eyes.

"Well, yes, I suppose I'm asking you to move to Massachusetts." He smiled, graciously forgiving of her imbecilic ogle. "Like I said, think on it for a bit and let me know. We—"

"I don't need a few weeks," she interrupted, almost shouting her response. "I accept."

He chuckled again, looking pleased, and with his full, white beard and ruddy cheeks, he could have been Santa Claus's erudite brother. "Well, then, welcome aboard, *Dr.* Henley. By the way, it goes without saying that I found your dissertation—and oral defense—to be exceptional."

"Thank you, sir." She felt out of her body, like an apparition hovering over them, breaking into an overexcited Irish jig. The compliment was almost more valuable than the invitation to be a part of Amherst's faculty, and its import caused her to become light-headed. He reached over his desk and grasped her hand, and she shook with such vigor that he laughed.

"I have to go," he said, "but we'll get together in a couple of weeks to finalize everything. Again, it's good to have you, Dr. Henley." He stood up, and she rose with him before trailing him out of his office. In a dreamlike daze, she stumbled down the hall, drunk with joy. Only when she reached the courtyard did she realize that she was still grinning like a baboon.

"Hercules? What are you doing here?" Audrey shaded her eyes and stopped walking. A breeze picked up, rustling the canopy of trees above them, and it circulated the muggy late May air, its vapory denseness enveloping her like a blanket. Sweaty students with loaded backpacks streamed around them like intellectually curious, upright turtles. Hercules approached her, looking ill at ease.

"I've got an appointment with Dr. Kushner." She pushed her sunglasses to the top of her head and then fluffed out her red T-shirt, drawing Audrey's attention to the spots of perspiration that had darkened the cotton material.

"Who's that?"

"Someone Reynaldo suggested that I talk to." She rolled her eyes. "He's a psychology professor who doesn't think he makes enough money teaching, so he moonlights by counseling Chinese children who can't get along with their fathers." She rolled her eyes again, clearly annoyed, before squinting in the sunlight. "What are you doing here?"

"I just met with my thesis director."

"How'd it go?"

"He offered me a job at Amherst." She realized that she was grinning like an idiot again, and unable to repress her joy, she lunged forward and hugged Hercules. When she pulled back, she saw that her friend was equally excited, and her apple cheeks squashed against her eyes as she smiled widely.

"That's wonderful! Did you accept?"

"Of course I did. I think I screamed out that I'd take the position even before Dr. Rymer finished offering it to me." She laughed, allowing herself to revel in the delicious memory.

"That's awesome, Auds. Congratulations." She was still beaming, her already rosy cheeks burning into a deeper flush, and her obvious pride touched Audrey. "Have you told your parents yet?"

"No, but"—she felt herself cringe—"right now, they're probably too preoccupied with other things to think about my career." She looked up, not at all calmed by the peaceful swaying of the live oak tree branches overhead.

"Why? What happened?"

She let out a sigh, and the deep exhalation turned into a groan. "She had Victor sign a prenup. I tore it up."

"Really?" Her bushy brows rose, deepening the faint lines on her forehead. She was clearly affected by the news, and if Audrey had expected her friend to thunder her opinion on the matter, she was surprised instead by her uncharacteristic reticence. They regarded each other for a silent moment, and when it became clear that Hercules didn't plan on speaking, Audrey reached out and touched her arm. "Hey, what are you thinking?"

"I was thinking that"—she watched a group of students settle into the grass a few feet from them—"honestly, I'm surprised that he signed it. And I'm really surprised that you destroyed it. I don't know that I would've done either if I'd been in your situations." She shook her head, looking thoughtful. "I guess if you were testing him to see if he was after your money, you got your answer."

"I didn't need to test him, H. I already knew."

Hercules crossed her arms, stretching the fabric of her top across her broad shoulders, and she peered at Audrey, her expression a mix of skepticism and admiration.

"I envy you, you know that? You managed to find someone who hasn't let you down. I haven't found someone who I can trust like that."

Audrey let out a little sigh, as baffled by Hercules' impossible standard of trust as Hercules was likely confused by her easy acceptance of one's faithfulness.

"Hercules, you've got to let go of this idea that you can only trust people who are perfect. Everyone's going to disappoint you at some time, whether it's your friends, your business partners or your family. You don't trust someone because you think he or she's never going to let you down. You trust them because you know that they've got your back."

"It's that simple for you?" she asked, frowning.

"When it comes down to it"—she nodded—"yeah. It is."

Hercules sniffed, looking unconvinced. "Are you going to tell your mom that you ripped up the prenup?"

"I might as well. She's going to find out sooner or later, and I can't afford to let her think that Victor refused to sign it, which is exactly what she's going to think if I don't come clean." She tensed, feeling dread collapse her shoulders.

Hercules cocked her head, wiping another stream of sweat that was trickling down the side of her face.

"You want to know what I think?" she asked.

"Please."

"Let Victor re-sign the prenup." Audrey recoiled, and Hercules let out a sigh. "Look, I know you're all principle over reality, and in a way, I admire that, but you're putting Victor in an impossible situation. If you refuse to let him sign it, what's going to happen? Your parents are going to flip their shit, they're going to give you grief about marrying him, and you're going to hate them for giving you grief. And even if he doesn't say anything, Victor's going to wonder what the hell kind of family he got himself into. He's willing to sign it, and your parents will be happy once he does, so what's the problem? Isn't a lifetime of peace worth a freakin' signature?"

"It's not that simple, Hercules."

"It's as simple as your perspective on trust."

"That's totally different."

"Why should it be?" She fanned her face with both hands before pulling her frizzy hair into a tight ponytail. "I'm not saying that you have to take my advice. But you don't have to be so freakin' stubborn, either."

Audrey guffawed. "So says the most stubborn human being I know."

"If you think I'm stubborn, you should try talking to my dad." She glanced at her watch and then pointed to the psychology building. "I've got to meet this guy. What are you going to do?"

"I'm going to sign up for a few summer school classes. I'll have to audit them, of course."

"Which classes?"

"Korean Culture and History and the Introduction to the Korean Language course. Hopefully, they're not already full. Registration ends tomorrow." Hercules seemed surprised. "It's never too late to learn something new."

"Yeah." She concentrated on the ground and dug the tip of her sneaker into the dirt. "I might sign up for a few classes, too. Maybe I'll take a Chinese-culture class and try to understand why my dad walks around all day with a stick up his ass."

"You should," Audrey said. "Take the class, I mean."

"We'll see. I'll catch up with you later."

"Okay." She headed towards the humanities building, and Hercules turned in the other direction. After two steps, Audrey turned around. "Hey, Hercules?"

"What's up?"

"You should know that if you ever want to talk about anything, I'm always here. There's nothing that you can say that I'd ever repeat to anyone else, and I'd never judge or think less of you. I just wanted you to know that I've got your back."

Hercules nodded, looking encouraged by what she had to know was true, and her lips parted into a smile, her slightly jagged teeth glinting in the light.

"I'll call you later."

"See ya."

Audrey maneuvered her way around a row of hedges and walked towards a row of brick buildings. She thought about Hercules' advice, pondering its practicality, and as much as she wanted to stand firm on her own idealistic principles, the objective, rational part of her also knew that her friend was right. The exhilaration she had experienced from ripping the prenup to shreds had lasted but a moment, and a nagging dissatisfaction had almost immediately overtaken her self-righteous indignation, as if she had been instantly made aware that she had just committed a bridge-burning sin. Even worse, she knew that her impetuous action had undermined Victor's attempt to appease her mother, and if she had intended to express her unconditional love for him, she had instead obliterated his manifestation of the same for her. With a shoulder-shuddering sigh, she realized that she had to make things right with her mother. For everyone's sake.

"How much longer is your work going to be on display?" Audrey asked, gazing at Jimmy's lithographs. She was at the Nesbitt Gallery with him, where she was anxiously chewing her nails down to nubs. After she had left Professor Rymer's office and registered for a full load of summer courses, she had phoned her mother to tell her that she had destroyed the prenup. The call had gone straight to voice mail, and rather than delay the inevitable, Audrey had left the bomb of an announcement, along with her scheduled whereabouts and a pitiful request to call her back. As frayed as her nerves were, she needed to be in a psychologically safe place, and given Jimmy's unassailable good cheer, the gallery was as perfect a hiding place as she could imagine.

"It'll be here another week," he said, and then slumped, his slim figure bending like a reed. "I've had a couple of people say that they'd like to buy one or two pieces, but I won't sell it to them. If they're asking for one part of it, then they don't get it. They're not a *series* of work. You either buy all six pieces or none at all. The *group* is the piece." He gazed at her, looking beaten down. "Does that make sense?"

"Yes." She sat down on a bench in the middle of the room. Jimmy sat next to her and concentrated on his cuticles. Despite his youthful outfit of a double layer of green T-shirts and loose-fitting jeans, he somehow seemed more mature, as if the conflict he felt with respect to his art was aging him. "It's like a separated double triptych. Or whatever you call one with six pieces."

"*Exactly.*" He straightened and smiled at her. "See, you understand."

"I think I did from the start." She hunched over and straightened the hem of her wide-legged trousers. "You know, you might get more bites if you weren't asking for a leg as a down payment."

"Honey, I poured my life's blood into this. I'd actually charge more if I didn't feel so conflicted about capitalism."

Audrey laughed. "Are you working on something new?"

"Oh my God." He bolted upright and grabbed her hand. "You are going to *die* when you see what I'm doing now."

"What is it?" His enthusiasm was infectious, and she wondered how he had the energy to be so thrilled all the time.

"I'm not going to tell you," he said mischievously. His honey-colored eyes sparkled under the lights. "It's a secret. But it's for you."

"It is?" She smiled widely, immensely flattered. "Is that what you tell all of your girlfriends?"

"No, of course not," he said with a grin. "It's fabulous. It's just *gore-jess*. You'll see."

"When will it be ready?"

"Oh—it may be a while. It's pretty complex. And with all this shit with Kevin and the lawyers—I'd say another few months. Maybe a year."

"I'm not that patient," she said, nudging him.

"That's too bad." He sighed deeply, and from the serenity of his face, she could tell that he was content. "Sometimes I can't believe how lucky I am. Five years ago, I didn't think that I'd be able to live my dream." He motioned to his hanging lithographs. "This is my dream, you know. To be able to spend all day creating what's in my head without having to work a horrible little job. I worked at an insurance company for four years, saving up so that I could take a break and concentrate on my work, and if that doesn't suck the life out of you, I don't know what would."

She nodded and then straightened, taking in his lithographs and studying the rest of the pieces on the wall. As little as she knew about the creation of art, she understood the desire to follow one's passion, and she let out a deep breath before turning to Jimmy.

"My dream is to be a professor, and today, I got an offer to teach at Amherst."

"Did you really?" His eyes widened, and he clapped his hands together. "That's incredible!"

"I mean, it's not a tenure-track position or anything. I'd be an adjunct prof for next year's spring semester, and then the department would have to reevaluate, but yeah, it's something, isn't it?"

"Girl, you are awesome. Awesome! I never had any doubt that you'd make it to the top." He gazed at her wondrously, his smile spanning the width of his face. "I can totally see you as a professor. You're going to make a great one."

"How do you know?"

"I just do. You have that air about you. *Professor* Henley." He straightened up playfully, as if he were a student in one of her classes. "This is so great. Just when I was starting to feel down about my situation, you come along and give me inspiration."

"Yeah?" His comments flattered her, and his contagious exuberance magnified her accomplishment, making it seem grander than perhaps it was.

"You had a dream, you went after it, and you achieved it. Maybe my dream will come true, too." He motioned to his pieces on the wall. "Maybe someone will get what I'm doing and buy the whole damned thing already."

She gazed at the colorful blotches again, absorbing their vivid hues, and whether because of his unfettered adulation, her recent professional achievement or the fact that she had loved his lithographs for months, she decided to act upon the urge that had grabbed her the minute she had seen his work.

"I'll buy it," she said, smiling brightly. "The whole damned thing."

"What?" He shrank back, surprised.

"I should've bought it the first time I came out here. I've had my eye on it for a long time." She continued to smile at him, halfway expecting him to explode with joy. His face went blank before clouding with consternation, and when he didn't speak, she patted his knee, rousing him from his introspective quiescence. "Why do you seem so disappointed?"

"No, it's not that. It's just"——he sighed and held her hands in his—— "I know you're, like, independently wealthy and all, and money probably isn't an issue for you, but I don't want you to pity me, you know? I don't want you to feel like you have to like my stuff or feel obligated to help me, just because I'm struggling. Everyone struggles. It's okay."

"Jimmy, I'm really not that philanthropic of a person. If I didn't like your work, I wouldn't even bother."

"I know. I guess I worry about silly things, too. Like, I don't want you to think that the only reason I'm your friend is because you've got money. I'm not a gold digger. I'm not that person." His expression was as serious as any she had ever seen on him, and his eyes pleaded with her. "I don't know if you get a lot of that, but I imagine that you would. The world's full of vultures."

"Stop. My gold-digger radar's pretty strong. If I didn't like you, or if I thought you were a moocher, I wouldn't be here. It's not a bad thing to let a friend buy your work, especially when it's the most moving thing I've seen in a long time."

"You really like it?" he asked, looking at the series of orange and red blocks.

"I told you from the start that I did. And you yourself said that I got what you were trying to do. You can't stop me from buying your work, either. I've already decided where it's going to go in my apartment."

He regarded her, and his eyes roamed her face, as if scanning for pockmarks of insincerity. At last, he broke into a smile, cupped her face in his hands and kissed her forehead.

"You are my angel, Audrey, you know that? My angel!"

She laughed and tried to pry herself out of his grip. He refused to release her, and she could barely see through his shower of kisses. When he finally let go, she was still laughing, and she wiped his lip balm off her forehead before looking up at the front door. Her heart froze when she saw her mother standing there. She was gaping at them, her perfectly lined lips formed into a tight circle, and her usually pallid skin was now burning with neon intensity.

"Oh shit," Audrey said under her breath.

"What's wrong?" Jimmy asked.

"My mother's here," she whispered.

"Which one is she?"

"The one staring at us with the look of death."

Her mother walked towards them in slow motion, her image distorted by the gallery's bizarre lighting and Audrey's sickening awareness that she was the cause of her ire. Her cropped blond hair was almost white under the lights, her high cheekbones jagged in the shadows, and her slim frame sliced through the air like a razor against cellophane. Her eyes, normally the color of the Indian Ocean, appeared black, and even in what looked like a nonthreatening Chanel box suit, she seemed to be radiating a mercenary's energy. By the time she reached them, Audrey was trembling slightly.

"Audrey, may I have a word with you?" she asked, her tone making clear that the request wasn't negotiable.

"Mom, this is Jimmy," she said, placing her hand on his shoulder. She could hear her words warble, and he laid a reassuring hand on her back.

"It's nice to meet you," she said in a low voice, and then gripped Audrey's arm. "Would you please come with me?" She pulled her off the bench, and in a few quick steps, they were outside.

"I guess you got my message." Audrey felt her lips curl into a smirk, an ill-timed reflex that presented itself whenever she was horrendously uncomfortable, and she knew that the expression wasn't relieving any of the tension between them.

"I did. I can't believe—I don't even understand—did you really tear up the prenuptial agreement?" She stared at her, perhaps hoping to hear that the voice mail had been a ghastly mistake, a terrible figment of her imagination.

"I did," she said quietly.

Her mother's pale face practically glowed in the moonlight, and she sucked in a sharp breath, looking as if she was trying to control herself. "What possible—for what reason—why *on earth* would you do such a thing?"

"I don't know—it was—it just—" She fell silent, suddenly at a loss as to how to explain her rash impulse. As much as she had contemplated her situation, had carefully reasoned her instinctual compulsion, nonetheless her mother's stuttering apoplexy, coupled with her own miserable discomfort, was short-circuiting her brain, jamming the pathway between emotion and articulation.

"I know you weren't happy that your father and I asked Victor to sign it," her mother said, her cheeks flaming, "but I assumed that you'd realize that we were trying to look out for you."

"I know. But—I couldn't stand the thought of starting our lives with a prenup," she said, finally finding her words. "I didn't want a written reminder that we're somehow on unequal footing, and I didn't want for Victor to have to compromise like that. It wasn't fair. I couldn't help myself. The whole thing—it just made me sick."

"Audrey"—she sighed heavily—"we've already been through this.

Whether or not you think it's fair, it's how it has to be. It's for your own good."

"Why does it *have* to be?" Her mother didn't answer, perhaps too agog to speak, and Audrey felt her shoulders fall. "Because we're making a mistake by getting married, right? Because Victor has to be a gold digger." She stared at the graveled walkway, burdened by her mother's months-long admonitions. "I don't understand why you're so convinced that we're doomed to fail. I don't know why you insist on focusing on the worst possible scenario."

"Because you refuse to acknowledge that there *is* a worst possible scenario." Her voice strained with frustration. "You act as if everything with Victor is going to be wonderful forever. I hope that it is, darling. Nothing would make me happier. But if it doesn't turn out that way—if it turns out the way so many marriages do—I don't want you to be stuck. We're giving you an escape—we—" She looked like she was about to continue, but she pursed her lips instead, and the weight of her unspoken words found its way to the rest of her body, expressing themselves in the rigidity of her posture. For what seemed like an eternity, they stared at each other, mute, as if they both feared what might come next.

"Is that how you feel?" Audrey finally asked, daring for the first time to tread on the subject they had treated as unspeakable. "That you're stuck in a marriage that you can't get out of? That it was a mistake? That's why you keep describing the prenup as an escape, isn't it? Because if you had had a way out, you'd have taken it in a heartbeat."

"We're not talking about my marriage," she said wearily. "We're talking about yours."

"But you're using yours as a blueprint for mine."

"Audrey, your father and I—" She paused, clearly struggling for the right words. "We have our problems like everyone else—"

"They're not like everyone else's," she interrupted. "I'm not blind, Mom. And I'm not deaf. You barely ever see each other, and you never talk about him other than to make jabs at him." Her mother frowned. "When you say that I take after Dad because I work too much, or that he *used* to be kind and sincere, I *hear* you. I hear the judgment in your voice. I hear the things that you want to say, but won't."

"When have I ever—"

"I ignored as much of it as I could," she said, her words tumbling out. "I didn't want to think about it. I didn't want to deal with it. Your relationship with Dad—I thought that it didn't have to affect me. But it's affecting me now. It's screwing up what's supposed to be the happiest time of my life. And it's screwing up your ability even to support me." Her face was on fire, and despair caused her to tremble.

"Your father and I may not have the perfect marriage," she said, clearly as unhappy as Audrey was, "but no one does. We're still a family, Audrey."

"You and Dad don't even pretend anymore that we're some kind of functional family," Audrey said, unable to repress the bitterness in her voice. "We haven't been a functional family in fifteen years." Her mother flinched, but didn't say anything, and Audrey took in a deep breath, watching as artists and patrons wandered in and out of the gallery, alive and engaged with one another. Their joy sharpened the pang of disappointment that was stabbing her, and she rubbed her temples, suddenly exhausted. "Honestly, Mom, I don't understand why you didn't just leave Dad. I don't understand why you won't now."

"Because I can't," she said with a sigh that shook her frail frame. "Your father and I—we are what we are." The color drained from her face, leaving her eerily lifeless. "Maybe it would've been better if we had divorced. Maybe it would've been easier for everyone. But we chose not to. That's the decision I have to live with, Audrey, whether you think it's fair or right or anything else." She sighed again. "But you deserve better than that. You deserve to be happy."

Audrey looked away, unwilling to ask why her parents had agreed to continue a union neither likely wanted. She wasn't sure that she could handle the response, and given the strain in her mother's tone, she clearly didn't plan on providing an answer.

"What I deserve, Mom," she finally said, "what I *want*—is for you to be happy for me. I want to know that you're on my side."

Her mother stirred, taken aback by her plea, and she stepped forward tentatively and placed a thin hand on her arm. Despite the evening's humid heat, her skin was cool, and its unexpected chill sent a shiver down Audrey's spine.

"Darling," she said, "do you really question whether I'm on your side? I'm *always* on your side. No matter what." She kept her intense gaze trained on her, as if trying to spot lingering doubt. "Don't you ever forget that."

A car drove up, its heavy tires crunching against the gravel of the parking lot. It stopped in front of them, the driver's face shaded behind the tinted windows. Her mother glanced at him, clearly dissatisfied by the interruption, before turning back to Audrey.

"I have to go. I'm horribly late for the Children's Benefit." She brought her evening bag under her arm and stepped closer to Audrey. "Please, for everyone's peace of mind, have Victor re-sign the prenup." She kissed her cheek, slipped into the waiting car and disappeared, leaving Audrey to grapple with the things they had said, and the things they couldn't say. She sat down on the lowest step of the short staircase leading to the gallery, barely cognizant of her surroundings for the thoughts swirling in her head. Her mother's admonitions, as rote as they had become, hadn't imparted new information, and her declaration of support reminded Audrey of what she realized she had known all along. Yet, whether it was because her mother had dared to open up about her marriage, if only to the slightest degree, because she had vocalized what Audrey needed to hear, or something else, she understood her mother's pleas to execute the prenup, even if she didn't agree. Frankly, she had understood the rationale from the beginning, intellectually comprehended its value despite her visceral reaction against it. She sucked in a deep breath, stood up and walked into the gallery, realizing that Hercules, her mother and Victor were right—if she wanted peace in the family, she was simply going to have to yield to what everyone had already accepted.

Twenty

Whitney gathered an armful of paper and formed yet another pile on the unending table that took up the center of the conference room. She had been examining documents, sheet by sheet, all morning, and her eyes were failing her. Fatigue consumed her. If she could just get through the remainder of this box, she would reward herself with a cup of coffee and a cigarette. For once, she was glad to be holed up by herself, away from prying eyes and loose lips. People may no longer have been gossiping that she was ready to file a lawsuit against the firm for racial discrimination, but she still didn't feel completely comfortable in the hallways where the secretaries were likely on the lookout for telltale signs of a future plaintiff.

As she placed the stack next to twelve other towering loads on the conference room table, she heard distinctive steps trouncing on the marble floor. Only one person made that kind of noise, and she wasn't in the mood to deal with Will Strong. She looked up in time to see him walk through the door.

"Lee! Those documents almost ready?" He surveyed a wall of boxes, stared at the piles on the table and then glared at her.

"Almost," she said, "if by *almost*, you mean nowhere close."

Will glanced at his watch, his jowly features smashed together in a grimace. "How much longer will it take?"

"At least another two weeks," she said, wondering if he expected the task to be completed in the next few hours. She had spent the last week in the conference room, arriving before seven in the morning and leaving after midnight, and she had managed to make it through only thirty-three boxes. Sixty-seven more boxes had yet to be touched, and if she didn't receive assistance, the next two weeks were going to be long indeed.

"I can't believe how badly James fucked this up." He scowled at her.

"I don't like to fire lawyers, but his screwup was ridiculous." He edged his furry eyebrows upwards. "You know what I mean?"

"Yes, sir." She didn't feel comfortable talking about James's departure. The last time she saw him, he had dumped blame on her and had gotten her fired, and though she felt that he was a crappy human being, he still had a wife and three kids to feed. She hoped that he had found another job.

"I won't be hiring him back, that's for *damned* sure," Will shouted. His face flushed with what Whitney assumed was fresh anger at the memory of the departed associate. "Anyway, with the first-years coming in soon, you'll get some help."

"Unless they're coming today, I'm not sure how anyone's going to help me with this project."

"Well, today's your lucky day," he boomed. Lashing his head about, he scanned the hallway for someone. Or something. Whitney sighed as he stormed down the hallway to retrieve whatever he had lost.

"God," she muttered, and returned to the documents. A moment later, the earsplitting ringing returned, and Will reappeared at the door. He had apparently found the person he had left behind, and Whitney gawked at the man standing next to her boss, feeling as if Will had dragged someone out of her faded memories and into the office.

"Whitney, stand up. I'd like for you to meet Kyle Brett." If she had paled at the sight of her lone Austin groupie, then Kyle was whiter than the paper on the table. He stood like stone, gaping at her as though a bespectacled elephant were marking documents for confidentiality. Will didn't notice anything strange.

"Kyle, this is Whitney Lee. She's my best goddamned lawyer, and she'll be showing you the ropes. She knows this case inside out, so don't feel shy asking her for help." He beamed at her with pride, and when she didn't move, he frowned. "Lee, what's the matter with you? Come over here and shake this boy's hand!"

Whitney stood up, too stunned by the introduction to think clearly. As zealously as she guarded her personal life from her work one—going so far as to prohibit her friends and family from visiting her at the office—Kyle's sudden emergence disoriented her, and his appearance,

particularly now that it was transformed by a gray suit and conserva-
tive haircut, confused her. His very presence breached the uncrossable
line she had drawn between her Boerne & Connelly persona and the
one she embodied at Mason's, and she walked towards the lawyers,
discombobulated by the unexpected blending of her disparate worlds.

"Nice to meet you," she said, and extended her hand. Kyle stood
frozen until Will slapped a heavy hand onto his back, and he jerked his
arm out and grasped her elbow.

"Boy, what kind of handshake is that?" Will shook his head. "All
right. I'm introducing Kyle to the rest of the litigation team, and then
I'll send him back this way. He can help you with the document review." He turned to Kyle. "Don't fuck this up, you understand? Whitney here can tell you what happened to the last lawyer who screwed
up this project."

She watched with unabated shock as Will dragged Kyle down the
hallway and introduced him to the other associates. What was he doing here? She recalled that while they were in Austin, he had explained
that he was a law student, but even if he had graduated in May and
had decided upon her firm, his walking around the hallways in June
made no sense. First-years didn't typically join the firm until September or October. They had bar exams after all, and out of sheer terror,
they tended to lock themselves in their apartments or the library for
months on end, studying from sunrise to sunset, taking breaks only to
pray that they didn't fail.

"Oh—my—God," she said as she slowly made her way back to the
table. If she had felt any sense of urgency before to scurry through
the mountain of documents that piled in the room, she now felt as if
she were moving in slow motion, and she sank into her chair and stared
into the hallway, trying in vain to digest the strangeness that was this
Monday.

Kyle walked over to Whitney, looking spent after having shaken at
least thirty hands in the last hour, and she imagined that his back was
sore, and probably bruised, from Will's incessant pounding. He eased

himself into a seat next to her, his deep, blue eyes giving color to the otherwise clinically white room, and she regarded him, remembering how attractive she had found him in Austin. He took in the sparse decor of the room before gazing at the table, and from his puzzled expression, it was obvious that he didn't have the faintest idea what she was doing.

"We're going through these boxes for privilege," she explained. Her heart was beating so fast that she felt her chest move. After the astonishment of their unlikely reunion had worn off, her mind began to process the fact that her Austin hottie was now in Houston, at *her* firm, in *her* office and on *her* case. She may not have shared Scott Yang's conviction in epiphanies, and she certainly didn't understand Hercules' inspiration in horoscopes, but she still wanted to believe that all events—no matter how trivial or absurd—occurred for a reason. Hell, she had professed as much at her parting dinner with Scott, and she glanced at her document-reviewing partner now, wondering if his flirting at Mason's had been the beginning of a sickeningly cute romance she would have gleefully welcomed.

"Privilege," Kyle repeated. "And you're marking the documents?"

"Yes. If it's attorney-client, stick a red flag on it. If it's work product, put a blue flag on it. If it's both, then put both flags on it. That's all Will wanted, but he has a way of forgetting things like trade secrets, so I'm putting green flags on anything that deals with reactor processes. We'll decide later if they need to be produced. Our client owns a petroleum refinery, and they're being sued for patent infringement. We're producing documents in waves, but we still need to get through them as fast as possible."

"Okay." Kyle's forehead crinkled as he pulled a sheet from a stack on the table. "How do you know if it's attorney-client privilege?"

"Here." She handed him a piece of paper. "This is a list of all the lawyers who worked on the deal, so if you see any communication that has these names on it, put a red flag on the document."

He studied the memo, and for the next few minutes, they shuffled through their share of documents without speaking. The marbled conference room seemed almost stuffy from the mausoleum soundlessness, exacerbating the awkwardness between them, and if Kyle caught her constant glances, he didn't acknowledge them.

"This morning was a little weird," he finally said, breaking the silence.

"Yeah." She lowered her document. "I thought you were in Atlanta."

"I went to school at Emory," he said, clearly surprised that she remembered. "But I'd always planned on coming back to Houston."

"Did you clerk here?" she asked, looking at him quizzically. "I don't remember ever seeing you in the office." The firm brought in three dozen law-school students for a summer program that was basically an eight-week inebriated interview. If the recruit proved that he could make it through the internship without throwing up on a partner, a permanent offer arrived in the mail after his last day in the program. Like other firms, Boerne & Connelly promised to give their summer associates "real world" experience. In reality, they did little to no work, began drinking at four and spent their evenings in Houston's finest dining establishments and hotels. The program was one long drunken orgy of partying, and she couldn't believe how many of the clerks fell for the firm's trick. By their first week as full-time lawyers, most associates realized that they had unwittingly handed the devil their souls, and miserably spent their sixteen-hour days trying to please their masters.

"I summered at another firm. But I didn't like the culture there, so I interviewed again and decided to work here. Actually, it works out better this way, because my fiancée's at the firm where I clerked, and they've got an antinepotism policy. Eventually, one of us would've had to leave."

Fiancée. Whitney tried not to react. He continued to leaf through documents, apparently not at all affected by his behavior in Austin, and she stared at him, wondering if he even remembered having hit on her.

"Congratulations," she finally said. "On your engagement."

"Thanks."

"How long have y'all been together?" she asked, trying not to sound judgmental.

"About four years." He smiled. "We got engaged last Christmas."

Her stomach sank to the floor, and as hot as her face was, someone may as well have been searing it with a blowtorch. Given the way he had approached her at Mason's, had enchanted her with his singularly focused attention, she never would have imagined that he was in a relationship. His spring-break indiscretion embarrassed her, made her feel abhorrently foolish, and the praise he had lavished on her that night suddenly seemed cheap, invalid. She continued to gape at him, horrified, and if his earlier flattery had made him beautiful and charming, it now rendered him vulgar and uninteresting. She didn't know why she was so offended. After all, she hadn't thought about him since the Valedictorians' trip, and she certainly didn't care about his moral rectitude. Even so. She sucked in a deep breath and concentrated on the task at hand, digesting the obvious fact that his arrival didn't import anything greater than a freakish coincidence. And as small as the big-firm legal community was, she wasn't sure that their chance meeting even qualified as a coincidence.

"I can't get over the fact that you're here." He shook his head, looking awed. "I would never have guessed that you were a lawyer. I thought you were a singer."

"I *am* a singer," she said too loudly. "I'm a creature of many talents."

He laughed. "How long have you been here?"

"Three years." She stuck a red flag on her document and placed it on a two-foot-high stack.

"That's a long time to be at one firm. I know a lot of people who couldn't take it after their first few months. Most of my class already knows that they don't want to be at a firm for more than a couple of years. It's kind of sad. Actually, I would think that it's opportunistic if I didn't know how horrendous the environment can be."

She stopped what she was doing and looked at him, surprised by his seriousness.

"It didn't used to be that way," she said. "It used to be that you went to a firm for life. But the last two salary bumps made everyone's expectations impossible to meet. There's so much resentment from both the associates, who feel like they're working to death, and the partners, who hate the fact that the associates are making so much money at such a young age. Everyone resents each other, and no one trusts anyone anymore." She shrugged. "It's not just at Boerne and Connelly, though. It's everywhere. I think the attrition rate's close to ninety per-cent across the country."

"You're still here," he said with a smile.

"My class started with twenty-two associates. I'm the last one standing." She glanced at him, wondering if he was put off by her nega-tive assessment of the industry.

"Well, I plan on being here forever." He leaned in, as if he was about to tell her a secret. "You know Will Strong? I want to be him one day."

"You're joking," she said, certain that he was teasing, even if his voice didn't carry any sarcasm.

"I'm serious. He's the managing partner at a really prestigious firm. He's made it in an industry that's known for burnouts. He's got a crazy roster of incredible clients. Everyone knows that he's an awesome liti-gator. That's what I want."

"For everyone's sake, I hope you don't turn out to be like him at all."

"You sound like my parents," he said with a chuckle. "They hate that I'm a lawyer. Or will be after I pass the bar."

"Really?" She thought of her own family, who treated her profes-sion as the noblest of undertakings. "Why?"

"Everyone in my family's a doctor—well, almost everyone—and they're convinced that the medical industry took a dive because of sue-happy plaintiffs' lawyers. They hate that they have to pay so much in malpractice insurance rather than on equipment and patient care, and they think that I'm feeding the beast. I don't know how to con-vince them that I'm on their side. And I really don't know how to convince them that this is what I want to do, you know?"

"You really want to do this?"

"Yeah. I do."

She turned back to her documents, unable to believe what she was hearing. As much as associates shouted their false allegiances to the firm, behaved outwardly as if their jobs were the most important aspect of their lives, they had uniformly decried their situations behind closed doors and plotted escape routes with the same desperation as prisoners of war. Everyone knew that the only reason more lawyers didn't leave was the outrageously lucrative salaries, partners included, and as miserable as everyone was, Whitney had almost dismissed the possibility that someone might actually harbor an interest in lawyering, or that a Boerne & Connelly lifer might have slipped through the rest of the transient ingrates. Kyle's unadulterated enthusiasm shamed her, underscored the leechlike quality of her own service to the firm, and she sank deeper into her chair, dismayed by her attitude and by his spotlight on it. She considered his arrival again, wondering if he had been sent, not as a romantic replacement for Scott, but to serve as a fortuitous source of inspiration. After all, if he could pursue his own professional desires in the face of familial objection, why couldn't she?

For the next few quiet minutes, they huddled over the table, flagging and marking and setting aside documents to be produced. Despite their uncomfortable introduction, she was glad that he was next to her, aiding in the project. Her days, while harried with too many deadlines, tended to be isolating, and she welcomed her document-reviewing partner, even if she didn't completely understand him.

"Hey, I meant what I said in Austin," he said. He spoke quietly, and she had to strain to hear him. "You know, at Mason's."

"What's that?"

"I told you that my uncle would love your performance. He did."

"Did he?" She continued to peruse the client's documents, barely paying attention to what Kyle was saying. She vaguely recalled that he had told her that he had connections to the music industry, but so did everyone else in Austin, most of whom prided themselves in scamming uninformed, starry-eyed songbirds out of cash and credit. She didn't need that kind of hookup. Besides, she was already working with Tate Philips on mixing her demo, cautiously feeling her way into the area of her life that scared her most, and the Philips family had their tentacles embedded in at least four independent record labels.

"He would've found you already if I had gotten your phone number. I tried, actually, but you left before I had a chance."

"You could've asked Chris," she said, turning to the next sheet on combustible-fuel generators. "He's in charge of booking gigs there."

"I did. He wouldn't give me your info."

"He probably thought you were just a drunk looking for a hookup." She felt herself smile, moved by Chris's safeguarding. "He's pretty protective of me."

"I noticed." He leaned in closer. "Look, my uncle's been giving me endless shit about you. He's got a really good eye for these kinds of things, and when he saw your video, he flipped out. He'd kill me if he knew that I'd run into you and didn't try to persuade you to meet him."

"What label is he with?"

"Train Tracks." She froze. "Have you heard of it?"

She stared at him for a long moment, too flabbergasted to respond. Of course she had heard of it. So had anyone with any real aspiration of a music career free of commercialized impediments and wholesale alterations to the purity of her work.

"He works for them?" she asked, feeling out of sorts for the hundredth time that day.

"He founded it, actually." He shook his head. "He left his medical practice to start it, which I guess is a good thing. He didn't give a shit about his patients. All he cares about is music."

She sank back into her seat, unable to stop gaping at him. Her mind was spinning with incredulity, and a surge of adrenaline caused her heart to race. Her plan—which she had begun to execute when she had returned from the Valedictorians' trip—was to record her five best songs onto a demo CD. Chris had given her free rein of the Philipses' recording studio, and Tate was already demonstrating his expert sound-engineering skills. In her precious few spare moments, she had compiled a press kit, complete with her bio and black-and-white picture, and as soon as her tracks were ready, she intended on sending her work to two dozen small labels and entertainment lawyers, knowing full well that most, if not all, would send back a form letter thanking her for her interest without reciprocating in kind. Train Tracks had been at the top of her solicitation list, the label best known for its generous handling of its artists and unwillingness to usurp creative control. Feeling as if God were striking her with lightning, Whitney gawked at the new associate who was now working for her.

"He wants to meet me?" she asked.

"Yeah."

"Okay, then," she said, still feeling as if she were dreaming. "Tell him that I'll meet him."

"You will?" He brightened, managing to look excited and relieved at the same time. "Just let me know when, and I'll give him a call."

"Okay." She turned back to her documents, too thrilled to focus. No one would believe what had just happened, least of all her, and she imagined that her friends would characterize her as incomprehensibly lucky, the opportune beneficiary of the cosmos's fortuity. But she knew that Kyle's appearance wasn't serendipity, and as much as a realist might proclaim that what seemed too good to be true probably was, she believed that the situations that presented themselves with the most ease were also the ones that were designed to occur at the time they were meant to. She glanced at Kyle again, and if she had originally imagined him a romantic partner, or the product of sick chance, she now regarded him as the conduit dream maker who had been sent to save her.

Twenty-one

"**I** am *not* paying more than ten bucks a pound for the veal, and I sure as hell am *not* going to pay more than twenty bucks for the venison. Who'd you talk to, anyway?" Hercules stared at Reynaldo Gonzales, then back at the game-meat price list, and then at her watch. Time had slowed to a crawl, and seven hours still remained before her date with Robert. She fidgeted wildly in her seat, sending bouncing shock waves through the banquette and over to Reynaldo.

"He's new." He placed a steady hand on her shoulder, and she stopped jerking about. "He's taken over Texas Traders, and those are the new prices." He retrieved the price list out of her hands and scribbled on it, his fountain pen scratching like a claw against the card stock.

"That's going to cut the profit margins by more than three percent." She flipped through an Excel spreadsheet of operations costs. "Either you talk some sense into—what's his name?"

"Jonathan Grazier."

"Either you talk some sense into Jonathan Grazier or we find another vendor." Her shoulders clenched, and she began to shake her leg again. "You let Jonathan know that Justin charged seven ninety-five for the veal, and that he and I have a long-standing relationship. Tell him that it's a small community, and I can make sure that no one uses him. Considering what he's charging, I doubt anyone would use him anyway."

"I will, although I won't use quite those words."

"I want the final prices by tomorrow."

"Okay." He adjusted his tie and pulled out a glossy file. Immediately, Hercules brightened.

"Is that the catalog?" She yanked it out of his hands.

"These are the finals. Manufacturing starts next week."

"Awesome. When do we see it at the store level?"

"Six months from now at the latest."

She looked up. "Six months?"

"At the latest. I'm pushing them to speed it up, but it could be that long." He reached out and placed a reassuring hand on her arm. "I really doubt it'll be that long, but that's the worst-case scenario."

Frustration hung in the air like a heavy cloud. The past two months had been an aggravating game of hurry-up-and-wait, and now that the final selection of Hercules Cookware had been decided, all that was left for Hercules and Reynaldo to do was to sit back, twiddle their thumbs and try not to bite their nails into stumps.

"What can I do, right?" she muttered as she perused the catalog of pots and pans. Her signature was etched into the bottoms of the items, and the catalog opened to a glossy eight-by-ten photo of her. She studied her picture, unhappy that her face had no angles. The image would have been better in black-and-white, so as not to show off her freckles. She was silently criticizing the unfortunate disproportion of her eyes and cheeks when Reynaldo spoke.

"Oh, I got you a spot on *The Houston Early Show*." He took out his BlackBerry. "For the nineteenth. You can promote Dragonfly Deux's grand opening." He looked at her, and Hercules felt his chastising stare. "Without any F-bombs this time."

"When's the last time you heard me use the F-word?" She pored over the fluted pans in the Acceleron prototype catalog, and when she finally looked up, he was smiling at her, his full lips stretched halfway across his face.

"Why are you looking at me like that?" she asked.

"You're right. You *haven't* cursed, or at least cursed as much, for at least the last six months. And you seem calmer than you did a few weeks ago. I take it that Dr. Kushner's been helpful."

"I haven't gone to see him."

"What?"

"I *went*, actually, got to his office, but then I decided that I don't need a shrink." She shrugged and crossed her arms. "Why should I pay five hundred dollars an hour to have someone listen to my problems when Whitney and Audrey will listen for free? Besides, a psychiatrist would never make herself vulnerable in front of me. She would never be able to share what's wrong with her life, and if I'm going to spill my soul to this person, I don't want her to stare back, all judgmental and shit."

"A psychiatrist wouldn't be judgmental, Hercules," he said, frowning. "That's the whole point. She's there to help you. I don't want you to repress your frustrations. I can't afford to have you snap in front of an investor, or at an Acceleron meeting, or on TV, for God's sake."

"Whitney and Audrey help me just fine." She smiled as cheerfully as she could, hoping to prove her case. "They bitch about their problems. I whine about mine. We've gotten to be a lot more open with each other, and I think that we're all benefiting from it."

"You're actually talking to them about your father?" he asked, his skepticism beginning to thaw.

"Yes, and about other things, too."

He let out a deep breath. Concern still lined his face, but he nodded and stood up.

"As long as you're not ignoring your feelings. I'm glad that you've got an outlet other than me."

"Yeah."

"I'll see you tomorrow."

She watched as he headed for the door, and thought about her father. Perhaps it was progress to unload her stress through her friends instead of balling it up until tears came, but she also knew that her deepening closeness with the Valedictorians wouldn't repair her relationship with her father. They had moved from a wretched silence to a resigned quiet, as if they were afraid that they might destroy the uncomfortable peace with unintended hurt or inevitable disappointment. They had effectively become dispassionate cohabitants, solitary roommates, and despite their impassive exteriors, she knew that an unending reservoir of feeling lurked beneath. She glanced at her watch again before pushing herself out of the booth. For now, their relationship would have to wait. She had a business to run. And a date to prepare for.

"What about these?" Whitney asked as she held a pair of jeans that had a delicate swirl of Swarovski crystal lining the hems. "I think they would look great with that top." She was in Hercules' walk-in closet, where fifteen pairs of already tried-on outfits lay in a heap on the floor.

"You think?" Hercules asked. "Okay, give me those." Nerves shimmied up her spine as she slithered into the ink-hued fitted denim, and she examined herself in a freestanding full-length mirror, unable to help comparing herself with her size 0 friend. She had always been proud of her size, confident of the power that emanated from her musculature and concrete bones, but during brief moments of insecurity like the present, she felt like a clumsy bowling ball next to her lithe pin of a friend.

Whitney turned to a shelf and searched for accessories that would complement her outfit. They had spent the last two hours in the bathroom, and though Hercules was loath to makeovers, she had to admit that Whitney had transformed her usually unmanicured self into an Asian Botticelli goddess. Plucked and preened and made-up, she felt more feminine than she had ever allowed herself to feel, and in her trendy jeans, silk blouse and three-inch black boots, she was surprised by how pretty she felt. Even her frizzy hair was lying right. Whitney tied a strand of red Lucite baubles around her neck, and as they gazed at her reflection, Hercules smiled. She was ready, and Robert was waiting.

"Thanks for doing this." She patted Whitney's arm affectionately.

"No, *thank you*," Whitney replied. "Y'all will have so much fun." Robert had no idea that his sister was in Hercules' closet, helping his date prepare for the night. Audrey, too, was in on the clandestine operation, and she was going to pick up Whitney in half an hour. The two would probably relax at a bar afterwards and drink themselves silly, and Hercules didn't doubt that they would gossip about how her date was progressing. She smiled wider as she thought about her friends.

"Okay, I think I've made him wait long enough." She smoothed out her sleeves.

"You look fabulous," Whitney said.

"I'll see you later." Hercules picked up a jeweled bag that complemented her jeans. "Wish me luck."

"No luck necessary." Whitney grinned like the teenager that she resembled, kissed her cheek and shooed her out the door.

"Wow, you look amazing," Robert said with what Hercules thought was astonishment as she made her way down the spiral staircase.

"Thanks. So do you." A mix of nerves, excitement and nausea wrestled in her stomach, and her heart lurched at the sight of her date. He, too, was in jeans, and having paired them with a white button-down shirt, he managed to appear casual and professional at the same time. His hair had been gelled and spiked, and she wondered if Whitney had spent the earlier part of the day coiffing her brother.

"I hope you like Mexican," he said as he opened the front door. From the corner of her eye, she thought she spied her father. She hesitated, staring at the edge of the wall that separated the foyer from the dining room. In a moment, the skulking shadow disappeared.

"I love Mexican," she said.

"Great. There's a little dive that I go to. It may not look all that fancy, but the food's really good." He opened the passenger side of his Toyota 4Runner and helped her into the seat. She watched as he trotted to the other side of the car.

"Where is it?" she asked.

"It's by Fifty-nine and Bissonnet." He started the engine. "It's not the best neighborhood, but I swear the food's awesome."

"I trust you." Had she been with anyone other than Robert, she would have tumbled out of the car and walked back into the house. She was an unapologetic food snob, and after what had happened to her in Austin, she had hoped never again to be subjected to cheap Mexican food. Besides, the little pocket in the southwest corner of the city wasn't the safest place to be after dark. Hell, she hardly dared to venture there in the daytime. Still, Robert was tall and strong, and if he couldn't protect her—well, she had five years of karate training under her belt. She just wasn't sure that she remembered any of the moves.

They sat silently, too nervous to speak to each other over the radio. This was ridiculous, Hercules thought. They had conversed countless times without incident, and tonight, they had nothing to say? She guffawed, attracting his attention.

"What's wrong?" Little lines of worry creased his forehead.

"Nothing. I was just thinking that this is so silly. I'm really nervous for no reason, and we've known each other for eons."

"I was just thinking the same thing." The furrows in his face relaxed. "Okay, we'll just pretend that we're an old married couple. Maybe that will get us talking."

"I've never seen an old married couple talk to each other at dinner," she said, and he laughed.

They pulled into the parking lot of the most run-down strip mall Hercules had ever seen. Bars encased every window, and a neon cowboy blinked at the entrance of the restaurant. EL MARIACHI, she read, and recalled that the *Houston Chronicle* had hailed the place as the city's best-kept secret. Judging from the ratty look of the eatery, she could see why no one talked about it. She didn't feel at all encouraged that he had invited her to what was bound to be a disgusting meal, but was instantly sunnier when Robert placed a hand on her lower back and guided her through the entrance.

They followed the host to a small table at the corner of the restaurant. They took their seats, and immediately, bowls of salsa and chips were plunked down on the table. No sooner had the salsa server left than a waiter arrived.

"*Buenas noches,*" he said, his dark features shining under the fluorescent lights. "Can I get the lady something to drink? Maybe a cerveza?"

"Yes," she said with a nod. Robert raised two fingers, and the waiter retreated.

"I've never been here," she said, taking in the piñatas, Mexican flags and pinball machine.

"I know it looks a bit—well, it's not Dragonfly, that's for sure," Robert said without the faintest hint of an apology, "but wait until you try their food. Actually, I'd be curious to hear a professional opinion."

"I heard that the crappier the place, the better the food," she said. She had actually never heard the aphorism spoken by a chef, and she would have preferred that he had taken her to a place that didn't require metal detectors.

"If that's true, then I think Dragonfly's the exception," he said. She felt herself smile, pleased with the flattery. It almost made up for the location of their first date.

Their beers arrived, and Hercules chugged on her Corona while watching Robert order. If people pictured Asian boys as short, scrawny honor-roll students whose only exposure to sports was academic decathlons, his long limbs and toned muscles served as a fierce physical rebuttal. She remembered how attractive she had thought him to be at Loyola, how she would stare as he sprinted across the school grounds with his lacrosse gear flapping at his sides. Time had only accentuated his chiseled good looks, and even now, the fluorescent lighting of the restaurant did nothing to uglify him. Boozy bubbles headed straight to her brain, and having been too nervous to eat all day, she felt immediately buzzed.

"Does all that sound okay?" he asked.

"What's that?" She blinked a few times, and he came into focus.

"I ordered a sampler of things so that you could try them. I don't know about you, but I'm starving."

"That's fine," she said with as much confidence as she could muster. Having been too busy drinking, she hadn't noticed what he had ordered. She hadn't even noticed that a waiter had come by. She felt ridiculous. Why couldn't she relax? Her head was spinning with nerves and alcohol, and she felt her face flush. It was suddenly too hot, and even though the restaurant was freezing, sweat beaded up on her neck. She reached for a glass of ice water just as he was grabbing a napkin, and in a moment of a lack of coordination, the water spilled all over the table. And all over Robert.

"Oh, shit," he gasped. His faded jeans darkened around his crotch.

"Oh my God!" She yanked her napkin off her lap and tried to dry him. Her clumsy fumbling probably gave the impression that she was trying to molest her date, and in her horror, she managed only to press down harder in the most inappropriate places.

"Here, I'll do it," he said, taking the napkin from her.

"God, I'm so sorry," she said, mortified.

"Don't worry about it." He offered her a kind smile. "It was cool and refreshing."

She laughed uneasily and helped him wipe the table. She prayed silently that the rest of the evening would transpire without any more disasters, and not knowing what they should discuss, she decided to talk about the one thing they had in common.

"So, do you like living with Whitney?"

"It's okay," he said with a shrug. "We have our ups and downs."

"Y'all seem so different." She sipped on her beer, careful to make sure that the bottle met her lips, and not Robert's water-soaked crotch.

"Yeah. That's what everyone says. Most people can't believe we're related."

"Really? Why?"

"I don't know. She's always been really easy with people, you know? Even if she's just sitting by herself on a bench or something, random people always come up to her. I on the other hand—I've just been . . . ," he trailed, looking unsure of himself.

"More reserved," she finished.

"Yeah," he said. "Something like that."

"Well, there's nothing wrong with being reserved."

Robert smiled again. It was a beautiful sight, made all the more precious by his total lack of pretension, and Hercules wouldn't have minded gazing at his face for the rest of the evening.

"What about you?" he asked. "I bet it must've been nice to grow up as an only child."

"It's tough to say whether it was any better or worse than having sisters or brothers. I don't know. In a way, it might have been a blessing that I was an only child, at least financially. It was so hard for my family as it was, and there were only three of us. I can't imagine how strained my parents would have been with another mouth to feed." She glanced over at him, worried that she had said too much. She didn't know why she was babbling about such a private matter, and she wondered if he found her directness off-putting. He nodded thoughtfully, and his graciousness put her at ease.

"Yeah, I think it was a little tough for my parents to send both of us to Loyola for four years," Robert said. "I heard that the tuition's almost thirty grand a year now."

"That's insane," she said, outraged by the fee. "You know, I'd never thought that I'd go to a private school, but my mother insisted on Loyola. I don't know what I would've done if I hadn't gotten a full scholarship. Actually, I might have been the only student who received financial aid." She thought about the extreme material disproportion between her and the rest of Loyola's privileged students, and even though she didn't regret having attended such a posh school, she sometimes wished that she had been oblivious to how the other half lived. The disparity stuck with her still, and she knew that the economic gap was at least one reason why she pushed herself so hard with her businesses.

"There were others," he said unconvincingly.

"Well, to answer your question, I sometimes think having had a sibling would've made my life a little easier," she said, reaching for her beer. "It would've given my father someone else to criticize. He's crazy, and he has a way of making *me* crazy."

"I know what you mean. My parents spend so much of their time dogging my sister that they leave me alone for the most part. I think that's atypical in Korean families. Older sons usually get the brunt of it."

"Why is that?"

"It's just how it is," he said, tapping his long fingers against his beer bottle. "Those are the cultural expectations."

"No, I mean, why do they dog on Whitney so much?" She took another sip of her beer and then placed it as far away as she could. She was woozy, and she couldn't afford to be insultingly honest tonight.

"I have no idea. Maybe they think she's got more potential." He rolled his eyes. "God, they wouldn't stop bragging when she graduated as a valedictorian at Loyola. It was obscene. Sometimes, I think they make it too obvious who their favorite child is."

"I'm sorry," she said, placing a hand on his arm. "I thought you graduated pretty high in your class's rankings, too."

He looked over, and she yanked her hand away. She felt so self-conscious all of a sudden. Had he wanted her to leave her hand where it was? Was he disappointed that she had retracted the touch?

"I graduated sixth," he said easily, apparently unaffected by her behavior. "My parents weren't what I'd call *thrilled*." He sat pensively for a moment and then shrugged. "Well, what can I do? It's not like their affection doesn't come without a price. Did she ever tell you what happened with her SATs?"

"No. I remember that she got a fifteen eighty, though." She was still impressed with the score, as if it somehow mattered now. It was a full two hundred points higher than hers had been, and she felt a ridiculous twinge of competitiveness.

"She took it twice, actually. The first time, she got sick or something. She was probably just hungover." He let out a rumbling chortle, and she could see the older-brother side of him. "Anyway, she left halfway through the test and when the score came, my mom basically gave her the silent treatment for two weeks. She wouldn't let her take it again."

"Why?"

"Because my mother's crazy, too."

"What did she make on her first one?" she asked, unable to help herself.

"I'm not sure, but I remember thinking that there was no way she could've gone to Duke with that score." He chuckled. "You don't remember this? She was a mess for weeks."

"She never said anything about it."

"Oh." He was absorbed in his thoughts, and he shook his head, obviously reliving the memory. "For whatever reason, my mother wouldn't budge. Absolutely refused to let Whitney take it again. She ended up borrowing money from me to pay the fee and then snuck out on a Saturday morning to take the SAT again." He slapped the table and guffawed. "Is that not just the most ludicrous thing you've ever heard?"

Hercules stared at him, unsure which part of his story was supposed to be ludicrous. The entire episode sounded insane. She had no idea that Whitney had taken the exam twice, or that her mother was a loon. Had she known, she might have commiserated with her about her father sooner.

"That's not the worst thing they've ever done to her." He took a long sip from his beer bottle. "Sometimes, I don't get them, either. My mom was a psychology major in college, and I used to wonder if she thought putting obstacles in Whitney's way would make her try harder to get around them. I don't think my sister's wired that way, frankly, and my mother's never explained why she's so hard on her. Who knows. Maybe it's an Asian thing."

Hercules thought about her father's constant criticisms. Was it possible that he was likewise harsh because he expected much of her? On the surface, the idea seemed like a cop-out, a romanticized defense of atrocious parenting skills, but she understood the psychology behind it, and she wondered if she didn't get her father more than she admitted.

"You know, sometimes I think my father's just harsh because that's how he grew up," she said. "I don't doubt that he treats me the same way his parents treated him. Maybe kids in China are immune to the criticisms, or maybe they interpret it differently, because it's nothing but hurtful here."

"I think there's a loss in translation," Robert said. "Both cultural and generational. That's why I talk to my parents all the time. Eventually, you kind of understand what they're getting at, even if they're not at all straightforward. Whitney doesn't accept that, and she's constantly getting on my case about tattling. But I'm not tattling." He looked as if he was defending himself. "If I didn't say anything, they wouldn't have a clue as to what was going on with her."

"You're a good brother," she said, smiling. Her previous anxiety was gone now, and she felt happy and light.

"I try to be."

"I think it would be nice to have a sibling, actually," she said. "You could tell each other things and not worry about the other not understanding. Y'all sound pretty open with each other."

"I think we are."

"What do you think of her wanting to be a singer? I saw her perform a couple of times, and I still can't believe how talented she is. I mean, I always thought that she'd do something spectacular with her life. I just didn't think that it would be so far from what she's doing now."

He frowned at her, perplexed, and she felt a jolt of panic race through her body.

"Shit," she said. "You didn't know, did you?"

"No. What are you talking about?"

"Whitney's going to kill me." She wanted to set back the clock, to travel back in time, and she cursed the honesty one beer expelled from her. When she looked up, he was still staring at her, completely bewildered. "I—she's really incredible." She was desperate to defend her friend, and she searched his face for a reaction other than confusion. "God, Robert, don't say anything to your parents before she gets the chance."

"Singing," he said under his breath. "Jesus." He snapped to and rested his hand on her leg. "Don't worry. I won't say a word. If they ever found out, they'd have simultaneous heart attacks."

"Thank you," she said gratefully. "You have no idea how crappy I feel for blabbing her business."

The servers returned with platters of beans and rice and meats encased in corn husks. Green and red and white items were brought to the table, at least half of the dishes still sizzling. The waitstaff withdrew from the table, and they dug in excitedly, Hercules not quite as animated as her date.

"Oh my God," she moaned and closed her eyes. She wanted to vomit. She had never imagined that beans could taste like fish, or that meats crisscrossed with grill marks could taste microwaved. The flavors danced in her mouth with the grace of a dancing elephant, and she grabbed her beer to chase away the rancidness of her meal.

"Is that a good *Oh my God?*" Robert asked anxiously.

Hercules looked at him, and his schoolboy eagerness crushed her. There was no way she could criticize his prized restaurant, and she would rather wolf down everything on the table than hurt his feelings.

"Good," she said as she covered her mouth. "*Oh my God* good." She glanced at him, wondering if he believed her. "You were right. This place is the bomb."

"That means a lot to me," he said, flashing another heavenly smile.

They ate for a few silent moments, and Hercules was glad for the blaring mariachi music that pounded from the kitschy jukebox. At least it masked the gurgling noises emanating from her stomach, and she kept a hand trained on her belly, halfway anticipating digestive mutiny. Not that it mattered. She couldn't have asked for better company, and if the chance of another one of his smiles required a rushed trip to the bathroom, or to the closest hospital, she would gladly accept the exchange.

Twenty-Two

Whitney smoothed her hair and walked towards the reception-ist's booth at Train Tracks, her dense heels echoing against the con-crete walls of the acoustically favorable building. Bright noon sunshine flooded the ultramodern lobby, its blinding light practically bleaching the pinewood floors and similarly hued Scandinavian furnishings. The sparsely decorated space looked more like an IKEA than a creativity-driven independent record-label company, and as blond and fair as the receptionist was, Whitney might as well have been in Sweden.

"May I help you?" the slim woman asked, her squinty eyes nar-rowing.

"I'm Whitney Lee." She glanced at her watch. "I'm a little early. I have a twelve fifteen with Terry Rogers."

She smiled suddenly, perhaps no longer suspicious that Whitney was an unwanted solicitor, or, more likely, now attuned to the fact that she had an appointment with the label's CEO. She motioned to a row of black leather benches.

"I'll let him know you're here."

"Thanks." She sat down, crossed her legs and picked up a *Rolling Stone* from the pile of magazines that littered the glass coffee table. She felt as if she were skipping school, even though she was a professional with theoretical flexibility over her schedule, and even though she had worked all weekend so that she could take the Monday off. Giddy an-ticipation had prevented her from sleeping past five in the morning, and nerves and anxiety had made it arduous work to slip into her lucky Levi's, a sheer black blouse and her hand-tooled boots. Adrenaline had robbed her of prudence, and she had been surprised to find herself in Austin less than two hours after she had left her apartment. Turning into her mother for an instant, she had praised Jesus that no one had pulled her over and suspended her license or taken her to jail.

She flipped through the pages absently, unable to concentrate on the content therein. Instead, she gazed about the room, wondering if Terry Rogers had had a chance to listen to her demo, if his initial impression of her had changed or if he even remembered who she was. Just then, the receptionist called to her.

"Whitney, Terry will be out in a second."

"Okay." She placed the magazine back on the table, careful to return it exactly as she had found it. She didn't know how to act all of a sudden, and she jerked around in her seat, debating whether to stand or remain where she was. *What is wrong with me? For God's sake,* she scolded herself, *try to act like a normal human being.*

A frosted glass door opened, and a squat man no taller than Whitney emerged, wearing a faded T-shirt, cargo shorts, flimsy flip-flops and a smile that spanned his round face. He lumbered towards her, his four-hundred-pound girth causing the floors to squeak, yet despite his size and obvious old age, he carried himself like a sprite. There was a lightness to him, as if joy had halted his aging process and had renewed his knees, and he bounded towards Whitney like an excited Labrador with his hand already extended. She shot out of her chair and met him halfway.

"You must be Whitney Lee," he said, shaking her hand with such force that she feared a dislocated shoulder. "Good God, I'm so glad that you look just like your picture. You never know these days, you know what I mean?" He laughed merrily. "People airbrush like crazy, or they abuse Photoshop, and when I actually meet them, they look like their picture's ugly cousin." He laughed again. "Can I get you something to drink? Water? Coffee? Gatorade?"

"I'm fine, actually." His jolliness was relaxing her, and if she had expected to meet a suit-wearing, number-crunching marketing monster, or a hippie, freewheeling weirdo, she was glad that Terry reminded her of a gleeful child instead.

"Why don't we go back to my office? If you change your mind about that Gatorade, I'll have Cynthia fetch us some."

She followed him through the door, down a wide hallway and into his office. In stark contrast with the Spartan environment of the lobby, his work area overflowed with personal effects. Pictures of what she assumed were his wife and children littered whatever space they could on his desk, bookshelves and side tables, framed awards took up more space, and boxes of CDs littered the floor. She walked towards a guest chair that faced his desk, careful not to step on anything. He, on the other hand, didn't seem to care that he was destroying his mail under his feet, and he walked behind his desk and plopped down, still looking enamored of her.

"Do you know why I started Train Tracks?" he asked, the beverage offer apparently the extent of his small talk. "It's because I couldn't stand to listen to the garbage people were calling music. And I definitely didn't want my grandkids listening to it, either. Kids these days are already so stupid, and I'm convinced that the trash they're bopping their heads to is making them stupider. You know what I mean?"

She smiled, tickled by his personality. His frankness reminded her of Hercules, and even though she had only known him for a few minutes, she found herself drawn to him.

"I don't mean that all young people are stupid. Kyle, my drunk of a nephew who was stalking you"—he lunged forward—"did he creep you out?"

"He was fine," she said, unwilling to criticize the person who had led her to Terry's office.

"That's good to hear. The last thing I need is for my lawyers to tell me that a beautiful girl like yourself is complaining that some pervy perv is following her around with his cell phone out. Anyway, that kid's got a good ear. A great ear. Too bad he isn't interested in working for me." He shook his head, looking disappointed. "At least he still has the good sense to go to clubs. And he's really got an eye for talent. The last six guys he insisted that I see turned out to be megasellers. Packed venues and rocketing sales—that's what I like. And you're going to be my seventh stallion." He rummaged through a pile on his desk and pulled out her demo before shaking it like a drying Polaroid. "*This* is music—pure, unadulterated, nongarbage music."

She crossed her legs, almost knocking over a pile of CDs on the floor. "You have no idea how glad I am that you like it."

"Of course I do. You're a musician looking for a label. You want people to like your work. You want *me* to like it. You wouldn't be here otherwise." He leaned his chair far back so that his stomach obscured his head, and popped her CD into a wall of stereo equipment behind him. In a moment, her music began to play, and he closed his eyes, his heavy breaths—snores, really—convincing her that he was asleep. When the song ended, he straightened, looking refreshed from the short respite. "Okay, so this is what's going to happen. I've got a lot of faith in you, and my nephew has a lot of faith in you, so I'm going to take a chance and offer you a contract. I can't give you a giant advance like the Big Four can, but it'll be enough to get your album recorded. Recoupable, of course. On the flip side, we'll be splitting net profits down the middle."

"Just like that?" she asked, jarred by the casualness with which he was handling the entire deal. As many musicians who had struggled for decades to find a place in the recording industry, she felt almost guilty, as if her big break had come too soon, even if her big break was a tiny label deep in the hills of Texas.

"Well, I'll have to approve the recording you turn in, and we'll need to talk about marketing and the thousand other things that go into this, but yeah—it is just like that. I like, I buy." He stood up and walked to where she was. "Leave me your contact information and I'll send you the contract in a few weeks. I know you're a lawyer and all, but you'll still want to get an entertainment lawyer to look it over. Oh, and at any point between now and the time we both sign it, we're free to walk away." He waved his massive paws at her, jolly again. "Not that I want that to happen, but you know."

"I don't even know what to say." She was trembling again, this time out of uncontrollable excitement rather than trepidation, and before she could control herself, she flung her arms around him, her fingers barely reaching around his broad shoulders as she squeezed him in her embrace. At last, she let go, and she saw that he was beaming at her.

"I like you, Whitney. You're going to go really far. Now, how about that glass of Gatorade?"

Whitney walked into her parents' house, exhausted from her day trip to Austin. She had followed the speed limit on her way back, and what with that as well as Houston's road-rage-inducing traffic, she had taken the last four hours to contemplate her future. The events that had taken place since the Valedictorians' trip—her having performed at Mason's, Kyle Brett's fortuitous presence in the audience, his familial connection to Train Tracks, Terry Rogers's instant appreciation for her and her music—had occurred so easily. Too easily, in fact. When she viewed them in succession, her calling in life seemed glaringly obvious, and by the time she had reached Houston's city limits, she realized that she couldn't keep her dream from her parents any longer. Still, that she was convinced of her path did little to allay the nervousness she felt, and she shuddered as she thought of how to approach them.

"Mom? Dad?" She walked into the family room, where her parents were watching *The Sopranos.* Robert was sitting at the kitchen table, hunched over a stack of data. "Hey, what are y'all doing?"

"This is so good," her father said, glancing at her for half a second before turning back to the TV.

"This is what I get for lending them the first season on DVD," Robert said. "They're on the fourth season now. I don't think they've slept all week."

"Shhh," her mother hissed, frantically motioning for him to be quiet.

Whitney watched as her parents stared at the TV like a couple of children glued to a video game. Never in a million years would she have imagined that the staunch members of First Presbyterian Korean Church of Houston would have found a consuming urge to practice what they had preached against for years, and she was agog at their total fascination with the series despite its violence and language. Too jumpy to join them on the floor, she remained where she was and decided to share her life-altering decision in between episodes twelve and thirteen.

At last, the credits rolled, and her father stretched his arms over his head. Her mother was already fumbling with the remote control, trying to skip to the next episode.

"Mom? Dad?" Whitney asked. "Can I talk to y'all about some-thing?"

"Hmm?" Her mother rose and walked to the kitchen, her bleary eyes confirming the new addiction that had subjugated her.

"What is it?" her father asked. Robert looked up from the table.

"I wanted to tell you," she said, willing her voice to be confident and strong, "that I—I, uh—maybe you should sit down first." She was suddenly petrified.

"What's going on?" he asked. "What did you want to talk to us about?"

She took a shaky breath and closed her eyes. When she opened them, they were staring at her with slight creases between their brows. *Here goes,* she thought.

"I've been thinking about things for a while, thinking about life, what you expect from me, what I expect from myself, and I realized that I have to live according to my own plans." She was blurting her words inarticulately, and her parents' frowns deepened. "I've never told you what I've been doing, but I should have. See, I've been writing my own music since law school, and I've been singing at local clubs for the last—oh, I don't know—almost six years now. I'm really good at it. I'm certainly much better at it than I am at being a lawyer. And I just got back from Austin, from this really fantastic record label—they're going to sign me." She looked up nervously, unsure how she was hoping her parents would react.

"What does singing have to do with anything?" her father asked. "What in the world are you talking about?"

"Whitney, how can you go to clubs?" Her mother's little eyes bugged behind her glasses. She had apparently stopped listening after she had caught the word *club.* "We already talked about this. You shouldn't go to places like that. It's dangerous. It's horrible."

"The places I go are just fine," she said, hearing her voice strain. "I don't know how to ease into this, so I'll just say it. I want to sing pro-fessionally. I'm not interested in being a superstar, but I want to have a career in music. I want to record an album, and I want to perform before audiences. This is what I was meant to do in life. You only get one shot at it, and like you were saying before, happiness is more important than anything else."

"Who said that?" her mother said, her eyes instantly bloodshot. "What happiness? What does that have to do with anything?" She stared at her in disbelief. "Is this one of your jokes? Are you being ha-ha funny?"

"No." She wrung her hands together, unsure what else to do with them. "I know the situation y'all are in, financially, I mean, and Robert and I've talked about what we're going to do to help. You don't have to worry about money, because we'll take care of you." They stared at her, even more flummoxed. "What I'm trying to say is that I've considered my decision from every angle, and I've thought about all the factors and consequences that go with something as risky as a music career. I'm not rushing into something that I dreamed up yesterday. This is what I've decided to do with my life, and you have to let me live it my way, Mom. You have to let me grow up."

"This is—this is just beyond—it's incomprehensible," she stuttered. Her face had drained of color, and her ashen skin accentuated the blackness of her eyes. "You *are* already grown up. You're a lawyer. You're a lawyer at a prestigious firm, and you have a prestigious future."

"Maybe. But . . ." She hesitated, uncertain whether she should disclose that she intended to quit her job, as well. Her shoulders heaved under the burden of secrecy. She had to tell them. "I don't want to be a lawyer. I haven't wanted to be one in three years. The firm's killing me—the stress and the hours are killing me. I don't want to be your age and feel like I've wasted my life. I don't want that kind of regret. I'm sorry. I've made my choice, and the choice is to quit my job, too, so that I can concentrate on what really matters to me. At least for the next few years."

They gawked at her, unblinking, perhaps unbreathing, as well. She worried that she had just traumatized them, that she had frozen them with her news. They continued to stare at her, perhaps without really seeing her, until her mother snapped to.

"Do you have any idea how lucky you are?" If she was shocked before, she was now livid. "Do you have *any* idea how hard it is to make it in this world? Not everyone has the luxury of a secure job or a bright future. Why do you think we sent you to Loyola? Or to Duke, or Harvard, or MIT? Because we were *rich*? Because we really need to brag about you and your brother to our friends?" Her skin had regained its color, and in stark contrast with the pallor of before, it was now the shade of a ripe mango. "It's because life is *hard*, Whitney. A good education is the only way to survive. We gave you that education so that you'd be prepared for life."

"I understand that. I appreciate everything that you and Dad have done for us. But it's unfair for you to say that you prepared me for life, only to demand that I live the one *you* want me to live." She felt desperate, and she didn't know how to explain what she was feeling so that they would understand. "I need to be my own person. I need to make my own mistakes and experience my own triumphs."

"This is the most irresponsible thing I've ever heard," her mother seethed. "You're throwing away everything we ever did for you. You're throwing away your life. How can you trade what you have now for— for—" She shut her eyes, and Whitney imagined that she was picturing the strangest kind of nonsense she would have pegged her music for, the kind of noise Terry would have described as fuel for the stupidification of the country's youth. After a few shoulder-shuddering breaths, she blinked and stared at the ground, regarding it with the same disgust as if someone had just defecated on the carpet.

"Mom, please try to understand."

"I don't need to understand. Who's ever heard of a girl—a *lawyer* who's almost thirty—wanting to be a singer? What, so you can dance onstage with four other girls like I see all the time on—what's that—MTV?"

"*Mom*," she said, trying not to aggrandize their argument with her exasperation, "who said anything about other girls? Do I even look like I'm interested in the stuff you see on TV?"

"Whitney, stop. I can't listen to this anymore." She shot her a caustic look before storming out of the room. Halfway down the hall, she halted, stumbling about as she tried to figure out her next steps. She hadn't kissed her, and for a moment, Whitney thought she might return.

Thirty-year-old habits died hard, and as she continued down the hall and into the bedroom, Whitney realized that tonight would be the first time her mother had left her kissless.

She exhaled as though stress could be released through sighs. She sighed again and glanced at the kitchen table, where Robert was gawking at her. His face contorted, and she was about to walk over when her father cleared his throat, reminding her that she still had to reckon with him.

"Whitney," he said quietly, "is this what you really want to do? This—singing?" He had fallen into a chair in the family room and was now looking at her with disbelief.

"Yes," she said, and sank into a couch across from him.

"I see."

They sat silently, and unease permeated the air. His shoulders hunched, and for the first time, Whitney saw her father defeated. She sighed again, miserable. The last thing she had wanted was for her parents to feel betrayed, or, even worse, dismissed. Still, there were more scandalous things she could have done, more atrocious ways she could have behaved. In the grand scheme of things, her career choice wasn't so onerous, and as she regarded her father's worn eyes and beleaguered face, she wondered if her pronouncement had, in fact, been the most egregious slap to his face.

"I wish you would reconsider," he finally said.

"Dad, I've been considering, and reconsidering, what I want to do for the last three years."

"Well, I wish you would reconsider one more time."

"Would it really be so bad that I pursue what I *want* to pursue?" She reached for his arm, and he didn't pull back. "Don't you trust that you've raised me to make good decisions?"

"Where did you even get the idea to do something like this?" He took off his glasses, rubbed his eyes vigorously and then replaced his spectacles. His brows knit, highlighting a bulging vein in his forehead. It was obvious that he was trying to remain calm, but his face betrayed the consternation he felt.

"I've thought about it since college. I've been dreaming about it since law school." He peered at her, his expression demanding more of an explanation. "Normal people would go to concerts and say, *Wow, that was great*. I'd think, *I need to do that*. I obsessed about it whenever I saw musicals or listened to the radio. I even thought about it when I went to karaoke bars with my friends."

"But that's just—everyone thinks they're a star at the karaoke bar. It's a hobby. That's all." His face reddened, and he didn't bother to push up his slipping glasses. They teetered at the tip of his nose, making him appear even more like a dissatisfied school principal. "There's stability in your law job, Whitney. There's no stability in a singing career."

"Maybe not, but I have a record contract. That's something, isn't it? It's a start." He didn't respond, and she leaned closer towards him. "Dad, it's really what I want to do." She felt like a child in his presence, or more accurately like a stunted adult mired in a state of arrested development. It was strange to think that she was twenty-eight years old, given that she still clung to her parents for their approval. Maybe their close relationship had retarded the natural course of her maturity. After all, they would always regard her as their baby, and in a way, she still regarded herself as such, too.

"When are you going to grow up?" her father asked. "Life isn't always about what you *want* to do. There are so many responsibilities that you'll face, things that you can't even imagine yet." He straightened and regarded her. He didn't appear furious like her mother, but his disappointment, apparent even in his gentle expression, cut through her like a piano wire. "Life is so hard, Whitney."

"Dad . . ."

"Whitney, please—not now. I just can't. We'll talk about this later." He stood and walked down the hall, likewise refusing her a kiss.

"Jesus Christ," Robert said from the kitchen table. She started, having forgotten that he was even in the room. "Jesus fucking Christ."

She stood up and walked over to him. He gazed at her in a daze as she took a seat next to him.

"Let's go home," he said. "You'll ride with me." He stood up and gathered his designs. "Come on."

"What about my car?"

"We'll get it tomorrow. I want to talk to you."

"If you're going to try to convince me to change my mind, I don't want to hear it," she said, remaining where she was.

"Whitney," he said sternly.

She looked up and saw that he wasn't in the mood for dissension. With a shoulder-heaving sigh, she nodded and rose.

"Fine."

They walked out the front door without saying a word, and she watched, slightly numb, as he threw his belongings into the backseat. By the time she climbed into the car, he was already starting the engine, his face like stone.

"Are you mad?" she asked, wondering if he was also distraught by her decision.

"No, I'm not mad," he said flatly. "Although you should have waited for a few months."

"Why would it matter whether I waited? We'd still be where we are now."

"Maybe from now on, you should run your decisions past me."

"Why?" she asked, annoyed with his patriarchal attitude.

"Because then I could tell you whether your timing was terrible or not." He rubbed his face before turning to her.

"What are you talking about?" She was suddenly worried. "What happened?"

"Tonight was probably not the best night to tell them that you didn't want a steady job," he said quietly. "You know, as a lawyer."

"Why not?" She scooted to the edge of her seat, pushed to its frame by anxiety.

"NASA restructured Dad's division," he said, his dark eyes piercing hers. "And in the process, it decided to do away with a lot of positions. Including Dad's."

"What?" she gasped. An icy tremor chilled her spine. "When did this happen?"

"Yesterday."

"Robert!" She lurched forward, and the seat belt strained against her torso. "Why didn't you tell me? I would *never* have brought up any of this if I had known!"

"Calm down." He reached across and pushed her body against the seat. "They told me not to tell you."

"Why would they do that?" Her breaths quickened, and her face flushed with indignation.

"They didn't want you to worry." He stared ahead as he navigated around the nine o'clock traffic.

"This is insane," Whitney huffed. "I'm not some kind of mental patient who can't deal with problems. If Mom and Dad had told me—"

"You know as well as I do that they're never going to treat you the way they treat me, okay? You're their baby. You'll always be their baby, and if that's some kind of burden to you, too bad. We should all be so lucky to have problems like that." He threw a disapproving look at her, and against the dim lighting the moon provided, he looked just like their father.

"So, they have no income now, is what you're saying."

"Yeah. They basically have nothing, actually." He shook his head. "What kind of bullshit is that? Dad's worked his entire life, has two doctorate degrees, and now they've got nothing. They're thinking about selling the house."

"But they love that house," she said, feeling panicked.

"Well, they can't afford it now," he snapped. He met her gaze, and his consternation dissipated somewhat. "At least they have us, right? And dad will be eligible for social security next year."

"They're not going to sell it," she said stubbornly. "It's the one nice thing they've ever allowed themselves."

"Unless you've got a money tree that I don't know about . . ."

"I told you that I considered everything before I decided to quit my job." She felt her shoulders clench, and she looked up, meeting her brother's stare. "They'll keep the house. I'll take care of it. If you can pitch in, great."

"Fine," he said tensely. He didn't argue with her, but she could see that he was straining to control himself.

She leaned against the headrest and gazed out the window, contemplating how she was going to make ends meet all around. True, she had enough in her bank account to make a severe dent in her parents' mortgage, and the Train Tracks advance would help somewhat, but she certainly didn't have unlimited resources. Maybe her mother was right. Her job, onerous as it was, *was* a blessing, and it had, in part, given her the ability to help her family. Yet, she also knew that she couldn't stay. She imagined herself at the firm five, ten, fifteen years later, and she already knew that she'd feel diabolically resentful of her situation. It was probable that she would transfer the bitter animus to her parents, and at the end, what good would any of it do? She turned to her brother, who was still glaring at the road.

"If everything goes to shit, I can always find another job as a lawyer."

"Yeah." He placed his elbow against the doorframe and rubbed his head. "And maybe I can go into the private sector and find a job that pays more."

"Mom and Dad will be fine."

"Everything will be fine," he said, not at all convincing.

She leaned against the seat and closed her eyes. God, she hoped he was right.

Twenty-Three

Audrey stood at baggage claim at George Bush Intercontinental and checked her watch. Her father would be landing any minute now, and a mix of nerves and anticipation caused her stomach to tingle. He had called her last night from Caracas, and for the first time in her life, he had requested that she pick him up. Usually, he had a driver wait for him, or a staff of handlers ready for his arrival at Covington, a private airport where his jet brought him home. As little time as they spent together, and as devoted as he was to his overbooked itinerary, she couldn't imagine what could have compelled him to shuck his routine, and she checked her watch, wondering what on earth she was doing there. Just then, her cell phone rang, interrupting her thoughts.

"Hello?" she answered.

"Guess what?" Jimmy squealed in a high-pitched voice. "Oh my God, you are going to die!" He was clearly ecstatic, and she felt herself smile, no longer surprised that even at eight in the morning, he managed to be jubilant.

"What's going on?"

"So, I ran into this guy—his name's Nathan Evangelista—have you heard of him?"

"The name sounds familiar."

"Well, he's this incredible man. He's like the patron saint for us starving artists. His house looks like a museum, and he goes around and commissions work from artists that he likes. Anyway, he saw my work at the Nesbitt and had the gallery get in contact with me. He wants me to do a piece for him!"

"That's great," she said, excited for him.

"He's going to pay me more for the work than what I would get from the house with Kevin, and with you being a supporter, too—it's just—I can't even talk, I'm so happy. I never told you, but I'd been stressing something major about money—God, now I don't have to get a job, which was what I was planning on doing when Nathan called. I can totally create without any distractions. It's like a fairy gave me the best wish I could've ever asked for."

"You didn't need a fairy. You're incredibly talented."

"You *gore-jess* thing, *you're* my fairy. You've been like my fairy-godmother muse since the day I met you."

She chuckled, watching as a stream of weary business travelers emerged through the space station–esque revolving door that led into baggage claim. Her father appeared, clad in a black suit as always, and after rubbing his eyes, he approached her, each purposeful stride carrying an almost feral energy.

"Jimmy, I've got to go."

"Are you busy tonight? I want to show you what I'm working on."

"I can meet you at the Nesbitt."

"Actually, I want you to see my studio." If possible, he sounded even giddier. "I rented a little place off of Richmond, and that's where I'll be spending most of my time. Can you believe it? Me with a studio? It's in the Hancock Building, fourth floor. Do you know where it is?"

"I do. How about I drop by around eight?"

"Perfect. You're going to die when you see the place."

She hung up just in time to embrace her father, his broad shoulders like concrete. He had been a star athlete in college, and even though he was nearing sixty-five, he still had the physique of a football quarterback. He had less hair than the last time she saw him, a few fine strands covering an otherwise bald head. She was suddenly awkward, and she tried to stave off the discomfort she felt around strangers.

"Hi, Dad. How was your flight?"

"Terrible." He glanced at his watch. "I'm starving. Have you had breakfast?"

"No."

"Let's get something to eat after I get my bags."

"Okay. Do you want to go to the Petroleum Club?" The club was Houston oil families' version of the *Cheers* bar, where every million-

and billionaire knew one another's names and business. Her father practically lived there when he was in town.

"No," he said too vehemently. "I don't want to run into anyone." He looked at her, and perhaps noticing her anxious face, he smiled broadly, his forced expression unnatural. "I don't want us to be interrupted, that's all. Why don't we go somewhere like—ah—"

"Café Brazil?" she suggested.

"What's that?"

"It's where I spent a lot of time working on my thesis. A lot of college kids hang out there on the weekends. It's a bit eclectic."

"Yes," he said with a curt nod. "Let's go there."

"Is everything okay?" she asked nervously. He was obviously preoccupied, and she worried that his business trip hadn't gone well. Perhaps more than business wasn't going well.

"Everything's fine," he said tensely. "I'm just tired."

They waited in front of the grinding steel carousel and collected his luggage. He didn't speak as they carried his three suitcases and two garment bags across the parking lot, other than to ask a few superficial questions about her health and first graders, and by the time they reached the Lexus GX that she hadn't driven since her trip to Austin, she was convinced that something was wrong. She was driving out of the airport when he spoke.

"You know, I've always liked that Victor of yours."

"Really?" Perhaps she shouldn't have been surprised, given that her father had taken the time out of his busy schedule to give him investment advice, but his outward utterance took her aback nonetheless.

"He's a good man." His BlackBerry vibrated, and he took it out of his pant pocket, glanced at it and then laid it on the dashboard. "The night before your mother's Remission Celebration, he called me and asked for my permission to marry you."

"I had no idea."

"Frankly, I wasn't expecting it. Kids these days seem to have forgotten about the little things that mean so much to my generation." His BlackBerry vibrated again, and he busied himself with it for a moment.

"He had asked for your mother's permission, too, but she said that she'd think about it."

"I'm not surprised."

"I told him to go ahead and ask you anyway."

Her spirits rose, as high as the overpass that she was traversing. They had never discussed her relationships before, whether because he was too busy or because he didn't care, and she was delighted for having achieved something worthy in his eyes, even if she hadn't agreed to marry Victor for her father's validation.

"He's got a good head on his shoulders. He listens to my advice and makes prudent choices with his investments. And he values hard work. There are so many men his age who have no idea what it means to take pride in what they do, and those are the ones who actually have jobs. Half of our friends' kids are still searching for themselves." He snorted derisively. "A thirty-year-old who's still searching for himself—what bullshit."

"Well, I'm glad that you like Victor," she said, easing into a parking spot at Café Brazil. "You have no idea how much that means to me."

They hopped out of her SUV and walked into the restaurant. A disheveled host motioned lazily at them, and they followed him to a booth in the corner. Her father gazed around, and if he was appalled by the dingy surroundings, he didn't say anything. He checked his watch again, the third time in the last half hour.

"I don't have much time," he said. "I've got a ten o'clock meeting."

"Dad, it's Sunday," she said, already knowing how feckless her words were. If there was one person who worked every day of the week and twice on Sunday, it was her father.

"What's good here?" he asked, squinting at the menu.

"Everything."

"What do you usually get?"

"I like their omelets."

"Sounds good to me." He waved at a waiter, who was deep in conversation with the host. The host looked up and poked the similarly bedraggled server. He walked over, and when she saw her father's contemptuous expression, she worried that he found her taste in restaurants lacking.

"Can I help you?" he slurred, barely looking at them with half-closed eyes.

"I'd like the Spanish omelet and a pot of coffee," he said.

"I'll do the same," Audrey said, and handed her menu to the waiter. He nodded without taking notes and left. In a moment, he resumed his conversation with the host, and she wondered how the kitchen would know to beat some eggs.

"Is this where young people spend their time?" her father asked, almost to himself. His dark, bushy brows knit together as he took in the tobacco-stained walls and gaudy prints of faux-Gauguin women, and in his usual outfit of a Brioni suit, Ferragamo loafers and a Rolex President watch, he couldn't have been more out of place.

"Dad, why are we really here?"

He focused his attention on her, and his lips curled into a small smile. "What, a father can't take his daughter to breakfast?"

"You've never before." She wasn't trying to accuse. She was simply pointing out an obvious fact, and even her father couldn't pretend that the day was anything but completely out of the ordinary. He nodded, perhaps recognizing the futility of pretense.

"I heard that you tore up the prenup."

"I did. More than two months ago." Nerves welled again, and she fidgeted in her seat, crumpling the paper napkin in her lap. She didn't ask if her mother had been the source of the information, and she didn't blame him for being months behind on the family's goings-on. He was the patriarch of the family, after all, the provider who was constantly away, and she had long grown accustomed to his detachment from them. "Victor re-signed it, though. Did you get it?"

"My lawyers did a few weeks ago."

"Are you mad?" she asked tentatively.

"About what?"

"That I destroyed it the first time around."

He peered at her, his impassive face impossible to read. "Your mother put you in a difficult position without any context. Frankly, I would've been surprised if you *hadn't* torn it up." He frowned, looking

aggravated. "She meant well, but she's never been good about expressing herself the way she needs to in situations like these."

"Did you talk to her about it?"

"No, but I assume that she presented the prenup as an ultimatum.
She probably told you that you were naive, or that you don't know how
the real world works." He continued to regard her, and the intensity of
his gaze made her feel as if he were scanning her thoughts. "She doesn't
understand that there's a difference between oblivion and impulse, and
she probably couldn't see past your initial reaction to realize that ripping up the prenup was your way of processing what we'd asked of
you." He shook his head. "I didn't need to be mad, because I never
doubted that you would eventually agree to it. We needed to know
that you were protected, you needed to show us that you were serious
about Victor, and he needed to prove that he was serious about you.
And as methodical as you are, I knew that you wouldn't elope without
signing the prenup. It wouldn't help the situation, and you weren't
about to destroy your relationship with your mother. There was simply
no way around it, and you understood that."

She stared at him, bowled over by his ability to size up their
months-long situation in thirty seconds, and she suddenly realized why
he terrified her friends. It wasn't because he was harsh or even because
he tended to appear cold. They were scared witless in his presence
because he had an inhuman ability to assess people, to evaluate their
expressions and mannerisms and instantly know the next twenty steps
they were bound to take, like a chess player who could picture an entire match even before the first move was made. He was intimidating
because he was always right, whether in his measurement of people or
business, and if she was slightly cowed by his startling perspicacity, she
was also glad that she didn't need to explain herself.

Her father leaned against the vinyl siding, clearly deep in thought,
and he checked his watch again before focusing his attention on her. He
seemed as if he was about to speak, but for the next minute, they faced
each other quietly. Finally, he drew in a breath and leaned forward.

"This conversation was a long time coming, Audrey."

"What conversation?"

"The one we're about to have." He glanced about, as if worried that someone was eavesdropping. "Where the hell's the coffee?" He shook his head, aggravated by the unhurried underlings, and turned back to her. "Your mother and I almost divorced ten years ago."

"Did you?" She concentrated on her lap, wondering if her voice was as flat as it sounded in her ears. A part of her wanted to bolt out of the restaurant, to continue to treat their strained relationship as if it had nothing to do with her. Yet, another side—perhaps the mature one that knew that she couldn't ignore reality forever—anchored her in her seat, steadied her for an explanation she was sure she didn't want to hear.

"We had fallen out of touch with each other. We stopped communicating, stopped pretending to be a couple. I was busy with work, and she was busy with—well, whatever the hell she does all day. She wanted me to be this person that I'd never been, and I was disappointed that she wasn't who I thought I'd married. We felt like we didn't even know each other anymore. When you left for college, it became obvious to both of us that we weren't a family at all. She wanted out, and as bitter as things had gotten between us, I can't say that I blame her. Then, the cancer came back."

She stared at him, feeling as if he were recounting someone else's history.

"We decided to put the divorce on hold until she got better." He was absorbed in his thoughts, and he seemed to have forgotten about his omelet altogether. "When she was well enough, we began to discuss the division of assets, and the more we talked, the more lawyers we dragged into the whole mess, the more we realized that separating wouldn't do either of us any good. Everything we had was tangled up in family trusts, and besides, we had our reputation to consider. At the time, your mother was on the board of the Defense of Family League, and she couldn't let anyone know that she was in the middle of a divorce." He shook his head. "The worst of it was that the entire mess was killing your mother—physically affecting her health—and the way things were going, I thought for sure that she'd be dead by the time we figured out a way to separate."

"I remember that," Audrey said under her breath, recalling several years when her mother's frailty bordered on hospitalization.

"The stress, the lawyers, your mother's health—it wasn't worth it, and as ridiculous as it may sound to you, we decided to stay together."

Audrey knew that she was gawking at him, but she couldn't avert her eyes, and she didn't dare to interrupt. She didn't know what to think, but she was beginning to realize that he wouldn't take her to the Petroleum Club because he didn't want his friends, all phonies in their own right, to know what their family was really like.

"But we made a deal," he continued in a voice he likely used in his business negotiations. "We would remain married and make appearances together when the occasion called for it, but for all intents and purposes, we would be emancipated from each other. She would live her life, and I'd live mine. No strings attached. And we'd certainly owe no accountability to each other. In a way, we're the happiest we've ever been, and when we see each other, there's no acrimony anymore. At least, not as much as there used to be." He shrugged. "It's not what I would call conventional, but that's the relationship we have."

"Why are you telling me this?" she finally asked, heartbroken. It was silly to feel so crushed. After all, she had known all her life that her parents weren't exactly normal, and she had to admit that cordiality, however artificial, was infinitely better than wall-shaking arguments and shattering glass. Still, so long as no one acknowledged the dysfunction of their household, she could pretend to have a Rockwellian existence. Now that her father had peeled back the shiny veneer of outward appearances, she felt as though she were left with a counterfeit family.

"Because you need to understand where your mother's coming from, and you need to know that we both have your best interests in mind. Even if it sometimes doesn't seem that way."

A waiter returned with two heaping plates of eggs, plunked them down on the table and then left, apparently unconcerned with their orders.

"It's about goddamned time," her father muttered. He shook the salt container violently over his plate before stabbing at it with his fork. After a bite, he reached for his coffee. "You're right. This is good."

"Thanks for taking me to breakfast." She meant it, and she was grateful for their time together. It was strange that someone with a machinelike efficiency, someone who floated into her world once in a blue moon, should convince her that he cared for her, and she was doubly surprised that his ostensibly unfeeling explanation had highlighted just how much her mother loved her.

"You're welcome." He swallowed hard and pointed his fork at her. "By the way, all of that stays between us."

"Of course."

He took another bite of his omelet and then guzzled his coffee. After pouring himself a third cup, he coughed, rubbed his fatigued eyes and gazed at her absently. She could almost feel his exhaustion, and she watched as he pushed his plate away before motioning for the waiter to bring the check. The server trudged to their table, looking still half-asleep, and her father pulled out two twenty-dollar bills and handed them to the undeserving boy. After another sip of coffee, he turned his attention to her.

"So, tell me, what's going on with you these days?"

"Well"—she considered—"I finished my thesis." He didn't seem to know what she was talking about. "For my doctorate in English lit."

He smiled, genuinely pleased. "That's wonderful. It's early, too, isn't it? Your program wasn't supposed to finish for another year."

"Yes." She felt her face flush, beyond thrilled that he remembered. "I got an offer to teach a seminar at Amherst. It's just an adjunct position for the spring semester, but it might help getting my foot in the door."

"Audrey, don't ever apologize for stepping-stones." He looked at her intently for a moment, as if to impart the importance of his counsel, and then relaxed, the crow's-feet around his eyes deepening as his smile returned. He gazed at her, as dreamy as the hard-nosed businessman was ever going to get. "My daughter, the professor."

She felt her cheeks burn with pleasure. He had beamed at her perhaps a handful of times in her life, and that *look* might as well have been the Holy Grail. It meant more to her than the opportunity to teach at Amherst, and she wouldn't have traded his expression for any amount of money in the world.

Twenty-four

"Robert's, like, the best kisser, too," Hercules said. Her voice was shrill and high-pitched on the line, in stark contrast with her usual deeply resonating tone. Whitney repressed the urge to gag, and she willed the image of her brother's amorousness out of her mind.

"H., will you swear that from now on you never tell me anything about my brother that involves any part of his body? It's making me physically sick." She nudged the receiver against her shoulder and flagged a document with an attorney-client-privilege marker.

"Sorry." She giggled, still in a bubbly cheerleader mood. "Hey, we're thinking about moving in together."

"Already?" She dropped a pack of Post-it notes. "Y'all have only been dating for a couple of months."

"I know, but things are going so well." She paused. "I finally know what Auds was talking about when she said that Victor was the one for her. I think Robert's the *one* for me. I just have this feeling."

"Well—if you know, you know, I guess. I'm glad for you."

"I am, too." Through the line, Whitney could tell she was smiling. "So, when are you going to pull the trigger?"

"Today. Right now."

"I wish I could see you quit. You should mess with your boss a little. Turn the tables on him."

"I'm not that sadistic."

"You should be every now and then. Good luck. Call me later."

"I will." Nerves tingled against her skin, so strong that she felt unsteady. She hung up the phone, stood up and then straightened her skirt. As she headed down the hallway and towards Will's side of the building, she felt more anxious now than when she had originally interviewed for the job. When she arrived at his office, she smoothed her hair for the tenth time, cleared her throat and then knocked on his doorframe.

"What?" he asked, not bothering to look up from his desk. He was dressed even more formally than usual, and he had accessorized his usual pin-striped suit with a blazing red power tie and crocodile loafers. She noticed that he had added a heavy gold bracelet to match his gold Rolex. All he needed was a fedora to complete the pimp-tastic ensemble.

"Will, I need to talk to you."

He looked up, and aggravation immediately etched his features.

"Where are we on those documents? This morning's deposition blew the fuck up because plaintiff's counsel didn't bother disclosing that he was producing another ten boxes of shit. I could kill that son of a bitch." He fumed for a few seconds before calming down. "It was going so well, too. I caught the witness in a lie, Lee. You should've *seen* me in action."

"I'm actually not here to talk about the documents." She strode into his office, which was easily ten times the size of hers, and sat in one of the oversized wingback guest chairs. He glared at her, apparently offended that she had entered without an invitation. "I wanted to tell you that—"

"*Boy*, I heard you giving someone hell this morning," a booming voice said out of nowhere. She turned her attention to the door, dismayed to see Chuck Johnson, a similarly pin-striped partner, standing there. He was leaning his three-hundred-pound heft against the frame while resting his elbow on his bloated belly. His sausage fingers gripped a Styrofoam cup, and after twitching his lips like a cow chewing cud, he spit into it.

"You heard, did you?" Will bellowed. He leaned back and lifted his feet onto the desk with a gut-shaking thud. "*Boy*, you should've seen it. I took the plaintiff's deposition this morning and caught him in a bold-faced lie. He made up a witness who he swore would testify at trial. Can you believe the balls on that boy?" His voice was amplified in the expanse of his office, louder than Whitney had ever heard.

"Witnesses," Chuck said before spitting into his cup again. How he was able to speak clearly through a mouth of Copenhagen was beyond her. "*Boy*, you never can tell what they'll say. Or whether they even exist." His voice matched the decibel level of a jackhammer, and as Whitney sat between the two grizzly-bear-sized partners who were shouting at each other in their heavily twanged accents while abusing the word *boy*, it was all she could do not to cover her ears.

"*Boy*, this reminds me of a case I had last year when I was chairing the committee on client development," Will said. "The plaintiff was suing on the basis of age discrimination, and it turned out that his boss, and his boss's boss, were older than he was. His key witness turned out to be a mole for the company."

"I forgot that you chaired the client-development committee," Chuck said. "This must have been when I was heading up the executive-compensation committee."

"That's right," Will said. "I remember because that was when I was also heading up the recruitment committee."

Whitney watched as Will and Chuck compared notes on who had chaired what committee and when, and even though neither acknowledged her presence, or even cast a sideways glance in her direction, she knew that their boasts were intended for her. She had been at the firm long enough to appreciate the delicate egos of these partners who feared that if they didn't constantly belt out their résumés before an audience, the associates might forget how important they were. She wanted to join their ruckus with a high-pitched *Who effin' cares?* Instead, she waited while gazing out of Will's wall-to-wall windows and thought about her recording contract. It had arrived earlier that week, and she had taken it to Tate Philips's entertainment lawyer, an unimposing man who made up for his size with his enthusiasm. Per the agreement, she had a year to turn in her first recording, and she was fantasizing about her upcoming studio session when she heard a pounding noise.

"Earth to Lee!" Will was shouting, slamming his palm onto his desk.

She looked up to find that Chuck had left. Will was glaring at her again, his self-laudatory speech and fraternal smile replaced by an irritated scowl.

"What do you want, Lee?"

"Sir, I just wanted to let you know that I'm giving my two weeks' notice, and that my last day will be September first. I'm sorry for taking up your time."

"What the hell are you talking about?" His scowl deepened, threatening to cave in his face. He yanked his legs off the table and shot up in his chair. "You're not quitting. Who's going to review the documents?"

"Kyle Brett's got a pretty good grasp of the issues now. And since he's two years my junior, it'll be cheaper for the client to have him go through them."

He squinted at her, and his narrowed eyes made him appear even more ursine. In a moment, the faintest sliver of a smile spread across his jowls, and he wagged a finger at her.

"You are a crafty one, Lee. I always thought you were a born negotiator. What is it this time? Do you want more money? Hell, you're making more than most people ahead of you. What? You want a bigger office? More vacation? What can I throw at you to make you happy?"

"Nothing," she said, and then rose from her chair. "I appreciate everything you've done for me, or tried to do, anyway." She crossed her arms. "I don't think I'm cut out to be a lawyer at a big firm, and there's really nothing you can do to keep me here."

"What?" he exploded. He lurched out of his chair, and a few sheets of paper fluttered onto the floor. "What the hell are you talking about? How can you quit?"

"Because I need to do what's right for me." She didn't know why he was taking the news so poorly. Attorneys came and went from the office as seamlessly as if the entire firm were one revolving door. She had never heard Will throw a fit because someone had decided to mosey along a different path.

"You are throwing away your whole life," he said, his anger boiling over now. "You walk out those doors, and you'll never know what you could've become here. I had great hopes for you, Lee. You weren't a quitter like so many before you."

"I hope you don't think of me that way." She didn't really care how he thought of her. "I need to get back to work, but I wanted to let you know. I'll submit a formal resignation letter by the end of the day."

She headed to the door, but not before he sank into a massive slump on his desk.

"Who the hell's going to take up the diversity initiative?" he asked no one in particular.

Who, indeed? Whitney thought as she walked out of his office.

"Hey, what's up?" Whitney asked as Robert entered the apartment. She had her feet up on the coffee table and was watching *The Tonight Show* in a tank top and a pair of Loyola gym shorts. The late August air was nothing less than stifling, and even with the air conditioner on full blast, the living room was sweltering.

"Not much," he said. "We went bowling."

"Who won?"

"She did." He plopped down next to her. "She's really good."

"And competitive," Whitney said with a grin. "She probably cheated."

"I know she did." He laughed and rested his lanky legs on the table.

"I'm glad you had a good time." She smiled at him, truly pleased for his happiness.

"Hey, Whitney?"

"Yeah."

"I never thanked you."

"For what?"

"For setting us up."

"I didn't set y'all up," she said. "You're the one who called her."

"Well, in any case, thank you."

"You're welcome."

They watched as Jay Leno bobbled his head throughout his monologue. Robert rested his head against the fluffy edges of the sofa, smiling faintly. Whitney couldn't remember the last time he looked so content, and from his soft sigh, she could tell that he was peaceful, as well. It was a nice change from his usual seriousness.

"Mom and Dad asked about you today," he said.

"They did? What'd they say?" It had been several weeks since she had visited them. After she had told them that she wanted to sing professionally, she hadn't reached out to them, and they hadn't called to invite her over. She knew that they needed time to shake off their initial hysteria, and she hoped that their silent treatment was coming to an end.

"They asked if you were okay. I told them that you were fine."

"How are they?"

"They're fine, too. They're calming down." He glanced at her. "At least, they're not as hysterical as they were before. They're actually starting to understand what a big deal it is to bag yourself a recording contract."

"Yeah?"

"Yeah." He was looking at her with a mix of curiosity and awe. "Hercules said that you made a demo tape and sent it around."

"That was part of what I did."

"Do you have another copy of it? The demo, I mean."

"Yes."

"Give it to me. I want to listen to it."

"Are you serious?" she asked, surprised by his sudden interest in her music.

"Yes, I'm serious. Hercules said that you were really good."

"Okay. I'll burn you a copy tonight." Hercules' compliment cheered her, and she was doubly encouraged by Robert's request for her recorded songs. As far as she knew, he limited his radio selection to the occasional NPR program, and she couldn't picture him blasting anything with a melody on his ancient CD player.

"Anyway," he said, "Mom and Dad are starting to chill. They're still pissed that they won't have something to tell their friends at that ridiculous reunion of theirs, but they're not talking about disowning you anymore." He glanced at her, perhaps worried that she might take his comment literally. "They were just venting, you know. They'd never disown you."

"You know what? That's fine. I've made my peace with the whole thing."

"Peace with what?"

"If Mom and Dad don't support me, that's okay. I can't spend the rest of my life worrying about making them proud. I'm twenty-eight, Robert. I'll be twenty-nine in two months. I'm an adult, and I finally realized that I wasn't going any further with my life because I was so hung up on Mom and Dad telling me that they were proud of me."

He stared at her, and his expression made clear that what she was saying made no sense at all.

"Why do you care so much what they think? I stopped worrying about it a long time ago."

"I care because I care," she said. "And even you don't buy that you stopped worrying about what they think."

He grunted and returned his attention to the TV. She considered his question. Why *did* she care so much? Maybe it was simply the umbilical tug of nature to desire parental approval. Maybe it was because they were at the top of the list of those she admired. After all, they had come to this country with enormous cultural handicaps and had still managed to make a place for themselves without whining about their travails, without complaining about their obvious difficulties. Perhaps she saw them as survivors against harsh odds, already victors in a race for which she was gearing up. Whatever the reason, Whitney knew that their opinions mattered a great deal, but that they could also no longer influence the course of her life.

"For what it's worth," Robert said, the irritation now gone from his voice, "*I'm* proud of you."

Whitney leaned over and kissed his cheek. For what it was worth, so was she.

Twenty-five

Hercules stared at the TaylorMade golf club. She had no idea what difference a forged iron made in a player's swing, and she wasn't even sure that golf clubs were an appropriate gift. She had never shopped for a boyfriend before, and she wanted to surprise Robert with something nice for his birthday. Something expensive.

"What do you think of this one?" Audrey pulled an enormous club out of a bag. "My father uses it, and he can drive the ball over three hundred yards with it."

"I have no idea," she said, staring at the club as though it were an alien-probing device. "I don't know anything about golf. I've never played before. I've never even watched it on TV."

"Never?" Audrey looked surprised. "It's on all the time on at least ten different channels."

"I haven't watched TV in forever. I just don't have the time." She thought about her schedule, about Dragonfly, which was busier than ever, Dragonfly Deux, which was finally set to open, and Dragonfly Trois, which was still in the works in Austin. Her thoughts ran to Hercules Cookware and her upcoming morning-show appearance, and the longer she dwelled on her list of things to do, the more panicked she felt about the task at hand.

"Well, you're not missing out on anything." Audrey returned the three-foot-long rod and selected another that looked just like it. "I didn't know Robert played."

"He took lessons in grad school, but he hadn't kept up with it until really recently. Now he wants to teach me." Her heart beat faster as she thought about their next date. "It's weird. Golf's all he talks about and all he watches these days. And the way he obsesses over Tiger Woods is completely unnatural." She spoke lightly, and with the confidence of one who knew that she had a great man.

"Welcome to relationships," Audrey said with a laugh. "Is he any good?"

"I have no idea." She shoved her fists onto her hips, stressed by the importance of her task and her unfortunate ignorance on his favorite pastime. She felt unimportant in the store, a barbarian without the appreciation for the sport, and in a yellow T-shirt and faded jeans, she didn't feel that she was even appropriately dressed for the occasion. Audrey, on the other hand, looked as if she had just returned from a tournament in her green argyle cardigan and tan skirt, and as she practiced her grip on several clubs and began to swing, it became obvious that she had grown up on the links.

"What are you looking for in a club set?" Audrey asked, watching herself in the mirror as she whacked at an imaginary ball.

"I wouldn't even know how to answer that. I just want him to know that I spent a lot of money on it."

"Okay." She straightened up, looking thoughtful. "I have no idea what kind of player he is, so it's a little tough to pick something out."

"Really?" Hercules' face must have fallen, because Audrey immediately pointed at a leather carrying case emblazoned with the Nike swoosh.

"If he's so taken with Tiger Woods, why don't you get him a set of Nike irons? A lot of people I know love them. And if Robert doesn't like them, or if they don't fit, he could always bring them back here and exchange them."

"That's brilliant." She walked over to the chosen equipment, and when she saw the price tag, she was overjoyed. They were the most expensive items in the store, and she took the steep cost as a sure sign that they were meant for her boyfriend.

"Did you want to buy him some balls, too?" Audrey asked, pointing to a wall of boxed sets.

"Sure."

"I highly recommend these." She picked up a shiny, metallic box, its red cover the only difference between it and the hundreds of other choices available for purchase. "My father kept going on about them, so I tried it last weekend." She placed the package in Hercules' basket. "Who knew that a ball could make such a difference?"

"Y'all play together?" she asked, feeling a surge of envy.

"Counting our game last week, we've gone out two times."

"That's two more times than I've done anything with my dad." She sighed heavily, causing Audrey to stop shopping and look at her.

"How's it been with him at your house? Are things smoothing out?"

"Actually, we haven't talked in"—she considered, cringing as she did so—"almost four months."

"How's that even possible?" she asked, stunned. "Y'all live together."

She shrugged. "He rarely comes out of his room, and I'm always working."

"So, you two have had absolutely no contact since he moved in?" Audrey asked, still shocked.

"Well, I put his diabetes medications on the kitchen counter in the morning, and when I come in at night, they're gone. That's the extent of the relationship we've got right now." Audrey looked as if she was about to say something, but Hercules continued. "I'm going to talk to him, though. This afternoon, actually."

Audrey stared at her for another moment, her disbelief still on display. "Well, I hope that y'all find a way to communicate. I mean, it doesn't have to be perfect, you know? It just has to be."

"Yeah. I guess." She tapped on the club set before bringing it closer to her. "Thanks for this."

"You're very welcome." She smiled widely. "Hey, if y'all ever want to play a scramble with me and Whitney, you should know that I've got a killer short game. And bunkers? Forget it. I'm a master with the sand wedge."

"I'll keep that in mind, even though I don't know exactly what the hell you're talking about."

They headed for the cash register, and it took two trips to load everything Hercules had bought into Audrey's SUV. She was eager to surprise Robert with her gift, and as she squeezed the last bag into the car's massive cargo space, her thoughts wandered from her boyfriend to the other man in her life. Time and distance had done much to dissipate her aggravation towards her father, as did her talks with her friends and Reynaldo. Her father didn't have a similar outlet, and she wouldn't blame him if he was angry with her for having retreated for so long. Still, she wanted to make their relationship right, and she was determined to do so, even if it meant letting him live his life his way.

Hercules tumbled into the foyer with Robert's gift. After propping the Nike golf clubs up in the formal dining room and placing her bags on the ground, she walked into the living room, her gait light with a mix of anxiety and giddiness. Robert was coming over in a few hours, and she couldn't wait to see his reaction to the present. Until then, she was going to spend some quality time with her father. No blown-up frustration, no harsh words. Her previous plan to subjugate him to her will clearly hadn't worked, and her desire for him to conform to her image of a father had only deepened the rift between them. Perhaps a change in her attitude was overdue.

She walked into the living room. The TV was on, and a Chinese news program enlivened the otherwise still house. For the first time in ages, her father was sitting on the couch, in a beige rugby shirt and sand-colored trousers, and despite the room's warmth, thin camel-hued socks hugged his feet. He barely glanced at her before returning to his show, and the sight of him flooded her with shame. Regardless of his hurtful way of speaking, she couldn't believe that she had effectively given him the silent treatment for so long, and she sank into the sofa next to him tentatively, racking her brain as to how to hold a normal conversation.

"So—I hired three chefs for Dragonfly Deux," she said. Her words sounded forced, and she tried to mask her discomfort, wondering if he sensed the tension she felt.

He didn't respond.

"I still need to find another person to staff the kitchen," she continued, her words coming quicker. "And then I've got to hire servers and busboys."

He still didn't respond.

"I thought you'd be interested to hear what was going on." He looked at her, perhaps perplexed by her sudden chattiness, and she babbled on. "I'm working on my third restaurant, you know. It's going to be in Austin, and my line of cookware's debuting next month. It's a really, really big deal, Baba. I think Mama would be proud of me. I hope you're proud of me." She felt self-conscious, and she wondered why she was rattling off her résumé. Perhaps it was because she felt small next to him, and even if the entire world were showering her with accolades, she hadn't sufficiently impressed him to eek out a compliment.

His thin lips pursed together, deepening the lines around his mouth. She sucked in a sharp breath.

"I'm really sorry that I haven't talked to you in a while," she said almost under her breath. "I should have, and I know that, but I didn't—I just couldn't—" *Deal with your criticisms anymore,* she finished silently.

He was still silent, and she watched the TV absently, wishing that he would say something. Anything. After a few moments, it became clear that any conversation between them would be one-sided, and she let out a disappointed sigh and dropped her shoulders. Perhaps she would have to be content that they hadn't argued with each other tonight. It was a baby step, but it was a step nonetheless. Suddenly, her father spoke.

"Why do you hate me so much?"

Hercules turned, startled by the question. "I don't hate you."

"The way you treat me sometimes, I think you do."

"Well, I don't."

"Then why do you look at me the way you do?"

"Like what?"

"Like that."

"Baba, I don't hate you, okay? I don't understand you sometimes, but that doesn't mean that I don't love you." The assertion of her familial duty to love him felt artificial, and it occurred to her that she hadn't professed any kind of affection towards him in nearly fifteen years. She was already aware that he had never initiated a similar sentiment, either.

"Why does it matter so much to you that you understand me? It's not important whether you understand. It's only important that you respect and obey."

"It's hard to respect someone when you don't understand them," she said, careful not to sound accusatory. "If the motivation behind a person's actions and speech are respectable, then it doesn't matter how he says it. I would still respect him."

"Xiao-Xiao, why do you have to make everything so difficult? I am your father. Why do you have to question what I say? Why can't you just accept it as it is?"

She breathed deeply and tried not to get upset. Perhaps she would never be able to convince him that his way of thinking had isolated him, or that his attitude was largely responsible for what he considered to be life's inexplicable misfortune. She already knew that there was nothing she could say that would change his outlook, so she rested her hand on his lap and nodded.

"Fine. I'll accept things as they are. I'll accept you as you are. I don't want to fight with you anymore, Baba. I just want to live peacefully."

He nodded stiffly, and if he was pleased, he didn't show it. A surge of rashness overtook her, and though she knew to leave well enough alone, she couldn't help but apprise him of what she had bottled up for years.

"Sometimes, I just wish that you were proud of me, you know? I work so hard to make you happy."

He looked at her, his weathered features crinkling with surprise. "I shouldn't have to tell you. You should just know, Xiao-Xiao."

"Well, I'd still like to hear it. You have no idea how much." She motioned around the room, her arm heavy with longing. "I've achieved all of this—I've earned it—but honestly, I'd give it up in a heartbeat just to hear you say that I've done something good."

He stared at her for a long moment, looking as if he was confused by her desire, and his tufted hair waved about his head as he examined the house. For what seemed like hours, his eyes roamed the space, taking in every lamp, every piece of furniture, the outrageously ornate fireplace and the pristine greens of the moonlit golf course. He sighed heavily, his lips settling into a thin line as he drew out his breath, and then turned to her.

"Xiao-Xiao, isn't it obvious how proud I am of you? We came to this country with nothing, and look at everything you have now. I couldn't succeed as a cook, and you are a famous chef. What I couldn't do, you did, and did it better than I could have even dreamed was possible. How can you not know how proud I am? How can you not see that everything you do is good?"

"It is?" She gaped at him, and as uncharacteristic as his encouragement was, she felt as if she were speaking to a ghost, a strange simulacrum of her father.

"Everyone admires you for your success. You don't need to hear it from me, too."

"Yeah, I do. You're the only one I need to hear it from." The statement stirred her father, and he looked as unsettled as he did flattered. Perhaps he hadn't expected that she should value his opinion, or that his words should carry any import. Or perhaps he hadn't understood that he could show affection without jeopardizing his own notions of respect. Whatever the reason, their exchange of support seemed to rattle him, and he focused on the TV, clearly still absorbed in what had transpired. It was obvious that he was at a loss for further words, as if their months-long silence hadn't prepared him for what he likely considered to be an uncomfortable emotional outpouring, and he kept his gaze trained on the screen, deep in thought.

She stood up and placed her hand on his shoulder, not realizing that she had done so until he patted it with his own, and she let it rest there for another second, shocked by his sudden feeling. When the TV fizzed to a commercial, he reached for the remote control, pulling himself away from her grip, and she turned and walked towards her room slowly, barely able to feel the wooden floor for the lightness of her steps. Maybe they might never have the close friendship of which she had always fantasized, and perhaps her father would never proclaim his paternal pride with the same frequency as his criticisms, but still, for the first time that she could remember, he had articulated his approval. And for now, that was enough. In fact, it was more than enough.

Twenty-six

*W*hitney was sitting on the plush couch in her parents' family room, trying to stave off the nerves that were eating away at her stomach. Her father had called earlier that afternoon and had asked that she stop by the house whenever she had a moment, a statement she had translated to mean in the next half hour. It had been almost six weeks since she had been to their house, and as she bit her nails into stumps on the couch, she wondered what had compelled them to reach out to her.

"Whitney, would you please come here?" her father called from the kitchen table.

She stood up and walked towards her parents. They were already seated, and with their bookish glasses, white shirts and tan pants, and matching black caps of dyed hair, they looked like real, live LEGO men. She sat down across from them, and under the simple domed chandelier that hung over the table, she felt as though she were in a suburban holding cell with two doll-sized officers.

"We wanted to talk to you about a couple of things," her mother said. She was perfectly composed, neither angry nor pleased, and her waxen expression was more unnerving than if she had begun the conversation with full-on fury.

"Okay."

"Robert told us that you know that I—that I lost my job," her father said, clearly still aggrieved over his situation.

"Yes."

"And you already knew about our investment with Commelast."

"Yes."

"So you understand why your mother and I were so upset that you were walking away from a very good job with a very good salary."

"I do." She felt as though she were being deposed, giving one-word answers to her father's inquiries. She didn't dare interrupt his train of thought, and she sat stiffly while he built his case.

"It's not easy to become successful in this country, or in any other country for that matter. It doesn't matter how good of an education you have, or how fluently you speak a language. Difficult times come for everyone, no matter what. But having a good education, *using* that education, it gives you an advantage in life, and it gives you more solutions." He pushed up his glasses and sighed. "I'm old, Whitney. I'll be sixty-three next year. Maybe it's too late for me to find another job or to land on my feet, as you say. But you are young. You still have every opportunity in front of you."

She gazed at her father before making eye contact with her mother. She felt so awkward, and their darted glances and averted eyes made her feel even more uncomfortable. She waited for him to continue, feeling every bit like a troublemaker in the principal's office.

"You already know all of this," he said. "Your mother and I, we tried to raise you to be a thoughtful person, and I hope we raised you to be an independent thinker, too. Maybe we were naive, but we always assumed that you would take after me and your brother, or after your cousins and friends. I would never have imagined that you would have ended up"—he cringed—"singing as a job. It was beyond our comprehension when you told us."

Her mother's lips pressed together until she was mouthless, and little lines creased around her eyes.

"Are you still going through with it?" she asked quietly.

"I am."

"So what's next?" Her father pushed his glasses up again, and her mother's face tightened further. "This whole—what do you call it?— recording business—explain it to me."

"You really want to know?" she asked, surprised.

"Yes, I want to know. I want to understand what my daughter does for a living."

She glanced at her mother, who still wore restrained consternation like a mask, before she turned her attention back to him. Perhaps sensing her diffidence, he sighed again.

"Whitney, contrary to what you and Robert think," he said, "your mother and I are not just monsters who say 'Do this, do that' and expect you to act like our robots. We don't understand what you do, and I'm asking you to explain it to us."

Her mother shifted in her seat, causing its wooden joints to creak under her weight. Despite her reserve, Whitney appreciated her presence, appreciated the effort they were both making. For the first time in an age, she felt hopeful, and even though she knew that they wouldn't be sitting around a campfire and singing hymns anytime soon, she also didn't feel as if they were excommunicating her, either.

"Well, I signed a contract with Train Tracks. You've probably never heard of it, but it's a well-respected independent label in Austin." Her mother flinched, perhaps put off by Whitney's use of the word *independent*, as if it were code for an outfit that operated out of the back of someone's car. "I have a year to record my first album, and after that, there'll be marketing and tours and whatever we think will make the record sell. Some of my friends own clubs here and in Austin, and they've got a lot of connections to venues in the South." She studied their impassive faces, unable to discern what they were thinking. "I'm not saying that it's the most incredible deal in the world, but it's a really big accomplishment."

"Are they going to pay you for all of this?" her father asked. "What are you going to live on while you're recording?"

"I got a decent advance, actually, which will go towards recording costs. . . ."

"How much?" her mother asked.

"It's—enough." As rarely as they discussed money, she felt deathly uncomfortable talking about the specifics of her deal, and she interlaced her fingers, hoping that her parents wouldn't push for details. "You don't have to worry about me financially. Not for a few years, anyway. I saved up a lot from Boerne and Connelly, and with my advance, I'll be fine. I'll be more than fine. I told you before that I thought about the big picture. I'm not going into this with blinders on."

Her mother stared at her for a few moments, her face still rigid with concern, and she turned to her father and whispered in Korean, just loud enough for Whitney to hear.

"She'll be okay, don't you think? Mrs. Kang's son just started at a big law firm in Dallas, and his beginning salary is close to one seventy."

"What does that have to do with anything?"

"She said that she saved up from her job. Mrs. Kang told me that the longer you work, the more money you make. I imagine that Whitney must have been making close to two hundred thousand dollars this year. Maybe more." She screwed up her face. "Oh, why does she have to walk away from so much money?"

"Woman, we've already been through this. It's what she wants. Besides, if she saved at least half of what she was making—"

"She didn't have any expenses other than her apartment and car. She doesn't even have school loans, since she was on scholarship. She should've saved more than that."

"And if she becomes famous as a singer—she could be the next Michael Jackson."

"Can she dance?"

"Of course she can. All singers dance."

"She might make more money than if she stayed at the firm."

"No wonder she can afford this house."

"And she's talented, don't you think?" her mother asked. "I couldn't believe it was her when I heard the CD."

"Who knew that she could sing like that?"

"Wait," Whitney broke in, sure that she had misunderstood their hushed Korean, "what are you talking about? You heard my demo?"

"Yes," her mother said. "Robert gave it to us."

"He forced us to listen to it, actually," her father said, looking almost pleased. "He didn't tell us who the singer was. We were shocked to find out that it was you." He shook his head. "I still can't believe it."

"Did you like it?" she asked hesitantly. She was even more nervous than when she had first arrived at the house, and she interlaced her fingers, feeling sweat dampen her palms.

His face flushed, and his lips curled into a faint smile.

"I loved it."

Whitney let out a deep sigh, realizing that she had been holding her breath until her father had responded with the most flattering compliment he had ever bestowed on her. Had Robert been at the table, she would have smothered him with the tightest hug she had ever embarrassed him with and showered him with grateful kisses. For all her harsh criticisms of his inability to keep secrets from their parents, she recognized the bonding value of his frankness, and she appreciated his unwavering championing of her to them. Whether he knew it or not, she was forever indebted to him.

"I've been thinking about things for a while," her mother said suddenly. "You know, about you, us, our situation, your situation. I was so upset the last time you were here that I didn't even hear you say that you were going to support us. Your father told me that you and Robert are paying for the house and for everything else, too. I couldn't believe my ears. We never asked you to do that."

"You shouldn't have had to." She felt nervous again. As visceral as her mother could be, Whitney could never quite tell what she was thinking.

"No, we shouldn't have had to. But children these days—it seems that no one has any respect for their parents anymore. We were just so . . ." She wiped her eyes. Good Lord, was she crying? Whitney had never seen the woman cry. Her father had once told her that even while suffering through thirty hours of labor, she hadn't so much as broken a sweat. "Balls of Steel" was how Robert had described the child-sized matriarch to his friends. And here she was, wiping a stream of tears away from her face.

"Mom? What's wrong?"

"Nothing's wrong," she said, trying to smile. "It just hit me. All these years, we've tried our best to take care of our children, and now they're taking care of us. We never raised you and Robert with the customs of our country, and yet you somehow developed the same responsibilities children in Korea learn. Maybe it's genetic."

"It's a good thing," her father said.

"So you don't hate me?" Whitney asked. It was a ridiculous question, she knew, but the thought had plagued her when she was left alone with her imagination.

"Why would you say something like that?" her mother asked, her brows raised high. "What could we have *ever* done to make you think that?" She gawked at her for a moment, and her expression turned angry. "We may not agree with the things you do, or the way you live your life, but don't you ever, *ever* think that your father and I don't love you."

"Yes, ma'am," she said, glad to see her mother back to her usual chiding self.

"A record deal," she said dreamily. "Just like Michael Jackson. What do you think our classmates would have to say about that?"

"Wouldn't that be something?" her father added.

Well, Whitney thought, that was more like it.

"Here's to friendship, our successes and our futures—whatever they may be," Whitney said as she lifted her glass of champagne. She was in a celebratory mood, made all the more jovial by the company of her friends.

"To all of that," the remaining Valedictorians chimed. They were in their usual booth at Dragonfly, and having gorged on Hill Country quail, macerated beets and fingerling potatoes, they were working their way through a second bottle of Dom Pérignon. The restaurant was extra frigid tonight, perhaps to relieve the patrons from the typical one-hundred-degree, one hundred percent humidity September evening in Houston. Although they had met and bragged about themselves at the last six dinners, their boasts had had a redundant quality to them. Only Hercules seemed to savor each time she had announced, and announced again, that Dragonfly Deux was almost complete, or that Dragonfly Trois had broken ground, or that Hercules Cookware was in the final stages of manufacturing. Whitney couldn't even remember what she had said by way of her accomplishments, but she recalled that the girls had applauded as heartily as if she had won a Nobel Prize. Tonight, she couldn't wait to apprise them of the tidings that had fallen her way, and she felt like shooing away the waiter as he placed plates in front of them. Before she could say anything, Hercules began to pound on the table.

"Dragonfly Deux is finally, *finally* opening next week."

"You sure?" Audrey asked.

"No more delays?" Whitney asked.

"No more delays," Hercules echoed. "And if there is, there's going to be all kinds of hell to pay. Someone's 'nads are going to land on my chopping block." Whitney and Audrey guffawed. "*And*"—she paused for emphasis—"Hercules Cookware's going on sale tomorrow. Y'all go to Macy's and check it out."

"Really?" Whitney asked.

"Really."

"I saw an ad for it in the *Houston Chronicle*," Audrey said.

"Isn't it fabulous?" Hercules nearly shouted.

"It is," Whitney said. "Congratulations, H."

They clinked glasses before guzzling from them. Whitney and Audrey exchanged amused glances. They had talked about the Hercules-Robert relationship before the chef had arrived at the table, and while they were thrilled for her professional success, they had been expecting a different announcement tonight.

"So, how's it going with Robert?" Audrey asked with a sly grin.

"Awesome," she said, beaming. "Wonderfully awesome." She pointed at Whitney. "My dad's supposed to meet your parents."

"On Saturday," Whitney confirmed. Her parents had twittered around the house, bumping into each other every which way in their excitement. A parent meeting could mean only one thing, and they were beside themselves that Robert was planning on proposing to Hercules. Whitney had already accompanied her brother to look at engagement rings, and if the families could dine together without erupting into a fistfight, Robert was going to take Hercules to a park and get down on one knee.

Beyond thrilled that Robert was finally getting married, her mother didn't balk at the short courtship. She had apparently even forgotten her rule about non-Korean spouses. Perhaps *forgotten* wasn't the right word. *Put in her place* was probably a more apt description. Robert had calmly explained that he was in love with a brash, thunderous *Chinese* chef, and when she started to object to the relationship, Robert, for the first time in his life, had stood up to her and said that his decision was final. Perhaps floored by his sudden assertiveness, her mother had backed off, and by the time he had intimated that they had been talking about marriage, she was as exuberant as she had ever been. So happy was she that she had even promised to refrain from discussing Hercules' size, suggesting diet plans for the wedding and producing baby pictures of her son. She was likely to break all three pledges, which was why her father had promised to keep a hand on her thigh. He might be an aging man, but he still could squeeze the shit out of his wife if she said the wrong thing.

"Auds, you're up," Hercules said, "although I'd like to say for the record that I really don't appreciate that you've decided to make me look like a freakin' sea cow at the wedding." She frowned severely, the expression doing little to hide her delight. "I thought the whole let's-make-the-bridesmaids-look-like-monsters fad died out years ago."

"It's not that bad," Whitney said. "The cut of the dresses is nice. The color—"

"Looks like someone splashed excrement on us."

"It's supposed to complement the ocean," Audrey said with a wide smile. "It's a sage brown."

"That's not even a color," Hercules said. "I'd rather go to your wedding naked than wear that awful thing you call a dress. You've got until next March, though. There's still time to change your mind and pick a color that won't burn our retinas."

Audrey laughed. "Complain all you want, but that's the color I've chosen. Trust me, it's going to be big next spring, although I don't know that I'm going to have a lot of use for fashion once I'm at Amherst. Oh, guess what? The department asked me to teach an Intro to English Literature in addition to the seminar I'm already slated to do."

"When do you leave for Massachusetts?" Whitney asked.

"Not until November or so. Classes don't start until January, but we'll need time to get settled."

"God, I hope you come back," Hercules said. "I mean, I'm really proud of you for going, but—" She reached for her glass and looked away.

"I know," Audrey said sadly.

They sipped from their champagne flutes, and Whitney blinked quickly to stave off her tears. She had known for months that Audrey was leaving Houston, but the formal announcement somehow solidified the fact that they wouldn't be able to phone her for an impromptu lunch or a spur-of-the-moment movie. She had no doubt that the spring seminar would turn into a tenured position, and as she drained her glass, she felt as though Audrey were saying good-bye for good.

"Is your mother okay with you moving fifteen hundred miles away?" Hercules asked, still unable to make eye contact with Audrey.

"I think so," Audrey said. "Although she's burst into tears a few times. I'm just glad that she's got my wedding to plan. It seems to be taking her mind off of my moving."

"She's planning your wedding?" Whitney asked, surprised.

"Yeah. It took her a while, and I think having the prenup issue out of the way helped, but she's actually happy that I'm getting married. She's flying down to the Bahamas the last week in February to make sure that nothing gets screwed up." She smiled, looking content. "I guess my mother's coming around will be my accomplishment this month. That, and the fact that my father told me that he's proud of me. It might've been the first time he's ever said so."

"Wow, I haven't heard you talk about your father in years," Whitney said.

"I can't remember when I've ever spent so much time with him. I actually went to Venezuela with him two weeks ago. He was scheduled to be there for a two-day business deal, but he flew me down for another week just to hang out and catch up." She sighed happily. "It was fantastic."

"God, Auds, I'm so glad to hear that," Whitney said.

"It's funny how things work out, isn't it?" she asked, swirling her glass of champagne. "I told my dad about Jimmy, and about how much faith I have in him as an artist, and guess what? Dad was actually looking for someone to create work to place in all of his buildings. They're talking about opening a gallery, too. Maybe in Caracas."

"Your dad's into art?" Hercules asked skeptically.

"He's into tax shelters." Audrey laughed, and then patted Whitney's arm. "Okay, I'm all tapped out of good news for this month. What's going on with you?"

"Well, it certainly doesn't beat a professorship at Amherst, or making an artist's dreams come true, but I'm going into the recording studio next week."

"You're going to be such a star," Audrey said. "I'm sure I'll hear you on the radio soon."

"God, I hope so. My parents hope so."

"They know?" Hercules asked.

"Yeah. I got the silent treatment for more than a month, but they know. And they're okay with it, I think." She chuckled. "They're actually doing a lot of research into the music industry. My mom keeps asking about escalating royalties. At this point, the only thing that she understands is that if I sell more, I make more money."

"*That's* what should've been your accomplishment this month," Hercules said. "I knew they'd come around. Hell, they'll probably make themselves crazy trying to up your sales. Which will be good for everyone." She finished her champagne. "I'm telling you, at the end of the day, all Asian parents care about is money."

"Lord, Hercules."

"That shit's the truth."

Audrey looked at Hercules, her head tilted as though she were experiencing an epiphany.

"You know what? That's the first time in months that I've heard you curse."

"I've gotten better, don't you think?" She smiled widely, and her teeth glinted under the lights.

"You actually sound like an adult," Whitney added.

"I *feel* like an adult."

"Well, then," Whitney said, raising her glass once again, "here's to adulthood."

"You're not packed yet?" Robert asked. He was standing at Whitney's door, looking mildly annoyed.

"I can't move into my new apartment until next week," she said. She fluffed a pillow and found a comfortable spot on her bed.

"Well, hurry up. Our lease is up on Tuesday."

"God, I can't believe you're moving into Hercules' house. I wish I could live there. Have you seen her pool? It's unbelievable."

"If you want, you could stay with us for a few days. She said that you're welcome until you get your living situation figured out." He surveyed several stacks of books, two heaps of clothes on the floor and the half-filled boxes in her closet.

"Thanks, but I wouldn't want to intrude."

"Really, Whitney, it wouldn't be an intrusion. Y'all have been friends forever."

"I think I'm going to stay with Mom and Dad for a few days. They've got a few miniseries that I could catch up on." She sat up and focused on the mess on her floor, sad that she and Robert would no longer be roommates. "I can't believe you're going to propose."

"Yeah." He cleared his throat violently, sounding as if he were choking on cat hair.

"Are you nervous?"

"A little."

"She's going to say yes, you know."

"God, I hope so." He crossed his arms and shifted uncomfortably. Judging from his awkward movement, Whitney realized that he was trying to convey a sentimental thought, and mushiness was not his forte.

"Just say it, Robert."

"I'm going to miss having you as a roommate."

"Yeah."

"Hurry up and pack your stuff, Whitney. I swear to God."

"I love you, too."

He rolled his eyes and left. As logical and unemotional as he tended to be, she couldn't imagine his proposing to Hercules, and she would've given anything to spy on what was inevitably going to be good happy-hour fodder.

She flopped backwards into the mound of pillows and stared at the ceiling. A strange giddiness began to consume her, and while there was no distracting the rest of Houston from the miserable September heat, she felt as though it were Christmas Eve. Next week, she would drive up to Austin and work on her album, and whether or not her friends truly believed that she would make it as a singer, she had no doubt that she was doing exactly what she was meant to do. Just as she closed her eyes, someone knocked at the door. Tate Philips was probably at the entrance, waiting to take her to Billy Bob's so that she could perform the dozen songs she planned on recording. She pictured herself on-stage tonight, surrounded by her parents, Robert and friends she had treasured since high school, and the thought of their cheering support made her surge with adrenaline. She hopped off her bed, grabbed her guitar and bounded out of her room. A show was calling for her, and she couldn't wait.

Off the Menu

Christine Son

A CONVERSATION WITH CHRISTINE SON

Q: This is your first novel. What inspired you to write this particular story?

A: At the heart of this story is the struggle of three women who try to reconcile the expectations and obligations they face from their environments, whether familial, professional or otherwise, and their own desires. More often than not, the two aren't consistent, and sometimes, one can preclude the other. I related to these women in that aspect, and I think that so many people—not just a second-generation Asian-American professional who fantasized about being a writer—can relate to this, as well. I can't tell you how many of my friends, some of whom are in their twenties, and some of whom are in their forties, feel as if reality has put a lockdown on their passions. As a result, we spend a lot of time talking about what we want to do when we grow up. Actually, that's all we talk about. That, and where we're going for lunch.

Q: Yes, thank God for the lunches, because it takes some of the stress off women's lives! The main characters in your book are Asian-American. Do you think the pressure is even greater for those women in general?

A: I'm not sure how much of the pressure is a result of society-fueled expectations of the Model Minority Math Genius, and how much of it is a function of being children of immigrants. Certainly, I felt that I owed my parents more because they had sacrificed much to give me the proverbial better life. So there was that need to succeed. Also, as generous as the Model Minority stereotype may seem, it assumes success, practically takes it as a foregone conclusion, and the systemic assumption of achievement sometimes stokes an irrational fear of failure. It was like taking the bar exam for me. Everyone at my firm kept assuring me that no one at the firm had ever failed. I was so terrified that I might be the first that I didn't furnish my office until after the results came out. And I had already made up my mind that if I hadn't passed, I would just disappear. Quit and just move to another state.

Q: *Fear of failure. I can relate to that. Does this play into the characters' motivations for keeping secrets from one another? Considering that Whitney, Audrey and Hercules are best friends, one would think they'd have no hesitation when it came to confiding in one another. Have you ever found yourself in this situation?*

A: Absolutely. This novel is the perfect example. I didn't tell anyone other than my husband that I wanted to write. I was a biology major turned lawyer who hadn't taken an English class since high school. What business did I have writing? I figured that if I never told my friends and family that I wanted to be a published novelist, I wouldn't have to feel their pity when I got passed up by publishers. It's a bit perverse, giving them so little credit, because if any one of them had told me that she dreamed of the same thing, I would never have thought of her as less fantastic for trying, regardless of the outcome. But we all fear public failure, I think. Funny thing is, once I told a small circle of my friends that I was staying up all night writing (they were concerned because I looked so strung out all the time), they blew my mind with their encouragement. And they let me in on their secret plans, which led me to realize how similar we all were, despite our outward differences.

Q: *Clearly there are many themes in this book that you explore and that you are familiar with firsthand. How much of the story is based on real life? Do you see yourself or any friends and family in your characters?*

A: Certainly the emotions, the feelings that the characters have, are based on real life. But other than Whitney's stint at a big law firm, nothing in the story is based on my life experiences. Many of the stories are a patchwork of bits and pieces of my life, of the lives of my friends, family members, colleagues, etc. I see a lot of myself in Whitney, who tries to do right by everyone while figuring out what she wants for herself. All the other characters are combinations of people I know and love, or those whom I know but don't understand. At the same time, I didn't want to create over-the-top characters that would require suspension of disbelief. For example, Whitney's boss has antiquated notions of diversity and often expresses himself poorly. Maybe he comes across as unbelievable, an ignorant boor in a suit. But if I were to form a character based on the many isolated conversations I've had with people like Will Strong, the product would be beyond unbelievable. And it would detract from the overall story. So I tried to strike a balance with respect to authenticity (and probably gave some real-life people the benefit of the doubt).

Q: *Will Strong is such a great character in that he's so awful! You just want to hit him over the head. He's particularly terrible in the scene where he fires Whitney, who takes the blame for James. I truly understood where Whitney was coming from when she did this, since she put her own needs behind those of her coworker, who appeared to have more on the line than she did. Do you think this is a trap that women often fall into at work or in their personal lives?*

A: It's hard to say whether women often fall on another's sword because we can't bear to see another person experience what we could consider to be injustice. I know plenty of women who would have let James take the blame, even if they felt awful about Will's harshness. And I know a few who might fling James towards Will as they tried to save themselves. But based on my experiences as a whole, whether work or personal, I think women tend to respond more strongly than men to circumstances like Whitney and James's. Maybe it's a maternal, protective instinct. Maybe it's our need to be perceived as team players. Maybe because of women's continued adversity in the workforce, we're more sensitive to unfairness and are thereby unable to do nothing in the face of it. It's a combination of all of the above and dozens of other reasons. You ask very deep questions.

Q: Off the Menu *is set in Texas. Why Texas?*

A: I went to high school in Texas, went to college in Texas. I love Texas and thought that the novel should reflect that. Also, everything that I needed for the story—big cities, outdoor activities, the space program, diversity and small-mindedness—can be found here.

Q: *You don't see a lot of books set in Texas, so it does feel fresh. I think the outsider's perception of this state is that it's filled with blond-haired, blue-eyed oil heirs. And that's because of the Ewings of* Dallas, *thank you very much. So it's an interesting surprise that this world of professional Asian-American women is set in Texas. Is there a large Asian population there? And do you think that minorities are faced with more challenges here than in other places, or is it an equal playing ground?*

A: I think there are more Asians in Texas than most people realize. There is also an enormous number of Hispanics. So, for me, I don't necessarily think of the blond, blue-eyed Cowboys cheerleader when I think of the state. Of course, that's not to say that we don't have a large population of your Ewing types. In terms of challenges, I think the difficulties are different. For example, when I was in school in North Carolina, I was one of so few Asians that most people approached me with a friendly curiosity. I was an individual rather than a stereotype. I love North Carolina. On the opposite end of the spectrum, California's Asian population is in the millions and is a significant voice in all areas. With that comes a lot of criticism, too. I remember hearing a passenger on a flight to L.A. complain about how Asians were overrunning the state and how it was such a problem. The statement really took me aback. Texas is somewhere in the middle. Personally, I don't ever remember feeling like my ethnicity put me at a disadvantage or that I was treated poorly because of it. I don't know if I'm unique in that aspect, or if I'm simply more oblivious than your average person.

Q: How long did it take you to write this book?

A: Well, I started the original draft in the fall of 2006. It was garbage. I reworked the story lines, cut out a character, changed the dynamics, changed professions, ages, everything. Other than the title, it became a completely different book. Three versions later, my agent said that she liked it. This was spring 2007.

Q: And what are you working on next?

A: I'm thinking about my next novel, the details of which are still swirling around a bit in my brain. I plan on focusing again on broad issues like race, gender, class, family and so forth. Not a terribly specific answer, I know.

QUESTIONS FOR DISCUSSION

1. Whitney, Hercules and Audrey have different backgrounds and interests, but there are some commonalities, as well. What do you think bonds them, and despite their friendship, why is there still a wall that separates them?

2. Hercules is very much an independent, modern and overachieving woman, but her biggest struggle is with her father, whose traditional and old-world outlook is hard for her to accept. Can you understand why? Could she have approached things differently with him? What do you think are some of the challenges that first generations face in assimilating into the new culture or country?

3. The three women are at turning points in their personal and professional lives where the decisions they make now will affect their happiness. They're pressured by what they think they should do and what their gut tells them. Have you ever felt at the crossroads where one decision you made affected which road you took in life? Did you follow your head or your heart?

4. Audrey's parents, though very successful professionally, seem to have had a difficult marriage. This affects Audrey's courtship and engagement with her fiancé. Do you think she made the right decision with the prenuptial agreement? What would you have done? And how has your own parents' or caregivers' relationship affected your own?

5. Whitney, Hercules and Audrey are all sympathetic characters with their own baggage, strength and resilient spirit. They're able to overcome their obstacles, but each handles her situation in a different manner. Which character do you relate to more and why?

Christine Son graduated from the University of Texas and Duke University School of Law. She works as corporate counsel for a Fortune 500 company in Dallas, Texas, where she lives with her husband. *Off the Menu* is her first novel.